Against all Odds

Amalie Hedwig Langmueller

RIVER VALLEY BOOKS
Pasadena, California

Published by:
RIVER VALLEY BOOKS
PASADENA, CALIFORNIA

Library of Congress Catalog Card Number: 98-91623

ISBN: 0-9665024-0-X

First Printing

Printed in the United States of America

PREFACE

All the characters in this book are purely fictitious. Any resemblance to actual persons, living or dead, is entirely coincidental.

There is no village of 'Madrone Flat' on the Eel River, neither is there a creek called 'Fir Creek' nor a 'Fir Mountain'. 'Hidden Valley' is a fantasy collage, created from true images of secluded, enchanting valleys and meadows in the mountains of Northern California.

The story plays some time in the future. It begins three months after intercity passenger service has been reestablished on the Northwestern Pacific Railroad–when sleek, modern trains make their daily runs between the San Francisco Bay Area and Eureka, 280 miles north, in Humboldt County. Science fiction? No, it's the opposite. Instead of inventing some new, imaginary rail technology, I am borrowing from the past. The story uses the old Northwestern Pacific passenger trains from the twenties to the fifties as models for the new, fictitious trains in the book.

The passenger service on the Northwestern Pacific Railroad was already alive and well at the beginning of this century. It reached Ukiah and Willits in Mendocino County in 1889 and 1902, respectively, and Eureka in 1914. 'Against All Odds', pictures a comeback of these trains between the San Francisco Bay Area and Eureka. The operating schedule is based on the 1923 schedule from Fred A. Stindt's books 'The Northwestern Pacific Railroad', but I took the freedom to reduce the traveling times, taking modern rail-technology into consideration.

Connecting the San Francisco ferries to the Northwestern Pacific trains at Port Sonoma, Marin County, is also borrowing from the past–from the very beginning of railroading in this area. In October of 1870, Peter Donahue inaugurated a ferry/train connection from San Francisco to Petaluma and Santa Rosa in Sonoma County. Reaching the north end of the San Francisco Bay, the ferry moved up the Petaluma River, to a place called 'Donahue'–named after its founder–located one third upriver between the Bay and Petaluma. From Donahue, passengers would travel by train to Petaluma and Santa Rosa. Later–by March 1872–the tracks extended another seventeen miles further north to Cloverdale.

Connecting future ferries with trains at Port Sonoma has been considered again during the past decade. Within half a mile of Port Sonoma, the Northwestern Pacific freight trains pass by on their way to the East Bay, Sacramento, and the nationwide rail system. To the west, the main north/south line between Marin County and Eureka is only three miles away. It is an ideal location for a ferry/train connection and I decided to use it in my story.

For many years, Sausalito and Tiburon in Marin County, just north of the Golden Gate, had served as ferry terminals for the Northwestern Pacific, long after the 'Donahue' connection had been abandoned. But now, the tracks to these two places are gone. Larkspur, seven miles north of Sausalito, is the location for the modern ferry terminal and is also the most southern point on the Northwestern Pacific tracks. The Larkspur ferries began to operate regularly in 1970 between Marin County and San Francisco and are equally appreciated by commuters and tourists. They could as well serve as a connection between future passenger trains and San Francisco.

What really will happen in the future–as far as connecting San Francisco to the North Coast trains is concerned–is everybody's guess at this time.

There is also the possibility of using 'Hi-Rail' buses on the tracks instead of regular trains or light-rail equipment. 'Hi-Rail' cars and trucks are commonly used for maintenance purposes or track inspections. They are equipped with regular car wheels in addition to metal wheels for use on railroad tracks. Within minutes, the vehicles can be transformed from rail usage to road usage. The 'Hi-Rail' buses would be ideal for commuters from Sonoma County to San Francisco, making the time-consuming transfer unnecessary.

A recent study concluded that building a second deck for trains on the Golden Gate Bridge is a feasible option. This would be the most attractive and efficient connection to San Francisco, but also the most expensive.

The fictitious story contains many passages of real railroad events and history. (See 'Source Notes' at the end of this book.) All Northwestern Pacific and California Western rail issues or events mentioned, up to May of 1998, are factual. Amtrak's Zephyr, and the Coast Starlight, as well as the California Western trains, are real, of course. And there is indeed serious planning going on to develop a high-speed rail connection between San Francisco and Los Angeles. A statewide ballot measure to secure funding is considered for 2000.

The exception are the fictitious 'regular Northwestern Pacific intercity and commuter passenger trains', which operate, so far, only in this story.

There has been no regular passenger service on the Northwestern Pacific line between San Francisco/San Rafael and Willits since 1958. Passenger service between Willits and Eureka continued until 1971, when it was also abandoned. However, freight service has been operating regularly over the years–with some interruptions caused by tunnel fires or floods from severe winter storms.

In April of 1996, the line was purchased by the public and in October of the same year, long-awaited weekend passenger train excursions from Healdsburg in Sonoma County to Willits in Mendocino County were inaugurated and ran for several weeks. In spring of 1997, the excursions were resumed, until a track inspection by the Federal Railway Administration forced the railroad to issue 'Slow Orders' of five mph, which made the continuation of the excursions impossible. Although the railroad is fighting a continuous financial battle, they have worked diligently on improving the tracks. There is hope that eventually, passenger excursions will be possible again.

Disastrous winter rains in 1997 and 1998, caused heavy damage to the line, and freight operations on the railroad were shut down for months. In spite of being eligible for state and federal disaster aid, the railroad has had lots of problems securing these funds. While highway repairs get funded and done immediately, the California Department of Transportation consistently neglects the railroad. Critics of the railroad maintain that supporting the Northwestern Pacific financially is wasting taxpayers' money, because the geological makeup of the Eel River Canyon supposedly makes it impossible to stabilize the tracks. They completely neglect to mention that the highways in the North Coast region are traversing the same fragile, geological formations and are damaged as badly by the winter storms as the railroad. In fact, mile per mile repair costs for the storm damage of 1996/97, was considerably less for the 280 miles of tracks than for the 912 miles of state routes in the four North Coast counties, while the carrying capacity of Highway 101 and the Northwestern Pacific is the same. For instance, in 1975, the railroad shipped a total of 75,000 carloads. This translates into 616 trucks per day, which is the present daily average number of trucks on

Highway 101 between Willits and Eureka. Fortunately, strong support for the Northwestern Pacific from the public and many legislators and public officials, recently influenced the California Transportation Commission to finally release some funding for rehabilitation. A private operator, Railways Incorporated, will take over the management of the Northwestern Pacific in early summer. The company has a good reputation and has already done an excellent job repairing last winter's the storm damage. The future looks a little brighter for the railroad.

Plans are under way to place a measure on the 1998 November ballot in the two counties north of the Golden Gate, Marin and Sonoma, to secure funding for commuter rail service. If the voters will decide in favor of this measure, approximately $200 million will be available for commuter rail in Sonoma and Marin county. Once this is established, one can expect intercity passenger trains from the Bay Area to Eureka to be the next step.

Since 1983, when the Southern Pacific Company first tried to abandon the northern portion of the Northwestern Pacific from Willits to Eureka, efforts had been made to acquire the railroad through a public agency. Many people worked on this project over the years and it is impossible to mention them all, except for a few names:

Brian Whipple, a private individual, had the courage to purchase the Willits-Eureka part of the line from Southern Pacific in 1984 and thus, prevent abandonment. Although the Interstate Commerce Commission in 1983 had denied Southern Pacific's request for abandonment, an appeal would most likely have succeeded eventually. Whipple tried very hard to make the line a success. He even inaugurated passenger excursions from Willits to Eureka through the Eel River Canyon that became very successful. Unfortunately, the rainy winter of 1986 caused many problems, and–lacking financial support–Whipple had to file for bankruptcy in 1986. During the five years, while the line was managed by a trustee, rail politics changed on the North Coast. Public support for regeneration of the Northwestern Pacific was on the rise, and the two legislators for the region, State Senator Barry Keene and State Assemblyman Dan Hauser, laid the groundwork with the appropriate legislation in 1989. Assembly Bill 1374 provided funding for short-line railroads, and Senate Bill 1663 created the North Coast Railroad Authority with representatives from Humboldt, Mendocino and Sonoma Counties.

In 1992, the North Coast Railroad Authority acquired the line from Willits to Eureka. The remaining part of the Northwestern Pacific, from Willits south to Novato in Marin County, and from there to Shellville in Sonoma County, was sold by Southern Pacific in April of 1996. The North Coast Railroad Authority bought the line from Willits to Healdsburg in Sonoma County. The southern part was sold to the Northwestern Pacific Railroad Authority–a joint powers agency with representatives from Marin County, Sonoma County, the Golden Gate Bridge District and the North Coast Railroad Authority.

One other name is forever connected with the fight for the Northwestern Pacific's survival: Ruth Rockefeller, the Mendocino County representative on the North Coast Railroad Authority since its beginning, a tireless supporter of the railroad.

In addition, there were countless others who helped: all the commissioners on the North Coast Railroad Authority, the Northwestern Pacific Railroad Authority, the Supervisors of the various counties, the California Public Utilities Commission, District One of the California Department of Transportation, the Cities of Willits, Fort Bragg and Ukiah, the representatives for the State Senate, State Assembly and the United States Congress, the many grassroots organizations who kept the support going all these years–and most important, the railroad's employees, who have worked diligently under often difficult conditions to keep the line running. Without everybody's dedication to rail, the Northwestern Pacific Railroad would not have a future.

And lastly, one word about the title of the book *Against all Odds*, which of course pertains to the fictitious events of the story. However, the title has a second meaning–it portrays the victory of the railroad 'against all odds', extreme weather conditions, geological instabilities–but most of all, against the forces who favor highways–the automobile and oil industries.

In my story, these odds have been defeated finally by the Northwestern Pacific Railroad. I hope that the book will inspire many readers to help securing a safe future for our railroads, where these 'odds' no longer exist, where the railroads will receive their fair share of transportation funding. We urgently need a balanced transportation system in this country, otherwise we will be left with a world that is paved from the Atlantic to the Pacific.
Amalie Hedwig Langmueller, May, 1998

Dedication and Acknowledgement

Without the help of many friends, I wouldn't have reached the point where, finally, this book could be published.

They spent many hours reading it for the story and the plot, they found typing, punctuation and grammatical errors, they made valuable suggestions for dropping weak and boring parts and for changes in the plot. They helped with typesetting, and with scanning the slide for the cover photo. They discovered inconsistencies and honed and filed, and thanks to them, the story became easier to read, easier to understand, and better all around.

I dedicate this book to all of them. Many, many thanks to: Regine, Peggy, Ruth, Neil and Rob in Northern California; my long-time friend and neighbor, Lily, in Santa Paula; Everett in Santa Barbara, and Clark in Baltimore !

I also want to thank everybody who supplied me with the many pieces of information I needed, not only to write the story but also to make the complete process work.

And lastly, I thank my husband for his continuous support, for patiently reading the manuscript again and again, and for taking the many photos needed to produce the cover photo.

A. H. L.

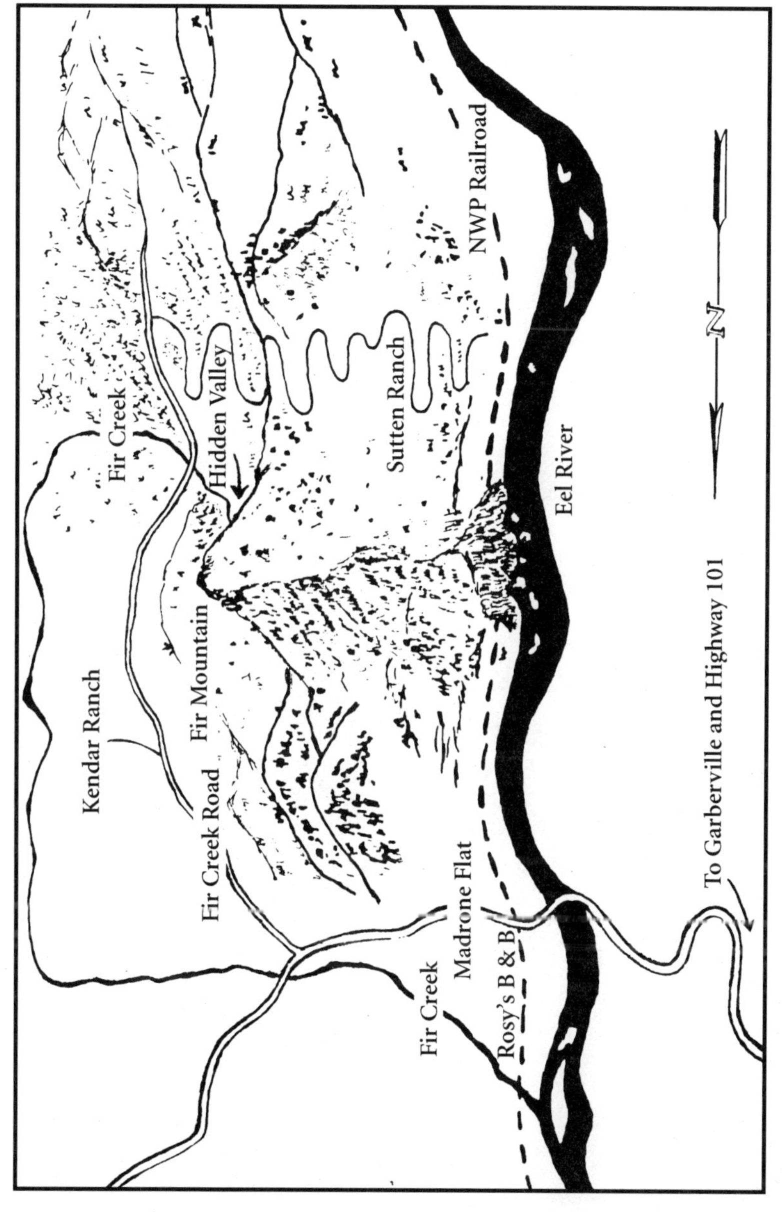
Kendar Ranch
Fir Creek
Hidden Valley
Fir Mountain
Fir Creek Road
Sutten Ranch
NWP Railroad
Eel River
Madrone Flat
Fir Creek
Rosy's B & B
To Garberville and Highway 101
N

CHAPTER 1

Amtrak's Zephyr, en route from Chicago to California, was winding its way along the Truckee River, climbing the eastern slopes of the Sierra Nevada. It had left Reno, Nevada, a few minutes after ten o'clock in the morning and would soon cross the border into California, scheduled to arrive in Oakland/San Francisco in the late afternoon. During the last week, a low pressure front had dropped a lot of rain on northern California, and the higher elevations of the Sierra had received a fair amount of snow. For early June, this was an unusual storm. Here, on the dry side of the Sierra, the weather seemed to have turned for the better today. Under a beautiful blue sky, the Truckee River sparkled in the sunshine. The high desert country looked fresh and pristine, and in the distance, the snowcapped peaks of the High Sierra glistened brightly in the morning light.

Julie Sutten enjoyed the scenery in the train's observation car, whose huge windows afforded an unobstructed view of the landscape. But she warily watched the small white clouds over the peaks increasing in size. They joined others to become bigger and darker, and by the time the train crossed the border into California, the clouds had formed a coherent grayish layer, promising more rain.

She had expected warm and sunny California weather and was disappointed that the last stretch of her journey would be marred by rain.

However, looking at the positive side, these late rains would keep the green colors of spring a little longer on the slopes and meadows of the Eel River Valley in Northern California where she was going.

It was a magic moment for Julie when the train entered California. She knew, she was home at last. Born and raised here, it was great to come back after four years of college in the east.

Julie had come by train all the way from New York. It had been a long trip, yet, she had loved every minute of it. During her college years, she had not been able to afford this luxury, spending that much time traveling. Although her grandfather–who had raised her after her parents had died in a car accident when Julie was only eleven years old–had paid her college tuition, Julie had to work for her living expenses. This did not leave much vacation time and every day had been accounted for. Now, with college behind her–she had graduated with a master's degree in archaeology–she had the time to take this wonderful train trip and to really experience coming home.

Julie had been looking forward to this last day of her train journey. It was great to see California again, especially from this perspective and at a leisurely pace–quite the contrary from speeding in thirty minutes from Nevada to San Francisco on a airplane. Yet, she felt sad when she pictured in her mind her arrival in San Francisco this evening. Tragedy had struck again in her life last December. She had come home for Christmas, and two days before she was to return to New York, her grandfather had been hit by a speeding car and died in the ambulance on the way to the hospital. He didn't have a chance crossing the street near his office when this car–driven by a drunken driver–suddenly appeared out of nowhere, racing through the red light.

It had been a devastating shock for Julie, because she had been very close to her grandfather. Since her parents' death, he had been father and mother to her. Julie was absolutely empty of any feelings when she finally had to fly back to New York. Her work was all that had mattered and she had buried herself in her studies, finished her thesis and graduated.

She now recalled the many times when she had come home for a visit and her grandfather had waited for her at the gates at the San Francisco Airport. She would miss him terribly in San Francisco and even more so up at his ranch at the Eel River. To stay for the commencement ceremonies without her grandfather in the audience would have been too painful. None of her other relatives could come. Julie's nine year older brother was living in Japan. Her aunt, her father's sister, lived in southern Mexico, and her maternal grandmother was not well enough to travel alone.

Emily and Bret Carter, who were part of her extended family and to whom she was very close, had offered to come to New York for the ceremonies. They lived at her grandfather's ranch in the Eel River Valley, and Julie was anxious to see them again and spend the summer with them at the ranch. As much as Julie appreciated their thoughtful gesture, she told them that she had decided to come home early, to California and the ranch. She knew how much Emily disliked flying. And Bret, who had worked fifteen years for an advertising firm in Manhattan, was not eager at all for a trip to New York–he had been very relieved when he turned his back on city life.

Her grandfather had been a wealthy man, the senior partner in a prestigious San Francisco law firm. But he had lived frugally and had raised her the same way. Julie had known that he would not leave her a fortune. He had willed most of his money to his daughter in Mexico–who was a physician–for her hospital in a poor, rural area. The rest went to various organizations that worked for social or environmental causes. Julie had inherited the old homestead at the Eel River and a small trust to pay for upkeep of the property. The 200-acre ranch had been owned by the family since 1912, when Julie's great-grandfather had worked as an engineer on the construction of the railroad through the Eel River Valley.

After spending the summer at the ranch, she expected to start work in September in the archaeological department of the University of California in Berkeley.

This evening, in San Francisco, her grandfather's partner and friend Fred Mendell, would be at the Amtrak station to pick her up. Fred had been with her grandfather's firm for over twenty years and was also a senior partner. He was a tax lawyer and, according to her grandfather, a very good one. Her grandfather had chosen him because of his competence and his personality and the partnership had worked well. Only politically had the two men differed greatly but had learned, over the years, after many heated discussions, to avoid these topics. Fred had been a dyed-in-the-wool bachelor, a very meticulous man, a little bit of a 'stuffed shirt', but a loyal friend of the family. To everybody's surprise, he had married two years ago when he was almost fifty. This evening he would discuss some financial matters with Julie, routine items pertaining to the ranch that would not take very long.

There was also a slight chance that Kim would be there to welcome her. Kim Brittany, a third-generation Japanese, was an old friend from high school and later, college. She was now a reporter for a weekly magazine and constantly on the go. She had promised Julie–in case she would not be at the Amtrak station in San Francisco–that she would visit her soon at the ranch.

Julie noticed that her fellow traveler, a young black woman who also had been on the train since Chicago and happened to sit next to her in the coach car, had entered the observation car. Julie had reserved a seat for her. The two young women had liked each other right away. They had similar interests, agreed on political and social issues and had shared several good meals in the dining car. Clara Winters was a year older than Julie, twenty-five years old, a school teacher, and going to attend a teacher's conference in San Jose. Before and after the conference, she would visit with her older sister who lived in the San Francisco Bay Area. She had never been in California and hoped to do some traveling once the conference was over. Julie had invited her for a visit at the ranch.

Clara Winters was an attractive woman, as tall and slender as Julie. Both had the good looks that come with kindness, intelligence, health and youth. Clara had not paid much attention to her appearance and had done very little to enhance her beauty. Her shoulder length, multi-braided hair was tightly pulled back into a ponytail. She wore faded jeans and a dark T-shirt, or gray sweat pants and shirt during the night. But now, as she came down the aisle, she looked gorgeous. She had changed into a long, colorful printed skirt that hugged her slender figure and gracefully flowed around her ankles. A snowy-white small T-shirt complimented the warm color of her skin. Beautiful long earrings and a necklace matching the colors of the skirt completed her outfit. Her many braids were hanging loosely down to her shoulders. Heads turned as she was walking toward Julie.

"You look absolutely stunning, Clara!" Julie exclaimed. "Are you celebrating our entry into California? Your skirt is beautiful, is it an African print?"

"Thank you," Clara replied, "yes, I feel like celebrating when I look at those magnificent peaks up there, I can hardly wait until we get into the mountains! But I also changed to please my sister when she picks me up in Oakland. She is kind of old-fashioned and will be delighted when I step from the train in a skirt rather than jeans. To answer your question concerning the print, it is and isn't an African print, the motifs are ethnic African, but the fabric has been woven and printed here. I work with a group of women in an inner-city, low-income neighborhood. We try to create jobs that not only pay well but also have some meaning. Someone came up with the idea to do some projects that would stress our African heritage and the fabric printing turned out to be a very successful one. We have a high demand for the materials and they are sold–made up as garments–in very expensive shops."

"Do you also make the clothes in your group?" Julie asked.

"We do some, and I always marvel at the many creative designs our women come up with and the quality of the sewing they produce. They are all very proud of what they are doing. We are also using the motifs for a line of stationary, but the fabrics and the garments are the main seller. This skirt I made myself and also made one for my sister. Would you be interested?"

"Sure," Julie replied. "The fabric is beautiful, and I know a little how to sew! A skirt is fairly easy to do, I don't need a pattern."

"When I get back to Illinois, Julie, I will send you some fabric swatches–I promise."

"You are very kind, Clara, thank you, I appreciate your offer."

After a short stop in Truckee, the train soon passed Donner Lake and was now gliding in and out of tunnels on the south side of Donner Pass, high above the valley, with a great view of the surrounding mountains. The sun still came through from time to time, but as the train continued westwards, the cloud cover became denser. At lunch time, Julie and Clara decided to forget about the dining car–the view from the observation car was overwhelming. They got some pizza and juice from the snack bar, and relaxed in their seats.

As the train descended the western slopes of the Sierra, the rugged, rock-strewn terrain of the pass area gave way to dense forests. The recent rains had done wonders, the forests appeared very fresh and moist all the way down into the oak-woodlands of the foothills. Julie explained to Clara the climate pattern that can be found all over California. Moist western slopes with dense vegetation and arid, desert-like eastern slopes, caused by the prevailing winds from the northwest which bring the majority of all rain storms to the state. As she explained that this was also the case in the Eel River area, where the moist red-wood forests on the western slopes toward the Pacific give way to the drier mountain ranges further inland, she remembered that she had promised Clara to draw a map of the Eel River area. Most likely, Clara would take the train, but in case she would come by car, she needed directions. Julie searched in her bag for a suitable piece of paper and started to draw a map and explained how to get there.

"This is Highway 101. You have to travel about two hundred thirty miles north from San Francisco, just beyond the town of Garberville. Turn off about eight miles north of Garberville for Madrone Flat, the small village on the Eel River north of our ranch. The narrow gravel road is marked 'Madrone Flat Road' and climbs up a steep slope. It winds up and up, seems to be going on forever. When you finally reach the ridge, you can see the Eel River way down in the valley. Now it's downhill until you come to the river. Right there is Madrone Flat. Just across the bridge, on the north side, is the general store, Post Office, restaurant, a bed and breakfast place and the train station. The people who run the place, Rosy and her husband George, know me well and if you feel lost, check with them. You then continue due east for about one mile and when you have left most houses behind, 'Fir Creek Road', a dirt and gravel road, turns off to the right–or south–which leads to our ranch. It is a fairly level road at the beginning, but starts to climb after about a mile or so. Another two miles and you cross Fir Creek which comes down from the western slope. Here the road becomes steeper. About a mile beyond the creek a road turns off to the right–to the west, climbing up a steep hill. From the ridge, you can look down to our ranch house. It is sitting in a large, hanging valley, way below the ridge but still about one hundred fifty feet above the river. Drive down the hill and you are there."

Clara studied the map and seemed satisfied. "Looks pretty easy. But where is the railroad I could use to get to your place, Julie?"

Julie took back the paper and drew a line parallel to the river on the eastern bank. "Here, these are the tracks. The Madrone Flat station is right there at the general store. Coming from the south, you can get out at our ranch, about three miles south of Madrone Flat. There is a small road from the tracks up to the house–here, I put it in. You can walk it in about ten minutes, leisurely."

"Sounds good," Clara decided. "But why is there no road from Madrone Flat along the tracks to your ranch? This would be so much shorter?"

"Well," Julie said, "you will see why when you get there. The mountain south of Madrone Flat, Fir Mountain, slopes all the way down to the river, where it ends in some steep cliffs. The railroad tracks lead through a tunnel there, no room for a road."

"I am really looking forward to getting up there, it must be beautiful country."

"I hope you will, Clara," Julie said. "I have no plans to go anywhere this summer–at least for the first four weeks–you can come any time. The problem is, that we don't have a telephone. My grandfather wanted to have absolute privacy when he was out there, and never had one installed when it became possible. Emily and Bret, who live there year-round–they sort of act as caretakers, but are more like family–feel the same way. They are lovely people, Emily writes books for children and Bret is the illustrator. Of course you can reach me by mail. I will write the address up here in this corner. But you can come any time. If you arrive by train, just get off at our station. Leave your baggage down there, we will get the it later by car. Just walk up to the house. I will make sure that someone is there all the time. Which week would be the most likely one for you to come, Clara?"

"Let's see–today is Wednesday. The conference will begin on Sunday and end next Sunday. The following week my sister wants to show me some sights–so I probably could come during the third week from this Sunday," Clara replied.

"What had you planned to see? You want to go to Disneyland?" Julie joked and her eyes twinkled. She grinned when she saw the disgust on Clara's face, "I was just kidding, that's probably the last place where you want to spend your time. I really hate those theme parks. They are as artificial as lunch meat you buy in supermarkets. Ground up, mixed, sterilized, awful!"

"I love that comparison, Julie. I have to try it on my kids some time.

They like both, lunch meat and theme parks. But it is difficult to get kids away from things like this, it's all they see on TV and most of them are hooked to those devilish boxes."

"Well, TV is something you don't find at the ranch, I can assure you!"

"Actually, I had already planned to get up into your area anyway, because I really would like to see some of the old-growth redwoods. Would there be any chance to combine this with a visit to your place?" Clara asked.

"Yes, we could take the train and go a little further north to one of the groves, do some hiking through the redwoods and come back in the evening."

"Sounds great to me–I am so glad I met you Julie, and you can be sure I will show up."

They both felt a little sad when the train finally left the mountains behind and the open plains of the Central Valley opened up. By now, the sun was gone and it was raining, which added another touch of gloom. Clara decided to go back to their coach and take a nap.

She got up and stretched. "I better go now and get some sleep, see you later."

Julie watched her walking down the aisle, and as she admired Clara's beauty and elegant bearing, she realized that she herself looked rather shabby and dumpy in comparison. She took stock of her clothes and felt that they needed a little renovation. Her jeans were crumpled and not too clean. Her light blue T-shirt had several stains and her shoes were comfortable but badly scuffed. Julie yawned, it was time to get herself cleaned up and put some fresh clothes on.

The Amtrak train had stopped in Sacramento, Davis and some smaller towns on the way to Oakland. Now it had reached the northern end of the San Francisco Bay and was turning south toward Oakland. Julie was back in the observation car after having spent some time in the bathroom, changing into a blue skirt, a white blouse with tiny blue flowers, and white sandals. She was wearing her dark-brown hair in a different style now. Instead of letting it hang down in two thick braids as she had before, she had it twisted into a heavy French knot, resting on her slender neck. She was just in time for catching the first glimpse of the Golden Gate Bridge and the San Francisco skyline. It had stopped raining, but the sky was still cloudy. From time to time the sun peeked through the hurrying clouds and produced some weird illuminations and even a wonderful rainbow. Because of the rain, the air was very clean and visibility high. The contours of Mount Tamalpais, the 2,586 feet high landmark mountain north of the Golden Gate, clearly showed the resemblance to the legend's sleeping Indian maiden. To the south, the City looked its best. It was great to be home again! Reluctantly she left the observation car, the train would arrive in Oakland soon. Her things were packed, she was ready to go. Now came the sad part, saying good bye. She was grateful to have had such a pleasant fellow traveler. When Julie returned to her coach, Clara was awake and just in the process of getting her things ready. She was really excited and happy to see her sister soon, but also felt sorry to have to say good bye to Julie. They hugged each other and promised to stay in touch. When the train stopped in Oakland, Clara had discovered her sister within a few minutes. She hugged Julie one more time, and was gone. Boarding the Amtrak bus for San Francisco, Julie got a last glimpse of Clara, holding a little boy's hand, and walking with a handsome couple toward the parking lot. OK, Clara was in good hands now, and if everything worked out well, she probably would come up to the Eel River in a few weeks.

Fred Mendell was at the Amtrak station to pick her up. To Julie's surprise, he gave her a big hug and as he was holding her, he said quietly and soothingly, "He is still here with us, Julie, even if we cannot see him, he is always in our hearts," and patted her gently on her back.

Julie was amazed and touched by Fred's sensitivity. Tears came into her eyes, she threw her arms around his neck, gave him a kiss on his cheek and whispered, "I was afraid of this moment, Fred, coming back to San Francisco. You have made it so much easier for me, thank you."

Fred had a message from Kim, who had to leave for Seattle this morning, but would come up to the ranch next week for sure. She had signed up for vacation. "You stay with us, of course, Julie. We'll take care of business first, some minor financial items concerning the ranch and by the time we're through, Doris will have dinner ready," Fred said. "While I try to get a cab, you wait here for your baggage to be unloaded, I will be right back."

She watched Fred as he walked toward some cabs. He was a handsome man, dark-haired, fairly tall, good features, good figure. A person one could trust but would not expect to have fun with. Why did he always look so serious as if he was carrying the whole world's problems on his shoulders? Did his clients' tax troubles rub off on him? He usually had been rather shy, especially with women. With her, he had an almost brotherly–or perhaps rather uncle/niece–relationship, and probably even now saw in her still his partner's little granddaughter. Yet somehow, he seemed to have changed, he never before had hugged her–had Doris finally got him out of his shell? It certainly had been a surprise, when he had come back to the office, after recuperating for several weeks from an appendectomy, and announced that he was going to marry his nurse. His colleagues had been skeptical and had even made some jokes pertaining to his inclination to hypochondria. But as soon as they met her, they changed their mind. Doris was a wonderful person, about five years younger than Fred. She had lost her husband to cancer many years ago and had raised two daughters alone. Julie had seen Fred only a few times since he had married, but her grandfather had told her about the change in Fred and gave a lot of credit to Doris for that. He had even joked that Doris probably would succeed in changing Fred into a liberal, after all, she had voted for Ralph Nader a few years ago.

Fred came back when her last suitcase came out. "OK, we have a cab waiting, Julie," he said and helped get all the baggage onto a cart.

"What happened to your car, Fred?" Julie asked after they had settled in the back of the taxi, "anything wrong?"

"I often walk to the office when the weather is nice, and it looked promising this morning, but then started to rain again. Besides, I hate to drive this time of the day, it is easier to get around in a cab. Oh, and you probably don't know yet that Doris and I bought a house in the Marina district. It is not very far to the office."

He was quiet for a while and then continued. "In late January, we started to look for a house and within three weeks had found the perfect place, near the Marina, fairly quiet, and clean air from the Bay. We already feel very much at home, you will like the place."

Julie was glad that Fred was going to talk with her at his house about the ranch. She was not quite ready to visit her grandfather's old office, it held too many dear memories.

A tempting aroma made Julie's mouth water when they entered Fred's house. Julie had heard rumors about Doris' culinary expertise and she was looking forward to dinner. Doris greeted her with a big hug.

"How about a cup of tea or coffee, Julie? Knowing Fred, you two will be sitting in his study for a while? Or would you rather have a glass of wine or sherry?"

Before Julie could answer, Fred had taken over, "I would love a cup of tea, dear , and I am sure Julie would too? And a plate of your good cookies?"

Julie nodded and Doris pulled her into the kitchen, where it smelled even more tantalizing. She started to make the tea, put cups and saucers on a tray and piled a plate high with crisp-looking chocolate-covered cookies. Fred had excused himself, he went to his study and expected Julie there in a few minutes.

When the tea was ready, Doris and Julie carried the tray and the teapot to Fred's study. Doris went back to the kitchen and Julie settled down in a comfortable armchair in front of Fred's desk. He mentioned some of the bills he had paid recently out of the fund her grandfather had left for the upkeep of the ranch–property taxes, insurance and a few other minor items. "You are welcome to do this yourself now, but I am glad to continue taking care of it. The contract with the Carters is good for another five years, so you really don't have to worry about anything and can spend a restful summer up there. Oh, here is one more item–the Carters had contacted me a few months ago because they had replaced the railing on the north side of the deck. I sent them a check for the lumber."

He paused, occupying himself with getting the file back in order and without looking at Julie, he said, "I am concerned that you will arrive at the ranch and find out that the Carters are gone, and you'll be by yourself."

Julie didn't know what he meant. "But Fred, why shouldn't they be there? Emily and Bret know that I am coming, they are looking forward to it. You know how much they love me, they are like parents to me and they never mentioned that they might not be there?"

"Well, I hope that they are back by now. They sent me a card from Seattle in May, thanking me for the check, mentioning that they had to leave on an unexpected business trip, but would be back by the time you came. They included a neighbor's phone number, in case you or I wanted to leave a message for them."

Julie didn't understand why she should worry about this. "I am sure they are back by now, or will be back any day."

But Fred told her that he had called this neighbor not quite a week ago to find out if they were back. The guy was not very helpful, he was just leaving and in a bit of a rush.

"He told me that he had not heard about the trip to Washington until he also got a card from them. He does not see them very often though, because he is sometimes gone for days, taking his invalid grandfather for therapy to Willits or Eureka. But he would certainly leave a message for them in their post office box or tell them, should he see them."

"Actually, that's what I did anyway," Julie replied. "Although they know that I am coming home earlier, I had written them a note about a week before I left, telling them when I would arrive and if there was any problem, to call you."

"But I have called the neighbor now several days in a row and can't get him even though I left a message to call me and to reverse the charges!" Fred complained.

Julie got a little impatient with him. He was apparently worrying about nothing. "Why are you so concerned Fred, that I might get to the ranch and Emily and Bret not being there? Of course, I would be very disappointed, because I am looking forward to seeing them again. But I am not a child and can stay alone for a few days, if not for the rest of the summer. I wouldn't enjoy it, but I could manage."

Fred explained, "If you take the train and they are still gone, you will be stranded with your heavy baggage at the bottom of the hill, down by the tracks. And it might rain again tomorrow, according to the weather report. Besides, it worries me to think of you being alone at the ranch, without a car, miles away from civilization. What would you do in an emergency?"

Julie burst out, "Oh Fred, you are really a worrywart, you are too overprotective!" the minute she had said that, she regretted it. Apparently she had overestimated the 'new' Fred. He put on his super-serious face and said stiffly, "I am very concerned about your welfare, Julie, and I am sure your grandfather would have felt the same."

Julie tried to mend the damage, "I am sorry, Fred, I know you mean well. How about trying to call the neighbor again?"

Fred quickly responded, yet again only reached the answering machine. He suggested, "How about stopping in Willits and visiting with your grandfather's friend, Frank… I can't think of his last name, he is a surveyor? He probably has a four-wheel drive car, perhaps even two, or knows someone who has and could rent it to you for a week or so. Then you can do the rest of the trip by car?"

Julie didn't understand his reasoning. "Why do I need a four-wheel drive? I probably could rent a car in Ukiah or Willits, if I wanted to drive in by car?"

"You forget, Julie, that we had a lot of rain during the last few days. The creek that you have to cross before you climb up the road to your ranch could be flooding the bridge. Remember, the bridge is kind of low, a regular car could get stuck."

Julie realized that in some ways Fred had not changed, but she did not want to upset him again and played along. Getting her baggage up the hill, alone, was no big problem, she just had to take her time. If it rained, she could leave it in the small building down by the tracks. But to drive a car she wasn't used to through a raging creek sounded much more dangerous. She would take the train to the ranch, and there was no question in her mind that Emily and Bret would be down by the tracks to meet her. Stopping in Willits, though, was actually a good idea. She always had liked Frank Rodgers. He had not been able to come to her grandfather's funeral because he had been in Southern California with his wife, visiting her mother. He had called her as soon as he found out and later wrote her a good letter. Also, he might know of some sites of archaeological interest in the area. Although this was not her specific field, she had planned to do some research concerning the history of the Native American Indians in this area during the summer.

"I guess you have a point there, Fred," Julie relented, and Fred immediately seized the opportunity.

"Very well, let's call Frank right away and find out if he will be there tomorrow."

Frank's son answered the phone. No, his father was not at home but would be there all day tomorrow and would be delighted to see her. He would for sure come to the station to meet her train.

Fred was satisfied he had done as much as he could for Julie.

"Well, that should take care of it for now, Julie. Let's see what Doris has created." He patted his stomach, "She cooks so well, I have a hard time to keep my shape," he grinned. "It always tastes so good and I can't resist."

Dinner was truly wonderful, Julie savored every bite. Afterwards, they relaxed on the small balcony overlooking the bay. Fred was refilling their wine glasses, when he told Julie that he had talked to her grandmother.

"Too bad your grandmother went on that trip, Julie, or we would have her with us tonight. I called her last week and wanted to remind her that you were coming, when she told me that she had signed up for the trip to Yosemite."

"I know, I also called her before I left. Had she been home, I would have stopped in Berkeley and visited with her. She promised she would come up to the ranch if I came down to get her, or if she could come with you. I hope you two will come up pretty soon?"

"We actually had planned to go up there by train in March," Doris said, "right after the intercity trains to Eureka started running. Unfortunately, I came down with a nasty flu and since that time it just hasn't worked out for us. But don't worry, we will be up there soon."

Julie felt good in Doris' and Fred's company. They were sitting outside on the balcony long after it turned dark, talking and reminiscing. It was a warm night without the slightest breeze and they enjoyed the view–millions of lights along the bay's shores and in the hills of Marin County, and the East Bay.

CHAPTER 2

Early on Thursday morning, Julie was leaning against the railing of the ferry as it was rapidly moving away from the San Francisco pier. Doris and Fred had come along to see her off, and Julie was now waving good-by to them. During the night, the clouds had rolled in from the Pacific. It was drizzling and visibility was poor. Only the midsection of the Golden Gate Bridge peeked through the fog, hanging there in midair, as if suspended by invisible cables from the sky. The water looked dark, it was windy and cold. Julie shivered. Her mood matched the weather. She had felt like crying when they arrived at the pier and she saw the gleaming white ship, with its large, golden letters 'Northwestern Pacific Railroad'. Why this senseless death so close to the fulfillment of his dream? For years, her grandfather had been a tireless supporter of the regeneration of passenger service on the Northwestern Pacific Railroad. He had been a member of several railroad clubs and had regularly attended meetings concerning the sale of the Northwestern Pacific Railroad to the public. In 1990, he had generously contributed to the Planning and Conservation League's transit initiative. This ballet measure was passed by the voters and large amounts of money for rail passenger service in California were made available. This had made it financially possible for the counties of Mendocino and Humboldt to purchase the northernmost piece of the Northwestern Pacific Railroad tracks from Willits to Eureka.

When Southern Pacific, the parent company of the Northwestern Pacific Railroad, had finally sold the remaining part of the line to the public in April of 1996, Julie's grandfather had been jubilant. Now the old Northwestern Pacific Railroad was in one ownership again. He had been one of the invited passengers on the celebration train in June. In October of the same year, the first passenger excursion train since 1968 made an inaugural run from Healdsburg in Sonoma–68 miles north of the Golden Gate–to Willits, another 70 miles to the north. And, of course, he was also on board.

Later, when the damage from the storms in 1997 and 1998 finally had been repaired, passenger excursions were reintroduced. Again, Julie's grandfather took every opportunity to ride those trains. But he wanted more, he wanted the real thing, reliable regular passenger service at reasonable prices for everybody. He was elated when regular commuter rail service in Sonoma and Marin County got off to a flying start. This was the first major step and soon intercity trains to Humboldt County would follow.

Julie remembered when he called her last year in August with the news that intercity passenger service between San Francisco and Eureka–which had been in the planning stage for some time–would start November 15. A new ferry was going to arrive in September in San Francisco.

"Now I don't need the car any longer, Julie! I only kept it to get up to the ranch." He told her, and sure enough, when she came home for Christmas, the car was gone. Only the date for the beginning of intercity service had been delayed to March 15. And then, tragedy struck and he never would make the trip he had worked for so hard.

Julie saw herself as the heiress of her grandfather's dream. At this moment, she felt his presence more than ever before. This train trip was the realization of her grandfather's hopes. It was not just a way to get there, it was a trip into her family's past, and a bridge to the future.

In spite of the rough seas, the ferry arrived at Port Sonoma, at the north end of San Francisco Bay, on time. To Julie's delight, she could see glimpses of blue sky–it looked as if the weather was improving. The northbound train was there, waiting and ready to go. Julie had checked her baggage through to Willits already in San Francisco and the transfer to the train took only a few minutes. She found a window seat and settled down, ready for the journey. Most of the ferry passengers had by now boarded the train. But Julie noticed a man outside her window, loaded down with several cameras and bags, nervously checking his wristwatch and looking toward the gangplank, which was now empty. Finally, just before the train was leaving, a woman came running down from the ship, received an angry look from the man with the cameras, and together they boarded the train at the last second. They entered Julie's coach and took the seats opposite from her. The woman greeted her with a cheerful 'Good morning' and asked whether the seats were still available. Her companion grunted a muffled 'Hello' and got busy stowing away their baggage. Julie could tell that he was furious. He gave an impatient shove to one of the bags when it didn't fit on the rack right the first time and then flopped down on his seat, staring out the window, seemingly uninterested in what his partner was doing. The couple was probably in their middle or late forties. The woman was attractive, with beautiful reddish-blonde hair, curling around her handsome, intelligent face in soft, natural waves. She was a little shorter than Julie, had a nice figure, and looked fit and healthy. It didn't seem to dampen her spirit that her companion–a slender man of medium height, with dark, graying hair and a small beard–was rather upset. She radiated happiness and positive energy and was either used to his mood swings or secure in her belief that whatever had made her late was justified.

Carelessly smoothing down her wind-blown hair, she sighed, "Wow, this was a bit of a rush, but...."

Her companion–still looking out the window–interrupted her, remarking gruffly, "That was the understatement of the year."

She didn't respond and continued, "... but I would give an 'A' to the first leg of the trip–the ferry left on time, arrived on time and the train left right on the dot!"

He almost spit out his response, "And you would have earned an 'F' had we missed the train, it certainly was very close."

Julie felt uncomfortable being the accidental witness to this evolving domestic quarrel. Should she look for another seat? But the train was pretty full. Then she remembered the *Ruth Rendell* mystery that Doris had put in her bag this morning at the ferry. She got it out and started–or at least pretended–to read. Fortunately, the woman, smiling radiantly, and touching her companion's hand, made an effort to restore harmony.

"I am sorry Josh, I really am," she said, trying to get through to him. "But if you would have seen who I ran into, you wouldn't be so crabby. This encounter I just had might add a few interesting lines to our story."

Noticing all their sophisticated camera equipment, and hearing the woman's comment, Julie assumed that the two were journalists. She had also seen that 'Josh' had been tempted to pull away his hand at first, then let her touch it and now she could detect a small smile on his lips. He even turned slightly toward his companion, and asked, still a little grouchy, "So, who was it?"

The woman, pleased that he came around, said, "You wouldn't believe it. Someone we have not heard from in years and had she recognized you, she would not have treated me like a long-lost sister. It was Elaine Jerkins!" she exclaimed and now had his full attention.

"What is she doing in the Bay Area?" he asked.

His companion told him that Elaine was now living in Santa Rosa, had married, and was working for a law firm in the city.

"So I asked her whether she was commuting by train and ferry every day...."

Josh interrupted her, saying, "And she probably told you that her BMW just happened to be in the shop today?"

"No, on the contrary, she told me that she has used the train since the commuter rail service started a year ago and how she loves it. That is really amazing, considering how she voted consistently against anything that had to do with public transportation when she was on the City Council. I wonder if she married a guy who completely changed her, or if she is perhaps running for public office–or has she finally seen the light? Anyway, her remarks might add some interesting points to our story. Down south, there are still a few people who remember her. So now you probably can understand why I tried to spend every available second with her–after all, we still made the train!"

"A good omen for our trip, don't you think, Helen? Meeting a converted anti-public-transportation person the first day. I'm glad that you took the opportunity–yes, after all, we made the train." He grinned and continued, "this waiting has exhausted me, and I am tired anyway. Bob kept me up too late last night with all his inside stories on transportation issues in Sacramento. Wake me when we arrive in Willits. I am going to take a nice long nap."

He kissed her and snuggled into his corner, closing his eyes.

Helen smiled at Julie, who had closed her book for a moment and watched the outside world go by.

"I hope we didn't disturb you with our little argument? We have been married for almost twenty years, and these short quarrels make life a bit more interesting. I am Helen Bender and he is my husband, Josh." She stretched out her arm to shake hands with Julie, who introduced herself too.

"What is your destination, Julie? Josh and I are taking this trip to write a comprehensive story on the Northern California railroads and we want to find out where people are taking the trains to and why, so I hope you don't mind me asking you?"

Julie didn't mind and explained that she was going up to the Eel River Valley.

"Great," Helen beamed. "So we will be in each other's company until we reach Willits. We are taking a short ride on the Skunk train this afternoon and will stay in Willits tonight. Tomorrow, we continue by train all the way to Eureka."

"That will be the same with me," Julie said. "I will visit some friends in Willits and then also continue tomorrow."

Helen told her that they were staying for two days in Eureka and then join a group of six people for a bicycle/van trip from Eureka to Redding. From there, Amtrak's Coast Starlight would take them back to L.A.

"Where are you going in the Eel River Valley? Is it a vacation trip?" Helen asked.

Julie told her that she was going up to her grandfather's ranch just south of Madrone Flat, at the Eel River.

"Actually, it is my ranch now, I inherited it from my grandfather who died last year. The ranch has been in the family for several generations and I consider myself more a steward of the land than…."

She was interrupted by Helen who excitedly jumped almost out of her seat. "Hold it, Julie. You are exactly the person I hoped to run into. Sort of an old-timer who could tell me some of the history of the area connected to the railroad. Would you mind if I taped what you are about to tell me?"

Julie laughed, "At twenty-four I am not really an old-timer! No, I don't mind being taped."

Helen retrieved her tape recorder from her oversized shoulder bag, checked the tape and apologized for having interrupted Julie. "Sorry about cutting you off. You were just saying that you had inherited the ranch from your grandfather and felt more like a steward of the land than…?"

"… than its owner–that's what I meant to say," Julie finished.

"Would you mind telling me when your ancestors started the ranch?" Helen asked.

"My great-grandparents bought the land in 1913. My great-grandfather had worked as an engineer on the construction of the railroad between Willits and Eureka for several years. He had married in 1912 and his wife was working as a schoolteacher in Ukiah. She often visited him on weekends and spent her vacations at the camps, wherever he happened to work. The wild country up there fascinated them and when a piece of land–next to the river and the railroad tracks, south of Madrone Flat–came up for sale, they bought it. They built a small cabin there, in a hanging valley overlooking the river. For a while, after the construction of the railroad was completed in 1914, my great-grandfather was still employed by the railroad, but eventually, he was faced with the choice to either move away for another engineering job or stay there and try his hand at ranching. It was a difficult decision, being raised in a city, ranching did not come easy to them. But they stayed there. A big garden with lots of fruit trees, berries and vegetables, and goats, pigs, sheep and chickens kept them more than busy. They were self-sufficient, and made a few dollars selling their surplus, taking it to Eureka or Willits by train. My great-grandmother taught school in Madrone Flat when a one-classroom school was established there, which added a small, reliable amount to the family income."

Julie looked searchingly at Helen. Was she still paying attention or was the family story getting too boring for her? An encouraging smile from Helen told Julie to continue. "Their first child, a girl, was born in 1915 and a son, my grandfather, five years later. The cabin eventually became a pretty nice house, and to supplement their income, they took in summer guests who arrived and left by train.

"We still have many of those wonderful black and white photos, slightly yellowed at the edges, that were taken at the railroad tracks, showing people arriving or leaving, often with the steam train in the background. The women–even in summer–wore formal, tight-fitting long dresses, and elaborate hats." Julie stopped for a minute, wondering again, if Helen was really interested in all these details?

"Sure, keep going, Julie, this is extremely interesting to me, I just love to hear what happened."

"The children went to school in the one-room school house in Madrone Flat, only for the last year of high school did they stay with friends of the family in Eureka, attending the school there. They went up by train on Sunday evenings and came back on Saturday mornings. Both were able to go to college on scholarships. My grandfather became a successful lawyer in San Francisco. But my great-aunt eventually came back to live at the ranch. She had studied horticulture in San Luis Obispo and worked for a while in a big nursery in Santa Barbara. Then her mother got seriously ill and she went home to nurse her. Although my great-grandmother recovered completely, my great-aunt remained at the ranch. World War II had just begun and her fiancee, whom she had met in Santa Barbara, died in the war. His death was a terrible shock for her. She needed years to get over it and never married. The garden at the ranch received her undivided attention and became a little jewel. Later, she taught school in Madrone Flat and occasionally did some landscape projects for clients in Garberville or Eureka. Both my great-grandparents died before I was born, but my great aunt was still taking care of the ranch during my childhood years. I grew up in the Bay Area. Every time we came for a visit, my aunt had planted something new and exciting. She died from a stroke a few years ago."

"I suppose when you were a child, the passenger service on the Northwestern Pacific Railroad had already been abandoned?" Helen asked.

"Yes, unfortunately. We always came by car, but again and again I heard those stories of the 'good old times' when one would go down to the tracks and get on the train.

"My grandfather lived in San Francisco, got married and had a son, my father, and a daughter, my aunt, who lives in Mexico. For them, the trains were still part of their lives. Whenever they visited their grandparents or aunt, they would use the train. Eventually, passenger service between San Francisco–or San Rafael in Marin County–and Eureka dwindled down to three times a week, and in November of 1958 Southern Pacific was allowed to abandon the passenger service between San Rafael and Willits completely. They still had to provide service from Willits to Eureka and a small train, the 'Budd Car', operated three times a week until 1969 when the service was cut to twice a week and was finally abandoned in April of 1971.

"Unfortunately, I never had a chance to ride the train. For a few years, already during the eighties and early nineties, there had been some passenger excursions from Willits to Eureka, and my grandfather had taken advantage of those trips, but somehow, I never made it. Now, I am closing the gap. After four years of college in the east, 'the fourth generation' is coming home on the train!" Julie said triumphantly.

"Do you know of other families that lived there for generations and were dependent on the train?" Helen asked.

"Yes," Julie was quick to answer. "The family who owns the general store in Madrone Flat has been in the valley as long as ours. I believe the grandfather of the present owner also came to work on the railroad construction and they all used the train as much as my family. They just opened a lovely bed and breakfast next to the general store, overlooking the river.

"Also, our closest neighbor's family has been in the area for a long time. They settled there years before the railroad was built. For them, and many others, the railroad was the lifeline to the outside world."

"You know, Julie," Helen regretfully sighed, "I wish we could cancel our reservation in Eureka and stop in Madrone Flat on Friday to stay in the new B and B! Unfortunately, this is impossible, we will meet with the other bikers in Eureka on Friday evening."

"When is the deadline for your story?"

"August first," Helen replied. "They want it for the September issue."

"You could come up by train on a long weekend. Take your laptop along and do some writing on the train. I'll be at the ranch until the end of August, you are both welcome to stay at our house," Julie said.

"Thank you for the invitation, Julie, but we would rather stay at the B and B to become acquainted with it and include it, hopefully, with places to recommend. Of course, we would visit you too at your ranch. On this trip, we are using the slower coastal route, next time we could use the inland route, the San Joaquin train, which is about three hours faster. I wish the new High-Speed trains from LA to San Francisco were running already. It is supposed to take only two and a half hours from San Francisco to Los Angeles."

"Wow, that sounds unbelievable," Julie responded excitedly. "How far are they with the construction? I haven't heard anything for a while."

Helen frowned, "I am not sure either when it is going to start running. All I know is that it goes faster than they had anticipated, which I like. It's a shame that we are so far behind Europe. They started the first High-Speed trains in the eighties.

Getting back to another visit–I am pretty sure we can make it. Do you have an address so I can contact the B and B?"

"Why don't you rather give me your address, Helen? I will send you their folder and some information on the other places in Madrone Flat as soon as I get into the village," Julie promised.

"Are your parents now at the ranch, Julie?" Helen asked and realized right away that she had touched a sensitive issue when she saw Julie's face clouding up. Julie looked down at her book, wondering how different her life would be if her parents were living at the ranch...

She finally said quietly, "My parents died in a car accident when I was eleven."

Helen felt bad to have stirred up sad memories and apologized. She looked concerned when she asked, "You will be all by yourself at the ranch, all alone?"

Julie laughed. "You sound like Fred, Helen! Do I look that helpless?" and explained who Fred was and that he, too, was worried she might arrive at the ranch and Emily and Bret still gone.

"You will see when we arrive up there both will be anxiously waiting for me down at the tracks!" Julie predicted. "They are acting–sort of–as caretakers, but they are almost like parents to me, I can't wait to see them again. Emily's mother was the sister of my great-aunt's fiancee. The two women had remained friends and when Emily, the daughter, came up to the ranch on a visit with her husband, my aunt invited them to live there. Being self-employed as author and illustrator, they enthusiastically accepted the offer and have lived at the ranch for over ten years. They are like family."

Helen observed the stop-and-go traffic on Highway 101 paralleling the train tracks. "It's amazing how many people still prefer to sit in this awful traffic, exposed to all the exhaust fumes, instead of riding the commuter trains. I use the trains in L.A. a lot and besides being freed of the stress of driving, I also very much enjoy meeting people. Look, we would never have met if it were not for the train! It brings people together in a friendly, relaxed atmosphere. This is one of the many advantages of public transit which hardly anybody ever considers. But in today's society, where fewer and fewer people talk to each other, it is very important."

After they had passed Santa Rosa, Josh woke up. Helen introduced Julie to him and gave him a short summary of what she had all learned about the history of Julie's family and the railroad. He was as delighted as Helen to meet a 'native'.

Josh invited the two women to the dining car for a snack. The selection at the buffet-type food-counter was impressive. Josh asked Julie if she could stomach a glass of wine so early? He wanted to drink a toast to the new train and didn't think that orange juice was appropriate. Julie liked the idea and picked out a cheese croissant, a good base for a glass of wine before ten o'clock in the morning. They settled at a table on the west side of the train.

After Josh had poured the wine, he raised his glass–it was real glass, sturdy and strong, adorned with the Northwestern Pacific Railroad logo–and announced, "Here is to a successful future of the Northwestern Pacific Railroad!" He pointed toward the countryside passing by and continued, "This is a fitting place to drink a good glass of wine, we are now entering the Sonoma wine country."

South of Healdsburg, the train crossed the Russian River, which was flowing swiftly westwards toward the ocean, the water slightly turbid because of the recent storm. By now, the sky was cloud free. It promised to become a beautiful day.

A large group of passengers–heading for two buses labeled 'Winery Tours'–got off in Healdsburg, where the historic station building had been restored recently.

The train passed through acres and acres of grape vines, their radiant green foliage in stark contrast to the yellowing grasses of meadows and fields.

These vineyards stretch out into the plains of the Russian River Valley, and climb up the lower slopes of the distant hills. Dark green hills in the west, the eastern edges of the Redwood forests that continue for thirty or forty miles all the way to the Pacific Ocean. The eastern hills are lighter in color, grayish-green. This area is drier and warmer than the Redwood region and not as densely forested. The hills are higher, with Mount St. Helena at 4,343 feet towering over all of them.

The three enjoyed the scenery, sipping their wine. Helen interrupted this complacent state. "Getting back to Madrone Flat, Julie, I have a question. You mentioned that you have many old photos that were taken with the train in the background. Any chance that we could borrow two or three to make copies?"

"Certainly, however our family always had the policy not to lend out any photos. I will go through our collection and pick out the best ones and have copies made for you."

"We will reimburse you for you expenses of course, Julie," Josh replied.

"No," Julie said, shaking her head. "Don't bother. This is my contribution to your story. Just write a really interesting and enticing article about the railroad. We want people to use the trains as often as possible. Also, you might put in a plug for the accommodations in Madrone Flat. This little community could use some extra income–and it's all locally owned."

Josh was looking out the window, watching the river. "That reminds me, have you two talked about 1964 when a catastrophic Eel River flood almost wiped out the northern end of the railroad?"

"No," Helen replied. "We didn't touch this subject yet."

Josh explained to Julie that during the last few days he and Helen had talked to a lot of people in the San Francisco area about the railroad. Rail fans, railroad club members, Golden Gate Bridge District Directors, Marin and Sonoma County Supervisors, Caltrans representatives, City Council members, transportation representatives from various environmental organizations, and others. Many of them had been involved in getting the commuter and intercity trains on the Northwestern Pacific Railroad established. Most of them were satisfied how the new system was operating and very much relieved that it finally had happened. But in many interviews, the 1964 flood had been mentioned. Could such a disaster happen again? "What is your opinion on this subject, Julie?" Josh asked.

"Well, the flood was long before my time, but I can assure you that I have heard many discussions about this disaster in my family. Whenever we had an extreme storm, the old flood raised its ugly head again and everybody worried. My opinion is really my grandfather's opinion. He talked to me about this matter often, especially during the last few years, when more and more money was invested into the rehabilitation of the line. Some people were extremely critical and insisted that every penny spent was a waste of taxpayers' money. My grandfather's main argument against that kind of reasoning was that the disaster of 1964 had not singled out the railroad, it also had played havoc with the roads. There was not one Highway bridge left on highway 101 between Willits and Eureka and the roads were severely damaged and often nonexistent.

"Still, the arguments against the railroad continued. Again and again it was pointed out that it was insane to build a railroad through a canyon where the soils were so unstable that even without a severe flood, slides would occur. Grandfather argued that the highways in these mountains were subjected to unexpected slides as well. Highway 101 has a history of bad slides which cost many millions of dollars to fix. One time–I believe it was around 1990–a large section of 101 south of Willits collapsed and the highway was closed for almost a week to all traffic. And this happened in May, not in the middle of winter during a heavy storm. It had rained only a few inches."

"I happen to remember that very well, Julie," Helen said, "because we were on our way to Oregon and had spent the night in Ukiah with friends. We found out the next morning, when we started driving north, and had to take the long detour of over one hundred miles to the coast, to Fort Bragg, and then back on Highway 20 to Willits and Highway 101."

"There are also natural disasters where railroads have fared much better than highways," Julie said and referred to several major earthquakes. "Just a few hours after the earthquake struck San Francisco in 1989, both the Bay Area Rapid Transit and Caltrain from San Francisco to San Jose were operating again. But the Bay Bridge had collapsed and many major roads in the area were closed for a long time. A little later, another earthquake shook Humboldt County. The tracks and a major railroad bridge south of Eureka were actually quite close to the epicenter. The bridge was unharmed and a fairly long slide, which had covered the tracks, was cleared within two days. But one of the highway bridges in the area was badly damaged and had to be rebuilt."

"This was the same situation when we had the earthquake in Los Angeles in 1994," Josh agreed. "The new light rail system had no structural damages at all and Metrolink was operating the next day again. Both carried enormous number of passengers who couldn't use their cars because the streets and roads were damaged badly in many places.

"Even a bad derailment of Southern Pacific freight cars at the epicenter was cleared for traffic within 48 hours, it was really amazing. Operations returned to normal long before repair on highways was even started. And yet, it has been such a struggle to get funding for railroads compared to funding for highways. In a state which is so vulnerable to earthquakes this doesn't make sense."

"I am afraid I got off the subject, Josh," Julie apologized. "You actually wanted to know more about the flood? Or rather, how did my grandfather feel about the possibility of a repeat of a 1964 flood? He realized that the combination of a record snowfall in the mountains of the Mendocino National Forest and a succeeding tropical storm with torrential rains had been catastrophic. But he argued that two man-made factors had contributed substantially to the flood and the damage–over grazing and over logging.

"Only too well did he know the region's history–how the land use pattern had dramatically changed when the first white settlers arrived and within a short time had driven the native people away from their lands into the reservation at Round Valley. While the Indians had treaded lightly on the land, the new ranchers did the opposite. Large ranching operations with huge herds of cattle or sheep were introduced and over grazing became a serious problem, which was already recognized around the turn of the century.

"Logging had accelerated dramatically after World War II. New big machines–bulldozers–opened up areas for logging faster than it ever had been possible. Many people believe that the worst logging occurred during the eighties, but in reality it was during the early fifties when the largest timber harvests took place. After the flood in 1964, Grandpa saw several examples of extreme erosion in the Madrone Flat area, where over logging or over grazing on the higher slopes had caused landslides which buried the tracks in mud or washed them into the river.

"The Eel River, together with its various arms and many tributaries, covers a huge area, a large percentage of it in the high mountains of the Mendocino National Forest. Unless bad land-use practices were prevented all over, one could not expect positive changes. Grandpa was also concerned about the decline of the fish population in the river. He was convinced that over logging and overgrazing was equally responsible for this problem.

"Public awareness about over logging was high in the sixties. There was a lot of pressure on the legislature to create more stringent forest management rules. As a member of the Sierra Club and the Save-The-Redwoods League, my Grandfather had participated in these efforts. So when finally the new Forest Practice Act was passed by the California Legislature 1973, hope was high that things would change for the better."

"But they didn't, right?" Helen interrupted. "We informed ourselves on the timber issues in Northwestern California before we started on this trip, because we don't know too much about this–having lived in Southern California all our life. We are also Sierra Club members and read the Club's literature on this general subject. Apparently, the Forest Practice Act had sound intentions but implementation was another matter."

"And, I guess in time, the rules were watered down and amended," Josh added.

"You are absolutely right, Josh," Julie said. "In the beginning, after the new forest act came out, my grandfather had been optimistic that things would change. But he was very disappointed when logging accelerated again in the eighties. Yet it never reached the same extreme proportions of the fifties, because there was not that much left.

"During the last ten years when passenger service on the Northwestern Pacific became a realistic goal again, Grandpa spent a lot of time studying the land-use history of the region. He became convinced that the 1964 flood would not have reached these catastrophic dimensions had man not destroyed the natural balance. The unrestrained, excessive logging reached its peak in 1955 and the following winter, when record rainfalls hit the area, the Eel River Valley experienced an extensive flood. Fortunately, the railroad escaped without major damages.

"Each following winter, heavy logging took its toll when the now exposed steep slopes continued to erode, and nine years later–in 1964–the damage was horrendous.

"In his research, he found out that logging in the Mendocino National Forest had dropped from over one hundred million Board feet per year to only about five Million per year in the nineties. Grazing had also dwindled down to 10 percent of what it had been seventy or eighty years ago. Of course, there is still a lot of land–forest land or range land–in private ownership in this area were logging and grazing decisions are determined by the individual owners. But overall, my grandfather was cautiously optimistic that even with the same kind of weather conditions another flood might not be quite as devastating. He repeatedly talked about this subject, wrote letters to newspapers in the region to make the public aware of the danger to the railroad if one continued with bad and unwise land use.

"And I guess, I am doing the same now? Talking to you and hoping that you will include this issue in your article and perhaps change one or the other person's attitude when they read your story," Julie concluded, looking hopefully for signs of support from Helen and Josh, who nodded in agreement.

Another passenger, who had passed their table a while ago and had sat down at the adjacent table, reading his newspaper, nursing a tall glass of beer and munching chips, approached their table. He was perhaps in his eighties, a tall and wiry man, dressed in jeans and a short-sleeved western shirt, his face and arms deeply tanned, indicating that he was spending a lot of time outdoors.

"Sorry folks, but I couldn't help hearing what you were saying, talking about the big flood. It brought back sad memories, because our ranch north of Madrone Flat had been badly damaged. You might have a point there about this over grazing business, young lady," he addressed Julie. "But we wouldn't have to worry about all this any longer, if they had let us build the Dos Rios Dam. The railroad would be safe and sound. That was a damn shame that they listened to some city slickers and gave up the project."

Julie was not happy about this interruption. She knew that this dam had been a very controversial subject. Her grandfather had been a fierce opponent from the beginning and hearing the story, she had agreed with him. Now she was afraid she might get into an argument with this stranger, because with Helen and Josh listening, she could not try to brush him off with some small talk. Judging from the questioning looks on their faces, neither Helen nor Josh seemed to know about the dam.

"You never heard about this dam project?" she asked Josh and Helen. Both shook their heads.

"This huge lake was proposed back in the sixties by the State of California as part of the State Water Project. The plan was to flood Round Valley and the Eel River Canyon all the way to the dam about three miles east of Dos Rios, a small community on the Northwestern Pacific route.

I do agree with you," Julie responded to the old man's statement. "The dam would have been a protection for the railroad against another big flood. But there was also a lot of concern whether in this region of unstable rock formations one could actually build a 'safe ' dam that would not some day fail and bring an even worse disaster to the area than the 1964 flood? I feel that protecting the forests from over-harvesting, and keeping grazing at a minimum, are still the best routes to go both for the railroad and the whole area."

"Too bad you feel like this about the dam, if you had seen the flood as I did you would have a different opinion. As I said in the beginning, I see your point about the over grazing, young lady," the old man argued. "Only, setting up laws about grazing or logging… I don't like the government telling me what I can do or not do. If it makes sense to me, I do it voluntarily and that's the way it should be. And I also don't like outsiders or newcomers tell me what 's right, I have lived here so long and know what's good for the country and my ranch."

"My family came to Madrone Flat back in 1909," Julie said quietly. "I am not a newcomer!"

The old man needed a few minutes to digest this information. Then he barked, "What's your name, honey? I know everybody up there!" Julie could tell that Josh and Helen were enjoying this little dispute. She answered promptly, "Julie Sutten." The stranger took off his glasses, wiped them clean on a big handkerchief, stared at her for a few minutes and exclaimed, "I'll be darned! You must be Gregory Sutten's granddaughter! I am Homer Morgan."

He grabbed Julie's hand and shook it. Julie introduced Josh and

Helen and invited Homer to sit down and join them.

"Thank you," he said. "I suppose you are going up to the ranch? Is your grandfather up there? I have not seen him for a while."

When Julie told him that he had died in December, she had not counted on such an outburst of his sympathy.

"What a terrible loss, what a loss. I admired him greatly, he was a good man, your grandfather was. How sad. I am very, very sorry, Julie. I feel bad that I didn't know about it, I would certainly have come to his funeral. We were in Mexico in December and January, otherwise I would have known."

He pointed a gnarled finger at Julie, "You are a chip of the old block, you defend what you believe in. This Dos Rios Dam business! We argued about it every time we met, back at the time when the issue was still undecided. But I tell you what. Your grandfather showed me on my land–after the big flood–where over grazing had eroded one slope and a small landslide had occurred. It was a lesson for me, after that I took better care of the land. Still, I think the dam would have been a good idea. Well, I guess, this is water–Eel River water–under the bridge by now. Who is living at the ranch now? You are not going to be there all by yourself?"Julie told him about the Carters and that they had lived there for several years, even before her great-aunt had died.

"Yeah, I hadn't even thought about them," Homer said. "I remember now, when we took the train down last week, the wife and me–she stayed at her sister's in Oakland for another week–we stopped at your ranch. A guy came on board who had been waiting there."

"This must have been Bret Carter," Julie said eagerly. "About fifty years old, tall and slender, right?" Julie asked, happy to hear that Emily and Bret were back.

Homer frowned, "No, "he said. "It was a short guy, about thirty or so. He had dark hair and a small mustache. I happened to see that he was using a commute ticket, explaining that he was a relative of the family and that the Carters would be back by the end of the week."

"Probably a cousin of Emily or Bret? "Julie shrugged, wondering if this person might still be there when she arrived? Anyway, this was good news, so most likely they would be back by the time she arrived. Helen and Josh took the opportunity to do an interview with Homer who thoroughly enjoyed himself telling them his stories. There was a short stop in Ukiah at the new and well-designed transit center where quite a few passengers got off and others boarded the train. The center was busy. A smaller train arrived from the north, and many people transferred from the train to the local busses waiting for them.

As soon as the intercity train left the outskirts of town, it started to climb up the ridge to Willits. Julie, Helen and Josh had gone back to their coach before the train had reached Ukiah. Homer was sorry to hear that they all would stay over in Willits, he had hoped to have their company until he arrived at his ranch. So he trotted along and sat with them for this last stretch.

It is a special experience to ride the train from Ukiah to Willits. From a 635 feet elevation in Ukiah the train climbs to 1,953 feet at the summit and then descends down to 1,377 feet in Willits. The view from the ridge is spectacular. Patches of forest dot the meadows in the valley to the west, and climb up the adjacent hills. Higher mountains, more densely forested, form the horizon.

Because of the late rains, the grass up here was still fresh and green, especially in the shady areas and wildflowers were abundant. Along the streams, the candle-like white flowers of the buckeye trees were in full bloom. Although Julie had made this trip up Highway 101 many times, seeing the area from way above the road was a new adventure.

CHAPTER 3

The train arrived in Willits on time. Homer Morgan had gone back to his coach, promising Julie to visit her sometime this summer, and–he chuckled–to talk with her about the dam.

Julie, Helen and Josh were waiting at the exit, ready to get off. As soon as the train came to a halt, the doors opened, and they stepped from the train. Helen and Josh, loaded down with all their reporter paraphernalia, said good-bye to Julie with a cheerful 'see you tomorrow, kid!' and strolled over to the office to pick up their tickets for the Skunk train.

So far, Julie had not discovered Frank Rodgers among the people waiting for the train. She walked slowly toward the baggage car at the front of the train, keeping an eye on the people who came in from the street, hoping to see a familiar face, but neither Frank nor anybody from his family showed up. An older, neatly dressed woman was walking along the train, observing the passengers who got off in Willits. Perhaps Frank couldn't come and this woman was his secretary? Julie stopped and watched her for a minute. No, she had just found her party. Two young boys came running toward her and she gathered them up into her arms. Julie fondly observed this scene, imagining her own homecoming the next day at the ranch, being welcomed as warmly by Emily and Bret when she would get off the train. She quickly turned and almost collided with a young man who was coming from the direction of the street, walking fast. He stopped, apologized and smiled at her, and continued along the train, scanning the passengers who came from the train.

The young man reminded Julie strongly of a colleague at Columbia for whom she had harbored a secret crush. For a second she thought it was him, although this was impossible. Benji had left Columbia last summer, going back to New Delhi. But this stranger certainly looked a lot like him–they were of the same height, similar built and coloring, and Julie realized to her dismay that she was blushing like a schoolgirl. She pulled herself together and kept going.

The smallest of her three suitcases had already come down from the conveyor belt. As she was concentrating on the various kinds of bags sliding down to the platform, someone tapped her lightly on the shoulder, and a male voice asked, "Excuse me, are you by any chance Julie Sutten?"

Julie turned around and to her utter embarrassment blushed again. The young man who had passed her a few moments ago was addressing her. She struggled to keep her emotions under control. With a stiff little smile she replied, "Yes, I am."

By then, the young man had taken off his sunglasses and without them, he became a stranger, the spell was broken. Julie felt normal again and noticed with relief that her cheeks were no longer burning. He held out his hand and introduced himself.

"I am Thomas Millon, a friend of Ken, Frank Rodgers' son. Frank had a client come in just when he was going to leave for the station to pick you up. So he asked me to meet you at the train, I happen to be visiting with them for a few days. I'm sorry to be a few minutes late. Frank had described you with short hair, which is not really true. He probably has not seen you for a while? The braids looks good on you, though, I like them."

Julie shook his hand, but was slightly annoyed. Partially, because she had blushed again, but also because she felt that his compliment was coming too fast–he had just met her, after all!

Thomas Millon seemed to sense her disapproval, "Sorry, I shouldn't have said that. Usually, I am not throwing compliments around. I just meant to explain why I was late, and when I looked at you, the remark about your braids slipped out." He seemed to be genuinely regretful about his lapse.

Julie couldn't help liking him and laughed, "That's OK. Yes, I used to wear my hair short and I guess I have not seen Frank since I started to let it grow. Sorry to confuse you."

They were interrupted by the baggage clerk who oversaw the unloading, pointing to two large suitcases, "Are those yours, Miss?"

Yes, they were and before Julie could say a word, Thomas Millon had picked up her suitcases and put them aside, out of the way.

"Do you have more coming?" he asked Julie.

"No, thank you, that's it."

"My car is across the street on the parking lot," he made a vague gesture in the direction of the street, picked up the suitcases again and started to walk toward the north end of the platform. Julie took the other suitcase and came along. The incidence had stirred up feelings which she thought she had overcome. She just hoped that she had not appeared too befuddled. When they reached the street, Thomas Millon stopped and put down the heavy suitcases for a moment.

"You must have rocks in here," he grinned and stretched. "Lots of books, I suppose? By the way, I am sorry I startled you when you were waiting for your baggage."

"Don't feel bad," Julie replied, "it had nothing to do with you. It just so happens that you resemble a colleague of mine at Columbia who was on sabbatical leave from India. When I first saw you, for a second I thought it was he."

As soon as she had said that she realized that perhaps Thomas, as an African-American, might be offended by being mistaken as an East-Indian. She started to apologize, didn't really know what to say and how to say it, blushed, and finally gave up, totally embarrassed.

Fortunately, Thomas didn't seem to mind, "Don't worry, I am not fussy about things like that. And besides, my great-grandmother was East-Indian."

Thomas' old car was of a nondescript color. Perhaps it had been medium blue at some time in the distant past, a few isolated spots still showed its original glory. But Julie was pleasantly surprised when Thomas opened the door for her. The interior of the car was extremely clean and orderly.

As they were leaving the parking lot, another train pulled into the station, and Thomas explained to Julie, "There comes the California Western, the Skunk train, from Fort Bragg. The Northwestern Pacific is waiting for the California Western passengers to make the connection, now the train for Eureka will leave in a few minutes."

On the way to Frank's office, Julie shyly observed Thomas Millon. He was of the same height as Benji, about five feet ten or eleven, and just as slender. His hair was curly and black. Julie liked Thomas' face. He was clean shaven, looked friendly and intelligent and his brown eyes had a warm, assuring smile. She figured he was about her age, he was probably at least five or six years younger than Benji, and better looking too, she added as an afterthought–in fact, very good looking. Was he also a law student, like Ken? Her thoughts were interrupted when the car stopped in front of Frank's office.

Thomas hoisted her heavy suitcases out of the trunk and carried them into Frank's office. The secretary welcomed Julie and told her that Frank would be through with his client in a few minutes.

Frank greeted her with a big hug. Julie liked him, she felt comfortable in his presence. He always seemed to be relaxed, never in a hurry. A short, slender man, he looked younger than he was, in spite of his almost completely bald head. His reputation as a surveyor was impeccable, and he was well respected in the community. Frank told Julie that Fred Mendell had called just before his client came in. He still had not heard from the Carters and was worried that they would not be back by the time Julie arrived up there. Frank explained to Julie that he could not help her with a four-wheel-drive vehicle. His Land Rover was in the shop and he needed his Jeep.

"Actually, the Jeep or any other car wouldn't do you much good anyway, Julie," he grinned. "Your grandfather would have loved what I am going to tell you."

Julie was mystified, what did he refer too?

"You will not believe it. Highway 101 is closed near Legett again, at the old slide area that has already swallowed millions and millions. It could take a week before they can get it open again. They are now advising everybody to take the train and more freight shipping will go by rail than ever before. Well, I am glad that we have the choice now, a few years ago, this would have been a total disaster." His voice belied the severity of the situation. Did he enjoy the fact that for once, the railroad surpassed the highway?

"The Jeep was Fred's weird idea anyway, Frank," Julie told him. "I had already decided to take the train to the ranch whether Emily and Bret are back or not. If the road to the ranch is still flooded by the creek, it probably would even be dangerous for me to drive in. The train is so much simpler, even if nobody is home and I have to drag my suitcases up the hill." She looked at Thomas and smiled, "I am not intending to carry them up the hill, full. I probably have to make several trips with the garden cart. Actually, Frank, I stopped in Willits mainly to visit with you, really! I have not seen you for a while and also was hoping that you might be able to tell me a little about historic Indian settlements in our area up there. You are very familiar with the whole area and have been in many remote spots. I will stay at the ranch at least for the summer and would like to take the time to explore the vicinity."

Frank was eager to help. "I'll be happy to tell you as much as I know."

He looked at his watch, "But before we get into that, I have to tell you what's going on here. We have planned a birthday surprise for Ken's girlfriend, Maria, a late lunch in Northspur, the halfway point between Willits and Fort Bragg on the Skunk train. The train leaves in forty minutes. Can you wait with lunch until we get to Northspur or are you very hungry? How about a cup of tea and some cookies?"

Julie was not very hungry, but gladly accepted a cup of tea from Frank's secretary.

"Back to your question about Native American settlements in your area. When we return from the train ride, we'll drive up to the house and I'll get my maps out and show you some places I know of. By the way, not only is Maria working on her master's degree in Indian History, she is also almost a full-blooded Indian. Her great-grandmother grew up near your ranch, somewhere along the Eel. She was a Lassik Indian, and Maria put together a marvelous collection of her stories. You must talk to Maria about this, she might be able to tell you more than I know.

Unfortunately, Linda and our daughter Iris are in San Diego, visiting my mother-in-law. They will be sorry to have missed you. Perhaps we will come up to the ranch and visit with you this summer. Do you have lined up a job in Berkeley? I remember your grandfather had mentioned that when I saw him the last time?""I have a good chance to get a job at UC, but it is not confirmed yet. They asked me to call them at the end of July. To be honest, at this point I am not sure if I want to do this anyway. Emily told me that the school in Madrone Flat is losing a teacher for a year, which gave me the idea to perhaps try to teach there temporarily. Of course, I don't have a teacher's credential, but I have a master's degree in archaeology now and have also a pretty solid background in chemistry. For an interim teaching job, I might qualify if they have not found someone yet. It would be like stepping into my great-grandmother's footsteps. After New York, I am tired of city life and the idea to live at the ranch at least for a year appeals to me. So I hope that by the end of July I will know what is available and what I want."

"Did Thomas tell you that he and Ken passed the Bar examination and both are now full-fledged lawyers?" Frank asked.

"No, he didn't. You must be proud of your son, Frank. And congratulations to you, Thomas," Julie shook Thomas' hand.

"Having just graduated from college myself, I know how you must feel. Where do you go from here? Do you already have a job?"

"Thank you, and congratulations to you too. I will start with an environmental law firm in Santa Rosa next month, I am really looking forward to it. The few weeks I have left I will take it easy. I'll take the train to Eureka next week and then do some backpacking in the Trinity Alps with Ken and another friend," Thomas responded. "How did you like the train trip, by the way?"

Julie couldn't help asking, "Which one, the one from New York to San Francisco or from San Francisco to Willits?"

"Wow, I hadn't been aware you were such a widely-traveled person," Thomas grinned. "I had been referring to the local trip. I would have liked to come up by train, but I gave up my apartment in San Francisco and have not rented a new one in Santa Rosa yet where I could have left my car safely. So how did you like the trip?"

Julie answered enthusiastically, "Great, it was wonderful! It is much more relaxing than going by car! I met a lovely couple on the train, both are reporters and they are doing a major story on the Northern California Railroads. Incidentally, they will also be on the Skunk Train, so you can meet them. They will continue tomorrow to Eureka."

Frank was happy to hear that, "Good, we need as much publicity for the trains as we can get. They will make life better for all of us. We will have less pollution and congestion on the highways and it is very comfortable to take the trains to the Bay Area and beyond. The last time I was down there by car I promised myself I would never do it again. Now I have been in the City already twice with Linda for a play and a concert since the passenger service started in March. We stayed overnight, it was like a mini vacation each time."

"Has Ken also found a job, Frank?" Julie asked.

Both Frank and Thomas looked at each other and smiled and Frank answered, "He will be working for a very prestigious law firm in San Francisco, one that you know very well. He got a job in your grandfather's firm."

"That's great!" Julie exclaimed. "I'm surprised that Fred didn't mention it?"

"Well, Ken wanted to do it on his own and not owe his job to his father's connections. So Fred probably still does not know about it, Ken used his San Francisco address. And besides, Fred is a tax lawyer, and Ken's field is environmental law, just like Thomas'."

"I have to tell you, Julie, that I had the great privilege to hear and observe your grandfather in court last year," Thomas told Julie. "When Ken applied for the job, he wanted me to get an idea what kind of a firm he would be working for. So he asked me to come along when he knew that your grandfather would handle a case in court. I was so impressed, that for a few weeks I considered applying for a job with your grandfather's firm myself."

Julie's eyes misted over. She was touched by Thomas' statement about her grandfather. "Why didn't you do it?"

"It wouldn't have been fair to Ken in case had they chosen only one of us and it would have been I. So I looked around and found this company in Santa Rosa. I feel pretty good about them, although they are certainly not in the same league as your grandfather's firm. But I liked the man who interviewed me and I expect to be able to learn something and to do a good job. Besides, I really like to get away from a big city for a change. Santa Rosa is still surrounded by semi-rural areas." Julie could tell that Frank was fond of his son's friend, he looked at Thomas with admiration.

Frank glanced at his watch, "It's time to go. We can walk, it isn't very far."

CHAPTER 4

Ken and Maria were already on the train, waiting for Frank, Julie and Thomas. Ken had just finished introductions between Maria and Julie, when Julie heard her name called. It was Helen who had spotted her and now introductions continued between Helen, Josh and Frank's party. They all went outside to the open observation car after the train started to move. Maria, Frank and Ken played tour guides. To Frank's surprise, Julie had never been on the Skunk train and it was also a new experience for Thomas, Helen and Josh.

Being a surveyor, Frank was especially familiar with the lay of the land, the topography and geology. He was also a registered, professional forester and knew a lot about the environment in general, the various microclimates and of course, was well acquainted with the tree species and shrubs.

While the train climbed up the eastern slope of the ridge which divides the Willits area from the valley of the Noyo River–through which the California Western Railroad winds its way to the coast–Frank made his party aware of the differences in the vegetation on the eastern and western slopes.

"As soon as we reach the western side of this ridge–a tunnel gets us through the last hill quickly–these oak woodlands you see here give way to a redwood and Douglas-fir forest, which are the dominant trees. In addition, there are under-story trees such as Tan oaks, red-barked madrones and various other oaks. Alders, maples and Bay trees grow along the creeks. Here and there, we can find some yew trees. The prevailing winds in our area come from the northwest, and they bring along the rain. Therefore, all these mountains receive higher rainfall on the western slopes than on the eastern slopes, which means that the eastern slopes are usually drier with less vegetation, but also colder in the winter and warmer in the summer than the western slopes."

"How much rain do you actually get here, Frank?" Julie asked.

"Well, there is quite a difference, depending on where you are. The highest rainfall is measured on the western slopes between the ocean and the inland valleys and the average amounts to between 60 and 80 inches. Both Fort Bragg and Willits receive less, and as you continue east from Willits, it gets drier also, until you get up into the western slopes of the next ridges.

"By the way, those bushes or small trees with the gorgeous, candle-like pinkish-white flowers are buckeyes," he explained, pointing at several of them right next to the tracks.

Bird watching was Ken's hobby and he made the others aware of a flock of wild turkeys and a red-tailed hawk. Maria added the human element to the story, telling them about the history of the area. She was a born lecturer. Her voice was pleasant, her talk lively and within minutes she was surrounded by a captive audience of other passengers who listened in.

"I want to give you a glimpse of my people's history. I will take you back not only one century to the time when the railroad was constructed, but several hundreds of years before any white people came to this land. We don't have books or pictures from these times, only stories that were passed on from generation to generation. My grandmother has told me stories that she heard from her grandmother, who was told stories by her grandmother and so on. Listening to her, I often envisioned this land three or four hundred years ago, its meadows, streams and forests barely touched by my people, people that lived in balance with nature.

"There were no roads, no houses or fences–no railroad and no tunnel. This slope here had no interruption, no cut–where the tracks are now–it flowed smoothly from the ridge all the way down to the creek.

Perhaps there was a narrow path winding its way up on this side of the ridge and descending on the western side, which eventually reached the Pacific. The path might also have been further north, in the next valley, or along the ridge, nobody knows for sure, we can only speculate, but we will never know how it was in reality. You imagine it differently than I do, but sadly, we all know that it is gone forever."

After this somber introduction, Maria gave a short summary of the California Western Railroad's history. Maria had grown up in Willits. As a teenager, she had worked for the railroad as a hostess on the train during the summer. On many trips, she had recited its history from the very beginning in 1885 as a logging railroad, starting in Fort Bragg, to the time it finally reached Willits in 1911. And onto the twenties, the thirties and to the present, through changing ownerships from Union Lumber Company under the Johnson family in 1885, to Boise Cascade in 1969, Georgia Pacific Company in 1973, Kyle Railways in 1987 and finally to a group of local business people from Fort Bragg and Willits in 1996.

"The California Western Railroad began originally as a logging railroad. But, it was quite different from all the other logging railroads up and down the coast which were built, pulled up and relocated again, depending where they were needed. All the others are gone now, only the California Western has survived. Although logging is no longer done by railroad, some of the milled lumber from the Georgia Pacific mill in Fort Bragg is still transported by rail from Fort Bragg to Willits, and from there on the Northwestern Pacific to the Bay Area and beyond. There is at least one California Western freight train operating once a week."

Frank added, "To me, it seems just a few years ago, but I guess it goes as far back as the seventies, when there was a freight train operating every day. I wish they would go back to that, it would relieve the traffic on the winding Highway 20. Sorry to interrupt you, Maria."

"I second your remark, sir," a man in Maria's audience spoke up. "We drove on Highway 20 yesterday, and the truck traffic was awful. If your county is interested in tourist dollars, they should try to eliminate some of that truck traffic."

A young woman, who had listened intently, suggested to her fellow passenger, "You don't have to drive on Highway 20 if you want to get to the coast. Take the Skunk Train from Willits to Fort Bragg, and at the coast, depend on public transportation, they have a pretty good bus system in this county. And if you don't like to drive on Highway 101 either, take the Northwestern Pacific train from the Bay Area. That's what I did and it was a lovely trip." She flashed her audience a brilliant smile and was rewarded with supportive nods.

Maria took over again, "Thank you for your input. I am glad you brought up the freight trains, Frank, I usually don't think of them. I guess I was too closely connected to the tourist trains.

"From the very beginning, the California Western encouraged picnic trips for the families of the workers on weekends. As the tracks were extended further into the woods towards the east, tourists would use the train to come to the coast. The main line from San Francisco had reached Willits in 1902 and had been extended to Sherwood, fourteen miles northwest of Willits, by 1904. From here, visitors would take the stage coach down into the Noyo River Valley and transfer to the train to Fort Bragg. This Sherwood extension had been planned as the first leg of the line up to Eureka. But when the construction began around 1909, the Northwestern Pacific engineers had worked out a new route farther east, along the middle fork of the Eel River.

"In 1911, the California Western tracks finally reached Willits and from then on, many people rode the trains from the Bay Area to Fort Bragg. The trips became very popular and in 1921, Pullman Sleeper Car service was added–an overnight train from San Francisco to Fort Bragg and back."

"Did they ever have Pullman cars on the trains to Eureka?" Helen wanted to know.

Maria hesitated, and Julie answered Helen's question.

"As far as I know, they offered sleeping car service into the forties. They had an overnight train from San Francisco to Eureka and back."

"On the Skunk train, the Pullman service lasted only into the late twenties, unfortunately." Maria paused and pointed down the steep slope to the south and up the equally steep slope to the north. "Imagine, building a railroad along rocky slopes like this with hand tools mostly. It's awe-inspiring! Whenever I look at those old photos from the construction days, seeing the guys at work with pick axes, shovels and wheelbarrows, I remind myself how lucky we are that the railroad got ever built. I am doubtful we could find workers today that would be willing to do this kind of a job without machines–what do you think, guys?" She challenged Ken, Thomas and some other younger men who were listening.

As the train was chugging up the hill along a steep, mossy bank, they saw wildflowers, which Frank identified as Pentstemons and Firecrackers lilies.

"Indian Pinks, my favorite spring wildflowers!" Julie excitedly pointed to several clusters of small, scarlet-red flowers.

"I like those!" Maria said. "Which family do they belong too?"

Neither Julie nor Frank could answer her question, but Thomas helped out, "The Latin name is silene californica, it belongs to the Caryophyllacea or Pink family and the order of Silene."

He noticed Julie's astonished look and explained. "Originally, I wanted to become a wildlife biologist. Eventually, I realized that many environmental issues were finally dealt with in court, so I switched to law but still kept up with biology, especially botany. This way I feel I am much better qualified to deal legally with many of the problems of species' extinction.

"That's laudable, Thomas," Helen said, "it means that you had to spend much more time on your schooling."

Thomas shrugged, "It's important to do things well. Now I am looking forward to my job more positively, knowing I can deal with the challenges. And you see," he joked, "it was worth it. I can answer your question. I agree with you, Julie, this little flower is very special. I also like it a lot, it is a very pretty, delicate plant."

The train had reached the summit at 1,740 feet altitude and the entrance of tunnel No.2 was looming ahead. The passengers had to leave the observation car and go back to the coaches during the ride through the tunnel because of the smoke. They all came out again after the train had cleared the tunnel.

As Frank had explained, they right away could see the difference between the eastern and the western slope. The area was more densely forested and soon they noticed the first redwoods.

"Do you happen to know some more exciting history, young lady? Like train wrecks, bad fist fights and the like?" An older man was challenging Maria.

Maria hesitated, but then said, "Well, all of this was so long ago, I might as well tell you. I don't know of any serious accidents on the railroad during which passengers got hurt. In fact, one of the conductors once told me, that in the thirty years he had worked the line, he never had a passenger on board who got seriously sick, like a heart attack, or was otherwise injured. They have had a good record. There was a runaway freight train back in the sixties, but the crew jumped off at the last minute. Over the years, especially during the winter, trains derailed. In general, they were usually back in operation within a few days or a week at the most.

"One of the worst tragedies that could have happened was prevented by a courageous Sheriff in Fort Bragg. To build the 1,122 foot long tunnel near Fort Bragg they had hired on a crew of Chinese workers. This angered the local workers. They threatened to beat the Chinese out of town–it had become a volatile situation. The Sheriff confronted the white workers, appealed to their common sense and asked who would be willing to dig the tunnel? Nobody came forward–but the tunnel had to be dug, right? So, if they wouldn't do it, why would they object to the Chinese doing it? Finally, the local workers relented and let the Chinese dig the tunnel without any interference.

"I heard of a gruesome story that involved the cook at the Irmulco Mill–which is a few more miles to the west–around 1915 or so. When the mill workers came into the big dining room for lunch, the main meal of the day, one guy walked by the kitchen stove where a huge pot of soup was sitting ready to be served. I guess he was very hungry and could hardly wait and so he dipped his finger into the soup and licked it off. The cook calmly took out his gun and shot the guy dead." Maria realized that her audience was shocked and skeptical too.

"It's hard to believe, isn't it? I guess life in those lumber camps was pretty rough. The person, who told me the story, lived here as a teenager with his family during the summer of 1918. His father, a mechanic, was responsible for the machinery. One time, the father was seriously ill with the flu and unable to work. The foreman told the seventeen year old boy to fix a machine that had broken down or his father would be fired. Working with his father, he had gained some experience, but now on his own he was very scared. He managed to get the machine going again and thus saved his father's job, but it had been a frightening situation. His sister, who had been twelve years at that time, told me the most terrifying thing she remembers, was the sound of the alarm bell. It went off whenever there was an accident at the mill, and unfortunately, that happened way too often.

And here is my last story–a real murder that happened right here, and not even that long ago. Are you brave enough to listen?" Maria pointed down the slope where one could see a few derelict buildings through the trees, rotting away.

"The owner of this property had a nice cabin here once, and during the summer she often lived here. In the winter, she stayed in town. One wet and foggy day in January in the late seventies, the motor car came from Fort Bragg on its way to Willits. As they reached this place here, they saw that the cabin was on fire, it had already consumed most of the building. They called in the fire crew, but the house was gone. When they poked around in the ashes, they found the charred remains of a man and the post-mortem showed that he had been stabbed to death. Later investigations revealed that two ex-convicts had shacked up in the cabin and one had killed the other. The murderer had gotten away. He was also killed a year or two later. You will notice that it takes a while before we get to any other cabins or houses. Somehow, they had found this isolated cabin up here and moved in, it turned out that they had lived there for at least two months."

The older man who had challenged Maria, said jokingly, "I hope we get out of here alive, this sounds really like Wild-West."

"Well, you asked for it," Maria countered, her eyes laughing. "I didn't realize that you have such a delicate constitution. But I can assure you, this is the only murder I know of, and as usual, it was drug-related."

"Do many people grow dope up here? "someone asked. "Sure, it is still a big crop," Frank replied. "As a surveyor, I have run into many plants or gardens. I guess it is grown where ever good soil conditions, water and secluded spots prevail, here as well as in the other counties to the north. I don't like it, because it often makes my job dangerous. I wish they would legalize the stuff!"

As the train was winding its way down the hill, they saw many beautiful sights. An exciting spot was the one hundred- and-six feet high 'Rock Wall'. The train went along a narrow ledge–the upper edge of this almost vertical slope, just wide enough for the train to pass. Because of the recent rains, there were still numerous small creeks rushing down the narrow gullies and canyons, tumbling over rocks as miniature waterfalls. In contrast to the oak woodlands east of the tunnel, this forest was much moister. The ground cover was lush and green. Eventually, the train reached the valley, where the Noyo River was winding its way through the meadows.

"From here on, the train will be the companion of the river until the tracks reach tunnel No.1, just east of Fort Bragg. There, the river makes a bend to the south and eventually meets the sea south of Fort Bragg. The railroad continues through the tunnel, along Pudding Creek and reaches Fort Bragg at the north end of town," Frank explained.

They passed several cabins and Maria pointed out the general area where the Irmulco Mill had been operating. A weathered sign on an old station building read 'Irmulco'.

"This was a huge operation between 1910 and 1930, with many buildings. There is nothing left," Maria explained.

"Is Irmulco a Spanish or an Indian name?" Thomas asked.

"Sorry to disappoint you, but it is neither. It is an abbreviation of 'Irwin and Muir Lumber Company'."

The next few miles to Northspur were quite different from the wide valley they just had passed. The canyon became narrower, the slopes higher. Again and again the train crossed the river on high trestles. One could catch glimpses of the steep banks, covered with mosses and ferns, shaded by the Redwoods and other trees, and deep below, the river running swiftly through its rocky channel or resting in dark pools of quiet water.

In Northspur, live guitar music created a joyful mood. The picnic area looked inviting with flowers on each table. The mouthwatering smell from the barbecue made everybody hungry. Frank had ordered lunch ahead of time and it was ready and waiting for them.

"This is really marvelous, Frank," Julie said enthusiastically, hugging him. "What a peaceful and beautiful place, I regret I never came here before. Thank you so much, for inviting us all. The train ride from Willits was great, I really enjoyed it. What is the rest of the trip like, Frank? The part from here to Fort Bragg?"

"The tracks run along the river all the way to tunnel No. 1, sometimes on the north, sometimes on the south side, crossing the river on a number of trestles. In many places, the valley is fairly steep and densely forested. It opens up closer to the coast. Although a scenic ride, it lacks the variety and excitement of the eastern part–the switch backs on the hill to Willits, or the 'Rock Wall'. I also like the vistas from the open areas and especially the view of the snow-covered high mountains east of Willits."

Helen and Josh had managed to get their lunch fairly quickly too and joined the others at their table. The food was delicious and they ate with great appetites. After lunch, they had some time left to stretch their legs and stroll around. Frank led them on a short trail along the railroad tracks into a group of huge old-growth redwoods.

Looking up the tall trunks of the magnificent trees, Julie said hesitantly, "You know, Frank, there is only one disappointing thing about this trip. In my mind, I had painted this valley full of big old trees like these here."

"I am afraid you are not alone in this, Julie. Quite a few people expect old trees here. You have to realize though, that the main reason for building this railroad was to open up the land for logging and get the trees out to the coast. As soon as the timber supply was exhausted, the tracks were expanded further into the woods. Before the advent of track-laying bulldozers after World War II, the railroad was almost the only way to get far into the forest. Fortunately, during the eighties, a scenic corridor was established along the line which protects a 160' wide strip on each side of the tracks from extensive logging and clearcutting. Although these trees here are almost the only old-growth trees left, there are quite a few second-growth trees along the line which are already of good size. Most of them hopefully will never be logged, they are too close to the tracks or the Noyo River. As the years go by, these trees will get bigger and bigger and people can enjoy them when they come through on the train."

The whistle of the locomotive called them back to the train and soon they were on their way to Willits. Again, they went out to the open car. Helen, who had listened to Frank at the big trees, came over when she saw him on the observation car.

"I have a question, Frank. Living in southern California one doesn't learn much about forest issues. Tomorrow morning we are going to visit one of the larger timber companies. We have an appointment with one of their foresters. Before we talk to him, I would like to get your opinion concerning the forests in your county. Is it true that the private industrial timber companies–who own about 600,000 acres in Mendocino County–have depleted your local forest lands?"

"Yes, it is true, Helen," Frank responded, sounding very concerned. "And this is not only my opinion, it is a fact that more inventory has been harvested–since WW II–than has been replenished by growth. I have a graph at home that would give you a good idea what has happened in this county since the first trees were felled. I'll look for it tonight and make a copy for Julie to give it to you tomorrow.

"Starting in 1860, the annual harvests were about 40 to 50 million board feet. They slowly increased to about 200 million board feet by 1910, stayed around this level until they dropped way down at the time of the stock market crash and the height of the recession. By 1940, harvest volumes were up again to almost 200 million board feet and climbed rapidly to reach an enormous peak of over one billion Board Feet in 1955.

"This was the time when the bulldozers were invading the forests, and roads were built into all the difficult-to-reach areas to get to the rest of the big trees, as I had mentioned earlier.

"From then on harvest levels declined again to about 400 to 500 million board feet in the late eighties. This was still way above the volume that had been harvested during the prewar period. The harvest volumes during the nineties have dropped to 200 Million Board Feet or less because the forests' productive capacity has been substantially decreased through past overharvesting.

"Yes, Helen, our industrial timberlands have been overcut at a frightening scale. The inventory today is only about one tenth of what it was many years ago. Actually, you don't need fancy statistics to find out what's going on. Anybody who has lived in this county for the last twenty-five years and has paid some attention to the logging trucks passing through town, knows that the size of the logs on the trucks during this time has decreased drastically. If they had slowed down with harvesting around 1965 to 1975, our second growth trees would be now between fifty and one hundred years old. Instead, short-term profit maximizing pushed the companies into continued inventory depletion, sacrificing future productive capacity of the resources and lumber quality substantially."

He paused, "Am I going too fast?"

Helen smiled, "No, so far I am with you, I'll interrupt if I am lost."

Frank continued. "Redwoods approach maximum productivity if allowed to grow beyond one hundred years of age. Cutting redwoods before this age is reached, jeopardizes the long term survival of the forest as well as its inherent wealth for the local population. We have already learned this the hard way when many people lost their jobs during the last few decades." Several other passengers had listened in and one man didn't seem to agree with Frank.

"Excuse me, sir, "he addressed Frank, "I have seen some forest land in your county today that does not at all fit the description you just gave. We drove from Fort Bragg to Willits this morning. From what I just heard, most of the land in this area belongs to the timber companies. I saw some pretty well-stocked forests this morning."

"I agree with you, sir, that this land on both sides of Highway 20 is in good shape," Frank responded. "However, the area you drove through is the Jackson Demonstration State Forest, it is not part of the industrial timber lands. The state has done a pretty good job managing this forest."

"I have another question Frank, do you mind?" Helen asked reluctantly.

"No, not at all, go ahead, Helen," Frank encouraged her.

"Repeatedly, I have seen beautiful advertisements by the leading timber companies. They show pristine forests, green meadows, clear streams, with captions saying that there is more growth in California's forests today than ever before. What does this mean. Are they lying?"

Frank sighed, "You are asking a crucial question, Helen. I'll try to give you a simple answer. When the timber companies talk about growth, they fail to specify whether they mean percentage or volume growth, and that's a big difference. Take a young tree, a seedling. It doubles in size from year one to year two. Can you tell me what the percentage growth rate is?"

Helen hesitated, then her face lit up, "That's simple, 100%, right?"

Frank beamed, "Yes, that's easy to figure out and to understand. And what would you say is the volume produced?"

"I guess it's pretty negligible? It's still a very small tree after one year, isn't it?"

"Exactly. The percentage growth is high but the volume produced is small. Now you look at a 120 year old tree. From year 119 to year 120 the percentage growth is very low, under 1%, but the volume produced is high, it is measurable in board feet, probably between 30 and 50 board feet depending on the site.

"Unfortunately, most trees on industrial timber lands today are often only 20 to 40 years of age. That means that the percentage growth is still fairly high, about 6% to 8%. So, if the companies are saying that their growth is high, they are not lying, but it is nothing to be proud about, on the contrary, it is a sad statement. It means that they have cut their big trees and only the young, low-quality, fast growing ones are left. Yet it sounds good and deceives the ignorant public."

Helen digested Frank's statement. "What would be your recommendation how the forest should be managed?"

"Our forests are in a critical phase. As I mentioned, we have over-harvested for many decades. Controlling the cut would be important, at least down to 2% of the inventory annually. This would maximize the forest's productivity and slowly build up its inventory. If the harvests were reduced to 1% of the inventory annually, a secondary forest with near old-growth characteristics would result eventually with all its favorable attributes."

"What are the favorable attributes of such a forest?" Helen asked.

"Long-term survival of the forest as a whole, and maximization of perpetual revenue." Frank replied.

"What is a 'sustainable' forest, Frank?" Josh asked."It is a forest that is still intact, a forest of diversity with trees of all ages and wildlife that is not compromised. A forest that really can 'sustain' itself. Unfortunately, the term is often used in a way that has little meaning, more like a slogan. It is a joke to talk about a 'sustainable' forest when the trees are cut on a thirty or forty year rotation."

"One more question Frank, and I promise this will be the last one. How do you feel about clear-cutting?" Josh asked.

Frank pointed down the steep bank they were just passing. "You can answer this question yourself, look down this slope, and look up to that high ridge over there. What do you think happens when you clear-cut these areas and next winter brings sixty to eighty inches of rain?"

Josh responded fast, "Erosion, slides, washouts?"

"Exactly, and that's why I don't like clear-cuts in these hills. If there is no vegetation left to hold the soil in place, it washes down into the river and the productivity of the land becomes poorer with each harvest. How many harvests does it take to turn the forest into a desert? We might be already close to the last one."

Both Helen and Josh thanked Frank for spending so much time with them.

"My pleasure, here is my card. Call me any time if you have further questions. Good luck with your story, send me a copy when it is out."

A young girl who had listened to Frank's explanations from the beginning, finally seemed to find the courage to ask a question. "But what about the fish? You only talk about the trees, aren't the fish also endangered?"

Before Frank could answer, the man who had previously challenged Frank, spoke up. "I can tell you, young lady, why the fish are gone. It's all those foreigners, those foreign ships, that are out there in the ocean overfishing our waters. And nobody gives a damn. Just as over logging depletes the forests, overfishing depletes the fish."

"I agree with you," Frank said. "We are overfishing our oceans, and you are right, this is one major reason why we have very few fish in the rivers now. But over logging is just as detrimental for the fish. Erosion from overcut slopes causes increased siltation in the rivers, and jeopardizes spawning. In addition, overcutting in the riparian areas opens up the tree canopy and raises the water temperature of the rivers, which is very harmful for the young fish, lethal in many instances. I am glad you brought up this question, my dear," Frank said to the girl.

A young couple had been among the listeners, and the man said in halting English, "I am a student from Germany. What you say is for me very interesting, because I study forestry science. But my English is not good, I have understood not everything, can I give you some questions?"

"Here is someone who can answer all your questions in fluent German," Frank said to the young man, and turning to Thomas, "I hope you don't mind taking over, Thomas? You know the answers as well as I do. I am around if you need some help."

To Julie's amazement, Thomas addressed the couple in what sounded to her like fluent German and soon they were involved in a lively discussion.

Helen and Josh expressed their appreciation to Julie. "I'm so glad that you and your friends are on this train. Frank gave us a great lecture. This trip will be an important part of our story. What a beautiful area! I had always heard about the Skunk Train and never had a chance to ride it. Look around, everybody seems to feel the same way, you see a lot of happy faces. I also liked the setting in Northspur–and the food, it was delicious. See you later, Julie. We'll walk through the coaches, perhaps we can interview a few other passengers."

Julie looked around. Frank was talking again with the passenger who had challenged him earlier and they were just walking toward the coach and disappeared inside a few minutes later. Ken and Maria had gone inside too. Julie had talked about her plans for the summer with Maria during lunch. She had promised to show her some places of historical interest on the map when they would be back at Frank's house.

"I hope you enjoy you trip with us?" the conductor addressed Julie. "Your first time on the Skunk?"

"Yes, it's the first time and it is great. I have been riding trains for several days now–from New York to Chicago, then to Oakland and up to Willits, and now this trip. And each one is very different."

"And I suppose the Skunk was the best of all?" the conductor joked.

Julie looked at him and grinned, "Sure–that's what you want to hear, right? Well, it certainly is not as fancy or as fast as the other trains, but it really gives you that feeling of being on vacation, being carefree, you know? A slow, relaxed ride through the beautiful redwoods, in addition to that festive atmosphere in Northspur, it is very enjoyable. I'll be back and I'm sorry I didn't ride it earlier."

"I can say the same, I really enjoyed it," Thomas supported Julie. He had just joined them.

"Is the train also running during the winter?" Julie asked the conductor.

"Sure, we have a daily train from Fort Bragg to Willits and back and I really can recommend it. After the first good rains in October, the meadows are getting green again, the river is filling up and all the small creeks are starting to run. From June to September we operate additional trains. You can ride daily from Fort Bragg to Willits and back or vice versa and you can also make two halfway trips from Willits or Fort Bragg to Northspur, like the one you took. Some of these trains are pulled by an old-fashioned steam engine. In addition, we have extra halfway trips to Northspur during the off-season. Here is our schedule. It lists all our trips for the entire year, including any special events. Glad to have you on board, I hope to see you again."

The conductor excused himself, he had to move on. Thomas told her that the young German was working for six months in Oregon at one of the State Forests. He had asked Thomas a lot of questions about the redwoods and had been happy to have found someone who could answer them in German. But their little boy had fallen asleep in his mother's arms and so they went inside.

Thomas was rolling his shirtsleeves down, "You look as if you are cold, Julie, shall we go inside?"

"That would be nice. It's getting a little chilly with the fog coming in from the coast. I forgot to take my sweater. The others went inside already."

There were a number of unoccupied seats, right in the first coach, where they sat down.

"It sounded as if you speak German fluently, Thomas? Have you lived in Germany?" Julie asked.

"Yes, I have spent some time over there. My mother is German and she raised my sister and me bilingually, so I learned it the easy way. I wish I could speak Spanish as well, because I have more use for it than for German."

"I can speak Spanish well enough to get around. My aunt lives in southern Mexico and I have visited her several times, two summers during my high school years. Still, I don't think I am as fluent as you seem to be in German. How did your mother come to the States?"

"It was actually my father coming to Germany, rather. He studied art for two years in Munich, and that's where he met my mother who was studying fashion design. And you know how it is, they fell in love .... "

Thomas left it at that, and smiled. Julie took up his unfinished sentence, "… married, and lived happily ever after?"

Thomas sighed, looking a little sad and took his time to answer. "Eventually they did live happily–after they had overcome a few obstacles. It took some time before they reached that point."

Julie felt embarrassed to have finished his sentence with such a banal expression. Why didn't she keep her mouth shut? Apparently, she had touched upon something she should have left alone. Julie couldn't help wondering what the obstacles in his parents' life had been. A German family who didn't like the idea their daughter marrying a black man?

She was startled when Thomas suddenly said, "You probably were thinking the obvious–a black man falls in love with a German girl, right?" he didn't wait for her answer but continued, "Yet it was the opposite–my father is white and my mother is black. And the obstacles were erected by his southern, very conservative family who was furious over his choice. Fortunately, my parents were both strong people and survived all these problems, and they are still very happily married." He was more relaxed now and smiled at Julie.

"Did your mother's family originally come from the states?" Julie asked, encouraged by his smile.

"No, they came from Africa in the forties. That's a long story, do I have time to tell you?"

He looked at his watch, "Well, I'll try. My grandparents came to Germany from South Africa right after the war. My mother was born in Germany. She grew up there and of course, speaks German like a native, and still does. My grandfather originally came from an area in the southwest of Africa which had been a German colony before World War I. He grew up on a ranch that belonged to the son of a German aristocratic family, Friedrich von Botha, who was the black sheep in the family. He had been strongly influenced by Karl Marx and became a convinced Marxist, to the family's embarrassment. They shoved him off to Africa to run their estate there. He fell in love with a young black woman who worked on his ranch and married her. She was awed by his ability to read and write and she asked him to teach her this skill. Being intelligent, she learned fast and this turned out to be the beginning of a school for Friedrich's farm workers. My great-grandfather benefited from this opportunity and eventually became a well-read man. When the Germans lost the war in 1918, their colonies fell under British and French mandates and the German owners lost their holdings. However, Friedrich's land was way back in the wilderness and he was left alone for over a year. Then, his father in Germany died and he received enough of an inheritance to buy some of the land back and to continue farming. His workers, whom he had always treated well, had stayed with him. Friedrich's son Budil was a few years older than my grandfather and they had become good friends. Budil took over the farm in the late twenties. He persuaded my grandfather to become a physician and offered him to pay his expenses if he would come back and establish a small hospital on the farm, which had grown into a huge operation. In 1932, my grandfather started to study medicine in Hamburg. But he had to transfer his studies to London in 1933 when Hitler came into power. He received his degree as a physician in 1938, just before World War II started.

"To obtain more knowledge in tropical diseases, he worked for two years at Albert Schweizer's hospital in Lambarene. He met a young nurse there–his future wife, my grandmother–who had come to Lambarene from South Africa. After getting married, they both returned to the Botha farm and worked there as a team for a few years.

"In the meantime, Budil–a convinced Marxist like his father–had gotten involved in the politics of South Africa and had moved to Johannesburg. His daughter took over the farm. Budil persuaded my grandfather to join him in South Africa and work together with him politically, because they had always shared the same socialistic ideas. My grandparents moved to Johannesburg in 1944 and in 1945, Budil was murdered. Although my grandfather worked as a physician, he was also active in the underground movement and life had become very dangerous. When he was offered a position in an East German hospital in 1946, he accepted right away. Not only would he be able to concentrate on his medical field, he would also live in the new, young communistic German state and he saw their future life through rose-colored lenses. So he came with his wife to Dresden where my mother was born.

"He soon realized the shortcomings of the system. Doing medical research, occasionally, he was allowed to attend scientific conferences in West Germany. Some of his western colleges finally convinced him to leave East Germany and even offered him a teaching position at the University of Heidelberg. So eventually, the family settled in Heidelberg and they are still there today."

Julie was impressed by his story and fascinated by Thomas. She liked him more and more and was anxious to hear the rest of his family's history. This family had been subjected to more than their share of historic changes.

"I often thought that our family is not the regular run-of-the-mill family. My maternal grandmother escaped with her parents–who were Jewish–from Hitler's Germany at the last minute. Later her husband, my grandfather, died when my mother was only two years old. My aunt, my father's sister, married a Mexican man and lives in Mexico and my only brother, who is nine years older, lives in Japan and married a Japanese woman. But compared to your story, my family history is almost boring! "

Thomas laughed, "I wouldn't call your family the typical all-American-next-door family either. But you are right, when I think of my grandfather's roots in Africa and what became of him as an adult, he went through many, many changes.

"The tragic part was that my father's family here was furious about his decision to marry a black woman. He knew that his parents, specially his mother, would welcome his wife with open arms, but the rest of the family would not accept her. So his parents came to Germany for the wedding and treated my mother like their own daughter from the very beginning. There was no response at all from my father's uncles, aunts or cousins, absolute silence. And this in the early seventies! They both finished their studies in Munich and then came to the States, where my father got his first job as an art historian at a museum in New York. Before he started, they went to visit his parents. My mother just wouldn't believe all these stories about racial discrimination and she was shocked when she experienced it right in her husband's hometown, dealt out by his own family. America to her had always been the land of the free, the refuge of the hunted. In Germany, she had not been aware of racial discrimination although as a black child she stood out in school and as a black young woman later in college. After experiencing the shock of the holocaust, Germans were trying very hard to practice tolerance during these postwar years. The Hitler regime had left them with a terrible guilt which continuously loomed over their lives.

"My mother was–and still is–beautiful. My favorite photo of her shows her in my grandparents' garden that summer when they came back from Europe. She is sitting on the lawn, wearing a simple white dress and a large white straw hat, young and very lovely. But the doors of my father's relatives were closed to my parents, although before this marriage the family had been very close. I guess this shadow over my parents' marriage lasted until we both were born. At that point, they had created their own family and recaptured their dignity and self-importance."

"Was you father the only child?"

"No, he has a younger sister and she welcomed her new sister-in-law."

"Did your father's greater family ever change their behavior?" Julie asked.

"Well, not really, although superficially they at least talk to each other if they meet. And they do. My father is now the director of a leading art museum in Washington and occasionally runs into his cousin who is a member of Congress. But in a way, they seem to live on different planets."

"I suppose your East-Indian great-grandmother belongs to your mother's side of your family?" Julie asked.

Thomas laughed, "You can be sure of that. If those bigoted Southerners would have had an East-Indian as an ancestor, she would have been quietly erased from the family tree. She was the mother of my maternal grandmother who came from Durban, the home of many Indians living in South Africa."

Frank came back from his discussion with the other passenger. "We are almost back in Willits, there is Highway 20 already. I hope Thomas provided good company, Julie? I am sorry I got sidetracked with this guy, but we had a good talk." Both Julie and Thomas thanked him again for the invitation and emphasized how much they had enjoyed the trip. After a short stop at Frank's office where they picked up Julie's small suitcase, they left for the Rodgers' house on Pine Mountain. Frank invited Maria and Julie into his study to go over the topographic maps pertaining to the area around the Sutten ranch. Both Frank and Maria offered many good suggestions for Julie's research. Frank made copies of map sections that could be of special interest to Julie. He and Maria assured Julie that they would soon come up for a visit and would love to help her. It was almost an hour later when they came out to the porch where Ken and Thomas were relaxing, enjoying the view. The green tangle of a profusely growing honeysuckle vine provided shade, filling the air with its delicate fragrance.

"Well, it's getting close to dinner time," Frank said, looking at his watch. "What do you prefer, Maria, a barbecue here or going to our preferred restaurant in town? It's your birthday, you make the decision."

Ken interrupted, "That's not fair, Dad, to leave it to Maria. Frugal as she is, she will not let you spend money on a restaurant and will vote for staying home. Which means that she ends up helping with the dishes and so on. Besides, we have two guests from out of town, let's show them that Willits has good restaurants. I'll call and make reservations, OK?"

The restaurant was a charming place and included a lush green patio in the back, filled with flowers, trees and shrubs. It was the perfect setting for dinner on this lovely June day. Picnic tables and benches were occupied by a number of customers. Ken had reserved a large round table in a corner where Maria's parents were already waiting–a surprise for Maria.

The food was delicious, the service pleasant and personal, and the dinner talk lively. Julie appreciated very much that she had decided to visit with Frank, what a nice group of people. And she added, to herself, that she was really happy having met Thomas.

The light on the answering machine in Frank's kitchen was blinking when they came back to the house."Fred called, Julie," Frank said, after he had listened to the message, "he still has not heard either from the Carters or the neighbor and he wants to know if I got a four-wheel drive for you. He wants you to call back, even if it's late."

So Julie explained to Fred that Highway 101 was closed and she was taking the train after all. She also mentioned that she had heard from a neighbor that Bret and Emily would be back this weekend. This finally calmed Fred down and he wished her a good trip to the ranch, but reminded her to call him next time she was going to Madrone Flat.

After she hung up, she told Frank what she had heard about Bret and Emily from Homer Morgan, who lived north of Madrone Flat.

"I bet he told you more than you ever wanted to hear about the Dos Rios Dam?" Frank asked. "This is his pet subject and he is still convinced that the dam would be the salvation of the railroad."

"How do you actually feel about this matter, Frank?"

"Well, I grant Homer that much that the dam would probably have prevented extensive flooding of the railroad tracks. But building the dam would also have been the worst environmental disaster I can imagine and I am forever grateful to Richard Wilson, a rancher from Covelo, who worked so hard to prevent its construction.

If we take better care of the Eel River watersheds and don't overharvest or overgraze them, even heavy rains will not erode the banks. Then the railroad tracks will be safe and the fish will come back, that's the only way to go."

CHAPTER 5

Julie woke up early. Except for some frog concerts, coming in intervals from the pond behind the house, there had been no sounds to disturb her sleep. A glance out the window promised another beautiful day. A few wisps of fog were still lingering over the valley, otherwise the sky was clear, the sun was shining. The fresh scents of early summer drifted through the open window.

When she came downstairs, the aroma of coffee guided her to the kitchen. Julie loved the smell of good coffee, although she was not an addicted coffee drinker–just an occasional cup was all she indulged in. Frank was taking some rolls out of the oven. He greeted her with a hug after setting the hot cookie sheet carefully on a rack.

Arranging the rolls on a blue and white ceramic plate, he said to Julie, "I just thought of a place you ought to look for signs of historic American Indian settlements that I forgot to mention yesterday. But, you probably will look there anyway because it is close to your ranch and is perhaps even part of it. One day, many years ago, your grandfather took me there. It's located northeast of the house. You climb up the slope toward Fir Mountain and descend from there into a canyon-like valley, I believe he called it the hidden valley."

Julie's face lit up, and her voice reflected how Frank's suggestion had taken her by surprise. "Thank you, Frank, I'm glad you brought this up,

I had not thought about it at all. I was there only once with my father, the summer my parents died. I recall that it was difficult to get there. Of course, I was only eleven at the time and I guess everything looks taller and bigger when you are small. We walked up the steep slope northeast from the house. The valley was beautiful, like a scene from a fairy tale the way I remember it, and just seeing it felt like a gift, like a reward for the hard work to get there. The creek cascaded down a high cliff into a small pond which was surrounded by mossy rocks and ferns, very lovely. I suppose one of the reasons why I have never been back was that it reminded me too much of my father. A week after we had been up at the ranch, he and my mother died in the accident. Unconsciously, I must have been afraid to revive the emotions I had shared with my father when we had entered this special place. So I have never been back–you are right, I should check there for signs of Indian dwellings, or rather, perhaps a ceremonial site? Thank you for reminding me, Frank, I will go there when I get to the ranch. Can I help you with anything?" Julie asked Frank, pointing to the rolls and coffee.

"You could wash the strawberries and place them in a bowl, Julie," Frank replied as he checked the coffee.

After she had cleaned the berries, Julie carried them outside to the deck where Ken and Thomas were setting the table.

They had a long, leisurely breakfast, good food and talk. But finally, Frank and Ken had to get ready to leave, they were meeting a client on his land north of Willits at ten o'clock.

"Thomas offered to take you down to the train, Julie. I hope you will excuse us for not seeing you off, but I doubt very much that we will be back in town before this afternoon. The County Museum opens at ten o'clock. You might spend some time there, I can recommend it highly. Oh, and I almost forgot, I found the graph I had promised to Helen, about timber harvests in our county. I made a copy for her, you can find it in the kitchen next to the telephone."

Frank gave Julie another hug and promised to visit her at the ranch this summer. Ken echoed his father's words, and then they left.

The County Museum offered excellent exhibits on Indian history and the early settlers of the area. Julie was sorry that they didn't have any time left for the railroad exhibit. It had grown substantially in size since she saw it a few years ago when her grandfather stopped in Willits for a 'steam-up' of the historic equipment. Soon, they had to leave for the train. This had been a delightful morning, especially Thomas' companionship. She really liked him and would have loved to spend more time with him, like staying another day. For a few minutes Julie entertained this idea, knowing very well that this was out of the question. But hadn't Thomas mentioned yesterday on the train that he might stop at the ranch on his way to Eureka? Or had he been joking? Had it been just a casual remark or did he really mean it, and perhaps she should invite him formally? By the time they arrived at the railroad station, she had gathered enough courage to ask him to be sure to stop at the ranch on his way to Eureka. His face lit up. He seemed to welcome her invitation and replied that he probably would come on Friday.

The train arrived on time, bringing Helen and Josh up from Ukiah. They were waving excitedly when they saw Julie.

Julie's baggage had to be taken into the coach, because she would not get off at a regular station. With Thomas and Josh around, the two heavy suitcases were stored away in no time.

Finally, the doors closed and the train was on its way. Julie settled down in her seat, opposite from Helen, at a window. Helen and Josh were telling her about their interview with the forester from the lumber company. Although it was a rather interesting topic, Julie hardly listened, Thomas was still foremost on her mind. He was much more important at this moment to her than learning what a timber corporation's 'Habitat Conservation Plan' would do to the company's over cut holdings. Julie remembered his face and his voice, things he had said this morning or last evening on the train, and the story about his family. She was happy she had stopped in Willits and met him. He was actually quite different from Benji. All they had in common was about the same height, and the same skin and hair color. Otherwise they looked very different, and had different personalities. Benji was much more conservative than Thomas and might even have been offended being mistaken for an African-American. She liked Thomas' easygoing tolerance. He attracted her because he seemed to be a responsible and self-confident person and he had a good sense of humor. The prospect of Thomas' visit next week made her feel good.

Her flow of thoughts was interrupted by Helen, who wanted to know if Julie would join them for lunch in the dining car. She gladly accepted. By the time they had selected their food and sat down to eat, the train had reached the Eel River canyon. What a difference compared to their trip to Willits yesterday! This was a landscape of great solitude and appeared wild and almost untouched. The vegetation was sparse. Gnarled oaks, twisted madrones and gray pine trees were scattered across the rocky slopes. The understory plants consisted of drought-resistant chaparral species like ceanothus, manzanita and chamise. There were still some wildflowers in bloom on the hillsides and the banks of the river. And because of the late rains, the grass had not wilted and yellowed as it normally would have done at the beginning of June. Under the trees, in the shade, the grass was bright green, interspersed here and there with clumps of Shasta daisies or other flowers. And way down flowed the Eel River, its waters dazzling in intense blue and turquoise colors. Helen and Josh were overwhelmed by the solemn beauty of the land.

"Are there any redwoods along this line at all, Julie?" Helen wanted to know.

"Yes, you will actually drive through them. The first trees start just north of our ranch. And as you get further north, past where the North Fork and the South Fork of the Eel River flow together, you will see huge redwood forests on the hills on both sides of the wide valley," Julie explained.

Although this southern part of the valley was drier compared to the area farther north around Madrone Flat, its characteristics reminded Julie of the hills around the ranch. Julie was happy and content, she was almost home!

"By the way, Julie, we had an interesting talk with the conductor on the train today, coming up from Ukiah. We were curious how the passenger count is shaping up. After all, the intercity train has been in operation only for a little over two months," Helen told Julie. "So far, they are very satisfied with the numbers. Tourists seem to make up the largest part of the passengers, individuals and groups. But the locals are also starting to use the train more and more. The conductor was quite pleased with the way things are going."

When they had returned to their coach, Helen and Josh expressed regrets that soon their companionship would end.

"I really hope that you'll be able to visit me," Julie repeated her invitation.

They both assured her that they had every intention to do so. The conductor came by to remind Julie that they would arrive at the ranch in about ten minutes. Josh and Helen helped getting Julie's heavy luggage to the exit, and waited with her at the door. Julie stared out the window to catch the first glimpse of the modest building that had served as a station for the ranch for many years.

"There it is!" she burst out, pointing to the small structure in the distance on the east side of the tracks. The train was slowing and as they came closer, they could see a man standing next to what appeared to be a Jeep.

"I guess your friends are back, Julie." Helen said.

But, as they were getting closer to the station, Julie realized that it was a stranger who was waiting for the train. "No, this is not Bret. I suppose it is my neighbor's grandson. I don't really know him. Well, at least I don't have to carry the suitcases up the hill," she tried to be cheerful about it, but Helen detected a note of disappointment in Julie's voice.

When the train stopped and the door opened, the man came forward and addressed Julie with a curt introduction. He was indeed the neighbor's grandson, Charles Kendar. He told Julie that Bret and Emily were not back yet, and that he felt obligated to come down and pick Julie up. After he had hoisted all the suitcases down from the train, Julie turned around to say good-bye to Helen and Josh before she stepped down too.

To her surprise both Helen and Josh had vanished, but at the last minute, Helen came running down the aisle, gave Julie a quick hug and slid a small book into Julie's bag. "Just a little keepsake from Josh, Julie."

As the train took off, Julie cast a closer look at Charles Kendar. He was fairly tall, like Bret, but not as slender, more muscular, with broader shoulders. She judged him to be about forty years old, a good-looking man, with an intelligent face, and dark, thick hair. But his facial expression was too serious, almost slightly bored or arrogant. He didn't look as if he would laugh easily. Although it was rather warm, he was dressed in a long-sleeved western shirt. His pants were also of western cut, made from wool, looking expensive. All his clothes were immaculate, perfectly color-coordinated. Julie knew that his grandfather had been a wealthy investment banker. Perhaps Charles was too, she wondered? She was afraid she was imposing on him. The expression on his face told her that he was picking her up only because he really didn't have any other choice. Julie was surprised that Bret and Emily had given his telephone number to Fred. At least, he was quite strong. With little effort, he loaded the suitcases into his red Jeep. He was also very polite, opening the door for Julie to get into the car, then he got in on the other side and slowly and carefully–because the narrow road was still soft from the rains–drove up to the house.

When he explained that he had just come back to his ranch, he became a little more human. "I was gone for several days with my grandfather. You probably know that he had a stroke. I have to take him for therapy on a regular basis. I didn't get your message until this morning when we came back. The Carters are not back yet, apparently, nobody was there when I drove by thirty minutes ago, so I decided to come down and pick you up."

"Do you have any idea why Emily and Bret had to make this trip? They had not mentioned anything in their last letter about going away, so it must have been an unexpected reason why they left," Julie asked, anxiously waiting for a satisfying answer.

"Unfortunately, I have not the slightest idea. I had not seen them for a while–at least several weeks–when I received a card from them from Seattle," Charles replied, concentrating on the road. "They are charming people and I always enjoyed their company. We have been inviting each other a few times for lunch or dinner. But I have been gone a lot too, taking my grandfather to Willits or Eureka for therapy every few weeks."

"I am sorry that we bothered you with all these telephone messages, Charles. I very much appreciate that you came to the train, being so busy. Can you imagine how many trips it would have taken me to get the suitcases up the hill?" Julie laughed.

Charles hardly responded, he didn't seem to have much sense of humor, just a trace of a smile showed around his narrow lips.

"Well, I am glad I could be of service," he replied stiffly.

When they arrived at the house, he was again attentive, swiftly unloading her suitcases and carrying them into the house. Julie offered to make a cup of tea or coffee, but he declined, he had to get back to his grandfather. Julie didn't mind. Although she was thankful for his help, he didn't strike her as a very sociable person. She had been surprised to hear that Emily and Bret had invited him several times.

After he was gone, Julie stepped away from the house a few yards and stood there for a while, looking at the beautiful old building she was responsible for now. The family had always kept it in good repair. Julie recalled all the summers when she helped with cleaning and painting. Bret and Emily were constantly busy keeping things in good shape. Julie noticed that they had freshly painted the shutters since Christmas, the last time she had been up here with her grandfather. Originally, it had been a two-story house with a big attic. When Bret and Emily moved in, Julie's grandfather had hired a contractor to make the attic into a very attractive two-room studio and bathroom for them. But they also used the downstairs rooms–the cozy kitchen, which was especially bright and friendly in the morning when the sun was streaming through the large east-facing bay window–and the west-facing living room with its French doors, its simple, functional furniture upholstered in cheerful, flowered chintz. The study, facing to the north and east, was not used by the Carters, because they had their own study upstairs where they did all their work. There were two small and two larger bedrooms on the second floor and all still contained some of the original furniture dating back to Julie's great-grandparents.

Julie entered the house and noticed that it smelled musty as if it hadn't been aired for some time. She opened the windows in the kitchen and the living room, as well as the French doors leading to the big deck overlooking the river way below, and the windows in the study. Walking through the house, she noticed that everything was in good order as always, just a bit dusty. After all, Emily and Bret had been gone for about two weeks. She peeked into the refrigerator. It was empty and smelled moldy. The freezer compartment held a few sticks of butter, a package of chicken breasts and a package of croissants. The propane gas refrigerator needed to be defrosted, a thick crust of ice was covering all the walls. Julie took one stick of butter out to thaw and made a mental note to clean the refrigerator as soon as possible to get rid of the smell and the ice buildup. The cupboards in the kitchen were well stocked with staples and the pantry shelves were filled with rows and rows of home-canned vegetables and fruit in old-fashioned glass jars. Being too far away from Madrone Flat, the house was not connected to the Pacific Gas and Electric grid system. Her grandfather had installed an alternative energy system several years ago. A number of photo-voltaic panels were arranged on a tracker which changed its position automatically with the sun to obtain the maximum yield. There was sufficient electricity for normal use, but an electric freezer would have consumed too much energy, therefore canning was the logical choice.

So there was plenty of food in the house, except for things that needed refrigeration, like cheese, eggs–and bread. Perhaps she should bake two loaves at least? Emily and Bret would certainly stop at Rosy's store in Madrone Flat to stock up on perishables before they came home and they would love the fresh bread. She got the recipe from Emily's file box and checked for the ingredients. Yes, everything was there and the gas was turned on when she checked the stove. Julie got out a big bowl for the dough and set to work. After she was done with the starter, she had to wait about twenty minutes and went outside to take a look at the garden.

Not only were there ripe strawberries but also raspberries and blueberries. Julie discovered asparagus, lettuce, carrots and sugar peas ready to be harvested. Plenty of everything, including weeds all over! She would do some weeding as soon as possible. Julie snacked for a while on the raspberries and her thoughts went to Emily and Bret, thankful to them for doing all the hard work in the garden. She went back to the kitchen to knead the bread. This done, she covered the dough to let it rise and decided to have a cup of tea and some cookies and relax for a while out on the deck until it was time to finish the bread.

While the water was heating for the tea, Julie went upstairs to take a quick look at her room. It also smelled musty and Julie opened the French doors, leading to the small balcony above the downstairs deck. Otherwise her room was in good order, although there were no sheets on the bed. This didn't look like Emily at all, they really must have left in a hurry. Emily was always well organized and had everything ready in plenty of time before company arrived–the beds made, the room clean and fresh flowers on the table. The whistle of the tea kettle in the kitchen interrupted her when she had just stepped into the hall to open the door of the big linen closet. Julie quickly slid down the wide banister of the staircase to the first floor and rushed into the kitchen. She turned off the gas under the sputtering kettle and made the tea. While she got the tray ready to take out to the deck, she remembered Josh's book and pulled it out of her bag to take it along and then went outside.

The pillows for the old Adirondack chairs on the deck were stored in the living room. She picked up two pillows, placed them in a chair for comfort and settled down. Although she deeply appreciated her peaceful and beautiful surroundings, she felt sorry for herself. In her mind, she had pictured this scene quite differently. Emily would have had the table covered with one of her embroidered table clothes and used her best china for the tea setting. There would have been a scrumptious berry pie, some whipped cream and a pot of delicious, fragrant hot tea. They would have been talking about Julie's graduation, her thesis, her last weeks in New York, Emily and Bret's new book in progress, and many other things. Instead, she sat here all by herself. Charles had been a disappointment in explaining this unexpected trip. Julie had hoped to find at least a quick note from the Carters, but there was nothing there.

She told herself not to dwell any longer on things she couldn't change anyway. Pretty soon, Emily and Bret would arrive and the cozy tea scene would become a reality, just a bit delayed. Being alone, she focused her undivided thoughts on her parents, her great aunt and her grandfather who had left this beautiful piece of land in her stewardship. The air was filled with the fragrance of the old-fashioned roses that her great-aunt had planted in big wooden tubs all around the edges of the large deck. Down in the garden the plants were either natives or deer-proof, there was an abundance of foxgloves, in many colors. Being poisonous, the deer didn't touch them. Roses would not have lasted long there, but up here they were safe. A huge Wisteria was climbing up to the deck on the south side along the railing, but it was through with flowering by now. On the north side, a star jasmine was in full flower and its fragrance mingled pleasantly with the fragrance of the roses. Its vine-like branches had climbed up to the second story and were growing along the balustrade of the balcony outside Julie's room. As she looked up, she noticed that the swallow's nest under the eaves was occupied as always and one of the parents was just diving down for more insects for the baby birds. This nest had been there as long as she could remember and each spring the arrival of the swallows was greeted with joy.

Julie could not think of any better place to be than up here on this deck, surrounded by flowers and seeing the river way down in the valley. How often had she yearned to be here instead in the dinky apartment in New York City. She had to pinch herself to be sure that it was true that she really was out here in the Eel River canyon.

The last five days had been a whirl of impressions. She had seen the whole country and met so many interesting people, and this brought back her thoughts to Thomas. Julie knew that she liked him a lot–had she fallen in love with him? It was good that a week would go by before he came. This gave her a little time to sort out her emotions.

The tea was good, it tasted better than anyplace else, the water made all the difference. Josh's little book was a short history of the Northwestern Pacific Railroad, up to date, including the new passenger service. As she opened it, a small piece of paper fluttered to the floor and disappeared in the space between two floorboards. Julie almost felt too lazy to get up, but after all, it probably was a friendly good-by note from Josh, and she could not just neglect it. With regret, she heaved herself out of the comfortable chair, walked down the steps and found the paper right away. Just as she grabbed for it, she heard a weak meow, meow. Buttercup! How could she have forgotten Emily's cat! She looked around but didn't see the animal. Only when she called his name several times, the large, orange-striped tomcat slipped out from under an old bench. He looked a little thin, didn't they leave him enough food? When he came up to her, she bent down, petted him, and finally picked him up and cuddled him. The cat purred and purred, licking her hand, he seemed to be happy to have company. Julie noticed that both the water dish and cat food dish were there, completely empty. To her surprise, the basement door was not locked and she found an almost full bag of liver-flavored cat food in a cupboard. While she replenished Buttercup's dish, he didn't even wait for it to be completely filled, but pushed his nose into it and ravenously ate his food. Julie watched him for a while and then remembered why she had come down here. The note was in her pocket and she started to read it:

Hello, Julie,

Please be careful concerning the guy who is picking you up. I heard you saying that he is not your caretaker and that you don't know him. I am pretty certain that he is the con man whose trial I covered three years ago. He was sentenced to four years in jail for robbery, but might be out on parole already. I'll find out when we get to Eureka and will give the conductor a letter for you tomorrow

morning with more details.
Just be careful! Sorry about the bad news,
Josh

She had to read the words twice before they made sense. Her first reaction was that Josh must be wrong, after all, in three years one can forget details. Had he really seen and heard enough of Charles in those few minutes? Charles didn't strike her as a warm or likable person, though he had been helpful and courteous and seemed to have friendly contact with the Carters. But a criminal? Of course, if he really were a con man, that could explain it. These people were good in deceiving others and putting up a perfect front. Julie thought of Fred. His worst nightmare about her being alone at the ranch had come true. It was almost funny–but was it really? All of a sudden, the peaceful atmosphere had disappeared and Julie found herself wishing even more anxiously than before that the Carters would return soon. If they really had social contact with Charles–as he claimed–they would know if Josh's suspicion had any merit. She felt restless and somehow had no desire to go back to the deck. As she walked up the stairs, Buttercup came with her. The cat's presence felt comfortable, there was at least someone to talk to, even if he couldn't talk back.

The bread dough had risen well and she could form the loaves. She placed them in the pans for another rising and preheated the oven.

In the meantime, she carried her suitcases up to her room. It took a while because she had to do it in installments, but finally the hall was cleared.

While the bread was baking, she went into the garden and picked berries, lettuce and asparagus, including some chives and parsley. Every time she heard the sound of a plane, she thought it was a car and scanned the road on the eastern hill to see if the Carter's car was coming down the slope.

The bread turned out beautifully and she couldn't resist eating a slice, still hot, with butter–it tasted delicious. By eight o'clock, she decided to eat, she was too hungry–a green salad and some asparagus soup with bread, and berries for desert.

When Emily and Bret still had not come home by the time she had finished her meal, Julie started to feel some anxiety. During the night, when the temperature dropped, the wooden parts in the old house–the ceiling beams, the floorboards, the oak boards of the stairs–would start making weird noises, creaking, moaning and groaning sounds. She was used to that and normally it didn't bother her. But with Josh's warning in mind, each sound would be amplified and she probably would worry all night and not get much sleep. Julie almost laughed about herself when she realized that she had that frightening image in her mind of a guy, resembling Charles Kendar, sneaking around the house in the dark. The idea was hilarious. Nevertheless, she couldn't shake off the uneasiness. Perhaps she should look for a sleeping bag and camp down by the river? She had done that many times. It was great to wake up early in the morning, hearing the birds sing in the bushes and trees along the river banks, watching the mist whirl above the waves, and eventually feeling the warmth of the first rays of sun. No, she couldn't do that. Down there she wouldn't hear Emily and Bret coming home. Her glance went out the window, traveling up the road to the eastern ridge. Up there, north of the road, was a fairly flat area with many small to medium size fir trees, a pretty spot. She could hide behind a clump of trees, nobody would see her from the road, yet, she was close enough to hear a car coming up the hill from Madrone Flat, and she probably would not miss the Carter's car, even if they came in the middle of the night.

It was getting dark soon, there was not much time to spare. Julie hurried upstairs and quickly found a sleeping bag. She changed into sweats, took the bag and a flashlight and walked up the hill. Buttercup had disappeared earlier, probably doing his nightly hunting, he would not miss her. Even going at a good pace–Julie was in top shape–it took a while to reach the ridge. There was still plenty of light to look for a good spot. She found it within a circle of small fir trees. A thick layer of fir and pine needles blanketed the ground, it felt comfortable and smelled good. A peaceful spot. Way in the distance, the snowcapped peaks of the Mendocino National Forest glowed pink in the setting sun and deep down in the valley the silver band of the river shimmered in the fading light.

CHAPTER 6

Earlier in the afternoon, when the train had stopped at the Sutten ranch, Josh had immediately recognized the man who was standing at the station, waiting for Julie, as the con artist whose trial he had covered a few years ago. Afraid that the man might also remember him, Josh had turned around quickly and gone back to his seat. Helen was surprised and annoyed about Josh's disappearance, how could he be so rude? She rushed after him, ready to drag him back to the door. Josh cut her short. He frantically scribbled the last words of his note to Julie, slipped it into the book and handed it to Helen, indicating that he would be at the exit in a minute, which, of course, hadn't happened.

After the train had continued its journey north, Helen went back to her seat. She was furious. Before she even sat down, she started to question Josh. Why had he been so impolite not to say good-bye to Julie and had just vanished? She finally calmed down after Josh told her at least three times to listen to him.

"Helen, I am very worried about Julie," he said urgently, "I got a good look at that guy who picked her up and I didn't like what I saw a bit. He was not Bret, her friend, but her neighbor's grandson whom she had never met, right? And that means that her friends are not back and she is alone at the ranch. I hope that I am wrong, but I am afraid that this is the same guy who was convicted of armed robbery, whose trial I covered about three years ago, remember? At least, he looks like the spitting image of that con man. He was involved in a robbery and someone got killed. They could not get him for that, he had a really good lawyer. His sentence was four years and he should still be in, but probably got out on parole. I could swear it was him. That's why I disappeared, I was afraid he might recognize me. His voice also sounded very familiar. So, I wrote a little note in that history book you gave to Julie, warning her to be careful. Tomorrow morning I will send a letter down with the train, giving her more details, after I have made a few phone calls."

Helen stared at Josh with wide eyes and her reply was a shock to Josh because he was convinced that he had done the right thing. "I think you are crazy, Josh. What a terrible thing to do! Although I do remember the case, I don't remember the guy. This man looked rather decent, I am sure he is not your con man. Perhaps he was not too friendly, but he didn't strike me as a dangerous person. You only will frighten Julie. I would not have given her the book had I known what you wrote. But yes, you are right, the caretakers have not come back yet. The guy who picked her up is the grandson of Julie's neighbor whom Julie's friend Fred in San Francisco called. He felt obliged to come to the train to help Julie with her baggage. That was very nice of him. It's been some time since you covered that trial, you probably have forgotten exactly what he looked like. Besides, what would a con man do in this isolated area?"

"Helen, I am afraid I am right. I attended that trial day after day and I saw that man very well and I heard him talking, I am very concerned. As soon as we get to Eureka, I will call Sid, he can find out easily if Kendar–that's his name as far as I remember–is still in jail. If he is, I made a bad mistake. If he is out, he must be on parole and it might be difficult to find out anything tonight, and tomorrow is Saturday. In any case, I will write a letter to Julie and give it to the conductor on the train tomorrow morning. He can drop it off at the ranch. Hopefully, her friends will come back today and she will not be alone. But wouldn't you agree that if I am right, it's good for her to be on guard?"

"Well, maybe you are right, though I feel really sorry for that poor girl when she finds your note and her friends have not come back and she is alone, miles and miles away from the village. We should have gotten off the train in Madrone Flat...."

"And what? Walking back to her ranch and finding out that the caretakers had just arrived? For heaven's sake, Helen, get real," Josh angrily replied. "Julie is not that helpless. She is a grown woman. And besides, this guy is not a rapist or a mass murderer. He has no reason to harm her. I just want her to be careful!"

"But you said he killed someone!" Helen insisted.

"I did not, I said that during the robbery, where he was involved, someone got killed. What happened was that Kendar had befriended the manager of a jewelry store to the extent that he knew all about the alarm system. When he was ready to make his move, he worked together with another guy who carried a gun, supposedly against Kendar's wishes. Anyway, the manager showed up unexpectedly, attacked Kendar's partner and was killed in the struggle. Kendar maintained that he had not known about the gun, his cohort said the opposite. Kendar got four years in prison, the other man twenty. Kendar had not been in jail before, but in the past had a number of charges against him which always got dropped because they could never be substantiated. Supposedly, he had swindled several people out of their money–women mainly–with all kinds of schemes. Apparently, he was a master of disguise and usually the witnesses who were to testify against him could not swear that he really was the felon. I warned Julie because I think he is potentially dangerous. Yet I am not that much worried and besides I hope that I will find out from Sid that he is still in jail."

In the meantime, the train had stopped in Madrone Flat for a few minutes and was now on its way again. Although Helen and Josh had planned to get a good look at Rosy's bed and breakfast place, right near the station, they had gotten sidetracked with Kendar and completely forgotten to look out the window.

"I just got an idea, Josh," Helen said and Josh sighed, "*What now?*"

"You remember what Julie told us about the woman who runs the general store and the B and B in Madrone Flat? Rosy? She is also the postmistress. If you do find out that Kendar is out on parole, we could call her and find out whether Julie's friends have come home."

Helen was pleased with her suggestion. Josh didn't understand the connections.

"How would *she* know whether they came home? I don't get your logic."

"If they have been gone for two weeks, the first thing they will do when they return is check their mail. All Rosy has to do is check their box. If it's empty, they are home, right?"

"Not a bad idea, except Rosy most likely will not disclose this information to strangers on the phone, have you thought of that?" Josh countered.

"Well, yes, you are probably right. We could find someone else to call whom she knows, like Frank Rodgers in Willits for instance. Anyway, that's a possibility. Here is another idea. Julie mentioned that Thomas wants to visit her on his way to Eureka next week. I think the two like each other. Did you notice when we left Willits, telling her about our interview in Ukiah? She didn't listen at all, she was still in Willits in her mind, dreaming of Thomas. I don't blame her, he is a good-looking guy and I like him too. If I were twenty-four, I guess I would also fall in love with him."

Josh made a sad face, but his eyes were laughing, "I wish I had known you when you were twenty-four, young and beautiful."

"Oh, Josh, you are too much, I was twenty-five when we met, have you forgotten?" Helen played right along, knowing only too well he was joking. "Nevertheless, observing Julie and Thomas in this early stage of their relationship–and somehow I have a hunch that this might become more serious–makes me feel old, and I almost wish I were twenty-five again, as when I first met you."

"I know what you mean, Helen, I felt a little jealous too, seeing this romance blossoming in its very beginning. But each age has its merits, and a long-lasting relationship is something precious, at least that's the way I see ours and I know how much you cherish it. too. Don't you?" He put his arm around her and hugged her for a few minutes. Helen snuggled up to him, placed his face between her hands and touched his lips with a long kiss.

But the next moment, she bounced back to their previous topic. "If we call Thomas and tell him of your suspicion, I bet he would come up right away."

"I have to hand it to you. You are never lacking ideas, Helen. I really think you are taking this too far. Just as we have this debate here, Julie is probably welcoming her friends back. I will call Sid as soon as we get to Eureka, and until then, let's rather concentrate on our trip, otherwise we have not seen anything of this beautiful country!"

Helen agreed with Josh on his last statement, besides, they couldn't do anything about Julie until they reached Eureka. Soon, they noticed the first Redwoods and a little later, they reached the confluence of the two arms of the Eel River. It now had become a big river in a wide, green valley–a peaceful, pastoral landscape.

As soon as they arrived at their bed and breakfast inn in Eureka–a well-restored Victorian house–Helen wasted not even one second to admire their room–the call to Josh's friend Sid came first. Her patience was tested, Sid was not home, his wife expected him back in an hour.

"Let's go for a walk, Helen. The old town section is rather picturesque. I know you get fidgety sitting around, waiting until we can call again," Josh suggested. They leisurely strolled through town, visited some shops and took many photos of the historical, Victorian houses.

Unfortunately, Sid was not back when Josh tried again. While they were gone, a bottle of wine, nicely cooled, with crackers and cheese had been brought to their room. Josh poured a glass of wine for Helen and himself, picked up some crackers and cheese and lay down on the bed with a newspaper. Helen took her glass out to the small table on the balcony, sat down in a comfortable white wicker armchair and put her feet up on a matching ottoman. She sipped the wine and delighted in the view of the small but exquisitely landscaped garden below and Humboldt Bay in the distance. For Eureka, it was a warm day. Helen luxuriated in the sunshine and savored the aromatic mixture of fragrances drifting up from the garden. She dozed off, until the shatter of some blue jays woke her up. A slender, white cat was slowly winding its way through the flower beds, completely ignorant of the bird's protests.

"This is the most enjoyable trip I have taken for a long time, Josh," Helen said, addressing Josh inside the room. "What makes it even better is the prospect of doing it again later this summer when we visit Julie. And this place here really tops it all, what a beautiful house. I love the white furniture and the blue and white flowered bedspread and cushions. It is simple and practical, and at the same time cozy and cheerful. I hate bed and breakfast places that are overstuffed with fake antiques.

Though I wish I didn't have to worry about Julie, it really puts a damper on my state of mind. Don't you want to try to reach Sid again? Josh? Josh?"

Josh didn't respond. Helen had turned her back to him and hadn't noticed that he had fallen asleep. She got up and walked over to the bed, kissing him lightly on his forehead, which woke him up.

"I am sorry to wake you, Josh, but it's been over thirty minutes since you tried to reach Sid, perhaps he is home now." Sidney Welsen was a parole officer with the Los Angeles Police Department and a good friend of Josh. He most likely knew or could find out fast if Kendar was still in jail. Josh sighed and sat up, reaching for the telephone. This time Sid was home. Helen listened as Josh related their story and concern to his friend. She gathered from Josh's answers that the guy apparently was out on parole. When Josh hung up, he looked depressed.

"I really had hoped to be wrong. As you probably already have realized, Kendar is out of prison and Sid believes that he was released to Santa Rosa."

"How is that possible?" Helen asked, "didn't he commit the crime in Los Angeles?"

Josh shrugged. "Connections!" he muttered, "everything is possible".

"So what do we do now, Josh? How about my idea to call Rosy to find out if Julie's friends came back in the meantime?" She grabbed the telephone book and opened the yellow pages.

"Hold your horses, Helen. Let's first talk about what we want to ask her–*if* she will give us any information."

But Helen had already made up her mind. "Here is the number," she said. "I know exactly what to say and what not to say."

Josh gave up and lay down again, listening to her conversation. Helen could be extremely charming and was using this art now talking to Rosy. She explained who they were and that they had befriended Julie on the train coming up from San Francisco. Before she could go on, Rosy told her that Homer Morgan had already given her a full report about meeting Julie, Helen and Josh on the train.

"One of his sons lives about an hour east of here in the hills, he came down to take his dad back to his place for a few days. While he got some repair done on his car, Homer hung around here and told me the latest news."

Realizing that she had won Rosy's trust, Helen tried to make her understand why they were worried about Julie. She told her that when the train had arrived at the ranch, a stranger was waiting there to pick her up instead of the caretaker couple that Julie had expected to be back. They were wondering if Rosy by any chance knew whether Bret and Emily had come home in the meantime? Rosy didn't even have to look into their box, she knew that the Carters had not come back. From Helen's description, Rosy assumed that the stranger was Frederick Kendar's grandson and assured Helen that he was all right. When Helen heard the name, her heart sank. But she didn't interrupt Rosy who told her that Kendar would come to the store once in a while, when he was getting the mail. Rosy felt he was kind of aloof and perhaps a little arrogant. He never talked much, she said, and she did not know him well. Yet, he seemed to take very good care of his sick grandfather, he was always considerate and respectful with the old man. At the end, Rosy promised to drive over to the ranch tomorrow afternoon. She hadn't seen Julie since last December when her grandfather had died, and she wanted to visit with Julie anyway for a while, even if the Carters were back by then.

Helen thanked Rosy for her help and put down the receiver, looking dismayed. "So, they are not back, Julie is alone and the man who picked her up is Kendar. You were right, Josh. My God, this is awful. Perhaps, after all, we should call Thomas to come up sooner, what do you think?"

"I think we should get something to eat and continue this discussion over dinner, Helen. We are going to meet the other bikers at eight o'clock, and there is not much time left. Besides, I am rather hungry, what about you?"

They chose a small seafood place within walking distance from their B and B. Tonight, they were on their own, but tomorrow evening the bicycle group would have dinner together. While they were eating their salad, Helen talked again about calling Thomas.

"What did Rosy say about Kendar?" Josh asked.

Helen told him as much of the conversation as she remembered. "Unfortunately, there is no question about the name, she repeated it several times. She does not know him well. Although she thinks that he is a little arrogant, she believes he is all right. He treats his ailing grandfather very well. I didn't want to bring up the fact that he might have been involved in a major crime, after all, I have no idea how people are interconnected in these little towns."

Helen mentioned that Rosy had already heard about them from

Homer Morgan.

"You did very well, Helen!" Josh said, "it was good you didn't spill all the beans."

The main course was served and for a while they were completely absorbed in eating. Both had ordered grilled salmon which was delicious.

"I guess I will tell Julie in the letter, which I promised her for tomorrow morning, that the man whose trial I covered, has indeed been released from jail. Whether he and the man–who met her at the train-are really one and the same, is something I am not completely sure about, but the resemblance is there. I will not mention his name for now. In any case, she should be careful if he comes back to the ranch. I am sorry to give her cause for worry, but I feel it is always better to know of a possible danger. What do you think?" Josh asked. "In addition, I agree with you to call Thomas tomorrow and tell him what we know. Perhaps he can come up a little earlier. Who knows, the caretakers might be delayed and not show up for several days?"

Helen put her hand on Josh's, "Thank you, I feel much better doing this. It would be horrible if something happened to Julie."

Next morning Josh got up early and walked over to the railroad station. The conductor was friendly and promised to drop off the letter at Julie's ranch. But when Josh called Frank Rodgers, he was not so lucky. Thomas had gone with Ken and Maria to Santa Rosa early this morning and they would not come back until Sunday evening. Frank himself was not home either. A neighbor who was cleaning the house had answered the telephone. They decided to call Frank back later.

CHAPTER 7

The sound of a car engine interrupted Julie's sleep on Saturday morning. Could that be Emily and Bret? Her watch showed ten minutes to six. She scrambled out of the sleeping bag, stood up and listened. The sound seemed to come from the Fir Creek road. Julie expected the car to come closer, to drive up the eastern side of the ridge where she was camping, but, as she walked over to the road, looking down into the valley to the east, she noticed that the sound of the car had become fainter. This side of the hill was densely forested and it was impossible to see the road except for the first fifty feet just below her. The sound became louder again when she walked back to her campsite, and became louder still when she walked slowly along the ridge to the north and up towards Fir Mountain. She could hear it clearer and clearer. Julie was confused. This couldn't be the Carter's car, and as far as she knew, there was no other road coming up the hill than the road to the ranch. All of a sudden, it was quiet, apparently the car had stopped and the engine had been turned off. Perhaps an early fisherman, trying his luck down by the bridge? Fir Creek was flowing down from Fir Mountain, through the hidden valley Frank Rodgers had reminded her of, down to the Fir Creek Road, crossing the road under the bridge and continuing down the eastern slope.

It was quiet and peaceful up here and the view was breathtaking.

Julie was pleased that she had camped out, thanks to Josh! With all the beauty around her, she didn't worry about Charles. Bret and Emily would come home soon, and somehow, she wasn't really afraid of Charles anyway. She actually felt silly now to have gone to all that trouble.

This morning, the peaks of the Mendocino National Forest looked dark against the light-blue eastern sky. To the west, the Eel River was still hidden by a light fog that was slowly disappearing as the sun heated the valley. Julie continued strolling up the ridge and eventually came to an area that most likely was the southern edge of the hidden valley. This side didn't look quite as steep as the northern edge from where she had walked in with her father. Although at first glance it seemed impenetrable with brush, vines, small trees and big trees growing together in an unrestrained abundance, it ought to be possible to find a path through this thicket down to the valley floor. But not today, Julie, she told herself, she needed at least a whole morning for this exploration.

Regretfully, she walked back to the camp to pick up her sleeping bag. After a leisurely breakfast on the deck, she walked down to the tracks to be there in time for the train from Eureka. Buttercup had come up for tidbits during breakfast. He now followed her down to the station, apparently happy not to be alone any longer.

She could hear the train in the distance. It stopped in Madrone Flat and soon was approaching the ranch. When the train emerged from the tunnel, she saw the conductor leaning out of one of the vestibules. He waved at her and dropped the letter off when the train went by. Julie picked it up, tore it open and read Josh's note with apprehension. Still, on this beautiful morning, she managed to keep her usual optimism. This was Saturday and if the Carter's relative, who had been at the ranch last week, was right, Emily and Bret would come back today.

The river looked inviting and she decided to go for a swim. There was nobody around. Julie shed her few clothes and dived into the clear water. It was cooler than she had expected, but it felt great. Buttercup eyed her suspiciously when she came out again. He certainly was not in the mood for a swim. She lay in the sun for a while until she was dry again and then dressed and walked back up the path, the cat trailing either behind her or making sudden jumps after real or imagined prey. Again, when she heard the sound of a small airplane, she thought for a second it was perhaps the Carter's car. When would they show up?

Just as she reached the house, a car was coming down the hill. To Julie's disappointment, it looked like Charles' car, and indeed, it was. Julie pushed Josh's letter deep into the pocket of her skirt and tried to look as relaxed as she could. He seemed to be even more aloof today than yesterday, but greeted her with a short nod.

"Good morning, I have a message for you. Thought I'd come right over, I am sure you are anxiously waiting for the Carters? Bret just called from a place in eastern Washington. They are delayed and will not be home until tomorrow. They hope to be in Portland by early afternoon and will go on until dark and then drive the rest tomorrow."

Julie tried to hide her dismay with a false cheerfulness, "Thank you so much, I really appreciate that you came all the way over to let me know. I am sorry that we bother you with our problems. Could I offer you a cup of tea or coffee today?" To her relief, Charles declined the invitation and took off a few minutes later.

Another day before she would see them! Her anxiety was growing. But Charles' short visit had also given her some reassurance. After all, he seemed to be pretty civil–if not very sociable. She wondered what he would think of her if he knew that she had slept on the hill because she was afraid of him? Well, he could have the laugh. The camp-out had been a great experience, perhaps she should do it again tonight?

While she was picking berries in the garden, she again heard a car coming down the slope. This time, it was not Charles' car, but a light green pickup truck. A young man got out and came over to the garden. He was about the same age and height as Julie, slender, yet sturdy and strong. His face and bare arms were deeply tanned, he looked like someone who worked outdoors most of the time.

Pushing his blond hair away from his forehead, he smiled and introduced himself, "Hi, I am Andy, and you must be Julie? I don't see the Carter's car, have they gone to the village? I did some work for them earlier in the season, cultivating, weeding and so on. When we were through, I didn't see them for a while. But when they had to go on this trip up north, they left a note at my gate, asking me to do some watering while they were gone, which I did until last week when we had that unexpected storm. I have not watered since then, but thought I better check today in case they had not come back yet or you had not arrived."

"Nice to meet you, Andy," Julie responded, shaking his hand. "The work you did this spring has certainly paid off. The garden looks great. I had asparagus and a salad last night for dinner and berries for dessert. Thank you so much for your help.

The Carters are not back yet, but I just got a message from Charles, Mr. Kendar's grandson, that they will be back tomorrow. I want to fill this bowl with berries to make a pie. As soon as I am through here, can I offer you a cup of tea?"

Andy accepted, and twenty minutes later they were sitting on the deck, drinking tea. He had no idea why the Carters had to leave so suddenly, he had not worked for them since the middle of April. Originally, he had come to clean up and paint the little house he was living in, his relatives' cabin in Madrone Flat. After he was through with the job, he stayed on, because he liked the place. Now he was putting in a garden and did some landscaping around the house. He was also doing landscaping projects in Garberville. With all these jobs he hoped to save a tidy sum. But by fall, he would need a more permanent job. Last year, he had finished college with a degree in horticulture. Andy's parents lived in Florida and owned a cut-flower nursery. His father had been seriously ill and the family had used up all their money, even took a second mortgage on their house. After working in his father's business for a while, Andy decided to come to California to earn some extra money to help his parents.

Andy's visit was a welcome interruption. He seemed to be a friendly, trusting guy, although Julie felt he was telling her too much about his family's history too soon. Was he lonely?

After he left, Julie made the berry pies she had planned earlier. Just as she was taking them out of the oven, another car arrived. Julie didn't believe her eyes when she saw Rosy emerging from her old VW. She rushed out to welcome her, this was a pleasant surprise.

"Oh, Rosy, I am so happy to see you!" Julie gave her a big hug after she had relieved her of the two large shopping bags she was carrying and put them in the kitchen.

Rosy Enderett was in her early fifties, a short, well rounded, extremely friendly and comforting woman. Her dark eyes sparkled with laughter, Julie had never seen her in a bad mood. Rosy was always ready to help and pitch in, wherever she was needed. She had been born in Southern Mexico, where her husband George had met her, after he had left Madrone Flat as a young man. Taking over his father's saw mill was not what he wanted to do with his life. He traveled for a year, meeting Rosy in the process, and they got married. George finished college and became a teacher. Rosy, being an excellent cook, started a small Mexican restaurant. When George's father became very sick, George agreed to come back to Madrone Flat and to help out. The saw mill was in bad shape and after his father died, was shut down. George and Rosy liked it in Madrone Flat and stayed, when George was offered a teaching job at the local school. Rosy again opened a small Mexican restaurant, which was now doing very well after the passenger service on the Northwestern Pacific Railroad had been reintroduced.

"How did you find out that I was here?" Julie asked.

Rosy laughed, "The grapevine is pretty good in these hills. I heard it first from Homer Morgan, who had met you on the train and then I got a call from your reporter friend Helen, who was very worried about you because a stranger had picked you up at the train. All your actions are well monitored, Julie.

The mail has not been picked up, which means that Bret and Emily are not back yet, right? I have the mail in the car in a large shopping bag. I also took some things along you probably didn't bring with you on the train–milk, butter, eggs and cheese? And I included some yogurt and cottage cheese."

She looked at her watch, "It is close to dinner time, I would like to invite myself, Julie. I have some enchiladas in the car, wrapped up in a blanket to stay warm."

Julie was moved by Rosy's generosity. She gave her another warm hug. "Come quickly with me in the garden, I'll pick some lettuce and herbs for a salad to go with it. I can hardly wait for your enchiladas, they are always so good. Dessert is right here, I just made two pies," she pointed at the two plates.

Ten minutes later, the two women were sitting on the deck, eating Rosy's delicious enchiladas with Julie's salad. Julie had opened a bottle of wine for the occasion. It was a very pleasant dinner.

"I am so glad you came, Rosy. Bret and Emily will not be here until tomorrow. Frederick Kendar's grandson brought me their message this morning. By the way, what do you know about Charles? I never met him before. He is kind of standoffish, isn't he?" Julie asked Rosy anxiously, who hesitated a little before she answered.

"You are right, that's the way I feel about him too. I don't know him well, but see him pretty regularly when he comes in with his grandfather. He first lived with the old man about five or six years ago, but then he was gone for a while and just came back last fall."

"I feel a little uneasy about him, Rosy. Josh–he is the husband of Helen, the reporter who called you–slipped me a note just before I got off the train. He warned me about Charles, after he had seen him at the station, waiting for me. Josh believes he recognized him as an ex-convict whose trial he covered a few years ago and who was sentenced to four years for a robbery. Is Josh right about his suspicions?"

Rosy didn't look very happy when she answered Julie's question. "Before I get into details, Julie, I am sure that Charles–whatever he did a few years ago–will not hurt you. As I said, he lived here some time ago, and in those years, I never saw him in the store. When he came down with the old man, he went into the bar across the street right away. Frederick got the mail, made some purchases and then sat at my lunch counter sipping his coffee, Coke or beer very slowly, waiting for Charles to emerge from the bar again. The old man was suffering a lot in those days. His grandson was letting him down continuously, yet, he probably was still hoping that things would get better. Then Charles was suddenly gone, and after some time we heard that he was in jail for armed robbery and that he had a record as a con-artist. And then his grandfather had the stroke....

"Last fall, Charles and Frederick came back to the ranch. Ever since then, Charles has taken care of him and is doing a very good job. The old man seems to be quite content, he looks well, and I have not seen Charles going into the bar any longer. Their housekeeper, who cooks their main meal and cleans the place, told me that Charles is writing a book. I really think he is a changed man, Julie. Now I can understand why your reporter friends called me, I had no idea that they had recognized him, they didn't mention this."

Julie had turned pale, when she heard Rosy mentioning armed robbery. "Armed robbery, you said? This does sound dangerous, Josh didn't mention this angle."

Rosy reassured her, "As I said, I think he is a changed man. Although he seems to be kind of arrogant or aloof, he is always very polite. Julie,

I am so sorry I told you all that. Why don't you come with me and stay with us until Emily and Bret come home? I have two vacancies, you can take your pick. You have your own bath, complete privacy."

But Julie declined the offer. After all, Rosy didn't think that Charles was dangerous and she herself didn't think so either. So why should she be afraid? She promised that she would visit her as soon as the Carters came home.

From the valley below came the sounds of the whistle, and the train rolling south. Rosy looked at her watch, "Oh dear, I told George I would be back in time for the later diners, I better get home. George took care of our guests and those diners that came in on the late trains. But we usually have some locals come in later when the train crowd is through."

"Is George doing this all by himself?" Julie asked.

"No, Denise is doing the serving and George is the cook. You might remember her, she is the fire chief's daughter. She is going to graduate from high school this month and this will be her summer job, but she helps out on weekends already. Denise is a lovely girl, intelligent, quick and very attractive."

Julie saw Rosy to her car. Sadly, she watched the VW winding its way up the hill and eventually disappearing behind the ridge. After Rosy's lively visit, the empty house was profoundly silent. For a few minutes, Julie experienced a touch of depression. Quickly, she caught herself and after cleaning up the kitchen, she decided to go down to the river again. The water was warmer than in the morning. Julie enjoyed a long swim and felt invigorated when she came out of the river.

Walking up the path, she was debating whether she should sleep again up on the ridge. Why not? It had been a pleasant experience. When she finally crawled into her sleeping bag, it was getting dark and she could see the first stars. Last night, she had been overwhelmed by the magnificent display of a myriad of stars in the sky, something she had missed in New York. It was as beautiful tonight and she was glad she had come up here again.

CHAPTER 8

It was still dark, when Julie woke up on Sunday morning. She contemplated the day ahead of her, letting her mind wander, dozing off and on, as the stars were getting fainter and the eastern sky was getting brighter by the minute. The air was chilly and after having her bare arms folded up behind her neck for a while, she snuggled back into the warmth of her sleeping bag. There was a lot of moisture in the air, the outside of the sleeping bag was damp and there were thousands of tiny dew droplets on the grasses and flowers around her.

The first rays of sun had just reached the top of Fir Mountain. Now it wouldn't be long and the ridge would be sunny too, it was time to get up. As she looked at her watch, she heard a car. This couldn't be Bret and Emily–unless they had driven through all night? It was five minutes to six, same time as yesterday. Going fishing again? The sound came from the same direction as yesterday. Julie walked up the ridge toward the edge of the hidden valley. Just as she arrived at the spot where yesterday she had tried to peek down through the jungle, hoping to catch a glimpse of the valley, the car stopped. It sounded as if it came right from below, next time she drove to Madrone Flat with the Carters, she had to take a closer look at that area.

It would be great to explore the valley this morning, trying to find a safe trail down. Julie had pondered about this a while ago, after she woke up. But it was a risk she should not take, alone, by herself. If she slipped or fell, nobody would ever know where she was. She would wait patiently until Bret and Emily were back.

Julie spent the morning sprucing up the house, cleaning the refrigerator, and later picking some vegetables. After lunch, she went again into the garden to do some serious weeding. The asparagus was disappearing under the grasses, dandelions, clover and other plants. She liked the work. Although the day was warm, she felt quite comfortable. There were a few larger trees outside the garden which provided shade and Julie adjusted her work areas to the tree's moving shadows. In between, she picked raspberries for snacks. Buttercup had joined her, cleaning and preening himself until he was satisfied with his appearance and settled down for a nap.

The afternoon glided into the early evening, and Emily and Bret had still not come home. Julie started to become nervous, and caught herself estimating again and again how much time they would have needed for the trip since they called Charles yesterday morning. She knew the area only from maps, she had never been in Oregon or Washington. Worried, she went back into the house, found a map of the area and carefully added up the mileage. She discovered that by now–it was seven o'clock–they definitely should be here, even if they had been driving fairly slowly and made frequent stops. Bending over the map again, adding up the numbers a second time, she arrived at the same conclusion. With the dreadful memory of her parents' fatal car accident, Julie easily worried when someone driving a car wouldn't show up on time. She tried to calm herself thinking of all kinds of harmless reasons why they could be delayed, and decided to go for a swim again to divert her mind for a while. Buttercup came along, watching her getting into that cold, wet stuff, convinced that a dry preening was preferable, much more pleasant and functional.

By the time Julie came back to the house–refreshed and in a more upbeat mood–it was eight o'clock. She ate a small sandwich with a salad and relaxed on the deck, reading a book until it got too dark. Should she sleep up on the ridge again? By now, she was more worried about Emily and Bret than Charles, but she was also curious whether the early morning car would come again on Monday?

It did indeed, at a quarter to six this time. The sound of the engine woke her up again and there was no question that it came from the same direction, the area between the hidden valley and the main road. It turned quiet after about five minutes of what sounded like laboring up a steep hill. Very strange! But this morning, Julie was not in the mood to occupy herself further with this puzzle. She had not slept as well as the two previous nights. It had taken a long time until she had fallen asleep, disturbed by bad dreams.

Realizing that she had not heard the Carters coming home during the night, she got up to look down to the house, to make sure that she had not missed their car. No, there was no car down there. What had happened to them? While she was walking down the road, she couldn't keep herself from imagining all kinds of frightful scenarios. Now she wished she had accepted Rosy's offer to stay with her, at least she would have had someone to talk to. Instead here she was, all alone, worrying herself sick. What had promised to be a great homecoming had turned into a nightmare–first the trouble with Charles and now this frustrating waiting for her dear friends.

As she ate her breakfast, she decided to wait until noon for the Carters to come home and then..., yes, what then? There was no telephone here and the CB radio was installed in the Carter's car. She had no other choice than to walk to Madrone Flat and use the phone at Rosy's store. If they had been in an accident, it would not be easy to find out because she would have to call the Highway Patrol in three states. And then it dawned on her that she didn't know their license number or the kind of car they drove, because they had planned to buy a new one. Well, there were still a few hours until noon and perhaps they would show up soon after all.

Her work in the garden was far from finished and during the next few hours she tried to focus on gardening instead of imagining the worst. When it turned rather warm by ten o'clock, she jogged down to the river for a swim. Coming back to the house, Julie noticed a piece of paper on the front steps, weighed down with a rock. A message! It was from Charles, and it was good news, but not what she had been so anxious to hear.

Hello, Bret, Emily and Julie,

sorry to have missed you all! Julie's friend Kim called last night, she will arrive on Tuesday on the afternoon train.

Hope to see you soon, Charles.

Julie had hoped that the Carters had left a message with Charles explaining their delay. This possibility was now out of the question. She was convinced that they would have called in case they had mechanical trouble, they were both responsible people. Everything pointed to a more serious explanation for their delay.

Back in the garden, Julie released her mounting anxiety by furiously attacking the weeds that were choking the strawberries. At noon, she was amazed how much she had accomplished, at least a third of all beds were free of weeds.

She decided to hop on the afternoon train to Madrone Flat, this way she had to walk only one way. The train was slowing anyway near the ranch because of the tunnel and the proximity of the village. However, before she left, she had a task before her that she loathed. She went upstairs to Emily and Bret's apartment to search for the license number and make of their car, expecting to be asked for this information by the Highway Patrol office. Fortunately, she didn't have to go through everything. The Carters had a large filing cabinet next to their main desk which contained personal documents. Easily, she found the file titled 'Car' and had all the information she needed.

Buttercup sat in the hallway, staring at Julie when she came downstairs. She almost felt like apologizing to him for invading the Carter's privacy. Unfortunately, she had to lock Buttercup into the basement, which he didn't like at all. But Julie was afraid that he might follow her to the tracks and then perhaps run after the train when she got on.

Sitting under a tree at the bottom of the hill facing the tracks and the river, Julie jumped a day ahead in her imagination, picturing Kim getting off the train and hugging her. They had not seen each other since last summer. In December and January of last year, Kim had been away in Japan on assignment. She had promised to stay for two weeks, and Julie was hoping that she would make this true.

She heard the whistle in the distance. Looking at her watch, the train was right on time. Better to go down to the tracks now so the engineer could see her as soon as the ranch stop came into sight. After a few minutes, the train approached around the bend about two miles south. It was slowing before she even waved. As it came nearer, she noticed the conductor leaning out of one of the vestibules, they must have seen her already. The train came to a halt and the conductor stepped down with the foot stool. Julie came forward to get on the train, and had the surprise of her life. Thomas came down the steps! He was carrying a large backpack and put his gear down to greet her. Julie was so happy and relieved by his unexpected arrival that spontaneously, she threw her arms around his neck and embraced him. She was still clinging to him when the train took off again a minute later and this brought her back to reality and she felt terribly embarrassed.

"I am sorry, Thomas, I didn't really mean to do this. I was just so overjoyed to see you because I have been alone here since I arrived. And now I am afraid the Carters might have had an accident. Actually, I was going to take the train to the village to call the Highway Patrol," Julie said, being startled by Thomas' sudden appearance. She now looked helplessly at the tail end of the train disappearing in the tunnel.

"I didn't mind your hearty welcome at all, Julie, in fact, I liked it a lot," Thomas smiled, and only reluctantly let her go, but then turned serious. "It sounds as if you had nothing but problems since you arrived? I hope you didn't have any major trouble with that guy who–according to Josh–had been in jail for armed robbery?"

"It was a bit scary to hear about this, especially since I was alone. I was glad that Rosy, who owns the store in Madrone Flat and whom I know very well, came over on Saturday. Although she was familiar with Kendar's criminal record, she tried to assure me that he had changed a lot and wouldn't hurt me. Josh and Helen had called her because they worried about me. They are a little overprotective, but they mean well. I am afraid they called you too?"

Thomas nodded, "Yes, they called Saturday morning. I had gone to Santa Rosa with Ken and Maria and we didn't come back until last night. So the minute I heard about it, I decided to come up. Josh, and especially Helen, were very concerned about you after they recognized that guy and knew you were alone."

"To tell you the truth, Thomas, I was not really all that afraid, because Charles made a fairly decent impression on me. He is not at all what you would expect of a con-man, like trying to win one's trust by being super-charming or overbearing. On the contrary, he is shy, reserved and not very friendly, but nevertheless helpful as a neighbor. And Rosy's judgment about him also gave me some peace of mind. After all, she sees him regularly at her store."

She was interrupted by Thomas, "Who is Charles, Julie? The message I got from Josh and Helen mentioned a Jason Kendar who picked you up on Friday and who is supposed to be an ex-convict. Is he the same person you are talking about?"

"Josh didn't mention a name in his note to me and Charles introduced himself as Charles Kendar when he came to the train last Friday. All I know is that his grandfather's name is Frederick Kendar. Perhaps being a con-man, he changes his names according to his mood?" she joked, but at the same time looked a little confused.

"Who knows?" Thomas replied, "In any case, we seem to be talking about the same person. Go ahead, I am sorry I interrupted you, I just wanted to be clear."

"Well, I was telling you about Rosy's opinion concerning Charles/Jason–whatever his real name is. Rosy offered me a room at her B and B until Emily and Bret came back, but I declined. Now I am really worried about them. I actually had planned to hop on the train to Madrone Flat and to call the Highway Patrol. Would you mind walking with me to the village?"

Thomas, of course, didn't mind. They stored his backpack behind some trees at the bottom of the hill and took off. On the way, Julie told him about the message the Carters had sent on Saturday according to which they should have been back last night at the latest. Thomas agreed with Julie's estimate. He had lived in Seattle and in Medford/Oregon for a while and had driven up and down the coast several times. He assured her that she was not overreacting. They easily should have made it home by early afternoon on Sunday, if they had reached Portland on Saturday afternoon. Something must have happened.

Rosy was happy to see Julie again and to meet Thomas. She was also concerned when Julie told her that the Carters had not arrived yet. Quickly, Rosy checked their mail box. No, they had not come by since Julie left the ranch an hour ago.

The calls to the Highway Patrol took some time. Julie started with calling the Eureka office. There was no report of an accident between the Oregon border and Willits that fitted either by name, license or car description. In Oregon, she had to call several numbers before she reached the correct office. Again, the information was negative. But the woman Julie talked to asked her to call back in about half an hour, in the meantime she would check the description of the Carters' van again on the computer. The call to Washington didn't lead to anything either, there was no report of an accident where a car like the Carters' had been involved.

As they were waiting for the thirty minutes to pass, Julie decided to call also Charles in case he had heard from the Carters since this morning. Looking at her face, Thomas could tell that the call was negative.

"He hasn't heard anything and seems to be very concerned that they have not arrived yet. He told me when Bret called him on Saturday, he could hardly talk because he had a very bad cold and supposedly Emily was even worse. Charles is wondering whether they might have gotten so sick that they had to stay in a motel to rest? Anyway, he asked me to call him should I hear anything about them. He really came out of his shell, I had judged him kind of arrogant, which he was not at all now, on the contrary, he was warm and caring."

Thomas told Julie about the trip to Santa Rosa. He had found a place to rent. "It's a small cottage set back in the garden of a larger house in the front. The area is slightly seedy, but this little house is really nice and quiet, sitting back from the street. And it is within walking distance of the office, so I don't need the car. During the last few years of law school, I worked part time as a private investigator for a large detective agency and needed the car a lot. That's why I happen to know the distances between Seattle and the Bay Area so well. One summer, I worked at their office in Seattle and some other time in Medford, in Oregon."

"That sounds interesting. What kind of investigation work did you do?" Julie asked.

"They gave me a wide variety of cases. Many had to do with insurance frauds, and some were divorce cases. But during the last year they put me on environmental investigations which gave me a good idea what to expect working in this field. I was never involved in something really dangerous, fortunately. It was all closely connected to law issues and so it was interesting for me and educational too." He looked at his watch and said, "I guess you can try Oregon again, it's been thirty-five minutes, Julie."

She dialed the number and asked for the woman she had talked to earlier.

"Ms. Sutten, I couldn't find any facts or real evidence linking your friends with an accident. We did receive some information though on

Saturday, in the late afternoon, about a van that supposedly plunged into the Columbia River around noon the same day."

Julie turned white and interrupted her, "Oh no, don't tell me it was their van!"

"I hope not, Ms. Sutten. But please, let me continue. The person who reported the incident, apologized for calling so late. He had been driving his mother from eastern Washington to Medford where her sister was seriously ill in the ICU of a local hospital. The caller had been following this van for some time, unable to pass it because the road was winding and there was a constant stream of oncoming traffic. All of a sudden–after rounding yet another curve–it had disappeared from the road, although there had been no turnoff or place to hide. Against the protest of his mother, he had turned around and checked the area again. The car was gone and the only explanation was that it had plunged down the very steep bank into the river. The river at this spot looked deep and was flowing swiftly and there was no sign of the car, any help would have come to late. He had meant to call sooner, but his mother had been anxious getting to the hospital. The driver remembered part of the license number and it matched the Carters' as did the color of the van. He also mentioned that he had seen two people in the vehicle. Unfortunately, someone interrupted him and apparently he was called away from the phone. He hung up before he gave any details concerning the location and did not call back."

"Don't you have 'Caller Identification'? Couldn't you find out his telephone number?" Julie asked, clinging to technicalities.

"Sure we do. The guy called from a pay phone at a local hospital. We called back a few minutes later and someone picked up the phone. But this person–a nurse who was just passing by–had no clue who the caller might have been. She promised to check with ICU and would call back if she found the visitor. We got a call from her on Sunday morning that she had not been able to trace the visitor.

"We have been searching both highways north and south of the river for possible skid marks in areas where such an accident could happen, and so far have not found anything. Of course, the investigation continues. Actually, I should not disclose this information to anybody except the close relatives. Please try to get in touch with your friends' relatives as soon as possible, and tell them to contact us. I still hope that this turns out to be a false alarm, but as long as your friends have not come back, we must take this information seriously. Could I have your phone number, so I can contact you in case we learn anything new?"

Julie explained that the ranch did not have a telephone and gave her Rosy's number. She also assured her that she would try to get the relatives' telephone number from information. Julie slowly replaced the receiver. She stared into space and started to cry. She wiped her eyes with the back of her hand, but the tears kept coming.

Interrupted by sobs and sniffles, she told Thomas what she just had heard. He put his arm around her in a gentle embrace and held her for a while.

"I guess I must try to reach Emily's sister and Bret's brother," Julie said, straightening up. "The trouble is, I am so distraught right now, I can't even remember their names. Emily's sister's first name is Bonnie, but her last name escapes me."

Thomas suggested that Bret's brother's name most likely was also Carter. "Perhaps you remember where he lives? If it is not too big a city, you might find him without a first name?"

"Sure, you are right, the name must be Carter too. And how could I forget the place where he lives! It is San Juan Capistrano!"

Thomas looked up the area code and called information. After he hung up the phone, he named the two Carters he had found numbers for, "There is a John and a Ralph Carter. Which do you think is the right one, Julie?"

When she heard the second name, Julie knew it was Bret's brother's name, "That's it, Ralph, I am very sure. I actually met him once. Oh, how awful, I hate to be the bearer of such tragic news!"

She pulled herself together and dialed the number. A woman answered the phone, she was Ralph Carter's wife. Julie had never met her, but the woman knew right away who Julie was, because she had heard about her from Bret and Emily. When Julie told her the bad news, there was absolute silence on the other end and then Julie heard her crying. She finally asked Julie for more details–could this really be true? Perhaps they had made a mistake? Julie told her all she knew and gave her the phone number in Oregon and Rosy's number. Julie promised she would call her back if she heard anything else or–it now sounded like a miracle–if they should still arrive. In any case, she would call back tomorrow. Ralph's wife promised to call Bonnie, Emily's sister. Julie finally hung up. Utterly exhausted mentally, she leaned against the wall of the phone booth for a few minutes. Thomas gently held her hand.

They went back to the store. Rosy was shocked and just couldn't believe it. Julie now remembered that Charles was also worried. Rosy volunteered to call him. There was nothing they could do anymore now and so they returned to the ranch.

They didn't talk very much on the way back, but the exercise restored some of Julie's energy. Even helping Thomas to carry his heavy backpack up the hill–she insisted doing that, because she had nothing to carry otherwise–seemed to require less energy than hearing the terrible news about the Carters and informing their close family.

Thomas was impressed by the house, "It reminds me of my grandparents' house in South Carolina which is also an old house, warm and inviting. But the setting of this house is really beautiful. I can see why you considered taking a teaching job at the local school. This is light-years removed from New York City, Julie! I wouldn't mind living here myself."

Buttercup was very appreciative to be let out of the basement. He took right away to Thomas, purring and waiting to be petted.

"Poor cat," Julie said, "he doesn't know yet how his life might change." She looked sad as she picked up her basket and went into the garden to get some things for supper.

While Julie picked lettuce and dug up some asparagus, Thomas inspected the tracker with the photovoltaic panels east of the garden, at the foot of the hill, close to the road.

"Is your house completely off the grid or are you still connected to Pacific Gas and Electric, Julie?"

Julie had completed her harvest and joined Thomas near the fence where he was watching the tracker, as it slowly changed its position, now tilted toward the western sun.

"We are completely on our own, we never were connected to the power company."

"But what happens if the system breaks down or if you have bad weather–many days without sun? Do you have a back-up generator?" Thomas asked.

"No, we don't, but in addition to the solar cells, we also have a small water turbine at the foot of Fir Mountain from where our water comes down. This runs day and night and is the back-up for the solar system during bad weather, in a way. It generates less power than the photovoltaic cells, but more than enough just for the lights. Bret is pretty good in maintaining the system. He studied it carefully when it was installed and understands its complexities. We also have a solar water heater up there on the roof," Julie pointed to the southern part of the house, and Thomas noticed the familiar box on the roof.

"Is this your only source for hot water?"

"No, it is actually one of three. All our excess electrical energy–once the batteries are fully charged–goes into a resistance water heater installed in our hot water tank. And the third source comes from the wood stoves–in the kitchen and the living room–which have water-coils in the fire boxes. So, we usually have plenty of hot water."

Thomas was amazed. He had read a lot about alternate energy and was very interested in its use. But having lived in an urban environment, he had limited practical experience, except with solar water heaters. This was the first house he had ever visited that was truly energy independent.

Julie had dinner ready within thirty minutes. "I had opened a bottle of wine when Rosy came over on Saturday. Would you like a glass, Thomas?" Julie suggested.

"Sure, that would be nice," Thomas replied.

He carried the tray with the plates, silverware and food out to the deck and Julie followed with the glasses and the wine.

Thomas was impressed by the meal, "You are an excellent cook, Julie, where did you learn this? Certainly not studying archaeology?"

Julie refused to take credit for it, "This is a simple meal, anybody could have done that. It only tastes so good because the salad greens, herbs and the asparagus, have all been harvested just minutes before preparation. The rice and the chicken didn't require any special skills. I did pick up a lot of cooking hints from my grandfather's housekeeper, Alma Reads. She is a wonderful person and a great cook. Grandpa hired her when my parents died and he had to take care of me. We had a very good relationship. This reminds me, I have to send her a note, she wanted to come up for a visit."

"What about this wonderful raspberry pie? You didn't get this out of a can, Julie?" Thomas grinned, helping himself to a second piece.

"Okay, yes I made it, but the berries were also fresh from the garden," Julie countered, "and a lot of credit should go to those who planted the garden. Bret and Emily are great gardeners. I still cannot believe it, somehow it just cannot be true," she had to fight her tears back.

When they had finished the meal, Thomas helped clear the table. He carried the tray back to the kitchen, which he admired. Especially the old-fashioned wood cook stove caught his attention. It had been bought by Julie's great-grandparents back around 1914 or 1915, and was still in good condition.

While they were doing the dishes–Julie washing them and Thomas drying them, stacking them neatly on the kitchen counter–he brought up the accident again. He was not satisfied with the scarce information Julie had received. Why, for instance, didn't the Highway Patrol in Washington State know anything about this matter? If they had indeed searched for evidence along the highway north of the Columbia River, the Washington offices should be involved. And did they try at all to track down the informer who had supposedly seen the accident, like talking to other people in the hospital who might have seen him when he made the call?

Julie pointed out that they probably had not told her all the details because she was not related to the Carters.

"I am sure they will be more forthcoming with Bret's brother or Emily's sister, Thomas."

"I hope you are right, Julie. Somehow I do not feel good about this whole matter. I have a friend in Medford who is a detective with the police department. Perhaps I can reach him tomorrow and have him check out the case. Of course, every minute that goes by without them showing up, makes it more likely for something very serious to have happened.

"Compared to this tragedy, having a neighbor who supposedly committed armed robbery, has become unimportant all of a sudden, especially when he has served his time and perhaps has changed."

"You are right, things are really turned around now," Julie said. "You can't imagine, Thomas, how much I appreciate that you are here. I would not have returned to the ranch today after hearing the terrible news if you had not come. Even with poor Buttercup locked up in the basement, I would have stayed at Rosy's. I hate to admit it, but I have camped up there on the ridge for the last three nights!" Julie pointed out the kitchen window to the ridge from where the road was leading down to the house. "You probably think I am crazy. When I found Josh's note about Charles being a criminal on Friday afternoon, I was really not too concerned. It gave me a little shock, but I managed to get over it fairly fast. Also, at the time I expected Emily and Bret would come home that day anyway. However, when it turned eight o'clock and they still weren't here, I started to worry a little. And you know, old houses have a life of their own. You can hear all kinds of these creaking and groaning sounds during the night. So I figured, I probably would sleep more relaxed camping out."

Thomas stopped wiping the dinner plate he held in his hand.

"I can't believe it," he said, looking incredulous, "You were afraid of sleeping in the house yet you thought nothing of sleeping all by yourself in the woods? What about bears or mountain lions?"

"As an environmental lawyer you should be better informed about the danger from bears or mountain lions. Bears are very shy, I have never heard of a bear attacking someone except if they smell food. And the bears in this area are not used to campers anyway, they are much shyer than those in the parks. And mountain lions are also very shy. The chance of being killed in a car accident is probably thousand times greater than to be killed by a mountain lion. Recently, I read that in the whole country only about sixteen people have been killed by mountain lions since 1906!

"Anyway, I really liked sleeping up there. The stars are magnificent! When I heard the next day that the Carters would not come home until Sunday, and when Rosy left after dinner and the silence in the house became almost depressing, I camped out again. And then on Sunday night I went up to the ridge again, because I liked it, but I also was curious whether that early-morning car would come again."

"What kind of car?" Thomas asked.

Julie explained about the car, how she had heard it every morning at the same time. And how she had been walking in the direction from where the sound came–along the ridge toward Fir Mountain–and ended up on the edge of the hidden valley that Frank had mentioned to her as a possible location of a Native American settlement or ceremonial site.

"I would very much like to find a path down into the canyon, but decided not to do it by myself, the slope is rather steep. Perhaps we can do it together when Kim is here?" she wiped her hands dry on a towel, "We are finished here now, let's sit outside again, Thomas."

As they were walking through the living room, Thomas stopped and admired the baby grand piano in the window bay on the left side of the French door to the deck.

"This looks like a very nice piano," he stepped closer. "May I?" he asked, and when Julie nodded, he opened the lid.

"A Bechstein!" he exclaimed, "that's a beautiful instrument. Do you play, Julie?"

"A little, for my own pleasure. It's my grandmother's piano, my father's mother's. She was an excellent pianist and started to teach me when I was six years old. She died two years before my parents. Grandma had always said that some day I should have the piano. It probably is out of tune. This is the only piece of furniture that I had moved from my grandfather's house after his death. Emily and Bret arranged the move, they knew I would love to have it here. There are other pieces of furniture still there that belong to me, and eventually I will get them. So far, I have avoided going back to the house. I should have visited Alma when I arrived in San Francisco. My brother inherited the house and Alma was willing to stay and live there. But I just couldn't go and only called her from Fred's house. Alma understands, and she will come up here soon to visit with me."

Thomas let his fingers glide over the keyboard, softly striking some chords, "It doesn't seem to be terribly out of tune. Good sound!" He played the first measures of Mozart's Concerto in A major, but stopped after a minute.

"Why don't you go on, Thomas? You play very well," Julie encouraged him.

"Some other time, I guess I am not really in the mood now. I would rather just listen to music. Would it be all right if I get a tape or CD out?"

Julie nodded, although in reality she didn't feel much like listening to music this evening.

"There is a little wine left ," she said, pointing to the bottle outside on the table, "shall I get two glasses again?" When Thomas accepted, she went back into the kitchen to get them. Julie was just pouring the wine when the music of Handel's Water Music sounded from the room. She was delighted by Thomas's choice after all. This music eased her grieving for Emily and Bret, and enhanced the joy she felt about Thomas being with her. When he stepped out on the deck, he looked at her with apprehension–had he picked the right music?

Julie smiled at him, "I like your choice, Thomas, this is one of my favorite pieces."

They sat there silently, listening to Handel, being entranced in their own thoughts, slowly sipping the wine–and enjoying being together. When the music died away, Thomas got up and turned the machine off.

"We could camp on the hill again tonight, Julie, and get an early start exploring the canyon and perhaps solve the mystery of the car as well–if it shows up again." he suggested when he came back out to the deck. "We probably can be back here by ten and then walk to Madrone Flat to make more telephone calls."

"To be honest, I actually had been looking forward to sleeping in my old room and my old bed again. But yes, I want to see the hidden valley and I am also curious about the car. So let's go before it gets dark."

She got a light rucksack from the pantry, packed some food for breakfast, and then they took off. They didn't talk much on the way up because the road was steep and they were walking fast to get up to the ridge before sunset.

They chose a camping spot quite a bit higher than where Julie had stayed. Thomas probably would have liked to hike all the way up to Fir Mountain, had it not been too late for that. The ridge was still getting some sun when they got there, but soon the sun would disappear behind the northwestern hills.

Up here, the landscape was dotted with rock outcroppings and the vegetation was sparse. One of the larger boulders provided a perfect backrest for sitting down. They watched as the evening sun turned the snowy peaks of the Mendocino National Forest deep pink.

"I never have been up there," Thomas said, "how high are these mountains? Have you been there, Julie?"

"Not recently, unfortunately. The highest peaks are about 8,000 feet high, and they are in the Yolla Bolla Wilderness area which is just southeast of here. I participated in a backpack trip through this area when I was still in high school and I have also camped twice in other parts of these mountains. It is very beautiful in early summer, until about the end of July. Later, it gets rather dry."

"Several times I was tempted to turn off from Highway 101 to the Covelo road and go from there across the mountains to the Central Valley. I never did, it was either the wrong time of year or I didn't have enough time," Thomas said with regret.

"You sure need time to do that, it is a long trip on a dusty, winding road. However, it keeps the mountains from being overrun with people."

The pink color was fading out and now the peaks were grayish white and getting darker by the minute.

Julie shivered, "I wouldn't want to sit on top of those peaks now, it must be freezing cold up there, I am getting cold even down here."

"You are still in short sleeves, put on your sweater and you will be warm, Julie," Thomas suggested.

"No, I know something better, I am going to snuggle into my sleeping bag, it is getting late anyway."

She took her shoes and socks off and slipped into her bag. Still leaning against the rock, she zipped the bag up to her shoulders.

"Okay, that feels more comfortable. What's that, Thomas?"

While Julie had crawled into her sleeping bag, Thomas had reached into the rucksack and was unwrapping what looked like a small box of candy.

"I am taking up my German grandmother's bad habits, who liked to treat my sister and me–when we were children visiting my grandparents in Germany–with a piece of candy before bedtime. And we loved it, of course. My mother used to be furious when she happened to notice it. Yet most of the time my mother didn't catch on, it was done very secretively. Like that, close your eyes and open your mouth!"

Julie did so and tasted a delicious piece of chocolate candy which Thomas had put between her lips.

"But of course, we were there only for visits, so the damage to our teeth was minor. This is one of the two small boxes of 'Mozart Kugeln' my grandmother sent me several months ago with a book for my birthday. So you can tell, I am really not addicted to chocolate. I had taken it along to share it with the guys on our backpack trip. But I would rather share it with you–I'll get a big Hershey bar to take along on our hiking trip. You care for another piece?" He smiled and offered her the open box.

Julie grinned, "Sure, why not, now that the damage is done anyway, thanks. But what does Mozart have to do with this chocolate?"

Thomas picked the small box–now empty–up again and showed her Mozart's picture on the lid. "It's made in Salzburg, Mozart's place of birth, that's the only connection I can see."

Thomas then told her about his visits with his grandparents in Heidelberg and his extensive train travels in Europe. He painted the European passenger trains in glowing colors, being reliable, fast, and fun. Getting into other topics, they discovered to their delight, that they shared many common interests–natural science, classical music and outdoor activities as hiking, cross-country skiing and canoeing.

They found that they had other similar experiences. Both had lived in the same big city, Julie until a week ago and Thomas until he was ten years old. It was fun to compare a ten-year old boy's experiences living in New York City to those of a twenty-four-year old woman. It turned out that here too they found some common ground.

"How did it happen that you came to California? Didn't you say that your parents live in Washington?" Julie asked.

"Now they live there, but after New York, my father worked as an assistant curator at the Oakland Museum, in the California Art's section. He also taught some art classes at UC. So I went to school in Oakland and then to UC in Berkeley. I was just starting my second year when my father got the offer from Washington.

"I guess you are familiar with the Oakland museum? For me, it was like a second home. Although my father worked in the art department, my main interest was the Natural Science section, or the California Ecology section, as they called it."

"Sure, I know it very well. I used to visit the museum quite often during my high school years and I always was very impressed. Art doesn't really interest me too much, but I did love those huge paintings by Alfred Bierstadt, scenes from the Sierra, like Yosemite Valley, they are overwhelming!"

Thomas had also decided to slip into his sleeping bag after he had strung up the rucksack between two trees some distance from their camp. As it got dark, it became cooler and a little windy. They admired the night sky and tried to identify the various planets and constellations and Thomas realized soon that Julie's knowledge was way superior to his own.

"You must have studied the sky for many years? Where did you pick that up? Not in New York?" he asked.

"Working for long weeks on digs in the southwestern deserts of Arizona or New Mexico, I spent many nights sleeping under the stars, out in the open, without a tent. That's why I didn't hesitate sleeping up here alone. The husband of one of our teaching assistants was an astronomer. Being very much interested in his wife's work, he often came along to our digs during the summer. She, on the other hand, also had a good knowledge in astronomy.

"So there we were lying in our sleeping bags, with the beautiful clear sky above us, being lectured by this husband and wife team, night after night. It was great, I learned a lot. Eventually, the stars and planets became familiar to me. I noticed the seasonal changes and I could understand how the captains of ancient ships had relied for centuries on the stars for navigation."

Thomas didn't respond, he was silent.

After a while–Julie had assumed that he had fallen asleep already–he spoke up, quietly, "Gazing up into the night sky and watching the millions of stars above us, makes me feel very insignificant. In spite of years of schooling, good achievements and success, compared to the gigantic dimensions out there in the universe I feel tiny, like a speck, very unimportant. I have often thought it would be good regular exercise for all of us to look up into the sky more often and become a bit more humble. It could teach us to see our worldly problems from a different perspective and prevent us from becoming arrogant.

"When you mentioned the possibility that you might want to stay here and teach school instead of getting a job in Berkeley, I questioned for the first time the wisdom of my decision to work as a lawyer, becoming mired in the quicksand of legal battles. Wouldn't a simpler life be a wiser choice? For myself and the environment? And tonight, under this magnificent starlit sky, I experience this doubt stronger than ever before."

"I just thought of my great-grandfather," Julie replied after a while. "He made the decision to stay here and live a simple life when the construction of the railroad was completed. He probably could have made a lot more money had he opted for another engineering job. Would he have been happier? From all I have heard about my great-grandparents lives, they were very happy here at the ranch. Don't misunderstand me, Thomas, I don't mean to say you should give up your profession. But once in a while, it is healthy to think of and even consider simpler solutions. They are often more rewarding to our mental and physical health than those that come with high returns–money, power and fame. You can become a good lawyer and still adhere to a modest life style."

Thomas took a while to answer. "That's the way I see myself now, Julie. That's what I am striving for, and I hope I will not lose it as life goes on. During my years of schooling, I met several lawyers who were the shining stars of their profession, but they had kept their integrity. They didn't succumb to the so-called high rewards. And I believe your grandfather was one of them. I very much regret that I met him only that one time when Ken asked me to come along to hear him in court."

They both were quiet, occupied with their own thoughts. Then Thomas yawned, his voice sounded tired, "Well, its getting late, we better get some sleep if we want to be up early. Good night, Julie."

"Good night, Thomas."

CHAPTER 9

Next morning, Julie's first thought was of Thomas when she woke up. What a relief that he was here. She tried to remain comfortably wrapped up in pleasant thoughts, but of course, it didn't last. Reality caught up with her as soon as she was fully awake, recalling yesterday's events. Every word of the devastating information she had received from the Oregon Highway Patrol Office invaded her mind. Yet, somehow, she still could not accept this information as final. Maybe it hadn't been Emily and Bret's car after all. Maybe their colds had turned really bad and they checked into a motel and both felt too sick to call? She knew she was grasping for straws, because the reality was so terrible and final.

It was great that Kim would come today and would stay at least for a week, because Thomas had to leave by Sunday evening.

With gratitude, she remembered the moment when Thomas stepped from the train yesterday. His presence had made the grief easier to bear, and she really liked him a lot. When she had embraced him after he got off the train–her cheeks burned remembering the moment–it had felt good and part of her wanted to hold him for ever. And later, when they had dinner together or listening to Handel's music–she had enjoyed being with him.

Her mind wandered and after a while, she fell asleep again. The swishing and flapping of wings woke her up. A Golden eagle was gliding over her, close by, sailing gracefully along the ridge.

"A Golden eagle, Thomas, look at the eagle!" Julie called out. Thomas didn't respond, and she discovered with surprise that Thomas was gone. His sleeping bag was open and empty. Her excited voice scared the eagle away. Swiftly, he dived down the slope and was gone a few seconds later. Julie sat up and looked around for Thomas. Where was he? Finally, she saw him. He was walking up the ridge toward the top of Fir Mountain. Julie knew what he was up to. The sun was still hidden behind the eastern peaks, but soon the first rays would reach the mountain top. He wanted to be up there for the sunrise! Too late for her to join him–she turned her sleeping bag around to face the mountain and crawled back in. It was always chilly before the sun was up. She looked at her watch, 5:40, still plenty of time before the car would come–if it came.

Thomas had timed his ascent well. A few minutes after he reached the top, the sun came up. Now it would not be long and the ridge here would be sunny too.

When Julie saw Thomas starting down, she got the rucksack that was hanging between the trees and walked up the ridge and met Thomas at the edge of the hidden valley.

His face lit up when he saw her, "I was debating whether I should wake you up, but you were sleeping soundly and so I took off by myself. It certainly was beautiful up there, very different though, from the colorful sunset last night. This morning, the mountains are not as clear."

"Did you happen to see the Golden eagle, Thomas?" Julie asked.

"Yes, I did. I watched him flying down towards our camp, I suppose he scared you a bit?"

"He woke me up and I called out to make you aware of it, and I guess chased him away. But I did get a pretty close look at him, this was a rare opportunity."

They stood at the edge of the hidden valley, looking down into the green maze of vegetation. It took a while to find the right spot from where they could penetrate the dense growth. Slowly, they made their way down through the trees, bushes and vines. The sound of running water became louder and louder the further down they walked. Eventually, they arrived on a narrow ledge and the valley opened up before them. It was lovely, enchanting–a natural treasure! At the steep, western slope, a creek cascaded down the almost sheer cliff in a spreading waterfall. It tumbled over rocks into a large clear pond. Surrounded by maidenhair ferns, yellow and red monkey flowers, fresh-green horsetails and many other shade and moisture-loving plants, it looked like a scene from paradise. The pond fed into a small creek, which meandered through the valley until it disappeared into a ravine at the eastern end of the meadow.

To Julie's and Thomas' dismay, all the flat areas and the gentle slopes of the valley had been cultivated and planted with rows and rows of small, fern-like plants, well protected by a fence.

Julie gasped, looking worried, "Is that what I think it is, Thomas?"

"Yes, I was afraid that we might find this, but I was not prepared for this volume," Thomas responded. "Of course, from up here, one cannot really be absolutely sure, the plants are still too small to identify them from this distance. Yet, what else could it be? This valley is too shady to plant any legal crops. I am sure it is not corn," he grinned.

"This is terrible, Thomas," Julie uttered, "to defile this beautiful valley with hundreds of marijuana plants, just to make money. This is almost a sacrilege!"

"I agree with you. I wouldn't have any problems with a few plants grown for medicinal uses. But this enormous cash crop is almost obscene."

"By the way, look over there, to the right, near the place where the creek disappears down the gully. Can you see the car tracks through the trees?" Thomas pointed to the eastern part of the valley.

"Yes, I see what you mean. This would explain the car I heard the previous mornings. I just wonder where it turns off the main road, I don't remember having seen a road branching off down there."

"They probably just blazed a trail up the slope. He is late today, it's already after seven o'clock Let's get out of here, what we are doing is dangerous."

Just as Thomas was saying that, they heard the sound of a car, plodding up the hill from the direction of the main road. They turned around quickly and climbed up the slope, hurrying to get away from the open ledge. They had almost reached a safe area of small Douglas-fir trees which they could hide behind. Thomas was stretching out his hand to pull Julie up the last few feet, when she lost her hold. A branch she had pulled herself up on broke off with a snap and she slid down the slope.

The car was inching its way into the valley. Thomas couldn't see it, but Julie caught a glimpse of it before she came to a halt at the level area. When Thomas started to slide down to help her, Julie begged him to remain where he was, "Stay were you are, don't come down, you will be too exposed and he will notice you. I will lie down here flat on the ground and I am sure he will not be able to see me."

From the ledge, it was still about a sixty foot drop to the valley and difficult to get up or down. There was no reason to assume that the person in the car would come up here, as long they kept quiet and couldn't be seen.

Julie had barely told Thomas to stay up there and that she was all right, when the car stopped and the engine was turned off. Now, they could not communicate with each other any longer. A few minutes later, the sound of a small engine could be heard, and then several sprinklers kicked on. There was nothing to do now but to be patient and wait until the watering was over. Thomas blamed himself for not having reacted fast enough when Julie slipped. He felt sorry for her, lying down there on the hard ground and not daring to move. He was anxiously waiting for the pump to stop. It seemed to go on forever. Finally, after more than thirty minutes, the sprinklers became quiet. A few minutes later, the car started up, apparently turned around, drove away, and soon could not be heard any longer. Thomas slid down the slope to help Julie, but she was already half way up to where he had waited.

"Are you OK?" he whispered, still under the influence of their close escape. Julie nodded and kept moving upwards. They climbed and scrambled up the slope as fast as they could, silently, not wasting any energy on speaking. When they reached the rim of the canyon and level ground, they straightened up and stretched out with a sigh of relief.

"That was a close call. Are you all right? It must have been terrible to lie still all that time." Thomas sympathized.

"It was not that bad. I was lying so close to the ground that I couldn't see anything of the valley, which meant, that he also couldn't see me. So I did move from time to time and didn't feel too uncomfortable."

"Nevertheless, we should never have gone down there in the first place. When you mentioned the car last night, after you had earlier explained the lay of the land, I had the suspicion that dope might be involved. I am sorry I didn't use better judgment, Julie."

"Do you really think that these people who grow the plants down there are that dangerous?" Julie asked.

"Its hard to say. Many people grow it only for their own use or to make a few bucks. However, this operation down there is well planned and will probably bring several million dollars. I would estimate that they have perhaps a thousand plants down there. This is a fortune and I don't know what this guy would have done had he seen us. He probably carries a gun. By the way, is the valley on your land?"

"No, as far as I know. I believe it belongs to Charles' grandfather. Their ranch starts at the ridge. Why?"

"If it is your land, you should report the plants. If they are raided, you can be made responsible and might even lose your property. If it is not your land, I would keep quiet, because reporting might also be dangerous to you. This business is so crazy. I wish they would legalize the stuff. Isn't it terrible that you cannot even go on a hike without risking being shot? And marijuana has a lot of healing properties and is probably less dangerous than alcohol, which is not only legal, but is even promoted in every magazine and newspaper. Our country spends over two billion dollars per year just to process marijuana arrests. Can you imagine? The prisons are filled with many small time drug offenders. There are actually far more people in federal prisons for marijuana crimes than for violent crimes. If marijuana were decriminalized, this plantation down there would not make any sense.

"When we get back to the house, Julie, you better check your deed, just to be sure that it is not your land."

Julie opened the pack and got the food out. They sat down, ate their breakfast and finally relaxed.

"Thomas, I believe the car that came into the valley was Charles' car," Julie said quietly after a while.

"Are you sure? Did you get to see enough of it?" Thomas asked.

"Of course, I didn't see it clearly, only for a few seconds, when I rolled down the slope, just before I came to a stop at the bottom. All I can say is, that it was a red car, short and square, like a Jeep. And that's the kind of car Charles has, a red Jeep. And it makes sense, because he is on his own property. Only Charles doesn't strike me as the person who would do this kind of physical labor that's involved with the operation down there. Perhaps he has hired people for that. But what concerns me even more, if I saw the car, the driver might also have seen me rolling down the slope. Too bad, I am wearing this red sweat shirt today, I really stick out."

"First of all, I am sure there are other red Jeeps around, don't focus too much on Charles' car. And second, I doubt the guy really saw you, he had to concentrate on the driving. Nevertheless, it might be a good idea to be careful for the next few days. When you meet Charles again–and if indeed it was him–you probably will get a feeling if he is suspicious of you."

"How long can you stay, Thomas?" Julie asked.

"You want to hire me as your bodyguard, Julie?" Thomas joked. "I wouldn't mind staying here for the rest of the summer. But I promised to be in Eureka by Sunday evening, on the late train, since we want to take off on Monday morning. But your friend is coming today, you will not be alone. And you'll see, nothing will happen. Just stay away from the hidden valley."

It was close to eleven o'clock when they came back to the house. Julie persuaded Thomas to walk alone to Madrone Flat and make the phone calls, because she had to prepare a few things before Kim arrived. Thomas felt uneasy leaving her alone, but she promised him to watch out for whoever came down the hill.

"I usually hear and see the cars coming down, long before they arrive here, Thomas. If I see Charles' red Jeep approaching, I'll go down to the river and hide there until you or Kim arrives. You really don't have to worry."

Thomas finally left, hoping to get back to the ranch station in time for Kim's arrival so he could help with her baggage.

Julie went upstairs to get Kim's room ready. She also checked out her Grandfather's bedroom where Thomas would sleep. Both rooms faced east, it was easy to watch the road.

Then, she went into the garden to get asparagus, peas, lettuce and herbs for dinner, picked berries for dessert, and cut flowers for Kim's and Thomas' rooms. Back in the kitchen, Julie made berry yogurt ice-cream and put it in the freezer. The vegetables had to be washed and prepared, to be ready for dinner later on. By now, it was well past noon.

While she was eating a quick sandwich, she heard a car and saw it coming down the upper part of the road. To her relief, it was Andy's small pickup truck. Finishing her lunch, Julie watched the car driving down the hill and when it had reached the house, she left the kitchen and walked to the front door.

"I just wanted to find out if you or the Carters might need my help in the garden or around the house. Have they gone to the village?" he said, looking for their car.

"No, they didn't...," Julie interrupted herself, because she noticed another car appearing at the crest of the hill. To her dismay, it looked like Charles' red Jeep! Julie's mind raced, what should she do? Sure, she was not alone, Andy was here, but did she want to pull him in, make sure that he stayed around as long as Charles was here?

She asked Andy if by any chance he was going back to Madrone Flat, and could she right away get a ride with him?

"Sure," Andy replied, "No problem."

She ran into the kitchen, got her handbag and scribbled a note 'Gone to the river', which she placed in front of the door, weighing it down with a small rock. When she slipped into the car, she explained to Andy that she wanted to avoid Charles–if at all possible. She crouched down on the floor so that Charles would not see her when the two cars passed. They met the red car about half way up the slope. Andy just waved and drove on. After the next curve, Julie felt it was safe to come up and sit down in the seat.

"What is your problem with that guy, did you have a quarrel?" Andy asked.

Julie hesitated to answer, how much should she tell Andy? Instead of answering his question, she asked him, "Do you know Charles Kendar?"

"Not really. He talked to me once for a minute when I was working in the garden and he came looking for the Carters who were not home. That was all," Andy replied, "but I know who he is. The Carters are quite friendly with him, they invited him for dinner several times. Emily told me that he is a professor at an eastern college, on sabbatical leave. I am surprised, that you are so much at odds with him."

Julie was amused, college professor on sabbatical leave? Was this one of his con-artist ploys?

"Rosy–the owner of the general store–told me that he just served a prison sentence for armed robbery."

Andy frowned, looking at her incredulously, and finally, replied, "Are you sure about that? I don't know him well enough to have an opinion, but I cannot imagine that the Carters would have such a good relationship with him if that were true."

Julie shrugged, "I don't know either, but that's what I heard. I am actually not so worried about that, because Rosy is convinced that he has changed a lot since he was released from prison. Also, he was quite helpful as a neighbor when I arrived on the train. However, this morning I happened to come upon a patch of his land that was well stocked with marijuana plants. Just as I discovered this, Charles drove in with his car. I tried to get up the slope and hide, but slipped down and there is a good chance that he recognized me, because I recognized his car. I am afraid that people who grow dope on a large scale can be quite dangerous. That's why I thought it would be better if I avoid him for a while."

"What are you going to do, Julie?" Andy asked, looking at her intensely.

"What do you mean? Do what? I am not going to do anything. If he grows that stuff on his land, it's not my business. I don't like it, but I will not do anything about it."

"Aren't you going to tell him what you saw?" Andy asked.

"Are you kidding? Why tell him? He might not have seen me after all! Please keep it to yourself, Andy. I really should not even have told you. I guess I owed you an explanation," Julie said, watching Andy's reaction apprehensively.

Andy didn't respond right away, they had just turned onto the main road and he busied himself with the car. Finally he laughed, "I wouldn't worry much about this, Charles probably didn't see you."

Julie scanned the slope to the left for signs of a road that might lead to the hidden valley. It was not very likely to be on the south side of the bridge, but she looked anyway.

Suddenly Andy stopped the car, muttering, "Damn. I have to talk to that guy over there for a minute, Julie. I'll be right back."

When Julie looked ahead, she saw a man leaning against the railing of the bridge, about hundred feet away. Andy moved the car back into a small widening of the road. He put the gears into park and got out, walking toward the bridge. Julie started to get a little nervous. Charles could show up any minute unless he had gone down to the river. She was not really afraid with Andy and this other man around, yet it would be embarrassing if Charles came by and saw her sitting in Andy's car. She was also concerned that Andy might get involved in a longer talk. There was not much time to spare to get to Madrone Flat in time to walk back to the ranch station with Thomas.

Andy had reached the bridge and was now talking to the man there. Although Julie could not understand anything they were saying–the car was still running–she could tell that this was not a friendly conversation. Even from this distance, she didn't like the looks of this man. He had a hostile and threatening expression on his face. What was going on? She glanced over to the left side of the bridge and beyond, apparently there was a turnout towards the hill. This would be the most likely spot where the road to the hidden valley would come out. Suddenly she noticed the man's car behind some trees and it gave her a shock. One couldn't see too much of it, but it was certainly a red car, and short and square like a Jeep! This was not Charles' car, because he was still at the ranch or even down at the station. So there was another red Jeep around, parked right there in a suspicious spot. Had she been wrong, suspecting Charles as the pot grower?

The conversation–or rather heated argument, judging by the faces of both Andy and the other guy–seemed to deteriorate. They were getting louder and louder. She could almost understand some words. Julie dared to turn off the ignition, she wanted to know what was going on. Fortunately, they didn't take notice, they were too embroiled in their dispute. Now she could understand words, and what she heard, horrified her. Apparently, this man and Andy were doing the pot planting operation together and the other man didn't seem to believe Andy, that Julie would not talk about it. He ordered Andy to take Julie to his cabin at the end of the road for interrogation, and Andy seemed to refuse. Julie was not only frightened because she was in a very dangerous situation, but she was also shocked because of the violent language the other man used. Never in her life had she heard such a barrage of obscene and vile words.

Suddenly, the guy had a gun in his hand, and was pointing it at Andy. By now, Julie was terrified. She knew she had to get away fast if she wanted to survive. Would they notice it if she got out of the car and ran?

Surely, they would come after her, they had too much at stake. What had Thomas said, several millions or more? She was angry with herself to have run into this trap. How could she get out of this horrible situation?

The man finally lowered the gun and tucked it away. From what Julie could gather, Andy had promised he would take Julie to the cabin. His partner advised Andy not to play any tricks. He ordered Andy to cross the bridge with his car, turn around there and take Julie all the way back to his cabin at the south end of Fir Creek Road. And he would make sure–pointing to where he had tucked in the gun–that Andy did what he had told him. Closing his demands with another burst of four-letter words, he walked to his car and disappeared behind the trees.

Andy came back, slowly, as if in deep thoughts. When he had crossed the bridge, he stood there for a few seconds, looking toward his car. Then abruptly he turned around and walked back to where his partner's car was parked.

Julie had watched in disbelief. This was the chance she needed, it was now or never! She knew she had to act fast. Quietly, she opened the door on her side, slid out and crouched down, using the car as protection from being observed. Sizing up the dense brush that lined the road, she had not much choice, it all looked thorny and impenetrable. She took a deep breath and pushed through, receiving scrapes and scratches on her arms, her face and tearing her T-shirt to shreds. Then she rushed down the slope which turned out much steeper than she had expected it to be. Sliding down, first upright, then sitting down, Julie hung on to branches, let go and grasped for others. The flight came to a short stop and then continued, gaining momentum which all of a sudden she could no longer control. She completely lost her balance and tried desperately to find a branch or vine to hang on to, but fell over head first. A sharp pain shot through her left leg and whatever had caused it, slowed down her fast descent for a few seconds. But a loud crack indicated that the short hold was over just as quickly and her downward plunge continued for a few more seconds, until it came to a dramatic stop. It felt as if all bones in her body had been broken, the pain was so intense that she fainted.

CHAPTER 10

Thomas ran all the way to Madrone Flat. During the last few months, he had often skipped his morning runs for lack of time. He had worked on a special project for the detective agency and wanted to finish it before he quit his job with them. This run was an opportunity to combine exercise with necessity.

Rosy was already waiting for Julie, she had two messages. Bret's brother had called this morning. He would fly to Portland in the afternoon. There was also a message from Emily's sister Bonnie, who had left her phone number.

Rosy insisted that Thomas should use her office to make the phone calls, "You will be much more comfortable here instead of standing out there in the phone booth, Thomas. And don't bother using your calling card, that's the least we can do to help in this tragedy, pay for some phone calls."

He gladly accepted her offer. As he settled down to make the first call, Rosy came back into the room carrying a tray with tea and cookies. She set it down quietly and left. Thomas made his first call to Bret's brother, Ralph Carter. His wife Roberta, answered the phone. After Thomas had introduced himself, she told him that her husband had already left, and would arrive in Portland at three o'clock. Ralph planned to contact the Highway Patrol Office first and then rent a car and drive along the

Columbia River, on both banks, north and south, to check out likely accident locations himself. Although it would be light until almost ten o'clock, he didn't expect to do both routes today. In any case, he would call back as soon as he either found or heard anything new or important, and would for sure call at the end of the day.

"Perhaps you could phone me around eight or nine tonight?" Roberta suggested to Thomas, "by then, I hope to have heard from him and you might be able to call him up and talk to him yourself."

Thomas promised they would do that. When Thomas called Bonnie, she answered right away. He could tell that she was still in a shock. Her voice was raw, she must have been crying a lot and was close to crying again. She managed to tell him that she would probably come up to the ranch within the next few days, unless she got an urgent call from Ralph to fly to Oregon. She had called the Highway Patrol in Oregon but had not received additional information. Thomas assured her that Julie would call her back, either tonight or tomorrow.

His next call was to Santa Rosa, to the branch office of the investigation firm he had worked for in San Francisco. He knew the office manager very well, and she was delighted to hear from him.

"Hi, Thomas, when will you start working here so we can have lunch together? I am dying to go out with a handsome young man!"

Cora Lanzen was in her late forties, an intelligent and competent woman. She used to work in San Francisco and had helped him a lot when he had started to work for the company. Her husband was also a lawyer and Thomas had been invited to dinner at their house many times.

He explained to her where he was at present and that he needed some information on a parolee. Did she happen to have any connection to a parole officer?

"I do, Thomas, I know this really nice guy, and he owes me a favor. What do you want to know?" Cora replied, and Thomas pictured her, smiling into the telephone, happy that she could help him. He told her about Jason Kendar, released on parole to Santa Rosa, but apparently living as Charles Kendar in Madrone Flat.

"When do you need the information, Sugar?" Cora asked.

"Yesterday," Thomas joked, "whenever you get to it, Cora. The only problem is, that there is no telephone at the ranch. I'll be here for another hour, but can call you back at home tonight, or at the office tomorrow."

"For you, Thomas, I'll get right to work. I'll try to get him as soon as I hang up and if I do, I'll call you right back. If you don't hear from me soon, call me back at home tonight." Thomas gave her Rosy's number and put down the receiver.

He relaxed for a while, drinking a cup of tea and eating some of Rosy's tasty cookies. He reflected on what all had happened since he got off the train yesterday at the Sutten ranch. Although he was truly sorry about the Carter's tragic accident, he couldn't help feeling good visiting with Julie. He had been captivated by Julie's natural charm from the moment he had met her in Willits, and when she asked him to stop at the ranch on his way to Eureka, he had accepted eagerly. Yesterday, when she had hugged him so enthusiastically as he stepped from the train, he sensed that she had not only embraced him because she was desperate, but that she liked him, too. Thomas was glad that he had come to lend some support, although the problem now was quite different from the one he had originally come for. The Carters' accident overshadowed everything else.

Julie had been so happy and full of expectations for a peaceful summer when they departed last Friday, and now the news about this terrible accident had changed her life completely.

The phone was ringing. It was Cora, who had managed to reach the parole officer.

"Mike Stainen, the parole officer, happens to know your guy well, Thomas, or rather your two guys. Charles and Jason Kendar are half-brothers who look very much alike. Charles Kendar comes down to Santa Rosa from time to time to visit with his half-brother Jason, because he is very concerned about Jason's rehabilitation process. Mike sees Jason Kendar almost every day, because Jason works in the yard of a farm supply store where Mike drives by when he goes to work. He often stops to chat with Jason. So far, he has been very pleased with the way Jason is conducting himself. The store manager also praises him highly. Mike saw him for sure Friday, yesterday and today in the morning. And the store manager has also confirmed, that Jason has been at work every day this week and last. Does this answer your question, Thomas?"

"You really made my day, Cora." Thomas thanked her for the prompt delivery. "When I start my job next month, I'll take you out to lunch and tell you the whole story. Thanks a million!"

Although the result of Cora's inquiry did not clear Charles from Julie's suspicion of being a large-scale pot grower, at least he was not the ex-convict who had been in prison for armed robbery.

Thomas directed his thoughts back to the Carters. Although he had felt uneasy about the Carters' accident from the beginning, he didn't want to worry Julie unnecessary. He had driven both routes, north and south, along the Columbia River, and he remembered, for long stretches, railroad tracks between the highways and the river. If there were places where a car could plunge right from the road into the river, they should be easy to check out, because there just were not that many. However, there was something weird about that telephone call reporting the accident. If it were a fake, what would be the purpose? Make the disappearance of the Carters less suspicious?

Thomas decided to call his friend Dean in Medford. Perhaps he could find out a bit more about the telephone call. Dean was at the office and within minutes, Thomas was talking to him about the accident and how he, Thomas, was involved. Could Dean perhaps check with the hospital whether they really had a patient in intensive care on Saturday who would fit the description being the caller's aunt, his mother's sister, as he had said?

To Thomas' surprise, Dean had already heard about the case, and he agreed with him that there were not many places along the river where this kind of accident could have happened. He also knew which hospital the call came from. Dean promised to drive over and get the information Thomas wanted. Because it was time for Thomas to walk back to the ranch, he gave Dean Rosy's phone number.

Rosy was busy in the kitchen with early dinner preparations when Thomas came in and brought the tray back.

"All done? Sit down and have some soup."

Before he could say anything, she had grabbed a bowl and filled it to the brim with steaming vegetable soup. She cleared a corner of the huge table in the center of the kitchen, put down knife, fork and spoon and urged him to sit down. Butter and bread–homemade, of course–appeared before him. Rosy poured herself a cup of coffee and sat down too. While he ate, she asked him whether he had heard anything new about the Carters. Thomas repeated the information he had received from Bret's sister-in-law and Emily's sister. He told her that his friend Dean might leave a message later during the day. The truth about Charles, as Thomas had heard it from Cora, was a big surprise for Rosy.

"I could have sworn that this was the same guy who lived up here several years ago and who got into trouble. They certainly looked like one and the same person, otherwise, I would not have confirmed what Julie had heard from her reporter friends. Though, I must admit, at the time when Charles, or rather Jason, lived here before, I actually never saw him very closely. He usually disappeared into the bar as soon as they came down here. Well, this is a lesson for me, next time I will be more careful with my judgment. At least, this will be one worry less for Julie. But I am sure glad that you are here now, Thomas, she needs your support."

Rosy was also suspicious about the river accident and harbored a tiny bit of hope that Emily and Bret were still alive. Both fell silent, occupied with their thoughts about this tragedy.

Walking back to the Sutten ranch, Thomas already spotted the red Jeep-like car when he was still in the tunnel. It was parked on the road between the tracks and the little station, pointing toward the hill. Charles Kendar's car? When Thomas came out of the tunnel, he saw Charles–at least he assumed it was him–sitting in the shade under a tree, reading a book. He was completely absorbed by his book, and didn't look up until Thomas was standing almost in front of him. Getting up slowly, while preserving with his left index finger the page on which he had been interrupted, he eyed him suspiciously. In a patronizing tone of voice he asked Thomas what he was doing here.

"I am Thomas Millon, a friend of Julie Sutten's, and I have been visiting with her since yesterday, when I came up on the train. I assume you must be Mr. Kendar, Julie's neighbor? Glad to meet you, sir," Thomas extended his hand which Charles accepted reluctantly, murmuring, "Yes, I am, how do you do?"

He looked quizzically at Thomas, "Millon? Did you say your name is Millon?"

And when Thomas nodded, he asked, with a slightly condescending glint in his eyes, pointing at his book, "I guess there is no connection between this Matthew Millon and you?"

Thomas had already noticed the familiar book cover, it was his father's newest book on art history. He was surprised to see Kendar reading it and being so preoccupied with it that he had resented his intrusion.

"Actually, yes, there is a connection, I am Matthew Millon's son," Thomas enlightened Kendar and couldn't help being amused seeing the arrogant expression on Charles' face change into disbelief, surprise and finally excitement.

"You are his son?" Charles exclaimed, "I admire this man, I have attended his seminars with great appreciation and I very much enjoyed talking to him. He is knowledgeable and a great lecturer and I am, of course, delighted to meet his son." He had a surprised look on his face when he continued, "but how…?" he looked embarrassed and stopped abruptly.

"Don't worry, it has happened to me before, Mr. Kendar. My mother is black, that's why. Is art history a hobby of yours or are you involved with it professionally?" Thomas asked.

"I am teaching art history at Cornell. Since last fall, I have been on sabbatical leave, working on a book and taking care of my grandfather who had a stroke last year," Kendar explained.

Looking at his watch, he continued, "The train with Julie's friend should arrive pretty soon, do you have any idea where Julie is? I came over to help getting her friend's baggage up the hill. My wife arrived last night and she is watching over my grandfather, so I am not that much in a hurry. Hearing the terrible news about the Carters, I came earlier because I felt that Julie probably needed some support. When I arrived at the house, she was not there. There was a note at the door that she had gone to the river, yet, I have not seen her, although I have been sitting here for a while," he concluded.

Thomas of course knew why Julie was not here, but he could not very well tell Charles. Still, if she was hiding somewhere, why didn't she come out now after he had arrived? Was she waiting until Kim got off the train?

Thomas was bewildered, lots of thoughts went through his mind. So this was Charles? Rather arrogant at first, as Julie had mentioned, but perhaps he was just annoyed at being disturbed. Otherwise he seemed to be a decent fellow. His red car was a Land Rover diesel, a rather old model. It certainly was not the same red car they had seen or heard this morning, that had been a car with a gasoline engine. This made Charles less of a suspect in the pot operation. Besides, it was rather unlikely that an art history professor from Cornell would grow pot in northern

California. But where was Julie? The train was supposed to arrive in a few minutes. He looked around–no sign of her. He could see the river banks to the north and south clearly, she was not down there.

"Have you looked for her since you came down here, Mr. Kendar?" Thomas asked.

"Yes, I have walked up and down the tracks, went to the river, sat there for a while and finally settled here in the shade with my book."

Using his hands as a bullhorn, Thomas shouted Julie's name into all directions several times, but without result. He started to feel uneasy, even if she was hiding because of Charles, hearing his voice should bring her out now. Charles, who apparently had not taken Julie's absence that serious, now realized that this young man had reason for concern.

One could hear the train approaching and within a few minutes, it stopped at the ranch station. The conductor helped a young woman get off the train. Kim Brittany was attractive. Her black, shiny hair was cut shoulder length and framed a bright, handsome and cheerful face. She adjusted quickly to the situation when Thomas explained that Julie for some reason was delayed and he and Charles would take her and her baggage up to the hill.

When they arrived at the house, there was no sign of Julie either and now Kim also understood that there was reason for concern. All three searched the house, the garden, the basement and the immediate area around the house, kept calling her name, but without success.

Thomas was desperate, what had happened to Julie? Had she been hiding when Charles came? And then, later, perhaps someone else had come to the ranch? Thomas' impression of Charles was fairly positive and he knew he needed help quickly to find Julie. So he decided to trust Charles. It was a delicate task to tell him of Julie's suspicion concerning the pot-growing operation and that she probably had been hiding when she saw him come down the road.

They sat in the kitchen, relaxing for a few minutes with cold beer and juice, while Thomas told the story. Both Kim and Charles were appalled, although for different reasons. Kim was, of course, very concerned about the safety of her friend, while Charles was extremely upset because he felt partially responsible for Julie's suspicion and its possible consequences. With a pained expression on his face, he explained that he had a half-brother who looked very much like him and who had indeed been in jail for armed robbery. He was also very angry to hear about the marijuana garden. There was no doubt that this was on his grandfather's land and he had not noticed anything going on there. Then, all of a sudden, he remembered that he had met Andy, who was coming up the road from the ranch, when he was driving down.

"Andy is a young man who has helped the Carters occasionally in the garden. They both liked him and were very satisfied with his work. When he saw me coming, he just waved and drove on. He was alone in his car, a small light green pickup truck," Charles told Kim and Thomas.

"I wonder if Julie took the opportunity to drive out with Andy when she saw your car coming, Mr. Kendar?" Kim suggested to Charles, "maybe she was hiding in his truck?"

Charles had not even considered this possibility, and he found the idea shocking that Julie would hide from him. But yes, she could have been hiding in the truck, he had not paid that much attention.

"If she did," Charles continued, "she either went with Andy to Madrone Flat and walked from there along the tracks to the ranch or she asked Andy to drive her back to the ranch after the train had arrived."

"Yes, I just came to the same conclusion. Perhaps you and Mr. Kendar could drive to Madrone Flat, Kim? And I will walk along the tracks. I hope that either the two of you or I will meet Julie. Can you spare a few more minutes to go to the village with Kim, Mr. Kendar? I really hate to impose on you again."

"Of course, no problem. Now that my wife is here, things are much easier. Although, I should stop at our ranch for a few minutes to let her know, will this be all right with you, Ms. Brittany? And one more thing, Kim and Thomas. Make it Charles, please, instead of Mr. Kendar, will you? So let's go, the sooner the better. Should I drive you down to the tracks, Thomas?"

"No, thank you, I probably will get to Madrone Flat almost at the same time you do, see you in about thirty minutes!" He gulped down the last juice in his glass, and was gone.

Charles and Kim left a few minutes later, driving up the hill. Charles drove slowly, stopping here and there, so they could scan the area on both sides of the road. Charles felt bad about Julie's disappearance and partially blamed himself.

"Both times I saw Julie–when she arrived by train last Friday and when I brought her the Carters' message on Saturday–I had very little time. The woman who comes in to cook for us and takes care of the house, could not stay very long because one of her kids was sick and I had to be back as soon as possible. So I guess I was impatient and not very friendly to Julie. I am also angry with the Carters for giving my telephone number to Julie and her attorney friend in San Francisco, thereby involving me with all these obligations. Sorry, Kim, I didn't mean this personally. I guess you got my number from Julie's friend Fred also? And of course, you had no way of knowing what the situation was like up here. It is quite a responsibility to care for a person who had a stroke, is wheelchair bound and cannot be left alone. I do not complain–on the contrary–I enjoy living out here, and fortunately, my grandfather is alert mentally and we like each other's company. We often have enjoyable conversations. But, although I have plenty of time to work on my book, I cannot leave the house unless someone is there to help him. Actually, it is not typical of the Carters to give my telephone number to Julie's friend. They always have been very considerate. Somehow they must have been in a big hurry when they left on that trip."

Kim sympathized with Charles and urged him not to feel guilty, she was sure they would find Julie soon.

Charles also told her about Jason, his half-brother, who was four years older. Jason's mother had been the girlfriend of Charles' father in high school who had run away with another man after baby Jason was born.

When they came to the bridge across Fir Creek, Charles stopped and pointed to the area north of the creek, on the left side of the road. "This would be the place from where one could reach the hidden valley, yet I doubt one could drive up there. I have to check out the place later. But look, there are quite a few tire marks, as if cars have turned around here recently."

Reaching the gate to his grandfather's ranch, he stopped, "It will take just a few minutes, Kim. If you don't mind, could you wait out here at the gate that we don't miss Julie should she come by?"

Kim agreed, certainly, this only made sense. She offered to open the gate, but this was not necessary, he had an electronic gate opener.

As Kim got out of the Land Rover, she saw indeed that the big gate was opening by itself. She watched as the Land Rover drove down the road, disappearing behind a small hill. The property looked well-kept and rather impressive. The huge double gate, as well as the fence on both sides, were painted white, all in top condition. In contrast to the main road, which was a gravel and dirt road, the long driveway was smoothly paved. Kim counted eight sheep feeding in the meadows on either side of the road. A few clumps of fir trees and oaks were dispersed more or less evenly on at least ten acres of fenced-in meadows. Kim caught herself wondering what kind of house was tucked away behind the hill? A new modern country house with all conveniences–or the old family homestead, lovingly maintained and restored through many decades?

The sun felt good, if she wasn't worried about Julie, she would have thoroughly enjoyed herself now, watching the pastoral scene in front of her and basking in the sunshine. The last five days in Seattle had been dismal. It had been rainy and cool all the time.

The sound of the Land Rover interrupted her thoughts–Charles was coming back. While they were slowly driving toward Madrone Flat, Charles finished the sad story about his stepbrother, which explained, perhaps, why Jason 's life had gone wrong.

CHAPTER 11

Julie's fainting spell had lasted only for a few minutes. When she came to, she was still hurting, but it seemed to be more tolerable now. She realized that at least her fall had ended in a spot where there was no danger of further slipping down. It was a level area of about three by eight feet, nicely padded with a thick layer of conifer needles and leaves except for a small rock outcropping on which she had partially landed with her left side. Eventually, she noted with relief that she didn't really hurt everywhere and that the pain was concentrated in her left arm and left leg.

She took stock of her body parts that still functioned. Without any pain, she could wiggle all her toes, her feet, the fingers of her right hand and could move her right arm and her legs. The worst pain was in her left shoulder, and specially her arm, which was still pinned under her upper body. Carefully, she rolled slightly over to the right to free her arm and then slowly pulled it up in an angle to her body. She was relieved when she found out that she could move her left hand and fingers, so whatever had happened was not too extreme. There was a bloody stain on her left jean leg that was spreading and she noticed a small twig, about 3" long, protruding from the center. The pain in her leg was bad, but compared with the pain in her arm, it was minor.

Now, the memory of the ugly quarrel between Andy and his partner brought back her fear. Although it seemed an eternity since she had left Andy's car, Julie noted–looking at her watch–that she had been unconscious not more than ten minutes. Any moment now, Andy would be back at his car and find her missing. The thought of these two men coming down the slope, searching for her and discovering her in this vulnerable state was almost unbearable. All she could do was to stay as quiet as possible and hope that they wouldn't find her. Fortunately, she was wearing a dark green T-shirt, which would make it more difficult for them to see her.

Suddenly, she heard voices–or a voice? It was rather faint. Apparently, she had come down the slope quite a distance. It sounded as if someone was calling her name–Andy? Julie remained still, she hardly dared to breathe. The shouts were repeated a few times and then ceased, no sign that he was coming down for her.

Julie relaxed for a few minutes but tensed up again when she heard a car approaching. Now, it became more dangerous. Most likely, the other man was there too. The faint sound of a car door being slammed made her cringe. Voices could be heard and another quarrel seemed to erupt. Julie clenched her teeth, she expected any minute to hear shouting nearby, the breaking of twigs and branches, rocks being dislodged, sliding down the hill and heavy footsteps coming closer.

To her amazement, nothing happened. Instead, car doors were slammed again and a car started up, apparently turned around and then careened off in the direction of Madrone Flat, and soon could no longer be heard. Julie couldn't believe it. Although she was lying here at the bottom of a steep slope, with a piece of wood embedded in her leg and possibly, a broken arm, she felt extremely lucky. She shifted her body around to be a little more comfortable and lay there absolutely still and listened, but there was no indication that someone was up there. The sound of the creek, somewhere to her left, was ever-present as its waters rushed down the canyon. Hearing the water made her thirsty, knowing only too well though that there was no way she could get there. Besides, if she was able to move at all, she should try to move to the right. The area around the creek was especially steep. She heard some bird songs, some chirping and twittering, and from the creek came the occasional croaking of frogs.

Kim had probably arrived on the train by now, and she and Thomas would soon be searching for her all over. Any chance that they would consider looking for her down here? Suddenly, she wondered why Charles had come to the ranch. Did he have another message to deliver? Perhaps that Kim would not come? That would be terrible for Thomas. It was bad enough that she was missing, Kim's presence would at least give him some support. Thinking of Charles, Julie was wondering now if she had missed the sound of his car driving by, back to his ranch. Or was he still down at the river? It was obvious now that Charles had nothing to do with the marijuana garden. But Thomas didn't know that yet. How would he react to Charles? Questions over questions–they made her dizzy. She had to concentrate on her immediate problems now.

As the area around her stayed silent without any sign that the two men were back, little by little, she felt safer, and little by little, she shifted her body around until she reached a sitting position that felt somewhat comfortable. She brought her left leg up to her body so she could reach the injured spot. It was difficult, because she needed her right hand so support her left arm. Carefully she touched the stick and winced. It was very painful, the piece of wood was well embedded in her leg, but the bleeding had apparently stopped, the bloody stain was not getting any larger. What she needed was a pair of scissors to cut the pant leg open, otherwise–if she would be able to move at all–the heavy denim would rub against the stick and make the injury more painful. There was a small pair of scissors in her handbag, and also a long scarf that would do as a temporary sling for her arm. She now remembered that she had grabbed her bag when she pushed out of the car. Most likely, she had lost it in her flight down the hill. Julie sighed–retrieving the bag was an impossible task.

Taking stock of her surroundings and turning around with great efforts to examine the slope behind her, something glittering way above caught her attention. Her hand bag! Julie could see the metal clasp through the branches of a small tree about fifteen feet above her. She had to try to retrieve it! Just move up bit by bit, slowly, carefully! And she managed to move, pushing hard with her right leg, inch by inch. It was very painful, but after about twenty moves she had come at least three feet closer to her bag. She rested for a while, still listening for any suspicious sounds, and moved again, inch by inch.

After three exhausting and painful moving operations, she was close enough to reach for the straps of her hand bag with a long stick–only she needed her right hand to support her left arm. She managed to wrap the bottom of her T-shirt around her left hand to support her arm and finally dared to reach for her bag and to pull it down. She felt like a survivor of a shipwreck on a small island, discovering a crate with food. Using the scarf as a sling, she could now use her right hand to find some of the goodies in her bag: two packages of Kleenex, a vial with about ten aspirins, a small chocolate bar, about five or six fruit-lifesavers and an open package of Swiss Herb Candies with ten pieces left. Not bad, the scissors were there too, it certainly had been worth the effort. She took two aspirins and swallowed them down with the help of a lifesaver.

Gingerly, she started to attack the heavy fabric. The scissors were almost too delicate to make a small hole to begin the process. It took forever until she had finally cut all the fabric free and it didn't look good. The bleeding had stopped, but there was no way she could pull out the stick. The whole area was swollen and sensitive, she had to leave it alone and try to get help as soon as possible. She had to continue moving, further up and to her right, where the slope appeared to become less steep and where she would be closer to the turnoff to the ranch. It would be a long struggle, yet, it was her only chance to survive. They would look for her everywhere but down here, she had to reach the road. Although, this could be dangerous if the two men came back, still looking for her. And what would happen if Thomas and Kim were searching for her down here and ran into Andy and the man with the gun? She refused to dwell on this chance encounter and rather focused on her survival. It was probably wise to stay in the shelter of the forest until it became dark. Then she could dare to cross the road and to make it up the hill.

Suddenly someone was calling her name. Julie froze. There it was again, it was Andy's voice. He repeated her name at least four times and Julie was afraid that any minute now she would hear the sounds of him coming down the slope. But nothing happened. A few minutes later, a car started up and drove off towards Madrone Flat, and then it was quiet again.

It almost seemed hopeless. She thought of Thomas and she knew now that she had fallen in love with him, and she was sure that he felt the same for her. When she had forgotten herself at the train yesterday and hugged him so spontaneously, and later, when he held her after she had received the sad news about Emily and Bret, she had noticed that he only reluctantly took his arms away from her. It was tempting to just lie here and think of him and then fall asleep.

But at the moment, there was no place for Thomas in her life. Thomas was the future. Her present life had no long-term future. Her present life and her present world was the spot where she was sitting now and the spot where she would be sitting in perhaps thirty minutes. It was this little piece of forest with its trees, shrubs and flowers and its creatures. With its moist, faintly moldy and earthen smell in the shady areas and its warm, aromatic smell of pine needles, mixed with the fragrance of blossoms, in the sunny areas. This was her small world now and she was part of it, enjoying its simple delights in spite of her pain, watching a bird or a lizard, or hearing the humming of the insects. This small world would nurture her spirit and would eventually make it possible for her to reach the top of the slope.

And so Julie continued, moving slowly and tediously–pushing, shoving, resting. Rewarding herself with a small piece of chocolate or candy, whenever she had accomplished about fifty tiny moves. Her arm was not hurting quite as badly any longer, the aspirin had helped and the pain in her leg was more tolerable. Whenever she was in a stable situation during the rest periods, she dozed off a for a while.

Eventually, the effect of the aspirin wore off, and the pain returned. She had just swallowed two aspirins again, when she heard a car coming from the south, driving very slowly. Was this perhaps Charles, coming back from the ranch? The car was driving by without stopping. Julie relaxed, this didn't sound like the two guys, they would have stopped and looked for her. Who else could it be? Someone coming with Charles searching for her? From the sound of the car, she could tell that she was getting closer to the road, although there was no way to see the road yet, the trees and the underbrush were still pretty dense here.

The next stretch of slope was not as steep but more open and she picked out a group of smallish ceanothus and manzanita bushes as her destination. Now she had to make sure to stay in places that offered good protection against being seen from the road as she came closer. On the other hand, moving on the gentler slope, she needed less energy to keep herself from sliding down. During her rest periods she soon felt better again, the aspirins had worked fast. Still, every little unplanned move of the leg or arm made her wince. Fortunately, the temperature was pleasant. Most of the slope was shady and on the cool side, and she enjoyed the short intervals in warm, sunny spots. She distracted herself from negative thoughts by observing the world around her, a chipmunk running down a tree trunk, a butterfly feeding on a flower or a spider weaving its web, and even a rabbit coming close, looking at Julie for a few minutes and then hopping off. She watched the animal with envy–if she could only jump like that! She identified plants around her, and was delighted when she discovered Indian Pinks flowering in a sunny spot. There were also some late Iris, a few Brodiaeas and Clarkias.

The next move brought her to a fairly level area where a clump of small fir trees provided perfect protection. Tired and exhausted, she fell asleep.

Suddenly, she was wide awake. She thought she had heard a car and listened intently trying to determine where it was coming from or going to. But now, there was absolute silence except for the familiar sounds from the forest around her. Had the car stopped somewhere along the road? Julie was reluctant to move on and get into the more open areas. This was the perfect hiding place and having heard the car, the dreaded image of the two men searching for her came back. It was safer to stay here for a while until she was sure that nobody was around. After a few minutes, she dozed off again.

Eventually, the pain in her arm woke her up. Should she take another aspirin? The pain-free intervals were getting shorter, she realized. Just then, she heard the sound of a car again, further down the road, it started up and was driving away towards Madrone Flat. Were the two men still around? And had they been looking for her again and finally given up now? She should stay here, play it safe, at least for a while. If she got as much rest as possible, perhaps she could wait with another aspirin a little longer. She lay down again and tried to relax.

CHAPTER 12

When Kim and Charles reached Madrone Flat, they didn't see any sign of Julie or Thomas. Charles parked in front of the General Store. Kim had expected a sleepy little village, but today, the area near the store was crowded with people, standing around in groups, talking. She noticed a sheriff's car parked near the fire station and two deputies talking to some men. Apparently, there had been an accident. And then Kim saw it and her stomach lurched–a red Jeep with a badly damaged front, attached to a tow-truck. She prayed that there was no connection between this red Jeep and Julie's disappearance. Charles had seen it too and she could tell by the grim expression on his face that he had the same thought.

Charles suggested, "Why don't you check with Rosy, the store proprietor, Kim? If Thomas or Julie are here, she would know. I'll try to talk to the sheriff and find out about the accident. I suppose you know her, don't you?"Kim nodded and walked over to the store. Rosy was busy with a customer, and neither Julie nor Thomas were there. When Rosy was available, she came right over to Kim and gave her a big hug. She couldn't believe the bad news and was very distressed, but assured Kim that she and her husband would help in the search if Julie were not found soon.

Rosy knew all about the accident. The red Jeep had plunged into the river and the driver had been killed. His passenger, a young man, had survived without being injured. Someone had taken him home a little while ago, he had been sneezing and coughing, probably coming down with a cold. Rosy didn't know the man who had been rescued and she hadn't seen the dead man. Both names were unfamiliar to her. There seemed to be no connection with Julie. But where was she? Kim left the store to look for Charles, who just came back from the fire-station, and then Thomas arrived, alone. He was as disheartened as they were that neither of them had found Julie. Seeing the red Jeep behind the tow-truck had also given him a shock and he was relieved to hear from both Kim and Charles that for sure only two men had been involved in the accident.

The two deputies Charles had talked to had been on their way to Trinity County and happened to come through Madrone Flat soon after the accident happened. The higher ranking officer–an African-American man in his early forties–was leaving alone now for Trinity County. His partner had to wait in Madrone Flat for a car from the mortuary to pick up the body. Charles' information concerning the accident was the same as Kim's, there really seemed to be no connection to Julie's disappearance. He suggested that they all should drive back to the ranch and do a more thorough search there. But Thomas disagreed. Considering that the vehicle involved in the accident was a red Jeep, the kind of car Julie had seen this morning near the dope plantation, they should at least try to find out who the guy was who had survived the accident. There could be a connection after all.

"I am very concerned about Julie's disappearance and feel that the situation is serious enough to mention it to the deputy–in connection with this accident. Let's go over and talk to him," Thomas urged the other two.

After introductions, deputy Earl Booth listened politely to Charles' narrative of Julie's disappearance.

"I am sorry to hear about this and hope that the young woman will be found soon," he said. Looking at his clipboard for help, he read off some of the more detailed information concerning the accident. "The dead man's name is Ned Gibson, according to his ID. Does not show a local address. 29 years old, born in Los Angeles. Would you mind taking a look at him?"

Charles, being the only one who might know the man, looked uncomfortable, but agreed to do so. The two disappeared through the station's open door and came back a few minutes later, Charles looking a bit paler than before.

"I do not know him," he explained to the deputy and Kim and Thomas, "but I am pretty sure I have seen him once or twice in his Jeep on the Fir Creek road. I have no idea though where he lived."

"The man who survived gave a statement to the Fire Chief," the deputy continued. "His name is Andrew Jonas and he lives here. I don't have his address, but Ben Wilson, one of the men who helped to get the car out of the river, took him home. I am waiting for Ben to come back–he had to change into dry clothes–and take me over to Jonas' place, I have to get a few more details from him. Jonas told the Chief that he hardly knew the driver of the Jeep. He had met him a few months ago when Gibson's car got stuck in the mud on Fir Creek Road. He helped him to get it out. Later, he met him once in Garberville. Today was the third time he had seen him, he ran into him at the Fir Creek bridge. They talked for a while and as Jonas was leaning against the railing of the bridge he was playing with his car keys and by accident dropped them into the rushing creek. Since he wasn't sure were he had put his spare key, and having an appointment in Garberville this afternoon, he accepted a ride from Gibson. But already one mile down the road he had been sorry he did–the guy was driving like a mad man and Jonas was not surprised they ended up in the river. According to Jonas, Gibson was either drunk or on drugs."

"When did the accident happen?" Thomas asked.

Booth looked at his clipboard and his wristwatch, "About an hour and forty minutes ago."

"How long does it take to drive from the bridge to the village, Charles?" Thomas asked.

"Ten minutes at the most, which would make it about an hour and fifty minutes ago when they met at the bridge where the guy lost his keys." Charles replied.

"What time did you arrive at the ranch, Charles?" Thomas asked, looking worried.

"I am afraid I see what you are getting at, Thomas," Charles said, looking at his watch. "I could almost have run into them. When you arrived at the Sutten station, I had been sitting there for about half an hour. I guess I drove down to the ranch about two hours ago, and that's when Andy came up the road. That means that he was near the bridge roughly at the same time as Jonas and Gibson… I don't like this coincidence, Thomas, "Charles said.

"And one guy is Andy and the other one Andrew, they could be the same person, right?" Kim added with fear in her voice. "What is the description of your Andrew?" she asked the deputy.

"Let me check–here it is. About twenty five years, blond hair, green eyes, slender… that's all I have," Booth said.

"That would fit the Andy I know–from what I remember," Charles responded. "We should really talk to him."

"There is Ben now," Booth said, pointing towards a tall, skinny fellow who had just parked his pickup truck next to the fire station. "I'll go with him and you three follow me."

Kim, Thomas and Charles hurried back to Charles' car. What they had just heard from the deputy troubled them deeply. It appeared as if Andrew and Andy were identical. Driving down to Julie's ranch, Charles had met Andy, coming up the road–and then Julie was missing. Was there a link?

At the turnoff to the Fir Creek road, Ben Wilson's car turned right, continued for another mile and then stopped. Earl Booth got out and came over to Charles.

"This is the place where Ben let him out. He lives way up there," he pointed to the long narrow driveway leading up the hill. "I guess you guys understand that I cannot take you along for now. I'll do my best questioning him and trying to find out if he is involved in the disappearance of your friend. Please wait here, if I need you, I might send Ben down. See you in a little while." He got back into the car and Ben drove up the hill.

"Is this Andy's place, Charles?" Kim asked.

But Charles didn't know. He had only seen Andy a few times at the Carters or passed him on the road, but never saw him turning in or out of a driveway.

It was getting too hot in the car. They sat down under a big Oak tree, which provided plenty of shade.This was frustrating, sitting here, doing nothing, while perhaps somewhere not too far away Julie might need their help urgently. To their surprise, Ben and the deputy came back after a few minutes.

The car stopped and Ben jumped out first, he was furious and shouted, "He is gone! This double-crossing jerk–he fooled me completely! I wish I hadn't listened and taken him up to the house. Right away, I would have realized that he doesn't live there."

Looking at Kim, Thomas and Charles, he saw the questions in their eyes. He tried to calm down as he told them what had happened.

"When we arrived here, Jonas and me, he asked me to let him out at the bottom of his driveway. He warned me that there was not much space to turn around up there–which I actually knew, because I had been to the house before. I know the owner vaguely, she once had a small fire in one of the outbuildings. She lives in Santa Rosa, and Jonas told me that he was caretaking the place. He said he could easily walk up the hill, it would be good to get some exercise. He was stiff from the cold water and sitting around after the accident. So I let him out and drove back to town. I am really very sorry about this, I can't believe that I was so stupid!"

Booth confirmed that indeed Jonas was missing. The house was still boarded up from the winter. There were no tire marks on the driveway or in the vicinity of the house, indicating that no car had been up there for some time. Charles, Thomas and Kim were very worried about this new development. If this Andrew had deceived Ben and had now vanished, it most likely meant that he had something to hide. And if he was in any way connected with Julie's disappearance, it was frightening.

"Where is the Fir Creek bridge?" Booth asked, and when told that it was just down the road, suggested, "let's all drive down there and look around. If we are lucky, we might run into him or see his car. After all, he didn't have a car, he had to walk, so he cannot have made it too far."

"I am afraid this will be a waste of your time driving to the bridge," Charles interrupted, "Kim and I drove by there just a little while ago, and we didn't see any cars on the road or by the bridge. Kim, Thomas and I should go back to the ranch as soon as possible and thoroughly search that area for Julie. She might have fallen and injured herself and time could be of the essence."

"I very much agree with Charles," Thomas said and was supported by Kim. "And I hope you two will find this Jonas guy soon," Thomas said, addressing Earl and Ben. "I am sure that there is some connection between him and Julie. If you run into anything important, you can reach us at the Sutten ranch, or leave a message with the Kendars. If we find Julie, we will also let you know."

"I guess you are right," Earl said, "Ben and I will stick around here for a while, questioning the residents in this area. Someone must have seen him and must know where he lives. This shouldn't be too difficult to find out. As soon as we discover Jonas, we let you know. But don't spend too much time looking for your friend without expert help. If you don't find her soon, come back to town and get more people to search for her, will you? Good luck, I hope you will find her!"

On the way back to the ranch, Charles stopped for a few minutes at his grandfather's ranch to let his wife know what was going on. At the Sutten ranch, they again combed the house and the surrounding areas, searching for Julie everywhere, calling her name over and over again. Convinced that she was not in the immediate vicinity of the house, they sat down for a few minutes to consider their next move. Thomas recapitulated the facts they knew and wrote them down, timing them as closely as they could.

"Next, we could go down to the river again, but perhaps we have to look for Julie in a very different place? We know that she wanted to avoid Charles. Perhaps she did get a ride with Andy when she saw Charles' car coming down the hill? If Julie tried to avoid you, she might have squatted down on the floor of Andy's car until you had passed, as we had already considered earlier. Andy could have arrived at the bridge about ten to twenty minutes later, right? That gets us back to that damn accident. There are too many coincidences–Andy and Andrew, the red Jeep, and the timing. Fortunately, there is not the slightest doubt that these two guys were alone in the Jeep at the time of the accident. But if she had caught a ride with Andy-Andrew, were is she now?" Thomas asked desperately.

"Perhaps this other guy in the Jeep did indeed meet them at the bridge as Andrew told the Fire Chief, only he didn't mention that Julie was there too, because… I hate to even think of what might have happened to her," Kim started to cry.

"Let's drive over to the bridge and look around there. If she did go with Andy, she might have gotten away from him after all, suspecting his possible connection to Gibson. There is certainly something fishy about Andrew-Andy, otherwise he would not have disappeared," Charles concluded as he got up, heading for the car.

All three carefully monitored the area adjacent to the road again as they drove up the hill and down to the bridge. They parked the car on the north side of the bridge and combed the area. Charles took over the northern portion of the road, Thomas the immediate vicinity of the bridge and Kim walked south. She was scanning the western slope above the road, checking for anything that looked suspicious, when she heard Thomas calling her. She rushed back to the bridge.

"I am sorry, I guess I should not have interrupted your search," Thomas said as he was pointing at the western end of the turnout. "I didn't find Julie, but look!" He walked towards a thicket of half-dead bushes and a number of small trees, bent down, and pulled out a small fir tree in a flower pot. "There are at least twenty of those here, the pots camouflaged by the dead brush. When you look beyond you can see some car tracks."

"So this must be the trail to the hidden valley where you discovered the crops this morning?" Charles asked Thomas. "What shall I do? If this gets raided, my grandfather might face a lot of problems. Should I report it?"

"I don't think that anyone would hold a man in a wheelchair responsible. Don't rush things. There might be others involved, too, besides the two guys. And after all, we don't even know if they were the growers. We only assume they were because of the color and make of their car. It might be wise not to disturb it for the time being, just keep an eye on it," Thomas advised. "But let's get back to our immediate job."

"It has been over an hour since we left Ben and Earl. I will just drive over to our house and call Madrone Flat to find out if they made any progress in locating Andrew, or Andy, for that matter. I'll be back very soon." With these words Charles got into the Rover and left. Kim and Thomas went back to continue their search for Julie.

CHAPTER 13

Voices woke her up–or had it been a dream, did she imagine things? No, there it was again, a woman's voice. It sounded as if someone was calling her name, it sounded like Kim? Julie was getting all excited and alert, sitting up and listening. And–oh, what a miracle–now she heard it clearly, it was Kim, calling her name. Julie was so on edge, for a few seconds she was unable to utter a sound.

Finally, she shouted as loud as she could, "I am down here, Kim, down here! Please come and help me to get up to the road!"

This time Kim's answer was much closer, "Tell me, where you are, Julie."

And Julie responded. This went on for a few minutes, back and forth and then she heard Kim's voice right above her, but still could not see her, "I am coming, Julie, hang in there."

And sure enough, a few minutes later she heard some twigs snapping, some scraping on the ground and a few stones rolling down the slope. Julie pushed the branches of the firs apart and called out to tell Kim where she was, and the next thing she knew her friend was kneeling in front of her.

"Poor Julie! I am so glad we finally found you. Did you break your arm?" and seeing the leg injury, she worried, "and what about your leg? This must hurt a lot?"

Gently, Kim embraced Julie in a compassionate hug, kissing her scraped and dirty cheek. Julie quickly told her what happened.

"How terrible! You were really lucky to get away, it could have been much worse. We have been searching for you since I arrived. But, I have to leave you here for a few minutes to get Thomas. It will be safer, if both of us get you up to the road. He probably could even carry you."

"Where is Thomas?" Julie asked.

"He is searching the area around the bridge for you, I was doing the southern part of the road. Oh, Julie, I really like your Thomas, he…"

"He is not my Thomas, Kim," Julie interrupted her and blushed, "I just met him last week in Willits."

"Well, perhaps he is not your Thomas yet, Julie. But this guy is very much in love with you, I can tell you. He was absolutely devastated when we found out that you were missing. Well, never mind, I better go and get him, you need medical care as soon as possible." She gave Julie another gentle hug and kiss and was gone.

Julie felt like in a daze, now she could relax, the ordeal was over. In her mind, she saw Kim running down the road to the bridge and telling Thomas, and then both of them rushing back to her. A few minutes later Thomas came down the slope. He was smiling with relief when he gave her a gentle hug but Julie saw the traces of worry in his face.

"You have no idea, how happy I am that we found you. We all were deeply concerned, especially after we heard about the accident."

"What accident?" Julie asked.

Thomas gave her a short run-down what had happened at the bridge in Madrone Flat with Gibson and Andy.

Julie was stunned, "I still cannot apprehend that Andy worked with that guy."

"Let's talk about the details later, Julie. We should now concentrate on getting help for you. I could carry you up the slope, but I believe it would be safer and more comfortable for you if we use a stretcher to get you up to the road," Thomas concluded. They heard a car coming on the road.

"That's Charles in his red Jeep, which is actually an old Land Rover," Thomas grinned, "I realize you don't know much about cars, Julie. Anyway, Charles has been extremely helpful, he has been with us, searching for you for hours. He was down at the station waiting for Kim when I came back from the village. He wanted to help with the baggage. His wife had arrived last night and so he could afford spending all that time looking for you, because she is taking care of his grandfather. We also found out that it is his half-brother who was in jail, apparently they look very much alike.

Kim went back to the bridge to get Charles, they are both up on the road now. I will leave now and talk to Charles, he should drive to Madrone Flat and get a stretcher. I'll be back soon, don't worry."

A minute later he was gone and then she heard the car take off. Kim came down with a large paper cup with water and Julie emptied it in one big gulp.

"Wow, you really were thirsty!" Kim exclaimed, sitting down next to Julie. "Thomas and Charles have left to get a stretcher. Actually, Charles will get the stretcher and Thomas is fetching Charles' grandfather's old Cadillac so we can take you to the hospital in style."

Kim then wanted to know more details. "But no, why don't you wait until Thomas is back, so you don't have to tell it twice. I am happy now to have you back, safe if not quite sound, and will wait patiently for your story."

She told her in detail about the accident at the river and of course, at this point Julie added her part of the story after all. Kim was amazed that in spite of her painful injuries, Julie had managed to crawl up the slope to where she was sitting now.

"You are courageous, Julie. This was very hard work, but it paid off. I wonder, if we could have found you if you were still down there, almost at the bottom of the slope. You might not have heard me calling or I might not have heard you. Oh, Julie, I am so glad we have you back." Tears came to her eyes as she embraced her friend again.

When Thomas came back with the Cadillac, he slipped right down to Julie. He brought along a bottle of cold apple juice, which tasted better than any she ever drank before. A few minutes later, Charles and Ben Wilson arrived in the Rover, unloaded the stretcher and carefully lowered it down to where Julie, Kim and Thomas were waiting. It didn't take long to get Julie up to the road.

But when Thomas opened the door of the Cadillac for Julie to get in, Ben Wilson objected. "If you plan to take Julie to Garberville in the Caddie, forget it, Thomas. You will never make it. There were two big washouts on the road, and although they are fixed, you cannot get through unless you have a good four-wheel drive."

For a moment, despair showed on Thomas' face, but then he insisted, "We cannot take Julie in the Rover, Ben. She is in a lot of pain. Would there be anyone who could perhaps loan us a more comfortable four-wheel drive?"

Ben scratched his head, "I wish I could help you. Most of the folks around here have rather rugged pickup trucks. They don't go for the more fancy four-wheelers. Perhaps we could put some extra padding in the Rover and you would drive real slow?"

Kim had listened to their exchange and her impatience showed in her face, "Listen, you guys, Julie is in pain and needs help as soon as possible. Why don't you put her in the Cadillac for now and take her into town. When we get there, we'll find out if there is another solution. If not, I am afraid we have to follow Ben's advice, making the Rover as soft as possible."

The transfer to the Cadillac was easy. After Thomas had helped Julie to get up from the stretcher, she got into the car all by herself. She felt extremely embarrassed when she saw Charles, and apologized that she had been so totally wrong about him. He just smiled and told her not to worry, it had not been her fault.

Charles and Ben went ahead, and Thomas, Kim and Julie followed at a slower pace. By the time they drove into Madrone Flat, Charles and Ben had already made a number of inquiries about getting another car, but so far, without results. Thomas and Ben helped Julie to walk to the fire station. Ben had called in a paramedic–he was one of the firefighters–and he started to take care of Julie's injuries immediately. He was sure that her arm was fractured. After he had put her arm in a padded sling which kept it immobilized and well protected, Julie felt much better. Then he took a look at her leg and before Julie knew it, he had pulled out the stick and then proceeded to apply a protective bandage.

"This should get you to the hospital. They probably will put in some stitches but for now you are all right." He also gave her some stronger pain pills.

In the meantime, Kim had gone to Rosy to get a few items to clean up Julie, and they both came back together to the fire station. While Kim was washing Julie's face and hands and combing her hair, the men were still trying to get hold of a better car.

Ben muttered to Thomas, "The Carter's new van would have been perfect, it's high enough off the ground, but...poor kid, she really had her share of tragedies."

"What about taking the evening train to Eureka?" Rosy suggested. The looks she received from the others were not encouraging. But Rosy kept going, "The train comes by here in forty-five minutes and you will be in Eureka about half past eight o'clock. Julie would be very comfortable on the train."

The fire chief had joined them, he had heard Rosy's suggestion. He added, "Normally the trip to Garberville takes about one hour and fifteen minutes, but it might take you twice as long because of those bad spots and if you drive especially slow. So you really don't lose much time using the train. I would go for it."

And that's what they did. They all got a bit to eat at Rosy's and soon after the train to Eureka pulled in.

Julie sighed with relief when at last she was able to relax in her seat on the train. Kim tucked her in with a few pillows and blankets which she had borrowed from Rosy.

Now they finally had the time to fill each other in on what had happened during the last few hours. Julie's first question was if they had heard anything from Emily and Bret. Thomas told her that Rosy had just given him a message from his friend Dean in Medford whom he had called this morning. Dean had found out that on the day when the call about the accident at the river came through, there was no female ICU patient in the hospital. So this had been a lie and most likely the accident was also faked, a red herring. Thomas also mentioned his phone calls to Bret's brother–or rather his wife–and that he planned to call back later this evening.

They all were quiet for a while. Julie wiped the tears from her eyes–this news was devastating. Later, they filled in details about Julie's narrow escape, the accident at the bridge and how the various events were most likely connected.

"I assume that these two guys panicked after you disappeared, Julie," Thomas said and explained to her how they had finally found her. "From what you said, you might have had a lead of ten minutes or so over them. When they came back and saw the steep slope and the dense vegetation, they knew they didn't have much of a chance of finding you, so they gave up and drove off too fast.

When we searched for you near the bridge, Kim noticed a spot where the brush along the road showed signs of recent disturbance, freshly broken branches, torn-off leaves on the ground. That's where she started to call your name."

Julie reached out and touched Kim's hand. Both women smiled at each other.

"By the way, Charles told me that the deputy has not been able to locate the place where Andy lived. They talked to a number of people, but nobody really knows him. Even Rosy has seen him only a few times. She had no idea that he had worked for the Carters. He must have kept a low profile intentionally. You don't know either where he lived, or do you, Julie?" Thomas asked.

Julie had no idea. She would never have suspected that Andy was involved, he seemed to be such a nice, friendly young man.

"Charles was really sorry that you had that extra worry about him, Julie–in addition to your worries about Emily and Bret," Kim said. "While Charles and I drove to Madrone Flat, he told me the sad story about his brother Jason. Charles is four years younger than his brother Jason. His father had fallen in love with a girl during his last year of high school. She became pregnant and his parents insisted that he marry her after he had graduated. They paid for her stay in an expensive home for unwed mothers where the child–Jason–was born. Two months later, shortly before the wedding, she ran away with the baby, supposedly with the gardener at the home. Charles' father started college, met eventually another young woman, married, and a few years later, Charles was born.

"When Jason was eighteen, he showed up at his father's house. His mother had died of cancer. The man she had run away with and later married, had never liked the boy and was glad when he left.

"For a while, Jason worked for his father, who was a lawyer, as an office boy. But when he was caught tricking one of his father's wealthy women clients out of money, his employment ended abruptly. His father generously offered to pay for college. Jason chose to study agriculture, managed to stay in school and eventually, graduated. After failing in several jobs, he persuaded his grandfather to let him manage his ranch here in Madrone Flat. Apparently, he played the gentleman farmer, didn't work, started drinking, until his grandfather threw him out. Finally, he ended up in jail."

"Wow, what a distressing tale, no wonder the grandfather had a stroke," Julie commented.

"But there might be a more positive ending," Thomas said. "I found out this morning that his parole officer is very encouraged, Jason seems to be doing quite well.

Soon after, Julie fell asleep and they had to wake her up when they arrived in Eureka. Thomas had called his friend in Eureka before they left Madrone Flat and he was right there to take them to the hospital.

Julie received immediate medical attention. The X-rays showed that the arm was broken. The padded sling the paramedic in Madrone Flat had strapped her arm in met the full approval of the emergency physician. He emphasized that she should keep her arm as quiet as possible for about three weeks when she should be back for reevaluation. She received five stitches on her leg wound and could leave. Thomas' friend took Julie and Kim to a nearby motel and then drove home with Thomas.

Before Julie settled down to sleep, she called Fred Mendell in San Francisco, who was probably already waiting to hear from her. Knowing Fred, she was careful with the truth and didn't tell him all the details, except that the Carters were delayed, that Kim and Thomas were visiting with her, and that she was not alone. Fred was satisfied and wished her good night.

Kim grinned, "Your call was a masterpiece of elimination, Julie. I just hope that Emily and Bret will come home again, otherwise you will have a problem explaining to Fred what you just said."

Julie looked tired and sighed, "I know, and I don't feel good about it. But had I told Fred the whole story, I would still be talking to him in an hour, and I'm exhausted and need to sleep. At least I didn't lie. I'll call him back in a few days and hopefully have better news by then."

CHAPTER 14

At first, Julie had no idea where she was when she woke up Wednesday morning in the small motel room in Eureka. Then slowly, the previous day's jumble of events came back to her mind. In spite of what had happened to her, she felt she had been lucky, while Emily's and Bret's fate seemed to be hopeless. If they had died, it would be a great loss for her and all who knew them, and Julie grieved deeply. Of course, with the new information Thomas had received last night from his friend in Oregon, most likely there had been no accident at the Columbia River. But what had really happened to them could be as final.

Then, she thought of the highlight of the day when Kim had found her. And she remembered what Kim had said about Thomas, how much he had worried about her and that she was sure he was in love with her.

Kim was up already and sat down on the bed when she saw that Julie was awake, kissing her lightly on her cheek.

"You look good, Julie, in spite of your ordeal. I'm sure you will be up and around soon. By the way, I like Thomas better and better. It was nice of him to come with us to Eureka. I'm sure he would not have come along if he didn't care for you a lot. After you had fallen asleep on the train, we talked about many things–sharing stories about ourselves, our jobs. We also talked about you, of course. This was a topic, he didn't get tired of. As I said, he really likes you. I hope, you two will stay in touch. We could get together from time to time. San Francisco, Berkeley and Santa Rosa–not too far apart. I am sure Martin would like to meet him too."

Julie looked a little distressed, "I hate to spoil your plans, Kim, but after all, I might not work in Berkeley this year." Julie said with regret.

Kim was very surprised, "Are you kidding? I thought you had everything wrapped up with the archaeological department at UC?"

"Not exactly. The grant is not expected to come through until the end of June and I am supposed to call back in July. In the meantime, Emily had mentioned in her last letter that I probably could do substitute teaching in Madrone Flat for a teacher who will be on leave for a year. I was not too crazy about this at first, but since I came home, I find this possibility very intriguing. It would be great to spend a whole year at the ranch. But the four of us could still do things together, it will be much easier and relaxing with the train now–provided of course, that this will really turn into a relationship with Thomas," Julie added, and couldn't help blushing again.

"Well, this is disappointing. I really had been looking forward to you living in Berkeley. Somehow, I can't believe it yet, Julie. But, I better get dressed or we will miss the train. I'll take a quick shower and then help you getting ready, so relax for a few more minutes."

As she got up, there was a knock at the door. It was Thomas with three cups of steaming coffee and some rolls and oranges.

"Ill leave you alone for a few minutes, I'm going to take a shower," Kim quickly said and disappeared in the bathroom."I hope I didn't wake you up, Julie?" Thomas asked, as he placed the food on a table. "How are you feeling?" he inquired, sitting down hesitantly at the edge of her bed.

"I slept fairly well, considering that I had to sleep on my back all night. I don't have any pain now and probably can do without pain pills. But I feel bad to have pulled you into this whole mess, Thomas."

"Don't you realize that I am glad I was there when you needed help Julie? And if you don't mind, I would like to stay at the ranch for another week. As you know, I have experience in investigations and can perhaps give some assistance in finding out what happened to the Carters. I talked already with Herb about this and we called Ken in Willits and postponed our hike for a week. They both feel that I should stay with you. In fact, both offered their help should you need it. How about some coffee? That's all I could get, there was no tea."

Julie gladly accepted a cup of coffee and a sweet roll, and so did Kim when she joined them. She was wearing a T-shirt that Rosy had lent her last night. Although a bit ample in size for her, Kim was thankful to have something clean to wear.

By seven o'clock they were on the train as it started its journey south. Thomas told them that he had called Ralph last night–it was disappointing.

"Just as I had expected, there are not many places where a car can plunge into the river–often the road is either too far away or there are railroad tracks between the road and the river. It was a cruel thing to fake this accident and the question is, why?"

When they arrived in Madrone Flat, deputy sheriff Calvin Stenton was waiting for them. He wanted to talk to them, especially to Julie. It had been late last night when he came back from Trinity County. When he heard that Julie had gone to the hospital in Eureka, he decided to stay at Rosy's overnight and talk to Julie this morning.

"I also would like to see the valley where you found the dope–Charles Kendar told me about that," he added, when he saw their astonished faces. "Since I have to drive back there anyway, I could come to the ranch and talk to you there, you might be more comfortable."

Five minutes after they came home, and Julie had just settled down in a lounge chair on the deck, Calvin Stenton arrived. Kim brought out a tray with refreshments and they all sat down.

"I talked to the Fire Chief, Ben Wilson, and Charles Kendar last night who gave me a rundown on what had happened here," the deputy sheriff began. "Earlier, deputy Booth had called me after he had returned to Garberville. Fortunately, I found out that you were all right–when I came back to Madrone Flat last evening. We still have not found this Andrew Jonas. However, a call came through to the fire station last night after you had left for Eureka. A muffled voice told the man, who had picked up the phone, to look for you on the eastern slope of Fir Creek Road, south of the bridge. He hung up right after that. The call came from Redding."

"Kind of late, about six hours after the incident. Anything could have happened to Julie in the meantime," Thomas said with disgust.

Stenton nodded, "He was certainly more concerned about his own safety, trying to get away as far as possible. Redding is a big enough town to disappear in, at least for a short time. And besides, in the meantime, he probably has spray-painted his truck in a different color and is on the move again.

I had just arrived here and happened to be at the station. I called Redding and asked them to be on the alert for the guy. Unfortunately, all we know is that he drove a small, light green pickup truck. Mr. Kendar doesn't know the make. Do you happen to know more about it, Ms. Sutten?"

Julie shook her head, "I never pay attention to cars, all I remember is the color–light green, as you said."

Stenton continued, "Also, from what I have heard, his real name apparently is Andy Taylor?"

Julie confirmed the name.

"Well, let's get to something else. There is not much we can do about Andy at the moment–I would appreciate if you could tell me exactly what has happened to you yesterday–for my records, Ms.Sutten."

Julie repeated the whole story again while Stenton took notes. When she was through, he congratulated her on being able to get away and not to panic. Stenton also asked her a number of questions in connection with the disappearance of the Carters. He had been informed about the possible accident at the Columbia, but seemed to be skeptical about it.

"We had received a bulletin about the Carters being missing on Monday late afternoon, apparently after you had called the Oregon Highway Patrol, Ms. Sutten. I called them back right away, because I was shocked when I heard the report and I wanted to know more details. My son has all the Carters' books and I admire their writing and artwork. I always wanted to meet them and here I received this terrible news. Late yesterday afternoon, Oregon alerted us again. Now, they no longer believe the story about the car plunging into the river, and feel that possibly some foul play is going on. They had sent this bulletin also to other counties in this area."

"I must admit, that I didn't believe the story about the accident at the river either," Thomas said. "Actually, I contacted a friend of mine, who happens to be an officer with the Medford PD. He found out that there had been no female patient in either intensive care or being seriously ill on Saturday in the hospital where the call came from. This part of the telephone call was made up and I am sure that the rest of the story is also not true.""I was not aware of all these details," Stenton said. "But back to your encounter with this man Gibson who died in the accident. You probably were very lucky getting away from him, Ms. Sutten. We might be in for a surprise when we get the fingerprints processed that I took last night from the Jeep."

"The question now is, what happened to the Carters and where? And is there an Oregon connection at all?" Thomas asked.

"There must be a connection," Kim said. "There is no doubt that the call about the river accident was made from a Medford pay phone, right?"

"You are correct, Ms. Brittany," Stenton agreed with her. "Most likely, whoever harmed the Carters made the phone call to prevent a possible investigation somewhere else."

"But they did go on that trip, they sent the postcards," Julie said.

"Postcards can be faked. Do you know someone around here who actually saw them leave? Mr. Kendar was not here when they left, from what he told me," Stenton said.

"They left a note for Andy!" The minute Julie said this she realized that it was anything but proof. "Sorry, that was stupid of me to say, it takes a while to get used to the idea that Andy is part of the problem. I can't help it, but I liked him and still cannot believe that he was involved with this.

"Do you see any chance that Emily and Bret could still be alive considering all these negative aspects?" Julie asked Stenton anxiously.

Stenton sighed, "We don't know. I am pessimistic. Someone went to the trouble to make it look as if they drowned in the river. Why? To cover up what?"

"Mr. Carter's brother flew up to Oregon yesterday and searched for signs of the accident along the river and was going to continue today. So far he didn't find anything, he was pretty discouraged. And I am sure he will not find anything, because there was no accident," Thomas concluded.

"There is one item you mentioned, Ms. Sutten, I would like to get back to," Stenton asked Julie again, "did you really hear Gibson telling Andy to drive you back to his cabin? Where would that be?"

"Of course, I didn't understand every word, they were too far away.

But they were speaking very loud, and Andy's partner especially was doing a lot of gesturing. He was consistently pointing into the southern direction of the Fir Creek Road, as if the cabin was somewhere south of the turnoff to our ranch. When you come down the road from our ranch, instead of turning left for Madrone Flat, you can also turn right. A narrower road continues to the south. I remember my grandfather mentioning once that back there someone had an old cabin. I have never been there, though," Julie explained.

"I would like to take a look before I leave, because if Gibson lived there, we might find some clues whether he and Taylor were the only ones involved with the dope planting. Could you come along, Mr. Millon, and wait for me at the turnoff until I come back? Going there alone could be a little risky if some other people might still be at the cabin," Stenton asked Thomas, closing his notebook and getting up.

"Sure, I'll be glad to help," Thomas replied.

"Also, how far is it to the valley where they planted the dope? Could you show me that place too?"

"It's easy to get in from the bridge area. We went in from this side, which is more difficult. They even drove in, as you know."

"Before you leave, Sheriff, I have one more question. What will you do now about finding Emily and Bret? You have to do something!" Julie begged Stenton.

"Honestly, at the moment I don't know what to do. When I get back to the office I will call Oregon again. We will declare the Carters as missing. Sending bulletins out might, hopefully, get a response in case someone has seen them. That's about all we can do right now. Of course, we also will do everything to find Andy, so far we still have no clues to where the man lived. Earl checked out all the unoccupied houses in Madrone Flat yesterday but didn't come up with anything. If Taylor stayed in any of them, he left the place in very neat condition so that nobody could tell he was there. We probably have to ask the absentee owners to come out and check their houses themselves, that might give us a lead," Stenton said.

"Perhaps Andy also lived at Gibson's cabin? I assume that your deputy didn't check that one, or did he?" Kim wondered.

"That's a good idea. No, as far as I know, Earl didn't go back there. I will look for signs when I go to the cabin," Stenton said.

He and Thomas got up and walked to the end of the deck toward the front of the house. Thomas had already disappeared around the corner, when the sheriff came back, addressing Julie again.

"I hate to even bring this up, Ms. Sutten, because I have the greatest admiration for the Carters as authors and artists. But I guess I have to ask you anyway. Do you think there is a vague chance that the Carters had any connection to this dead man? After all, he was apparently managing an extremely lucrative dope garden. Any possibility they were in this together and had a falling out?"

"Absolutely not, no way!" Julie cried out sharply, being visibly angry about his suggestion, "They are some of the finest people I know and have high ethical and moral standards. Both don't smoke or drink, they live rather modestly, even though they are quite well off. And this would be another reason for not getting involved in this kind of behavior, they earn plenty of money with their books, they have more than they ever need."

"Sorry, I didn't mean to tarnish their memory, but in our line of work we have to consider everything," Stenton tried to conciliate her. Julie didn't answer. He waited a few more seconds. then turned and followed Thomas, who was waiting in old man Kendar's Cadillac. A few minutes later, Julie and Kim heard the two cars taking off.

Julie cried, "How could he be so insensitive. And at first I first liked the guy!"

She rested her arm on the table, bent her head down and sobbed. Kim sat down and hugged her, gently stroking her hair. She was also upset about the sheriff's question, but could understand that he had to think of all angles. Knowing Emily and Bret well, she knew that any connection to the pot growing, as the sheriff had suggested, was preposterous.

Kim regarded the Carters almost as Julie's parents. The news about the accident was terrible. But now it was even worse, not knowing where and how–or even if–they had died. No wonder that Julie had collapsed, after all that she had been through yesterday.

Eventually, Julie stopped crying. She lay down on the lounge chair again and after a while, fell asleep.

CHAPTER 15

When Thomas returned, Julie and Kim were sitting in the kitchen. He sensed that their mood had changed. Julie looked as if she had been crying and Kim had a sad expression on her face, both were very quiet.

"What happened to you? You both look as if a goose walked over your graves." Thomas exclaimed.

"I am very angry, Thomas. Stenton asked me if there was any possibility that the Carters had been involved in the dope plantation. He inquired if there might have been a connection between Gibson and them. Can you imagine?" Julie could hardly contain herself.

"I too, have already considered a connection," Thomas replied. But when he saw the incredulous expression on her face, he hastened to add, "Of course, I am not talking about the Carters growing dope, but rather the Carters discovering the plants. Just just as we did yesterday morning–and being surprised by Gibson, that kind of a connection."

Julie looked at him, naked fear in her eyes. "I understand what you are saying, this would not leave any hope."

Thomas put his arm around her and kindly said, "Don't give up hope, there still could be a chance that they are all right."

Kim tried to change the topic. "What did the sheriff find at the cabin, Thomas?"

"Actually, I didn't wait for him at the turnoff, I went with him to the cabin. I told Stenton that I have a license as a Private Investigator and he agreed that I could come along. Anyway, it was obvious that the cabin had been lived in until very recently, although it looked as if only one person had stayed there. There was a single bed in a corner with a filthy sleeping bag, and that was it. If Andy had stayed there, he took his stuff along.

Stenton left everything as he found it, just dusted for fingerprints to check out if this really was Gibson's place. We found some maps of Oregon and Washington, otherwise nothing that would establish a connection either to Andy or to Oregon. We did, however, find lots of fertilizer in another shed behind the cabin, all recently purchased.

The inside of the cabin was a mess–dirty dishes, lots of empty beer and whiskey bottles, ashtrays filled to the brim–and the floor was dusty and dirty. When Stenton gets back to the office, he will check out who owns the place."

"Did you go to the hidden valley, Thomas?" Julie asked.

"Yes, it is so much easier to get in from the bridge. In ten minutes, you can be up there and it is easy going because of the car tracks. I doubt that anybody else is around to water the plants, they still look fine, but the ground is dry. It didn't look as if they were watered today."

"I have thought about this case a lot since you left, Thomas," Kim said. "The report about the accident at the Columbia River was made on Saturday around 5:30 P.M., but Charles got the call from the Carters on Saturday morning, around what time, Julie?"

"Charles got here at about 10:30, this means that Emily or Bret had probably called him around 10:00."

"At that time, they were several hours east of Portland. And in the late afternoon, they had most likely passed Eugene and were getting close to Grants Pass. The call was made from Medford, which is not too far away. I reasoned that harm was done to the Carters somewhere in that general area sometime between ten in the morning and five in the afternoon. But what you said a little while ago changes my whole concept."

Thomas did not respond to Kim's argument. He seemed to be lost in thoughts. Suddenly, his face lit up, "I got it! "he said. "Something had been bugging me. I am sorry I didn't listen to what you just said, Kim, I got sidetracked with my own ideas. I knew it was important, yet I couldn't remember what it was. It is only a small detail that I noticed as strange when I first entered this house. The calendars!" he exclaimed.

Julie and Kim looked at him, at a loss what he meant.

"The calendar over there on the wall next to the refrigerator still showed April and so did the one in the living room when I came here on Monday." Abruptly, he left the kitchen and ran upstairs. It slowly dawned on Julie and Kim what this could mean. When he came back a few minutes later, he told them that the calendar in his room also hadn't been changed from April.

"I can tell from your faces that you understand the importance of this calendar business. If the Carters had not left until the end of May on the trip up north , why hadn't they turned over the April pages to May, when they still were here? Could we take a look at their apartment upstairs, Julie? They probably have some calendars there also."

Reluctantly, Julie opened the door to Emily and Bret's place when they arrived on the third floor. There was a large calendar in their study which still showed the April page and the same was the case with a pretty flower calendar in their bedroom.

"I hate to make the suggestion, Julie. But could we take a look at their engagement calendars, if there are any around?" Thomas asked, pointing at the Carter's desks.

"I don't like to admit it, Thomas, I already did something similar when I looked for the license number of their van. I felt guilty when Buttercup saw me, he had followed me up the stairs."

As she was saying this, the cat came through the open door and jumped up on an armchair, sitting there very erect with his tail neatly covering his front paws, watching them closely.

"This is eerie, it almost gives me a chill seeing him sitting there, silent and yet talking loudly," Kim said. "Poor cat!"

The engagement calendars were found in a minute and the pages during the first three months showed only a few entries in Emily's, but Bret had made notes almost daily. He had reported events that had happened concerning the weather, work that was done or had to be done in the garden, repairs in or around the house and similar items. However, there were no entries after April 4th in both books except some short notes with times that looked like appointments or upcoming events. There was no mention of a trip up north.

The three looked gloomily at the two calendars. This was fairly convincing evidence about what they had surmised after seeing the other calendars still showing the April page. But none of them had dared to say it. It looked as if the Carters had left much earlier.

"Who actually told you that they had left on a trip to Washington in late May, Julie?" Thomas asked.

"They had sent a picture postcard to Fred in San Francisco, telling him that they were on a short trip and would be back by the time I arrived. Charles then told me that they had left a note at his gate just when they were leaving in May and Andy told me roughly the same. Both of them also received postcards. They also had left a note at Andy's gate... that means Emily and Bret knew where Andy lived! Was there a gate on the road leading to the cabin, Thomas?"

"No, there was no gate at all. So, Andy most likely did not live at the cabin. If it is true what he told you, the place where he did live had a gate somewhere. I should let Stenton know about this," Thomas replied.

"Well, it doesn't help us much one way or the other. Getting back to the letter the Carters left for Andy, it contained one hundred dollars for watering the garden should it be necessary while they were gone. From these three accounts, I knew that they were on a trip, although, they had not mentioned it in the last letter I got from them in New York."

"When was this, do you remember?" Kim asked.

"Well, let me think... I am not absolutely sure... I guess it was either the end of March or early April. I might still have it, only it probably would take some time to find it. But I just remembered something else I had completely forgotten! On the train up to Willits, I met an old guy who knew my grandfather–Homer Morgan, he lives north of Madrone Flat. When he had taken the train south about a week earlier–actually, it was the Monday before I came up–a young man flagged down the train at our station. He had a commute ticket and Homer happened to hear him saying that he was a relative of the Carters. They would be back from their trip by the end of the week, but he had to leave before they came home. He rode the train to Willits."

"That's strange, who was this person? When you and I talked to Bret's sister-in-law or to Emily's sister, neither one of them mentioned that someone of the family was up here! Of course, it could have been a distant cousin or someone else? But getting back to the timing of their trip, there is something wrong. Perhaps we should drive over to Charles and talk with him about the note he had received and maybe you should also call Fred, Julie. If he still has the postcard, please ask him to send it up," Thomas concluded.

The Kendars were just finishing a late breakfast. Charles' wife was a charming woman–petite, exquisitely beautiful and a gracious hostess. Within seconds, she had brought out cups and was pouring tea for the visitors. Thomas told them about his trip to the old cabin back at the end of the road and what they had found there. He then mentioned the discrepancy about the calendar entries, the calendar pages that had not been turned over, and the notes or postcards from the Carters. Unfortunately, Charles could not help either. At the time when the Carters left the note, he was in Willits with his grandfather for almost a week of physical therapy and found the note when he came back.

"Do you remember the last time you saw them?" Thomas asked Charles.

"I have to get my calendar to help my memory. I'll be right back." He left the room and came back within minutes with a leather-bound engagement calendar.

"Let's see, January 10th, they came over for lunch. Oh yes, here I ran into them at the store. I remember, because I have a note here about the frost we had that day, this was February 15. Let's see, they invited me over for dinner on February 26–it was a lovely evening. Then Granddad and I were gone until March 10th. On March 25th, they came over for lunch and we were sitting outside. It was a beautiful, warm day, and they were telling me about the work they had already done in the garden. Incidentally, they were very pleased with Andy's work and expected him again the next day."

He kept flipping the pages, searching for entries and finally gave up, "I believe this was the last time I saw them. We were gone in April several times and I drove over to their place in early May and happened to run into Andy who was doing some weeding and watering. The Carters were not home and Andy had no idea where they were either. He had gone there to see if they needed some help. When they were not home, he decided to wait for a while and, in the meantime, do some cultivating. I left a note at their door, and a few days later, they had attached a note to my gate, saying that they were sorry we had missed each other, hope to see you soon–or something like that. And then I found the note at the end of the month that they had gone on that trip."

"If we assume that something happened to them in April, all these notes and calls would have been made by someone else. Could this be possible, Charles?" Thomas spoke out what everybody dreaded. He saw the despair and fear in their eyes, fear about discovering the grim reality.

"Do you assume that Andy faked the notes and postcards, Thomas?" Julie said and her face registered her disappointment about Andy.

Thomas just shrugged his shoulders helplessly. "All the notes were printed instead of handwritten," Charles pointed out. "But I don't know their handwriting anyway, so I cannot make a judgment about this. The phone call last Saturday–I must admit–was a little strange. When I picked up the phone, someone was coughing badly and I said hello a few times before finally a very scratchy voice said, 'It's me–Bret'. He had a terrible cold and could hardly talk and told me that Emily was even worse. At the time, I didn't think much about it, but ever since all these events have happened, I have had some doubts about that call."

Charles' wife spoke up. "Did he really say, 'It's me–Bret'? Bret wouldn't say that, would he, Charles?"

Charles laughed, "Listen to our English professor. You really have a good point there, Nomi, Bret wouldn't say that. I am absolutely sure that the person who called said 'it's me', and I am sorry to say, it didn't strike me as strange at the time, it is just about all one hears these days."

"I agree with you, Charles. Bret wouldn't have said 'it's me'. But if they never left and something happened to them here, where does Oregon come in?" Julie asked.

"There is a slight chance that identifying the dead man might shed some light on where he came from and could perhaps explain the Oregon connection. I guess we have to be patient until then," Thomas replied.

And that was the end of their conversation for now concerning the disappearance of the Carters. Kim and Charles' wife Nomi quickly found common ground and slipped into Japanese for a few minutes. And Thomas and Charles talked about Thomas' father and Charles' work. Julie had walked outside where old Mr. Kendar was sitting in his wheelchair on the porch, reading a magazine. He recognized her when she introduced herself. They talked for a while about her grandfather until he fell asleep. Julie arranged a pillow behind his head so he would be more comfortable and went back in to tell Charles and Nomi that he was sleeping.

Nomi offered them lunch, but they declined because they wanted to be home at the time the train came through, in case Bonnie, Emily's sister, should be arriving today.

Charles begged them to keep the car until Julie was back to normal. This was the least the Kendars could do for their neighbors. Besides, the Kendars had another, smaller car which they would use for most trips.

Thomas left again right after they got back to the ranch. On the drive home, he had told Julie and Kim of an idea that had occurred to him while they were discussing the case with Charles.

"If we assume that the disappearance of the Carters and the dope plantings are related, Gibson might not have worked alone–except for Andy–and could have had some help in Oregon. How did he stay in touch with them? Calling them, right? But there is no phone at the cabin, so where would he have called from? A pay phone, of course. I have a good friend at the phone company who probably could give me the numbers in Oregon that were called from the few local pay phones. I want to find out how many pay phones are in Madrone Flat and get their numbers and then call my friend. If any calls were made to Oregon from here, she will find them. Of course, if he was very cautious and called from Garberville, we are out of luck."

"There is also the chance that Andy lived in a cabin with a telephone, he might have used that?" Kim suggested.

"That would mean that Andy was completely involved–I just don't believe it," Julie said. "What do you want to do then if you find these numbers, Thomas?"

"I'm not sure yet, it depends on where these numbers are–if there are any. I might have to drive up there."

So he left for Madrone Flat and Kim went down to the train. And indeed, the train stopped and Emily's sister Bonnie, together with her seventeen year old son Nick, got off.

They left her baggage at the station to be picked up later by car and walked up the hill. Bonnie was very different from her older sister. Emily was tall and slender, Bonnie was short and a bit on the plump side. She was a woman one would never get tired of looking at. Her features were beautiful and flawless. She bore a strong resemblance to

Boticelli's Madonna faces and radiated inner beauty, goodness and happiness, which was only slightly dimmed by a shadow of sadness now. Her son Nick was tall and thin, and looked and acted very mature for his seventeen years. Bonnie's husband was in Europe for several months and their daughter Esther had just left to join him. Nick was not quite through with school, but he was an excellent student and his teachers let him off early in this emergency.

When they arrived at the house, Bonnie and Julie had a tearful reunion. They sat outside on the deck and Julie and Kim told Bonnie what had happened at the ranch in the meantime. Bonnie was shocked when she heard what Julie had gone through. She could tell from observing her–Julie was lying on the lounge, her left leg propped up, her arm in a sling–that the injuries were painful when she made a wrong move.

Thomas came back soon. After introductions, he reported what he had done in Madrone Flat. Rosy had told him that there were four pay phones in the village: at the store, the train depot, the bar and the gas station. Thomas got all four numbers and had called his friend who happened to be there. She promised to get him the information by the end of the day.

Also, he had talked to Rosy about the Carter's mail. As far as Rosy remembered, the mail had been picked up regularly until the end of May when a note was left in their box telling her that they would be gone for about two weeks.

But then Rosy had interrupted herself. She remembered the package she brought along with the rest of the mail when she came over to the ranch on Saturday to visit Julie. This hadn't been picked up although she had put a notice in their box several times.

When Thomas had asked her whether she happened to recall when this package came, she told him that it probably had arrived around the end of April.

"This is interesting," Thomas said. "If indeed someone else had faked and sent out the postcards and left the other notes, this person also could have picked up the mail, at night, when nobody was around. But this person would not dare to ask for a package during office hours, right? So it was never picked up."

They told Bonnie about the theory they had just arrived at this morning, that possibly Emily and Bret had already disappeared in early

April and that most likely they had never gone on a trip. Unfortunately, Bonnie had not been in touch with her sister since the end of March when Emily had called her up. Bonnie had written a letter in April but had not received a response. She had not worried about it, because sometimes months had passed before Emily or Bonnie herself would finally sit down to write.

"If you feel up to it, Bonnie, you could go through their mail and bank statements. That might also give us some clues," Thomas suggested.

Bonnie's face clouded up, this was something she was not eager to do. "But if something happened to them in early April, who could have picked up their mail?" Bonnie asked.

"That's a good question. To open those number locks you need the combination. There is either information on this number in the Carter's desk and the person who masterminded this all found it and used it. Or, he was able to pick the lock of the post office door that leads into the mail room. Which is unlikely, though we could ask Rosy if there is an alarm system. When you look for financial statements you might also look for the box number. They might even have a file on it," Thomas said. Bonnie nodded and wiped her eyes.

"What about Andy, maybe the Carters had trusted him so much that they gave him the combination?" Kim suggested.

"Somehow I can't believe that Andy was that much involved, Kim," Julie responded. "When he started to walk back to his car, down at the bridge, just before he turned around again to go back to Gibson, he didn't look mean. He slowly shuffled along, his head down, as if in deep thoughts, trying to figure out how he could outwit Gibson. In fact, I had the feeling, that he was giving me the opportunity to get away."

Thomas looked skeptical, "I wish you were right, but he certainly played a trick on Ben Wilson. And you didn't answer him when you heard him calling your name, did you, Julie?"

Julie looked uneasy, "I know, Thomas. No, I wouldn't have trusted him, and yet… I just can't believe that he did all these terrible things."

"But, he decided to run, didn't he? If he didn't have a guilty conscience he would have stayed around," Kim countered, and Julie had to admit that she was right.

Later, when Julie helped Kim prepare dinner in the kitchen, Bonnie came in. She had a number of envelopes and bills in her hand.

"Thomas was right, there is some indication in these statements that after April 4 Emily and Bret might not have been here any more."

She was almost crying when she said this and they could tell that she probably had been crying upstairs, while she was going through their files.

"The last ATM withdrawal was done on March 29 at a Garberville bank. There was none after that. But, there were a number of purchases with their Visa card in May for fuel, motels and restaurants. The first purchase–for fuel–was in Garberville, the others in Oregon and Washington. The statement ends on May 22."

Thomas and Nick had come in and listened to what Bonnie had to tell. She had also found a file labeled 'Post Office Box'. It held paid bills and a slip with the combination number, so whoever was responsible for all these activities had had access to the combination of the lock. "We have discovered some other evidence," Thomas said. "Nick checked out the newspapers still lying around and there are none from after March 29. We went through the recycle stuff in the basement. There are numerous empty plastic containers for cottage cheese, yogurt and so on. They all have expiration dates and the latest we found was April 10. There is no question that around April 5 something happened. Will we ever find out?"

Meanwhile, Kim and Julie had dinner ready. They had set the table in the kitchen, it was cool and windy outside. Because of all the negative findings they had made, the mood was rather cheerless at the beginning of the meal. But the food was so good and well prepared that the atmosphere improved in time. Dinner was an excellent carrot soup followed by new potatoes, slightly browned in butter, with asparagus and venison goulash. Rosy had given Thomas a jar with home-canned venison earlier today. Her husband, George, did some occasional hunting. For dessert, the berry ice-cream Julie had made yesterday was well appreciated. They tried not to talk about the Carters, yet their presence in this house was too strong. It was almost impossible not to mention their names.

Thomas was ready to drive back to Madrone Flat after dinner. Who would like to come along? Julie and Nick decided to stay. Julie was tired and Nick wanted to go for a swim, in spite of the cool evening. So the other three left after everybody had helped with the dishes. Julie went into the living room and lay down on the couch with a book. Her mind wandered and she could not really concentrate, and finally dozed off.

She woke up when Kim, Bonnie and Thomas came back. They joined Julie in the living room, just as Nick was coming back from the river. Thomas had been successful with his phone call, his hunch had paid off.

He explained what he had found, "There had been twelve calls from Madrone Flat to places in Oregon between March and now. Two calls had been made from the local bar, both on the same day, to a motel in Bend, eastern Oregon, in early March. There was one call from the gas station to Portland, to a motel, also in early March. I have the feeling that these calls have nothing to do with the case.

"The other nine calls were all made to Medford. Eight to an address on Buckthorn Lane and one to what sounds like a used car dealership in downtown. The eight calls to Buckthorn Lane were made in early March, in mid-March, on April 5th and 6th, in mid-April, in mid-May and last Friday and Saturday. The ninth call, to the car dealer ship, was also made on April 5th. And I believe it was made by the same person who had called Buckthorn Lane. The first call to Buckthorn on April 5th lasted only one minute. The other number was called immediately after the first one and the call lasted ten minutes. The Medford calls were made at random either from the train station, the store or the gas station. All were made either at night or very early in the morning, with the exception of the calls on April 5th, which were made just before ten o'clock in the morning."

Thomas had spoken slowly and his audience had been able to follow him. They were trying to digest the information.

"I also talked to the sheriff. The man who died in the accident had a long and bad record. Since he was sixteen, he was in and out of prison. Until last August, he had been in prison for robbery, assault and rape. He violated parole a week after he got out. But Stenton couldn't find any connection to Oregon, except for the gun they had found in Gibson's pocket. It had been reported stolen in Tacoma, Washington, a few years ago, at a time when Gibson had been in jail.

"Stenton also found out that the property back here with the cabin where Gibson lived, has been leased for the year from the owner since February to someone in Seattle, Washington. The owner is a Mr. Mellet, who lives in Los Angeles. Stenton tried to reach the party who had rented the place, but the number is disconnected.

"I would like to drive up to Medford and see if I can find out who the people are behind the telephone numbers. I have a strong feeling that there is a connection. Don't forget, the call about the river accident was also made from Medford. Would some of you like to come along?"

Kim looked questioningly at Julie, but before Julie could respond, Bonnie reacted, "I heard that you have worked as a PI, Thomas, is that right?" she asked, and continued when he nodded, "I want to find out what happened to Emily and Bret, when and how. If they are dead–and we all are afraid that there is only a little chance that they are still alive–I want them to be placed to rest at a decent place where we can pray for them. I would very much appreciate if you could try to find out as much as you can. Can I retain you for this task? I have great confidence in you!"

"Thank you for your trust in me, Bonnie. But I will do this anyway–for Julie's sake and for all of you. I wouldn't feel comfortable being paid for this work, and besides, I might be completely off with the Oregon connection."

"All right, I don't want to hurt your feelings, Thomas. Would you at least let me pay for your expenses? You probably have to rent a car, stay in a motel several nights, eat and so on. I know you will start with a job soon, but I am sure both of you–Julie and you–have more or less exhausted your finances during the last months of school. So please, let me at least take care of these unexpected expenses, will you?" Bonnie pleaded with Thomas and to her relief, he accepted her proposal.

She continued, "I have the feeling that either Bret's brother or his wife will come here soon and I should stay put for at least a week, otherwise I would like to come along on your trip. Julie, if you and Kim want to go with Thomas, don't worry about me, with Nick around I am not afraid to stay alone. Although I don't think you are well enough, Julie. I'm sure it would be better you stayed here," Bonnie said, affectionately patting Julie's hand.

"I would love to come along," Julie said. "But I think it would be foolish, you are right Bonnie. My arm is still hurting quite a bit. I noticed it today, just coming over from Madrone Flat and going back to the Kendars. It's better to stay here and to support the healing process as much as I can. How about taking Nick along? I am sure you will be careful and not endanger him, Thomas?" Julie looked apprehensively at Bonnie and Thomas.

Julie's suggestion came as a big surprise to Nick. But then he looked expectantly at Thomas and saw only encouragement in his eyes,"That would be cool if you would let me come along, Thomas. I would love to help." Nick looked at his mother for approval.

"I'm confident that Thomas will not do anything risky, so if you want to go, Nick, that will be fine with me," Bonnie responded, and Nick glowed–he would be working with a real detective!

"I would like to help, Thomas, if you think you could use some extra woman power?" Kim said.

"Sure, three people can accomplish more than one. It will be safe, I have no intention of getting into a shoot-out. I just want to check out these people and having you both along for possible phone calls or whatever comes up would make it much easier than doing it all alone. And besides, I would love to have you both for company. I would say we should leave right away. No, not tonight, Kim!" Thomas reassured her when he saw the worried look on her face. "Let's leave tomorrow by train for Eureka. We can then rent a car there and drive as far north as we get. This way we could get to Medford by late morning the next day. How about that?"

"Why not use Charles' car, Thomas? I am sure he wouldn't mind?" Kim asked.

"I think this is stretching Charles' generosity a bit too much, Kim. And Bonnie and Julie would be here without a car. Who knows, they might need it. Besides, this old Cadillac is really a gas-guzzler and pretty conspicuous. I would rather use a small, nondescript car for this trip. My own car would be perfect, but it is now in Santa Rosa, too far to go."

"What do you plan to do when you get up there? What is your strategy?" Julie asked.

Thomas laughed, "To tell you the truth, so far I have no strategy, we have to be flexible. It all depends on what we find in Medford. The first thing I want to do when we get to Medford is check out Buckthorn Lane, get a feeling for the neighborhood. Then we also drive by at the other address in town. Next we stop at C and O..."

He was interrupted by Kim who wanted to know who C and O was.

"It stands for California and Oregon Investigators. It's the detective agency I worked for during the last few years while finishing school. Actually, they also have an office in Seattle, I worked there for a few months. Anyway, I want to talk to them and see if by chance they have any information for us. Then, I will look up my friend Dean at the Medford Police Department. He is a sharp guy and has his eyes open and he might know a thing or two. In the meantime, we can talk about the options we have. You, Kim, might pose as an insurance adjuster and talk to some of the neighbors, if Buckthorn Lane is suited for that. It wouldn't work, for instance, in a gated neighborhood or if it is a very run-down area. So we have to see how it all turns out. By the way, do you happen to have some more formal clothes with you, Kim? Like a suit and somewhat dressier shoes? Don't worry, this will be a safe job, I will not let you do things that could be dangerous."

"You forget that I am a reporter, Thomas. I often get into situations that are not super-safe. So I don't worry about that. But I have a suggestion, instead of posing as an investigator for a mortgage company, let me act as what I really am, a reporter. I have learned a trick from a colleague who used to work for one of the big tabloids. I don't want to burden your conscience with details now, but it is easy to get people to talk and most of the time it works. The clothes are another matter, I didn't bring anything formal along. One summer dress, it wouldn't be the right thing for Oregon. Could I borrow some stuff from you, Julie? I actually could do this as well in jeans and sweater or T-shirt, but a change of clothes might come in handy and being dressed more formally helps, especially with older people."

"Sure, I have a dark blue blazer," Julie replied, "and a plaid, pleated skirt that would fit you and several pairs of more dressy low heels."

"Great, I'll try the clothes on before going to bed. By the way, you might actually get company. My husband has vague plans to come to the ranch perhaps by the end of this week. I know you won't mind if Martin shows up all of a sudden. He will come by train and he knows how to get to the house from the tracks."

Next morning, Julie went through her grandfather's map file in search of road and street maps of Oregon and Medford and found all they needed. Later, Bonnie drove Kim, Thomas and Nick to Madrone Flat. Julie went along to see them off. She was sad that she had to stay home, not only because she wanted to help, but she would also miss

Thomas. Last night, they had sat outside on the deck, alone, talking, and listening to Handel's Water Music again, just like Monday night. She was glad that he and his friends had postponed their hiking trip one week.

They stopped at the Kendar ranch to let them know that they were going to Oregon and to introduce Bonnie and Nick. In Madrone Flat, Thomas called Stenton. He told him about the calls from Madrone Flat to Medford and that he was going up to Oregon to investigate the parties in question. Stanton mention that they had tried in vain to find any clue concerning Andy. He had talked to practically all absentee landowners, but nobody had rented out a place. So far the best lead had been a cabin on the Fir Creek Road, not too far from the place where Andy had been dropped off by Ben Wilson. Stenton confirmed that it had a gate across the driveway, after Thomas mentioned it. It belonged to some people in Eureka, owners of a small saw mill. They both were away for a few days. The secretary told him that their nephew had come up from Florida in January and lived at the cabin until late April when he had finished the repairs and painting he was supposed to do. This all coincided with the information Julie had on Andy. The cabin in question had indeed been freshly painted but there was no sign that someone had lived there recently. If this was the place where Andy had stayed, he had kept it very neat and clean, the opposite from Gibson's place.

The secretary had never met the nephew, she only knew that he was in his twenties. He had gone to Redding for another job when he was through in Madrone Flat. Stenton was going to follow up with another call in a couple of days, he had the feeling that he was on the right track. He also assured Thomas that he would leave the cabin and the plants in the hidden valley untouched until Thomas came back, just in case someone else was involved who might show up after some time. Of course, they would keep it under close observation.

Thomas gave Stenton the name and phone number of his friend who worked as a detective for the Medford police department, and also of the C and O agency in Medford in case any new information should be revealed. Stenton warned him to be careful, wished him good luck and hung up.

Thirty minutes later, Kim, Thomas and Nick boarded the train, ready for action, while Bonnie and Julie tearfully waved good-bye as the train was leaving Madrone Flat.

CHAPTER 16

Kim came back from the buffet car, carrying a box tray with three tall glasses of lemonade and three chocolate chip muffins. Thomas took a long sip of lemonade. After placing the glass on the small table extending from the window, he leaned back in his seat and admired the view. He looked at the redwoods that had replaced the drought-resistant tree species from the river valley further south.

"I love the redwoods, their beauty and grandeur! As much as I was impressed by the southern part of the canyon–the barren slopes covered with colorful rocks, spectacular oaks, madrones with dark-red trunks, and the various chaparral species–I feel more at home up here. Look at the hills close to the river or the higher mountains looming beyond. They are densely forested with redwoods and Douglas-firs, promising shady groves, lush meadows with wildflowers, and cool creeks, cascading down the canyons. And above it all, the deep blue sky. What beautiful scenery!"

Thomas' enthusiasm had awakened Kim's and Nick's imagination. They looked at the forested hills with new eyes, picturing the sylvan scenes he had described so vividly. Nick had even closed his book.

"And we can enjoy all this in perfect comfort," Thomas continued. "Going by train is really the most civilized form of travel, comfortable, clean and relaxing. In addition, trains are much safer than cars. It's incomprehensible that so many politicians are reluctant to provide funding for rail. Our society pays a terrible price for the delusive privilege of driving individual cars. I don't think there is one person in this country who has not suffered the loss of a relative, close friend or some other person he or she knew fairly well, from a car accident. We all know about the tragedies in Julie's life."

Kim asked, "When you say that trains are safer than cars, Thomas, does this take into consideration that many more people travel by car than train? I, of course, know of several people–besides Julie's parents and her grandfather–who either died in a car accident or were badly injured. In comparison, I don't know anybody who was involved in a train accident, because very few people still travel by train. But after all, there are train accidents."

"When you compare the two modes of transportation, you compare the miles traveled. Rail transportation has the same high safety record as air travel. How many people did you know personally that died in an airplane crash? Also, you live in the Bay Area. How many people do you know that died on BART, the Bay Area Rapid Transit? I am sure that many of the 250,000 daily BART riders would be dead now had they instead always used their cars for commuting. We talked about this last year when I was visiting my grandparents in Germany. Rail travel in Germany is extremely popular, everybody rides the trains. There are the very fast long-distance trains called ICE, the regional trains from the inner cities to the smaller communities further away or the trolleys and subways in towns. Yet my grandparents–who have lived there since the late forties–couldn't come up with one person's name who had been injured or killed in a train-related accident as a passenger. I think this speaks for itself, doesn't it?"

"I am glad that air travel is also safe, statistically, because I fly a lot and always feel a bit uneasy, especially after a crash. I just wish it were more comfortable–like this, which compares to first class air travel," Kim said, patting the seat next to her and looking at Nick, who sat relaxed in his corner, back to his science fiction novel again.

"Except at thirty thousand feet altitude you don't get much of a view, this certainly beats it, " she pointed toward the river, where two kayaks were swiftly making it downstream.

Nick sighed and closed his book reluctantly, wondering if perhaps it was a little rude of him to bury his nose in the book and not participate in the conversation. "You are right, Kim, this is better than first class flying, which I actually did once when they had overbooked a flight and wanted to bump me off. I was furious and they checked me in after all, putting me in first class. But you know why it is also better? It is so much quieter than on a plane, don't you think so?"

Thomas thought this was an interesting statement from a seventeen-year-old–an age when most of his peers reveled in extra loud music. He nodded and said, "And there is something else that makes train transportation more advantageous. Per passenger mile, planes use ten times more fuel than trains. Imagine, what this does to the atmosphere!"

Kim pointed to the slope on the opposite side of the river where a small herd of Holstein cows was grazing. "What a peaceful scene, it reminds me of Switzerland."

"I get the same reaction, Kim, I also enjoy these scenes. Unfortunately–taking a closer look–it is by far not as benign as it looks. do you notice those narrow horizontal lines running across the slope?" When Kim nodded, he explained, "These lines are signs of over grazing and the cows should not be kept on this slope any longer. This hill is in danger of eroding when the next big storm hits. It is sad when landowners don't have a feeling for their land any longer."

As the Eel River was flowing in a northwesterly direction towards the sea, getting closer to the cooler and moister areas of the coast, past the point where the main river and the South Fork of the river joined, the landscape of the valley slowly changed and eventually became wide open with the huge river spreading out. After crossing the Main Fork of the Eel River, the railroad stayed on the eastern bank. The train sped past several small hamlets, stopping once or twice for a few minutes. It also stopped in Scotia, a typical company town, neat and orderly, the seat of the Pacific Lumber Company which had been founded in 1880. The Murphy family had acquired the company in 1905. They had managed it wisely for the benefit of its workers, stockholders and the entire region. But in 1987, by means of a hostile takeover, the Texas junk bond millionaire Hurwitz became the new owner. In order to pay off his debts, he doubled harvests of the company's huge timber holdings–many of them still harboring old-growth redwoods at that time–and didn't consider the long-term, detrimental effect to the community and future health of the forests.

Near Fernbridge, the Eel River turned due west, flowing into the Pacific Ocean five miles further down stream. Soon, the outskirts of Eureka came into view and then the end of the line had been reached. Their car was waiting for them at the depot and within minutes they were heading north.

Neither Kim nor Nick had ever been north of Eureka on Highway 101 and both enjoyed the trip along the scenic coast. After dinner in Crescent City, they drove on until dark when they found a decent looking motel and stayed there for the night.

Next morning, they got up early and after a good breakfast, were back on the road. Traffic was light and they reached the outskirts of Medford shortly after nine o'clock. Kim had been studying the Medford street map and directed Thomas to leave the freeway at the first exit. Giving him directions and leading him through a maze of streets, commercial and residential neighborhoods, she finally announced that the next right turn would lead them into Buckthorn Lane.

"Okay, crew, be alert," Thomas said jokingly, telling them to be on the lookout without attracting unnecessary attention. It was a nice, fairly well-kept area, lower to middle-class neighborhood. He slowly drove through the street and soon they discovered the right house. The front garden was slightly neglected, in spite of the low-maintenance landscaping. There was no car parked in front or in the driveway. Downstairs, the curtains were drawn, nobody was in sight. The only person they saw was an older man, three houses down, working in the garden. He was doing some pruning, being watched by his dog.

"This is the perfect street to do your thing, Kim. I am sure you will find some people at home who are willing to talk to you and hopefully we will pick up information that gets us a step ahead," Thomas said after he had assessed the neighborhood.

Then they headed for the second address, the used-car lot. They soon had reached the general area which was not too far from downtown, and the street they were looking for. It was a slightly run-down section of town, but the condition of the street improved drastically as the numbers went up and the 'Used but clean and fast" dealership looked pretty decent. A new chain link fence surrounded the place. The freshly painted office in the back–its front door flanked by flower boxes–made a good impression. Thomas drove around the block to get another look before they continued towards downtown where he stopped in a quiet, well-kept street in front of the C and O office.

The receptionist took the three down a long, carpeted hallway to the office of Maxine Cooper, who was the general manager of this branch.

"Thomas, what a nice surprise!" she exclaimed, getting up quickly from behind her desk and shaking Thomas's hand. "Congratulations, I talked to Cora yesterday and she told me the good news that you passed the bar examination, and you got a job in Santa Rosa! It's good to see you."

After introductions, her secretary brought coffee and tea. When everybody had settled down, Maxine wanted to know what brought Thomas up to Medford. He told her why they were here. Maxine was an attentive listener. She was a handsome woman, about thirty-five years old, tall and slender, with blond, curly hair cut short. Before Thomas had even finished, she was already looking through her file box and then checking her computer.

"What a terrible situation for your family," Maxine kindly said to Nick, "I hope we can help a little, let me see what's in our files." Reading her screen she said, "I show nothing in my files on that Buckthorn address. This is a nice neighborhood. Our agency has not had any cases against residents in this area. The used car lot is different however. We have done four investigations for clients who had encountered problems buying from them in the last three years. The guys who ran the place were always slick, had the right lawyers and nothing came out of it. Now they have a new manager who has cleaned up the place and so far, I have not had any new complaints. Nevertheless, I don't trust him."

"Do you happen to know his name, Maxine?" Thomas asked.

"Let me see," Maxine said, working her computer, "OK, here he is, Merv Olson."

"He is the one who lives on Buckthorn Lane," Thomas said excitedly, "that explains the two phone numbers. What else do you know about him or the business?"

"I don't know where he came from. He has been in town for about a year, tries very hard to fit in, but has not succeeded yet. Several people I know are as suspicious of him as I am. The owner of the property and the business lives in Seattle. Although his name has come up, he was never involved nor did he show up here when there was trouble."

"He lives in Seattle?" Kim mused, "I wonder if there is a connection. You remember, Thomas, the person who rented the cabin in Madrone Flat also lives in Seattle."

"Well, let's call Stenton, he knows the name. Stenton is the local sheriff," he explained to Maxine. "Could I use your phone? Oh, by the way, what is the guy's name?"

Maxine turned to the computer again and read the name to Thomas, "Milt Undell is the owner's name. Go ahead, and make your call, Thomas."

Thomas called Garberville and happened to get Stenton right away on the line. From his responses the others could tell that he didn't get a clear-cut answer.

When he hung up, he explained, "It's a different name. I more or less expected that. If this Undell were indeed behind the rental, he would not be so stupid to give his real name. Of course, so far this is just a vague possibility. However, the interesting thing is that when Stenton tried to reach this man in Seattle, it turned out that the phone number was disconnected. He is going to call the PD in Seattle and let them check out the address, which is a Post Office Box.

"I have another question, Maxine. Could you find out if Olson owns the house on Buckthorn Lane or is it a rental. And if he rents it, who is the landlord?"

"Let me get my secretary. She will find out in a jiffy." Maxine picked up the phone and gave her instructions. Then she turned to Thomas, "What are your plans now?"

"Well, we have to be flexible. At first Kim will pose as an investigative reporter and try to interview some residents near the house and hopefully come up with some useful information. Depending on what Kim finds out, I might ask you if we can borrow your white van for perhaps one or two hours?"

Maxine frowned when she heard about Thomas's plans with Kim. But when she learned that Kim was a reporter and quite experienced, she changed her mind.

Maxine smiled at Kim and apologized, "I guess as a reporter you know what to do. I was just worried that you might get into trouble. I wish you good luck, I hope your investigation will answer some questions for you. And Thomas, you may borrow the van. Just don't tell me any details of what you plan to do. I trust your good judgment. Oh, and here comes Elaine with the info you wanted. It's a rented house and here is the name of the owner." She handed Thomas the note Elaine had given her. "I wish we could have lunch together, but I promised my husband to come home for lunch today, it's his birthday, I have to leave in a few minutes. I will be back around 2:30. If you need to make phone calls or anything else, feel free, there will always be someone here in the office."

She stood up, got her bag and jacket and they went to the front office. Kim was impressed by Maxine. Behind the pleasing, feminine facade was a woman who worked very efficiently, who didn't waste words and time. Kim disappeared into the bathroom to change into her formal clothes. When she came back, Thomas had called his friend Dean at the police department, they were going to meet him for lunch.

CHAPTER 17

Lieutenant Detective Dean Weaverly was waiting for them in a pizza restaurant. The place looked tiny from the street, but it extended all the way to the back of the building and was divided into three sections. In the last room, they found Dean Weaverly at a table next to a huge window. The room was attractive. The back wall was mostly glass, looking out into a patio with white-painted garden furniture, lots of shrubs, flowers and some smaller trees. There was more greenery beyond the patio–a small city park with lush green lawns, flowers, many trees and shrubs. Kim looked longingly out into the inviting garden, but it had started to rain.

Dean welcomed Thomas and his two companions with pleasure and firm handshakes. He was good looking–a tall, lanky man. His curly blond hair, worn fairly long, was a bit wild. He didn't wear a uniform or a suit and was dressed very casually in jeans and a plaid flannel shirt, with the sleeves partially rolled up. One probably would match him with any other profession than that of a homicide detective.

"Welcome to Medford, I wish you had a happier reason to be here. I have already ordered a super-size pizza, vegetarian with lots of mushrooms, which should be enough for all of us. Is that OK with you?" When they all agreed, he added, "I didn't know what you would like to drink. You have to go to the front counter and order it there."

After getting Nick and Thomas' orders, Kim got up and went to the front room. In the meantime, Thomas told Dean more details about the Carters, and what had happened to Julie. When Kim came back, they discussed the telephone call from the hospital. Dean had gone to the trouble to check out the other hospital in town, but there also had been no patient in intensive care last Saturday, who fitted the description. When Thomas mentioned the used car lot and the possible connection with the disappearance of the Carters, Dean became alert.

"Unfortunately, I can't tell you more than Maxine has told you already. We are looking at this new manager Olson with suspicion. So far he has been clean. What do you plan to do?"

Thomas told him that Kim would try first to check out the neighborhood. Depending on the outcome, they would make a plan. Dean looked uncomfortable and cast a worried glance at Kim.

"Be real careful, Thomas. Buckthorn Lane is a nice, peaceful neighborhood, but this Olson guy could be just the opposite. He lives with his girlfriend, supposedly quite a dish. And you speculate that perhaps even the owner of the car lot might be involved? This would make it much more serious. To tell you the truth, I wouldn't be surprised at all. I have a feeling–more than a feeling actually, based on some 'factual' rumors within the department you could say–that there is much more to these two guys than we care to know. Unfortunately, I can't do anything at the moment, I guess you understand? So far, there is not enough evidence for me to get involved. I agree that the timing of those phone calls from Madrone Flat to Olson is very suspicious and I am pretty much convinced that he has worked together with someone down there. However, the puzzle is not complete. Hopefully, you will find some clues when you check Olson out. Again, *be careful*, and if you run into any trouble, call me immediately, will you? We will be alert should anything new come up. When I get back to the office, I will discuss the situation with my boss, perhaps we can get something going."

The pizza arrived. It was scrumptious and they all enjoyed it.

After lunch, Thomas drove back to Buckthorn Lane and parked three blocks away from Olson's house. On the way over, they had talked about Kim's task and Thomas was sure that she would do an excellent job. He felt good about her and didn't expect any trouble. The rain had stopped and the sun came out again. Thomas and Nick watched Kim as she walked down the street. They saw her talking to a man for a few minutes who was working in his yard, and then she seemed to ring a bell next door and disappeared in a house.

She came out about twenty-five minutes later. An older lady walked her to the small gate at the sidewalk and they talked for at least another five minutes. Then she turned around and came back to the car.

"It went well, I think I got all the information we need." While Thomas drove back into town, Kim reported what she had learned.

"You probably saw me talking to the man who was working in the garden? He was hard of hearing and I had to talk very loud. That was not an ideal situation. So I cut it short and rang the bell at the house across from the Olsons'. I talked to an older lady who was very approachable. She told me everything she knew about the Olsons. They moved in last July. Most neighbors consider them married, but my old lady is convinced that they are 'living in sin', as she put it. In October, a young man arrived and lived with them until January. Just before he moved out–and she has not seen him since–he showed up with a brand new red car, the 'car with the dog', she said. At first, I didn't know what she meant, but then it came to me, a Cherokee Jeep with a Golden Retriever. Advertisement leaves it's marks, doesn't? This must have been Gibson. Her description fitted him exactly.

"The wife's name is Jessica and she is home most of the time, always wearing heavy make-up and fancy clothes. She doesn't go out a lot by herself because she doesn't have a car. My lady sees her every day, getting the mail. Once in a while she is doing a little yard work and occasionally walks to the neighborhood stores. When she goes out with Olson in the evening–at least once a week–she is always overdressed and on those occasions he drives a fancy car, like a BMW, Jaguar or Cadillac. He often changes cars. They get a lot of food deliveries–pizza, Chinese or Thai food–on a very regular basis, at least three times a week. The old lady is convinced that Jessica never cooks, just watches soap operas and reads romance novels. And that's about it. They seem to lead a fairly quiet life, hardly ever have company. "

"Great job, Kim. From what you heard, we can already infer that Gibson and Olson worked together. Gibson's description, the red Jeep, the timing, the telephone calls–all these things fit. I hope our next move will work out and bring us still closer to the truth. Now here is what we will do. You, Kim, take the rental car and drive to the used car lot, park it at least a block away. If you are afraid to go alone, I am sure Maxine would have someone to come with you for support. Pretend to be looking for a used car. Try to talk to Olson and tie him up as long as you can.

"I'll borrow a white van from C and O and go back to Buckthorn Lane, with Nick, posing as the rep for a cable company at the Olson's house. I hope Jessica will let me in. Nick stays in the van which we park near the Olsons' house. He will call the house exactly five minutes after he sees me entering the front door. Nick will pretend to be Ned Gibson's girlfriend. Can you give your voice a higher pitch, Nick? If that is too difficult, you could switch roles with Kim and you look for a used car and Kim comes with me?"

Nick grinned. This was a challenge he had been waiting for, something different, "Sure," he said, giving his voice a girlish sound, giggling, "I can do it. No problem. What do I have to say?"

"Excellent, Nick! You will tell Jessica that you were Gibson's girlfriend and that he was killed in a car accident. He had given you the Olsons' phone number, in case something should happen to him.

"She probably will brush you off, pretending you have the wrong number, or that she doesn't have any idea who Gibson is, something along those lines. Be persistent and get at least the message through that Gibson is dead. From Jessica's reaction to Nick's call we will learn several things, hopefully. First of all, we probably will find out if the Olsons knew Gibson and worked together. Second, did he do the dope project alone or was there someone else around down there who already told them that he died? If the Olsons don't know it yet, but know Gibson, we can conclude that Gibson worked alone down there. Then Jessica most likely will call Olson right away and that's why I want to be in the house to listen in if that should happen. So, if he should be called to the phone while he is showing you a car, Kim, it could be Jessica. It might be interesting for you to watch his reaction. If you have a chance, try to listen to his conversation, in case you realize it is Jessica who calls. I hope that I will be able to catch the conversation at my end if things work out well, but who knows, anything can happen. Stay around at the car lot for a while if you feel you can still learn something. Then drive back to C and O and wait for us. I'll get you a pager to wear. In case we should page you, drive to C and O and get help, we might be in trouble. But don't worry, I'm sure we will be all right.

Before Nick and I get started, we'll call the Olson's house as well as the business to find out who is where, just to be sure."

"But what about Emily and Bret? How will you find out about them, do you have any plans, Thomas?" Nick asked.

"So far, I have no plans, Nick. First, we want to establish whether Olson is really part of this, and then we have to find out how to get information about the Carters. Who knows, we might find out more than we expect, or nothing at all. Do you have any comments how to improve the plan and do you both feel comfortable in participating?"

Both Nick and Kim had no reservations. On the contrary, Nick glowed with excitement. Kim suggested that she should change back into jeans, sweater and wind breaker and wear a scarf over her hair, just in case Olson was home earlier and saw her when she talked to the neighbors. Nick felt that Thomas should also wear a pager while he was in the Olson house.

"If all of a sudden a car should arrive at the house, perhaps with some of Olson's buddies, I could page you and you could get out in a hurry," Nick said to Thomas. "And what shall I say to Jessica if she does not brush me off? If for instance she would like to get my phone number because Olson will call me back?" Nick asked.

"That's a good question, Nick. You are right, that could happen. OK, here is what you say. Tell her you are calling from Santa Rosa, you are on the way to the airport in San Francisco. You are flying home to Texas and will not be back until next week. You will call her when you come back. All right?" Thomas suggested, "But I am sure this will not be necessary. Good points, I am really glad you came along. I couldn't do this all by myself," Thomas said.

They had arrived at the C and O office ten minutes ago and had stayed in the car while going over the plans. Kim went to the bathroom to change, while Thomas talked to Maxine about borrowing the van. He checked their collection of uniforms and changeable signs for the van, and picked up the pagers. Finally, he and Nick drove off in the van for Buckthorn Lane, while Kim left about ten minutes later. On the way to the Olson's house, Thomas looked for a hiding place where he could put a sign on the van without being seen. He found the perfect place behind an old abandoned warehouse. When they emerged again, it was in the

NEW HORIZON CABLE SERVICE van. They stopped at the next gas station where Thomas went into the rest room. When he came back, Nick almost didn't recognize him. Thomas had changed into a chambray work shirt with the same name on the pocket flap as on the van. He wore dark-rimmed glasses and sported a trim Van-Dyke beard. They stopped near the Olsons' house. Nick climbed into the back of the van where he could look out through the tinted windows, but could not be seen from the outside. From the car phone, Thomas called the office in town first and asked for Olson. He was in, busy with a customer and couldn't come to the phone, which suited Thomas fine. So he was definitely not at home. He then called the house, disguising his voice, asking for an imaginary Linda. A woman answered the phone, telling him that he had the wrong number. So Jessica probably was also at home and the stage was set.

Armed with a clipboard, a canvas bag holding all kinds of measuring devices as an ampere-meter, a voltmeter, pliers and some wiring, Thomas walked to the Olson house. Nick watched him excitedly as he stood in front of the door, waiting to be admitted. As soon as Thomas entered the house, Nick checked his watch, ready for action. In five minutes, he would call Jessica from the car phone.

When the front door opened, a powerful wave of mixed perfumes enveloped Thomas' senses. The intensive fragrances almost triggered an impulse in his brain to run away as fast and as far as he could. He took hold of himself and tried his most attractive smile as he introduced himself to the woman–or rather apparition–who opened the door. She was probably only in her early twenties, but appeared older because of the heavy make-up that completely covered her face. Long, black, false eyelashes obscured her eyes. Her silver-sprayed hair was piled up almost as high as it had been the custom during the ornate period of the rococo. The floor-length caftan, made of a sparkling, wisp-like fabric, flowed around her figure in shrouds and veils of many colors. She wore the longest earrings Thomas had ever seen, crystal ornaments that wouldn't be too small for a lamp. He had a hard time not staring at her. Although he had interrupted a soap opera–he saw the flickering colors on a big-screen TV and heard pieces of the dialogue through the half-open door between the hall and the living room–Jessica didn't mind. She seemed to welcome the interlude. Here was a good-looking young man with a nice smile. She could try out her charm on him for a while before returning to TV's dream world. Graciously, Jessica invited him in. Thomas was just in the middle of explaining the advantages of his company's TV and telephone computer service, when the telephone rang. Jessica picked up the fancy, gold-colored old-fashioned telephone. A little early for Nick? Indeed, someone else called. Jessica didn't like the interruption at all and was quite rude to the caller who apparently wanted to talk to Olson. Impatiently, she slammed down the receiver. Thomas continued his spiel, hoping to get through before Nick called. Jessica was enchanted by what she heard–at least that's the way she reacted.

"Why don't you come into the living room and tell me more about it. This sounds absolutely fascinating." She was pointing toward the open door, when the telephone behind her rang again.

Now she was really angry, and picking up the receiver, she snapped a very short "Yeah?"

Thomas felt sorry for Nick and hoped he could deal with Jessica's impatience.

"Yes, this is the Olson's residence," Jessica responded, tapping her foot, ready to slam down the receiver again. Suddenly–after listening for a few moments–she became rigid. Her face mirrored the unpleasant news she was hearing from Nick. "Sorry, but I don't know who you are talking about, say it again?" She now became aware that she was not alone and turned her back to Thomas.

"Ned Gibson? No, I never heard the name." Jessica's voice was completely flat when she explained to Nick, "Yes, this is the number, but you must have it mixed up. Perhaps he lived here before we moved in?"

Thomas could see that she was very anxious to end this conversation, she couldn't wait to call Olson. She hardly finished her last response, "I understand that he died in an accident, sorry, but I don't know the guy," and firmly put down the receiver.

For a minute, she just stood there, absolutely still like a statue. Then she turned around and seemed to be almost surprised to see Thomas. Her mood had changed, she looked very upset.

"I hope you didn't get bad news, Mrs. Olson?" Thomas asked.

"Oh no, this was just someone calling the wrong number." She had collected herself by now and tried to smile at him, but didn't quite pull it off. "I just remembered that I have to make a phone call, would you mind waiting to check the phone until I am through?"

"Actually, I wanted to ask you to make a phone call so I can check the line while you speak. This would give me some idea if your system has enough capacity to be used for a computer service connection without installing an amplifier or rewiring. Would you mind if I test your line while you make the phone call?" Thomas asked.

She didn't seem to like the idea having him around while she called.

Thomas opened his bag and got out one of the meters. "I suppose you have another extension, don't you? I can work on this phone here and you can make your call upstairs or wherever you want. All I have to do is to connect this measuring device here and check it while a phone is in use."

She shrugged, gave him a halfhearted nod, and went into the living room, firmly closing the door behind her.

Thomas attached his 'measuring instrument' to the telephone and within seconds he heard her through the tiny loudspeaker, hidden in his ear, asking for Olson. When he answered the phone, Jessica burst out telling him about the call she had just received, that Matt had been killed in an accident. So for them Ned was Matt, and Jessica sounded as if nobody had told them yet that he had died.

"Listen, I happen to have a customer. Hang on for a second, will you?" Olson's voice was urgent. Was Kim the customer, Thomas wondered? Olson was back on the line within a minute and sounded very angry when he heard that Ned/Matt had given their telephone number to a girlfriend. He told Jessica that he would be home in thirty minutes and they would be leaving for California right away.

"When I come home, I want you to be ready to go, did you hear me, honey? And I want you to dress as plainly as possible."

"But Mervy, I just got the most gorgeous dress in the mail this morning and I did my hair in a new way, matching my dress. I want you to see it–don't you want me to look..."

He interrupted her rudely, "Can't you listen? We have to get down to that hick-town where Matt lived as soon as possible to see what we can save of his multi-million dollar operation. This is an emergency and you are whining about me not seeing your new dress? I'm mad enough about Matt already, don't let me get mad about you too. I wish I had never seen the guy, but the boss insisted on setting him up. In April, he got into this mess with the couple that walked into his plants. Now he kills himself driving too fast. Wait until the boss hears it, he'll probably blame it all on me. So come on, wake up and do as I tell you. Also, get rid of all that gook on your face, including the paint on your nails. When I come home, I want you to look like your sister, the Sunday school teacher. Don't take any clothes along that wouldn't meet the approval of your sister, that's easy to understand, isn't it? No tight jeans, no glittering stuff, no black underwear. We don't want to draw any attention when we get there. We must look as plain as possible."

"Okay, okay! Plain skirts, flat-heeled shoes and a baby-blue flannel night gown buttoned to the neck. I get the point. When you come home, I will look so ugly you'll be sorry you ever kissed me. This will be a fun trip! How long will we be gone? You want me to pack your things?"

"Well, pack some underwear and socks for me, the rest I will select myself. I guess we will be gone for up to a week–it all depends. We should try to get to Eureka tonight and check out the local newspapers if there is any mention of the accident. Then, we go to Madrone Flat tomorrow and nose around, playing tourist."

"You mean we are going to stay in that primitive cabin?"

"We are going to stay away from that cabin as much as possible. There are several new B and Bs in Madrone Flat, maybe we can make reservation from Eureka. But get going now, when I get home, we will leave. Oh, one more thing, get out the rings and put yours on, and take off all that knickknack jewelry, you understand?"

Thomas took the listening device out of his ears and switched the meter off. When Jessica came rushing out, heading for the stairs, he stopped her and told her that the test had turned out well and the capacity was adequate. Could they now do the other extension? She hardly listened to him, and while she was running up the stairs, she shouted down to him to come back some other time because she had to leave suddenly.

Thomas, of course, was not surprised about her reaction and satisfied how his plan had worked out. Nick had played his role well. He walked back to the van, where Nick was anxious to hear from him. Thomas explained to him how important the information was they had gleaned from Jessica's telephone call. Although it could not be used to prove anything legally, at least they knew now that there was definitely a connection between the Carter's disappearance and the dope plantation. Nick was an intelligent young man who right away understood the implications, and he was proud to have played a role in Thomas' detective work. They drove around the block and at a convenient spot Thomas removed the signs on the van. He wanted to go back near the house to watch Olson when he came home and possibly take a photo of him. He also wanted to find out the kind of car he was driving and get the license number. They didn't have to wait very long. About twenty minutes after Thomas had left the house, a light blue, late model Buick pulled up in front. A tall man jumped out and ran up the steps to the house, too fast to get a picture of him. Ten minutes later, Olson and Jessica came out again, each carrying a small suitcase. Thomas got the surprise of his life when he saw the woman. She wore sensible shoes with flat heels, a neat blue denim skirt with a slight flair; a crisp, white blouse and dark blue cardigan. Her hair, still showing some of the silver spray, was pulled back tightly into a ponytail. No make-up or false eye lashes. She looked pretty, much younger than in her seductive setup. Olson was quite a bit older than Jessica, probably in his early forties. He was almost the spitting image of Clark Gable, dark slick hair and a small mustache. Only now, he was lacking Gable's alluring smile, he looked angry and upset. This did not look like a pleasant trip for Jessica. Thomas almost felt sorry that he had heaped this trouble on her. He managed to shoot a few pictures before they took off.

He grinned at Nick when he put the camera back in place, "Well, I guess we can go back to California now too."

Kim was talking to Maxine when Thomas and Nick came back to the C & O office. Both were anxious to hear what had happened. After Thomas gave his report, he listened to what Kim had to tell.

"I recognized him as soon as I came to the office. Your description of Olson was accurate, Maxine," Kim began her story. "His portable phone rang right after he started to show me several cars. From the expression on his face I could tell that it was probably Jessica. He asked her to hang on for a minute because he had a customer. There was nobody else around to take care of me, so he was anxious to keep me there. I made it easy for him, telling him that I was not in a hurry, I would take a look around.

"So he continued his call. Of course, I tried to stay as far away as possible in order not to pressure him. On the other hand, I tried to hear as much as I could, and I did, because his voice became louder and louder. When he was through, I could tell he wanted to take off right away, he was real nervous. I guess he paged another salesman to help him out. This guy suddenly came out of the office and took over. Olson apologized that he had to leave for an appointment and took off. I left soon after."

"There is little doubt now that Olson and Gibson had worked together. And the remark, 'in April he got into the mess with the couple who walked into his plants', points to the Carters. We both heard it, and I am afraid we know what it means. Thank you so much for your help, Kim. This was very important," Thomas said.

He called Dean and brought him up to date also. Stenton was not in his office, Maxine offered to call him later. "I'll try to reach him, Thomas. He should know as soon as possible that Olson is coming south. Also that there is someone else involved at a higher level, the guy Olson calls the boss, as you said. I hope you find out soon what happened to the Carters. Perhaps you can trap Olson when he checks out the plantation, although this will be a delicate task. I hope everything will work out for you without any new trouble. Anyway, I am glad you pulled it off without being hurt. You really should stay in this line of work, Thomas, you are good at it. As a lawyer you will lose that skill. Good luck, and I hope to see you again in the not-to-distant future."

They again thanked Maxine for all her help, and then started their journey back to Madrone Flat.

CHAPTER 18

Kim was driving. Thomas had looked tired when he came back to the car after refueling, and Kim offered to take over.

"You had the responsibility for the whole operation, Thomas, and also the scariest part. What I did was what I usually do and it was easy, without any danger. Olson was actually very charming, I almost felt guilty coming in there, pretending to buy a car."

"Kim is right," Nick had agreed, "when you entered the Olson's house–although I found it rather exciting–I must admit that I was also a bit apprehensive what might await you there, going into the lion's den."

Thomas had laughed, "It was not a lion's den, it was a siren's den. I expected any moment Jessica would start to sing, hypnotize me, and enfold me in her silver veils and float away with me. She looked eerie, and she enjoyed having male company, trying out her new glamorous outfit and hairdo on me. When you saw her coming out of the house, Nick, there was nothing left of that alluring creature. She was all scrubbed and peeled clean to make a perfect impression on the people in Madrone Flat. Olson knows what he is doing. I just hope he does not direct his anger toward Jessica, because he was pretty upset about this Matt or Ned guy. But, thank you for taking over the wheel, Kim, I do need a nap."

He was now fast asleep on the back seat. Nick would have loved to continue his science fiction novel, but he felt somehow protective of Kim, and also felt obligated to keep her entertained with his conversation while driving. Knowing that Kim was a reporter, he actually had a number of questions for her. Nick was involved with his school newspaper and could use some professional advice. He was also curious about what kind of approach Kim had used to get her information so easily from the old lady across the street from the Olsons.

Kim laughed, "I knew you would ask me that question, Nick. As I mentioned, a reporter I know who had worked for one of the tabloids, told me the trick. In my line of reporting, I have no need for this kind of interviewing. I work mostly by appointment now–this was a special case for me. Anyway, I told that nice lady that her neighbors across the street had won big in a lottery and my paper wanted to do a story. This subject seems to intrigue people and they are usually eager to talk. But, I didn't mention the name of the neighbors, I just mentioned the address. After we had exhausted the topic, I repeated the address and pretended that my address was 'Buckthorn Terrace' instead of Buckthorn Lane where I was, interviewing her. And when at last I mentioned the name–using a different name than Olson–it also turned out to be wrong, of course. So I apologized for having taking her time, apparently we had talked about a different family. I would have to go back to the office and check the address again, but I would let her know what happened."

"And are you going to do that, Kim?"

"Sure, I don't like to let people down. In a few days, I will send her a pretty little note, telling her that the agency made a mistake, it was Medford in Pennsylvania, not Oregon. She will be flattered getting the letter and I got the information I wanted in the first place. That's the trick, pretty sneaky, isn't it? As I said, I don't have the need to use these methods, yet in this case I thought it would work better than posing as an investigator for an insurance or mortgage company."

"Gee, I am really disappointed in you, Kim, I would never have thought you would stoop so low," Nick joked, "though I must say, this is a cool idea, perhaps I will make use of it some day for the school paper. But don't feel bad about today. You didn't hurt anybody and it helped us to come a little closer to finding Aunt Emily and Uncle Bret–at least I hope so. And besides, the old lady probably enjoyed talking to you."

A few hours later, they stopped for a quick dinner break and eventually arrived in Eureka just before ten o'clock. When they drove into the parking lot of the first motel that showed a vacancy sign, they drove out again just as fast–the Olson's blue Buick was parked in front of one of the rooms.

"That was close," Nick exclaimed, who had spotted the car first, "they probably wouldn't recognize us, but I think it is better not to stretch our luck."

They finally found a room for Kim in a motel at the south end of town. Thomas and Nick stayed at the house of his friend Herb, who was eager to hear what happened in Medford. Herb had been in law school with Thomas and Ken. His father was also a lawyer who had an office in Eureka and Herb had just started to work for him.

Next morning, when they were heading for the train station, they passed the motel where the Olsons were staying. The Buick was still parked in the same place, they had not left yet. As soon as the train started to move south, Kim bought breakfast in the buffet car and carried it back to their coach. They enjoyed the hot tea and coffee, it was a chilly morning. The sky looked gray, the clouds were hanging low and the higher elevations and distant hills were shrouded in a dense fog. They were almost through with breakfast when the conductor came by to punch their tickets. It was the same conductor who had been on the train Tuesday evening when they had taken Julie to the hospital.

He recognized Thomas and Kim and immediately inquired how Julie was doing. "I hope Miss Sutten is all right? How is her arm? And I guess by now the Carters are back home?"

Kim reassured him that Julie was fine, just had to take things a little slower for a while, but that unfortunately, the Carters were missing still, and nobody had any idea what happened to them. The conductor was stunned, he had not heard the bad news yet.

"Were you on the train when that young man got a ride with you from the Sutten ranch south two weeks ago?" Thomas asked the conductor, "I remember vaguely that you talked with Julie about it on Tuesday evening."

The conductor quickly said, "Sure, I remember the incident very well, never had seen the guy before, ... "He hesitated for a few seconds and continued, "He used a commute card and told me that he was a relative of the Carters. However, he had to leave before they would come back on Friday or Saturday. Later, I had a little run-in with him. His commute card had been almost used up but was still good to Willits. When he stayed on the train to Ukiah, I told him that he had to pay from Willits to wherever he wanted to go, and he refused. We made a stop in Redwood Valley and I told him to get off the train or pay. Very reluctantly, he paid, using pretty obscene language. I must say, I was very surprised that he had anything to do with the Carters."

Thomas had listened with increasing interest and asked the conductor, "Would you mind taking a look at a photo and tell us if it is the same man you just talked about?"

Kim was confused. A photo? What did Thomas mean? And then it dawned on her. "Do you have one of Stenton's photos of Ned Gibson after… do you have one of those with you? You better tell him what kind of a photo it is."

Now, the conductor was bewildered. But when Thomas got his wallet out and handed him a photo of the dead man, he understood Kim's concern. He didn't flinch when he looked at the picture and gave it back to Thomas.

"Yes, that's the same man all right. Only he doesn't look quite as lively as he did on the train," he said with a deadpan face. "What happened to him?"

"He died in a car accident, drove his Jeep into the river. He is suspected of being involved in the disappearance of the Carters. Could you spare five minutes in Madrone Flat to call the sheriff's office in Garberville? Ask for Under Sheriff Stenton. If he is not there, just leave a message for him and tell him where and when he can reach you. Be sure to mention that you had seen Ned Gibson getting on the train at the Sutten ranch. Will you do that?" Thomas asked.

"Sure, I will make the call. Whatever I can do to help to find the Carters I will. There is no doubt at all that this was the same man. Sorry, I have to go on. I sure hope that you find the Carters soon. Please give my best regards to Miss Sutten."

When they reached South Fork, from where the railroad followed the North Fork of the Eel River, it started to clear up, and soon the sky was blue and the sun was shining.

"You look a little sad in spite of your exciting novel, Nick, what's the matter?" Kim asked.

"I am sorry that this nice train ride has come to an end. I would love to keep going and going. It's really fun and I have not been on trains a lot. I am envious of my sister. She is now riding trains all over Europe with my Dad–across the channel between England and France–through the tube, and so on."

"How did it happen that you didn't go?" Kim asked.

Nick shrugged, "My parents felt since I had been on a trip to Mexico last summer, it was Esther's turn now. Besides, I have to study a lot for my last year in high school. Of course, they are right–parents are always right, aren't they?" he said sarcastically, but then laughed. After all, he seemed to agree with them. "Even though the reason for this trip is rather sad, I enjoyed being with you. It was inspiring and I admire you a great deal, Thomas. And, you too, Kim," he added hastily, and continued, "You remember what that woman said to you in Medford, Thomas? You should keep working as a detective–I agree with her."

"By the way, Kim, I have some concern about what I did in Oregon," Thomas said reluctantly. "In contrast to law enforcement, private investigators have a little more freedom in gathering their information. When we tell Stenton what we found out, it might be prudent to emphasize what you overheard from Jessica's phone call to Olson. You understand what I mean, don't you? "he asked.

"Yes, I do, Thomas, and I agree with you. Don't worry, I will tell Stenton everything Olson said to Jessica. I have very good ears and could hear him well , even some distance away. And besides, you probably heard all what she said, didn't you?" Kim responded and smiled at Thomas.

The train stopped in Madrone Flat and a few minutes later at the ranch. When the conductor was helping them to get off, he told Thomas that he had reached Stenton and had reported his encounter with Gibson. Stenton would call him back in Eureka this evening to get more details.

They walked up to the house. Julie was outside on the deck, reading. She was happy to see them, but she broke into tears when she told them what had happened in the meantime. Ralph had arrived Thursday evening. He was upstairs now with Bonnie.

"It is terrible," Julie began, "I wish I didn't have to tell you. Ralph called the sheriff yesterday morning. He requested a search party with dogs to look for his brother and Emily. And he offered to pay for it if the police didn't have the funds to do it. Stenton reacted very fast and arrived with a dog trainer and two dogs in the early afternoon. First, they had the dogs search around here with no results. Then they went back to Ned Gibson's cabin and didn't find anything either. Finally, they went to the hidden valley. After a few minutes, the dogs were barking like crazy, they had found the Carter's dog. The sheriff took the dead dog back to the office and informed Ralph this morning that the dog most likely had been shot quite some time ago."

They listened with apprehension as Julie was telling the sad story. Although they were shocked about the dog, his death was not the terrible ending they had feared to hear. If the search dogs had not found Emily and Bret, maybe there was a little hope left? Thomas was just going to ask Julie for more details when the others came out to the deck. Bonnie had been crying again, her eyes were puffed and red. Julie introduced Ralph to Kim and Thomas.

"I don't want to sound callous," Thomas said, referring to what they had just heard from Julie, "but the fact that the search only resulted in the dog being found could perhaps give us some hope? Were the deputy and the trainer satisfied that the dogs had found all they could, or did they break it up for other reasons?"

"No, Thomas, they didn't rush off at all, "Ralph replied. "The trainer was convinced that the dogs would not find anything else. But I don't share your optimism, be it ever so small. They probably killed Bret and Emily someplace else."

Thomas then quickly told them what they had found out in Oregon and that the Olsons could arrive in Madrone Flat any minute now. It was important to have someone there to watch them. He suggested that Bonnie, Nick and Ralph should go because he and Kim were known to them.

"By the way, when you were up in the hidden valley yesterday, Ralph, did you cover up the entrance from the road again?" Thomas asked, just as they were going to leave.

"Yes, we did. Deputy sheriff Stenton was very concerned about this. He hopes to lure the other partners of this dope operation into a trap, and this might happen now thanks to your action. We put all the small trees back and then hid the pots with branches. Also, he treated Gibson's accident very low key and didn't mention any connection to the pot planting or the Carters to the press."

Thomas was relieved to hear that. In case the Olsons came, looking for the place where Gibson had done the planting, everything was back in place. He was convinced they knew pretty well where it was, otherwise they wouldn't have come south to California.

When they arrived in Madrone Flat, Bonnie introduced Ralph to Rosy and told her what had happened and that they were now waiting for the Olsons to arrive.

Before she even finished, Rosy interrupted her, "They have reservations with us, Bonnie. We got a call around nine o'clock last night, they said they were in Eureka."

Addressing Bonnie and Ralph, she continued, "The two of you could act as receptionist and maid if you wouldn't mind doing that? And perhaps get them involved in a conversation?"

Both were ready to do anything that would help the case. Rosy suggested that Nick should sit outside on the deck off the cafe. From there, he would have a good view across the river to where the road was approaching the bridge from the west.

"As soon as you see their car, call me, Nick. I then will tell Bonnie and Ralph to get ready for their guests."

Nick got a newspaper from the counter and settled down in a comfortable chair on the deck. Rosy took Bonnie and Ralph over to the B and B office. She produced a white apron for Bonnie and told Ralph how to register the Olsons when they showed up. Business was slow at this time and Rosy kept Nick company for a while until some customers showed up. Nick was just folding open his paper, when he heard a car coming. Looking up, he saw the Olson's blue Buick approaching on the west side of the river. He rushed in to tell Rosy and then hung around in the store, watching the parking lot. Rosy went over to the office and informed Bonnie and Ralph. She came back into the store just as the Buick turned into the parking lot of the B and B. Bonnie was dusting the railing along the porch of the office, when the car stopped a few feet away from her. She felt like an actress at opening night when she greeted Merv Olson with a cheerful smile as he got out of the car. Olson didn't look happy, but apparently remembered right then that he wanted to make a good impression. The sour expression on his face gave way to a false smile as he coaxed Jessica out of the car. Assuming that Bonnie wasn't looking, he gave Jessica a little shove to remind her what she was supposed to do. Her face lit up as if turned on by a switch, she smiled and cooed, "What a charming place, dear, you really have picked a beautiful spot. I will enjoy our stay."

Ralph came out to the porch and now it was his turn to welcome them and to invite them in. In spite of his efforts to start a cozy little talk, the Olsons didn't bite, they were not in the mood. After the formalities were taken care of, Ralph showed them to their room. Jessica emitted a flood of admiring shrieks when she saw the tastefully decorated room and the view of the river from the window.

"Let's stay a little longer, darling, not just one night. I love it, this is marvelous," she begged Olson.

Although he didn't seem to feel like it, Merv put his arm around her and also commented on the view. "Well, perhaps we should stay a second day if you like it that much." Ralph again had no luck getting a conversation going, so he gave up. He told them that lunch was served until two o'clock either in the small dining room behind the store or outside on the deck. If they showed their room key when placing the order, lunch was included in the room price. Except for a short thank-you, no talk developed and Ralph left. The Olsons emerged from their room half an hour later. They walked over to the store and after a lengthy discussion of the choices ordered lunch from Rosy. She promised to bring the food out to their table on the deck. Nick got a piece of pizza and some apple juice from Rosy and carried it out to his table. He sat down as close to the Olsons as possible, unfolded his newspaper, and while he ate his pizza and pretended to read, he watched the Olsons and tried to listen to their talk.

Five minutes later, Bonnie came out, carrying the Olson's lunch. As she was setting the plates and silverware down, the train arrived from the south. Merv and Jessica gaped, apparently they didn't know about the train.

Bonnie noticed it and proudly said, "Yes, this is our new passenger train service. It started in March and we are all very happy about it. I am expecting two couples by train who will stay here for several nights."

"I am not crazy about trains," Olson said, "you cannot beat cars, they are much more convenient, faster and reliable. But this road into your valley is awful, we almost didn't make it through some of the soft spots.

Some large rocks hit the bottom of the car several times. I can see why you like the train. Can't they pave that road and make it wider and less curvy?"

"We are actually quite happy that the road is not a four-lane highway. The valley stays quieter and the air cleaner. We already have had many visitors since March who have come by train and enjoyed the peaceful atmosphere. There are a number of nice trails where one can go for long walks without being bothered by any traffic."

Olson stared at her as if he was questioning Bonnie's sanity, and continued in his argument, "If your road was better, you probably would attract new developments to your community. Perhaps you could even build a golf course and that would certainly bring in tourists. I guess the train wouldn't hurt it, although it is noisy and you have all these people milling around," he pointed to the station where quite a few people were getting on and off.

"Don't worry about these people. In a few minutes, the train will be gone again and so will the crowd. But talking about cars, I am not so sure that they are so much better. Just a few days ago, we had a tragic accident here. A young man swerved off the road coming down from the eastern hill and plunged right into the river. They couldn't save him, he drowned."

Bonnie had finally found the right key to get them started. Nick was listening closely. He had not expected his mother to be such a good actress. Once the ice was broken, the Olsons tried to gather as much information about the accident as they could without attracting unnecessary attention. Bonnie played right along, charming them into asking more and more questions. She could tell that they were quite shocked when she mentioned that another man who had been able to save himself had also been in the car. This seemed to be news to them. They wanted to know whether they had been locals, both the victim and the passenger. Bonnie tried her best to convince them that the men apparently had just been driving through. She said that nobody in town knew the men and that the passenger had been a hitchhiker. This information seemed to put them at ease. Nick's admiration for his mother increased by the minute–he was sorry he couldn't videotape her performance. Yet he knew that she was not really play-acting. His mother was dead-serious. She was mourning her sister and Bret, yet pulling herself together and performing a splendid acting job, being friendly and polite to the people who were partially responsible for whatever had happened to Emily and Bret.

Now the Olsons wanted to know what they could do here, had Bonnie any suggestions? Bonnie gave them a few hints about walks they could take. Along the river, or east off the main road, along a road called Fir Creek Road, which had very little traffic. There were also kayaks available for rent. All this didn't seem to appeal to them very much, but they thanked her just the same. Bonnie left, the topics had finally been exhausted.

While they ate their lunch, they didn't talk very much. Nick heard only pieces of their conversation, they almost whispered to each other. Yet he understood that they were pleased about what Bonnie had told them. They finally left and Nick also got up a few minutes later and went into the store. Ralph was eager to drive back to the ranch because he expected the Olsons to go for a ride and check out the area, and he wanted to be ahead of them. On the way back, Bonnie informed Ralph about her conversation with the Olsons. Bonnie blushed when Nick praised her how great an acting job she had performed, she had not expected this reaction from her son.

Ralph grimaced, "I am afraid I would not be good either as an investigator or actor."

Bonnie reassured him, "This was not your fault. They were in a bad mood when they arrived. He looked ill-tempered and she was sulking when I greeted them. I guess they had a fight, over the road perhaps. By the time they came for lunch, they had relaxed a little. And the arrival of the train really set off the conversation."

Ralph stopped the car at a level spot after he had driven half way up the western slope to the ranch. "You two drive on to the ranch. I will stay up here for a while and watch for the Olsons' car. From here, I can see a car coming to the bridge or driving on to the dead guy's cabin back there. This is completely safe, Bonnie, you don't have to worry. There are lots of trees or bushes I can hide behind."

Right away, Nick offered to stay with him, he didn't want him to be there alone. They got out and Bonnie drove down to the ranch.

Thomas, Julie and Kim were out on the deck, finishing lunch. Bonnie gave them a quick report. When Thomas heard that Ralph and Nick were sitting up there on the hill, he decided to join them.

Bonnie slowed him down, "Wait a minute, before you leave, I want to fix some lunch. Nick had a piece of pizza but Ralph didn't eat anything."

Bonnie rushed into the kitchen and within minutes she had a basket with food and drink ready to take along and soon Thomas was on his way, walking up the road.

After Bonnie had eaten, she and Kim cleaned up the kitchen. Julie was tired and lay down and soon had fallen asleep.

Voices woke her up. The men were back. The blue car had shown up about an hour after Thomas had made it up the hill. The Olsons had stopped at the bridge, and had walked toward the hidden valley, but came back within twenty minutes. Then they had continued along the road toward Gibson's cabin and had stayed there a long time. After almost two hours, the car was finally coming down the road again. They did not stop at the bridge but kept going to Madrone Flat.

The men had just finished their story when Calvin Stenton drove up, in an unmarked car. Bonnie had made a lasagna which was ready to be served. They invited Stenton to join them for dinner and they all filed into the kitchen were the table was set.

Stenton wanted to get a report from Thomas about what had happened in Medford. Thomas outlined what they had done, praising Kim and Nick for their participation. He pointed out the important pieces of information they had obtained and that their action had served its purpose to flush out Olson. Stenton was pleased to hear that they were now in Madrone Flat, already checking out the area.

"From what you tell me, it seems to be pretty obvious that Gibson was doing his thing down here alone, except for Andy, of course. Otherwise, the Olsons' would have heard from Gibson's partner–or partners–that he had died," Stenton concluded. "And it also proves, in a way, that Andy was only partially involved, right? Otherwise he would have called the Olsons. Most likely, he was not aware of Gibson's Oregon connection. Too bad that he ran away, he really screwed things up for himself should we ever catch him."

Stenton also told them that the Carter's dog had been shot with the gun they had found on Gibson.

"What we need to do now is watch the plantation up there. I am sure this will be their next step, trying to drive up to the hidden valley and continue to take care of the plants. If they do, and we catch them in the act, we can nail them. Then we can put pressure on them, and hopefully get them to talk about what happened to the Carters.

"Unfortunately, I will not be able to get a deputy out here until tomorrow afternoon. We had a major burglary in Eureka yesterday where someone almost got killed. One guy was caught and two others are still out there, heavily armed. That's why we are short of manpower. Could you guys keep an eye on the place? But remember, so far, this is the only way to link Gibson or Olson with the Carters. As valuable the information is which Thomas, Kim and Nick gathered in Medford, we probably cannot use it against them, it would not stand up in court."

He smiled at Thomas, telling him that he read between the lines of his report.

"Even the records of the phone calls will not prove anything, because we cannot substantiate who made the calls. So be real careful that you don't mess up things and lose it. By the way, does one of you have a camcorder? If you could make a movie–while they are watering the plants, for example–we would have a very strong case against them."

"Couldn't they claim that the plants will be used for medicinal purpose and get away with it?" Bonnie asked.

"No way," Stenton said and Thomas nodded in approval. "First of all, they have trespassed and are growing this stuff on somebody else's property. And second, this is much too big an operation. They would have to show proof that they need to supply a whole hospital with the plants. And lastly, there seems to be a major crime committed–where are the Carters? They have disappeared. I am sure we will be able to prove that these same people are involved in their disappearance. No, I have no doubt that they will be indicted and eventually prosecuted if you can bring the proof I suggested. Don't get me wrong, we probably could also get them in a different manner, but this seems to be the easiest way. I trust Thomas, he will use good judgment. Just be careful."

"Perhaps two of us should start with the watch this evening. It doesn't get dark until almost nine. They might come back later." Julie suggested.

"I doubt it," Stenton said. "I stopped at Rosy's and she pointed the Olsons out to me. They had just come in for dinner. He had ordered a bottle of wine and part of it was already gone before they even had their salad. By the time they have finished their meal, they won't feel like taking on dangerous adventures."

"I have a good camcorder. Too bad I left it at home," Kim said. None of the others had one either.

"I could drive over and see if the Kendars might have one," Kim suggested, and after they were all through with dinner and Stenton had left, she took off for the Kendar ranch with Nick in tow.

Bonnie washed the dishes and everybody helped drying them. When the kitchen was cleaned up, they sat down for a night cap. They shared a bottle of wine, waiting for Kim and Nick to return.

CHAPTER 19

On Sunday morning, at day break, Ralph and Nick started out for the hidden valley. Kim and Nick had come back with the Kendar's camcorder the previous evening, and Ralph now carried it in his rucksack. Charles and Nomi had been eager to help and to hear details about the Medford trip from Kim and Nick.

Thomas had promised that he would relieve Ralph and Nick at nine o'clock. At breakfast, Julie surprised everybody with the announcement that her leg didn't hurt any longer, her arm felt much better, and she offered to go along with Thomas, because she also wanted to help.

Bonnie, very concerned, objected, "Don't you think you should be more careful, Julie? Climbing up and down the slope is not easy. Kim or I could go with Thomas."

As she was saying this, Kim–who was sitting next to Bonnie–stepped on her foot and smiled at her. Bonnie got the message, silently regretting her ignorance. She could understand that Julie wanted to be with Thomas as well as participate in the search for Emily and Bret. Nevertheless, she thought it was reckless of Julie to consider hiking down into the valley. Certainly, there were safer and easier to reach places where she could be alone with Thomas. But quickly, she switched to another topic.

"I'll fix you some lunch to take along, for Ralph and Nick also, if they want to stay around for a while. Perhaps, you should at least take the car up to the ridge, Thomas, so Julie doesn't have to walk all the way?"

Thomas was as surprised about Julie's decision as Bonnie. He didn't say it, but he agreed with Bonnie that it was a little risky. Yet, Julie had smiled so radiantly when she told them that she would come with him, he didn't want to spoil it for her. And besides, he would certainly very much enjoy her company. He just had to be extra supportive when they walked down the path to the ledge. Once they got there, she would be all right. They did take the car. At the ridge, Thomas turned off the road and continued up the slope until it became too steep and rocky. He slung the rucksack with their lunch on his back and firmly held Julie's arm so she would not slip as they walked up the slope.

After they had climbed about hundred feet, Thomas stopped. "How is it going, are you all right?"

"Sure, "Julie replied, "I'm fine. I just have to watch where I am going, but leaning on your arm helps a lot."

She stopped and looked into the valley, with a sad look on her face and tears coming into her eyes.

"How beautiful it is up here and the house down there looks so peaceful, in spite of the dreadful things that have happened. Everywhere, I feel Emily's and Bret's presence. It's as if I lost my parents a second time." Thomas patted her arm, "There is still hope left, Julie, as long as it has not been confirmed that they are dead. We will find out soon, I'm sure. Thank you for coming with me this morning. I was happy when I heard you saying it during breakfast. Though, to be honest, I think Bonnie was right to voice her concern. We have to be very careful walking down the slope, Julie."

They continued their walk up to the edge of the valley and then descended slowly and quietly, Thomas being ready to catch Julie the second she should slip. They made it down easily. Well before nine o'clock, they reached the place where Ralph and Nick were hiding behind some bushes. Both were reading and didn't hear them coming until they were almost upon them. It was a surprise for them to see Julie and they were glad that she had done so well getting down. So far, nothing had happened in the valley. Both were eager to leave and to get into the sun. The morning had been rather cool and sitting here quietly hadn't helped. Each of them took a sandwich and some fruit, which they would eat on the ridge where it was sunny. They left, promising to be back after lunch, unless Kim and Bonnie were eager to take over.

Thomas went down further to see if there was a better and closer observation place. He was back within a few minutes, claiming to have found the perfect spot. It was about ten feet above the ledge–the small, level area where the slope ended abruptly in a cliff, dropping off vertically down to the valley floor. There was a group of young firs, intermixed with some ceanothus bushes, which provided a good hiding place. Julie came down with Thomas but was afraid that they might be seen from the valley after all.

"OK, why don't you stay there, Julie. I will go down and see if I can spot you." He quickly walked down the narrow path to the valley, aware that the Olsons could show up any minute. When he reached the bottom of the valley, he looked up to where Julie was sitting, but couldn't see her at all.

"This is a safe place, Julie, don't worry any longer," Thomas said when he came back and looked through the binoculars. "Take a look, you can see the valley floor perfectly through the branches and yet, we are well hidden."

They spent the waiting time discussing what might happen if the Olsons were caught in the act. Would they talk? And did they really know? Or had the knowledge of the Carters' fate died with Gibson? Almost an hour later, they heard the sound of a car.

"This guy is foolish enough trying to make it up to the valley with his Buick!" Thomas said as they listened to the sound of a slow-moving vehicle, straining as it came up from the road.

All of a sudden it stopped, apparently it had reached its limits. Car doors were slammed shut, and then they heard voices coming up the hill from the direction of the bridge. At last, they saw two people walking into the valley, and Thomas whispered that indeed these were Merv Olson and Jessica. Thomas had tried out the camcorder earlier and was ready to shoot. He filmed the Olsons' movements step by step. When they had reached the center of the valley, Julie and Thomas could understand most of what they were saying. Olson apparently was familiar with the layout. Within minutes, he had located the pump. It was hidden in a wooden box with a green tarpaper roof, hinged on one side, which he was opening now. Jessica wore jeans today–kind of baggy as

Olson had requested–and a red and white checked blouse. Her hair was still tied into a ponytail. She didn't seem to be in a good mood.

"This place gives me the creeps," she complained, "this is just as cold and damp as Oregon. How long do we have to stay here?"

Olson was studying a small pamphlet, probably the instruction manual.

"At least an hour. These plants have not been watered since Matt died. They need a good soaking to survive. Imagine how many holidays in the Bahamas this stuff here will pay for, perhaps that will make you feel a little hotter?" He snickered, as he pulled the starter of the pump. After a few halfhearted turns, the pump rumbled on and six sprinklers came to life, watering the planted area.

"Shucks, the battery is empty!" Thomas exclaimed, trying to keep his voice down. He was checking out the camera, which had stopped recording.

Julie whispered "I remember Kim saying last night–when she came from the Kendar's with the camcorder–that there was a second, fully charged replacement battery in the bag. And I recall that she even took it out. Have you looked?"

"Yes, it's not there, someone must have forgotten to put it back in. I feel bad that I didn't check it out this morning. Well, I guess we have to go back and get it. Fortunately, this operation down there will be going on for awhile," Thomas replied. "Only, we have to be careful when we climb the first two or three yards. After that they cannot see us any longer."

"I am not coming along, why should we both leave, I'll stay here and wait, you can move faster."

"Are you crazy, Julie? I would never leave you here by yourself. Come on, let's go."

Julie finally convinced Thomas that it was better she stayed where she was. She was well hidden here, there was no danger. Very reluctantly, Thomas left. In a crouching position, he carefully moved up the first few feet but then could no longer be seen. Julie picked up the binoculars again and looked for the Olsons. They were sitting near the pump, relaxing. Olson smoked and Jessica was reading a paper back.

Suddenly Julie had to sneeze. At the last instant she managed to pull up her sweatshirt and press it against her nose to stifle the sound.

Fortunately, the sounds of the pump and the sprinklers were loud enough to cover up the sneezing. Though it gave Julie a little scare and she was hoping that Thomas would be back soon.

Olson had stopped smoking and was lying in the grass, on his side, apparently sleeping. Jessica was tickling him with blades of grass. Then she started to massage his back. He didn't seem to like that and pushed her hands away several times. But finally, he turned around and pulled her down to him, starting what looked to Julie like foreplay to a sexual interlude. She felt embarrassed to have intruded into their privacy and had just put the binoculars down, when all of a sudden the roar of the pump stopped. The sound of the sprinklers became quiet. Cursing, Olson got up and walked over to the pump. He was bending down, checking it out, when Julie felt another urge to sneeze. This time, it happened so abruptly that she could not muffle the sound. It reverberated like an explosion in her ears and when she looked down, she knew that at least Jessica had heard something.

Jessica looked around and excitedly said to Olson, "Did you hear that? There must be people around, I heard someone sneezing. "

Olson apparently had not heard anything. "You are always imagining things. That was probably a deer."

"A deer! " Jessica shrieked, "have you ever heard of a deer sneezing?"

"Yes, I have, in the zoo. Dogs and cats can sneeze too. Leave me alone for a a minute, will you? I have to figure out what's wrong with this pump."

Julie was relieved that Olson dismissed Jessica's interference. She just hoped that she didn't have to sneeze a third time before the pump was working again. But just in case, she held her sweater in her right hand, ready to press it against her face should she need it.

Jessica started to complain, "I wish we hadn't come down here. How much longer do we have to water the plants?"

"Not very long. When we are through here in an hour, we call the boss and tell him what happened. I am sure that he will have someone available soon who can take over Matt's job. All we have to do is find a place for this new guy to stay, either here in Madrone Flat or nearby. It is too risky to let him stay at the cabin. The police might have identified Matt, and in case someone has noticed that he lived back there, it is better to stay away from the cabin. Although we probably should get the fertilizer out of there. As soon as all this is arranged, we can leave."

"But don't call the boss from Madrone Flat, there are probably not more than two or three pay phones, and it would be easy to trace the calls should something go wrong. Don't you think?"

"You are a smart kid. You are right, we should go to Garberville and call from there."

"No, I hate this terrible road. How about taking the train to Eureka or Santa Rosa? I would like to do that–that would really be fun. There, I heard it again! Was that your deer again?"

The urge to sneeze had caught Julie completely by surprise. The sudden outburst seemed to be even louder than the last time. Although she pressed the sweater against her face at the last minute, it sounded terribly loud to her. She realized that both had now become suspicious. Olson got up from the pump and looked around but apparently didn't see her.

"I think it came from up there, Merv," Jessica said, pointing toward the slope where Julie was sitting. "I knew we would get into trouble," she wailed, "let's get out of here."

But Olson was not ready to give up several million dollars so fast. "You stay here, I'll check out the slopes. I still think it was a deer."

Julie saw him walking in the direction of the road from where they had come in. He stopped a few times, apparently listening, and then walked on. Now he was standing at the point where the road lead down to the bridge. Probably he thought that someone had walked up from there. Should she try to get up the hill? This was too risky with Jessica down there staring up the slope. If she moved, Jessica would notice her for sure. Besides, Julie was not able to move fast enough up the hill because she could use only her right arm to hold on to trees or branches.

The camcorder! It was lying there next to the rucksack, if they came up here and saw the camera, they would know right away why she was there. She angled for the rucksack, then for the camera and carefully–moving as little as possible–hid the camcorder at the bottom of the rucksack, under the food. Carefully, she draped the sweater she had taken off earlier around her shoulders again, and fastened some buttons to hide the fact that she was wearing her arm in a sling.Merv now came back from the road and Jessica was pointing in Julie's direction.

"Look over there on that slope, I am sure the sound came from there."

To Julie's horror, Olson walked toward the cliff, crossed the creek by stepping on some large rocks and then she heard him coming up the small path leading up to the ledge. Julie knew there was no way she could outrun him. She had to play the encounter cool and behave as innocently as possible. After all, Olson made a much more civilized impression than Gibson. If he would respond halfway decently, perhaps she could keep him talking until Thomas would be back. She pulled Peterson's bird book from the rucksack and was now sitting there, reading. The binoculars were at her side–she was posing as a bird watcher.

Olson's footsteps came closer, and soon he had reached the top of the cliff from where he could see her easily. Her heart was pounding like crazy, she was very scared, but pretended to be reading, and not paying any attention to him.

"Hey, what are you doing there, snooping around?" He yelled at her when he had reached the level area, looking up to her.

Julie tried to hide the fear in her voice and to make it sound as if she was completely surprised by his presence, "Gee, I didn't hear you coming. What do you mean, snooping around? I could ask you the same question. This is my neighbor's property here and I am doing some bird watching. Are you lost, where did you come from?" She managed to make her voice sound as loud and firm as possible, in order to impress Olson, but also to warn Thomas in case should he be on his way back. Olson stepped closer and looked her up and down.

"Are you here by yourself?"

"I don't see anybody else around, do you?" Julie snapped, hoping her response would make him less alert to watch out for another person.

"Are you that heiress who owns the big ranch over there?"

Julie figured that he had learned this from Gibson. That guy really had snooped around. She shuddered, the thought of Gibson entering the house, going through the Carters' and her belongings, was repulsive.

"It's my ranch, yes. Are you from Madrone Flat? How did you get here? Are you on a hike and got lost?" She tried to make her voice sound as natural as possible, but his reply told her that it didn't help, he didn't care.

"You must be pretty stupid if you don't know what I am doing here," Olson said, pointing towards the valley floor, "and I don't like people poking around, spoiling my plans. You know what happens to people that are too curious, don't you? I am afraid you will have to share your friend's fate. I am not willing to jeopardize this gold mine down there."

Julie realized that she could not expect any pity from him. She was as much a danger to him as the Carters most likely had been to Gibson. Her only hope was that Thomas would come back soon and rescue her, she must try to keep Olson talking as long as possible. If he didn't have a gun, Thomas had a chance to get him under control.

While this went through her mind, she noticed a man's figure emerging from above the path Olson had just come up. For a second, she thought it was Thomas. But in a flash, her feeling of relief was gone and changed to naked fear, when she recognized Andy. So, he was after all one of them and had come to help Olson. Julie's heart sank. Even if Thomas came back in time, one against two tipped the balance in their favor.

Olson apparently noticed the alarm on her face as she looked beyond him. He quickly turned around to see what had caught her attention. To Julie's utmost surprise, Andy had picked up a downed, good-size tree limb and approached Olson in a threatening manner.

"Leave her alone, will you? You are frightening her, go back to where you came from. You are trespassing, this is her property."

Olson just stared at him. He looked back at Julie, apparently at a loss what to do. Julie expected him any minute to pull out a gun, she was terribly worried. When he didn't move, Andy came closer.

"Didn't you hear what I said? Get lost, we don't want your kind around here, "Andy ordered him to leave. Olson still didn't move, he looked like being in a trance, but when his right hand moved toward his pocket, Andy acted. He dropped the stick and furiously attacked Olson with his fists, delivering a heavy blow against his right shoulder. As Olson tried to gather his strength to defend himself, another unexpected painful stroke hit his left shoulder. Olson was taller and heavier than Andy, but Andy was extremely agile and also in better physical shape. Most of Olson's strikes ended up in the air, with Andy slipping away at the critical moments. Julie could tell that Olson was hurting, he became slower and slightly disoriented. He did not seem to realize that he was moving closer and closer to the edge of the cliff as he was retreating, trying to get away from Andy's nonstop pounding. Julie's sympathies were certainly not with Olson in this fight. Yet, when he received another severe blow and again stepped backwards, she instinctively cried out in alarm to warn him. She was too late. He stumbled, tried to pitch forward, didn't make it and his next step ended up in space. They heard crashing and cracking sounds, a dull thud, and then there was silence.

Julie felt like waking up from a terrible nightmare. Just a few minutes ago, Olson had been standing here, inflicting terror on her. Now the place was empty, he was gone, as if wiped out by a higher force. She stood up slowly, as Andy was coming closer, wiping blood off his chin where Olson's fingernails had left a deep scratch. For a few seconds, they both stared silently towards the edge where Olson had disappeared.

"I am sorry that I scared you when I came up so suddenly. I saw the look on your face, Julie, you must have thought I was the devil. I just felt I had to do something when I heard him threatening you. But, I didn't mean this to happen. I saw his hand moving toward his pocket and was afraid he might have a gun."

"I also thought he was reaching for his gun, just like the guy at the bridge. You acted in self-defense, Andy, and probably saved my life. I don't know what would have happened if you had not come. I was terribly frightened." Julie said, handing him a Kleenex to stop the bleeding.

A high-pitched scream brought them back to reality.

"Merv, Merv, what happened? Oh Merv, they killed you." They heard a woman sobbing.

Julie looked miserable, listening to her crying, "His girlfriend, she is down there," she explained. Andy reacted fast.

"I better go down and see if I can help."

"I'll come too, I just can't move very fast because I have injured my arm," Julie promised.

Andy ran down the path and Julie heard Jessica screaming at him when he approached her. Eventually, her screams became fewer and fewer, and then Julie heard them talking to each other quietly. She took off her sweater and put it in the rucksack, together with the binoculars and the bird book, when she heard some rustling of leaves behind her. Thomas had come back.

"Have they left already?" he whispered.

Hurriedly, Julie told him what had happened. Thomas was shocked when he heard her story and relieved that she was all right.

"Andy probably saved your life. And he is down there now?" Thomas asked

Julie nodded, "He ran down when Jessica started to scream. I just wanted to go down there too. I am glad that you are here now, it will be easier and safer with your help."

"It would be better if you stayed here, Julie. This path is rather steep and rocky. Besides, you have to climb up again later."

But Julie was stubborn. With Thomas' help she negotiated the difficult spots, and they made it to the valley floor.

Olson was alive, but unconscious. Except for some bad scratches and bruises, there were no noticeable signs of injury, but he definitely needed medical attention as fast as possible. Before hitting the ground, he had fallen on some dense manzanita bushes which probably had saved his life.

Andy was surprised when he saw Julie coming down with Thomas. However, there was no time for introductions. Thomas acknowledged Andy with only a brief and–he couldn't help himself–not very friendly nod.

Jessica didn't look up at all. Thomas had to ask twice before she answered monotonously, while keeping her eyes focused on Olson.

"Where is your car?" Thomas asked Jessica.

"Down there," she pointed vaguely to the entrance of the valley from where they had come.

"You have the keys?" Thomas asked.

"He has them in his pocket," Jessica said.

Thomas gently pulled the keys out of Olson's pants.

"I am going down to your car and drive to Madrone Flat to get the ambulance. Do you happen to have a car phone?"

Jessica nodded.

"OK, I'll try to use it, but if it doesn't work I have to drive to the village. If he should regain consciousness, don't give him anything to drink and keep him as quiet as possible. I'll be back as soon as I can."

Thomas left, and within a few minutes they heard the engine starting up and the car driving down to the main road. Jessica didn't move, she was sitting next to Olson like a statue. She was holding his hand and petting his cheeks from time to time, sobbing off and on, while tears flowed down her cheeks. In spite of the heartache these people had brought upon her, Julie felt great pity for Jessica. In her present state, she was the opposite of the woman Thomas had encountered in her home in Medford. She looked very young and vulnerable and deeply in love with this man who got himself and her into serious trouble now.

All of a sudden, Jessica started to speak.

"I wish we hadn't come down here, to California I mean. I knew something would happen," Jessica whined. "And you killed him if he dies," she said, pointing her finger at Andy.

"Your husband threatened me, and my friend here just helped me. Your husband stumbled and fell down the cliff, nobody pushed him. It was an accident," Julie explained to her.

"But you were snooping around, that's why it happened," Jessica accused Julie.

Julie didn't respond to this accusation. After all, what could she say? She had been snooping, Jessica was right. But would Jessica admit that Olson had brought this upon himself? Not very likely. On the other hand, Thomas' and Julie's snooping was done in defense against the criminal acts committed by Gibson and Olson.

All three stayed silent. After a while, Andy told Julie that he wanted to show her something. He walked with her toward the entrance of the valley.

"I just wanted to talk to you, without her listening. Who are these people, anyway? I heard him threatening you and realized that you needed help. By the way, he did not carry a gun. I was too hasty in my judgment when I saw him moving his hand toward the pocket. Are they connected with the guy who drowned?"

"Yes, they came to take over the plantation. Don't you know them? I thought you had worked closely together with Gibson?"

Andy shook his head, "I'll tell you the details later, but I can assure you that I was only very superficially involved in this project. Did you hurt your arm when you went down that slope near the bridge?"

Julie nodded, "It's fractured, I also injured my leg, but this has healed already fairly well."

"I am very sorry, Julie, I really am," Andy said, shaking his head, "I don't know why I did such a stupid thing like working with that guy. I'll tell you everything later. But now I would like to leave here before the ambulance comes, in case they remember me from the accident at the river. My car is parked about halfway up your road, I can reach it by walking along the slope there." He was gesturing towards the hill where Julie and Thomas had come down from. "You can be sure, I will not run again, instead, I will wait at the ranch until you are back and then tell you my version of what happened. So as soon as we hear the car coming I would like to leave."

"Why did you come back, Andy? After you disappeared, we all suspected you to be a partner in this." Julie pointed toward the marijuana plants.

"I know, and I don't blame you. It was very stupid of me to run away. Finally, I realized that I had to come back and talk to Emily and Bret. After all, they know me well and probably would vouch for me."

"But don't you know that the Carters are missing? Didn't I tell you that day when you gave me the fateful ride to the bridge?" Julie asked.

"Disappeared? Emily and Bret? What do you mean?" Andy looked very unhappy when he realized that the Carters had not returned and could not help him. And he looked even worse when Julie finally told him the whole story.

"That's terrible, Julie, I had no idea."

As they were walking back, Julie assured him that it would be all right with her if he would leave before the ambulance came. She hoped that she could trust him now.

Olson was still unconscious, nothing had changed. He moaned once in a while, and Jessica would gently stroke his hand, sobbing quietly. Finally they heard a car coming. Andy got up, climbed the path to the top of the cliff and had just vanished from sight, when Thomas arrived. He announced that help for Olson would be here in a few minutes, and indeed they heard another car coming already. A few minutes later two men, carrying a stretcher, appeared at the entrance to the valley where Thomas was meeting them. Their eyes went wide as they saw the sea of medium size marijuana plants swaying in a gentle breeze.

"I guess I could retire on that!" one of the guys said to Thomas, "your stuff?"

"Do you really believe I would have called you if that were the case? The guy who got injured is responsible for this operation. He is lying over there."

They checked him out before lifting him. One of the two men was a paramedic. He frowned when he checked Olson's pulse.

"He needs help soon but I think we will make it to the hospital in time. You are coming too, Miss?"

Jessica nodded and trotted along as they were carrying Olson out.

"Wow, what a mess. I didn't wish him anything good, but now I sure feel sorry for both of them. All of a sudden, their dreams have crumbled. Where is Andy?" Thomas asked and looked skeptical when Julie told him. "Well I guess you couldn't have held him anyway. For his sake, I hope he is at the ranch when we come back.

Here is my suggestion, Julie. Instead of climbing up the slope and walking to the car, why don't we take the easy way out, walk down to the bridge where I left Olson's Buick and use it to drive back to the ranch? Jessica doesn't need it, she is going with Olson to Garberville and I still have the car keys."

"That's a good idea, Thomas. I am still shaky from the confrontation with Olson. Oh, Thomas, I wish I had listened to Bonnie this morning. Why was I so foolish to come along. I was endangering your life, too."

Thomas smiled and instead of an answer took her into his arms and kissed her. "I am glad you came along, Julie. Although, to tell you the truth, I agree, you should have stayed at the ranch, Bonnie was right. But I was so happy that you wanted to come with me and so I didn't interfere. I knew it was risky, yet I was prepared to carry you down the slope if I had to," he grinned. "Well, you weren't quite that helpless. Nevertheless, we were a little irresponsible. Fortunately, you didn't get hurt, and I didn't lose my chance to tell you that I love you. I just hope we will be more careful in the future." He kissed her again and Julie put her good arm around his neck and told him that she had loved him ever since she had met him at the train in Willits. They stood there in this blissful state for what seemed to be an eternity.

"I guess we have to come back to earth. Hopefully, the others by now have heard from Andy what happened and are waiting for us, Thomas," Julie said, and they started to walk down to the bridge.

Arriving at the ranch, Julie sighed with relief when she saw Andy's car parked in front of the house. They were all outside on the deck. The table was set for lunch and when Thomas and Julie came, Bonnie rushed into the kitchen to bring out the food. Andy had already told them what had happened and Julie and Thomas added the last part. Julie told them the story about her rescue and highly praised Andy for his brave interference. Thomas added that besides calling for the ambulance he had also called the sheriff, and Stenton had promised him to call Charles Kendar as soon as he had anything important to report concerning Olson.

During lunch, Andy explained why he had run away on Tuesday.

"What I did these last few months was the most foolish thing in my life. My father has been very sick for over a year. He is over the worst now, but his illness has swallowed all his savings and in addition my parents had to mortgage the house to the hilt. I finished college last year and tried to get an outside job instead of helping my mother run the nursery. My parents grow cut flowers in Florida, you know. Anyway, my uncle, who owns a small lumber mill in Eureka, offered me a well-paying job for the summer. So I came out here in February and did a lot of work on their cabin, about one mile north of the Kendar ranch."

Kim and Thomas looked at each other and smiled, because this was just opposite of the place where Andy had told Ben Wilson from the Fire Department to drop him off.

Andy continued, "My uncle paid me well for the work and in addition I worked for the Carters and some people in Garberville. I like the Carters a lot and was terribly shocked when Julie just told me they are missing. And apparently, Gibson and this Olson guy have something to do with their disappearance? When I heard Olson saying that Julie would have to face the same fate as her friends, I had no idea how serious this threat was. And I didn't know that with 'her friends' he meant the Carters.

"Anyway, one day in early March I met Gibson on the road when he was stuck in the mud, and helped him to get his car out. We had a beer together and I guess I told him a little about my parent's financial problems. That's when he offered me five percent of the profit of the marijuana crop if I would water or fertilize them every evening. He told me they were worth one million dollars."

Andy grinned, "I never have been in this line of work before, so I don't know the prices. After I counted them, I figured that he was probably right."

"I'm afraid he minimized the value–they are worth several millions, Andy." Julie interrupted him.

Andy shrugged, "I'm not surprised. Anyway, together with these other gardening jobs it looked like a very lucrative summer. Most likely, I would come out with a much higher profit than in my uncle's saw mill and a nice tidy sum to come home with. Gibson instructed me to keep a very low profile. In case the operation went sour and the plants were raided, we should be able to slip away unnoticed. How right he was!

"The morning you slid down the slope above the plantation, Julie, Gibson had seen you and worried that you might report the plants. He came over to my house and asked me to talk to you and find out if it really had been you and if you had seen the stuff. I had no idea Gibson would be waiting for me at the bridge when I gave you the ride. When I met him and told him that you wouldn't tell anybody, he didn't trust you. He wanted me to take you back to his cabin, supposedly to talk to you. Did you see that he threatened me with a gun?"

"Yes, that was awful and I knew then I had to get away," Julie said with a small voice, recalling this terrible situation.

"I felt the same," Andy said. "When I walked back to the car, my mind was racing. How could we get away from him? I was afraid he might kill you–and me too. I had never seen him in such a rage before. I had noticed that you had turned off the engine to my car and must have heard what was going on. After I had passed the bridge, I decided to go back to him, stalling him. I would tell him of some problem I supposedly had encountered with the pump the night before. This would give you a chance to get away because we both could not see you from where he had parked his car.

"First, he exploded when he saw me coming back, but I made the problem with the pump so real that he listened. He started to worry, asked questions and was not quite as edgy, rather concerned that the watering might be jeopardized. I tried to talk as long as I could, when all of a sudden he lost his patience. He screamed at me, ordered me back to the car, pushing me hard that I almost fell. Fortunately you were gone, Julie. I could tell where you had broken through the brush."

"That's exactly how I finally found Julie!" Kim exclaimed, putting her arm around her.

"And you called my name, didn't you, Andy?" Julie asked.

"Yes, I did, and I was glad you didn't answer, I pictured you either hiding somewhere down there or still running away," Andy responded.

"Didn't it occur to you at all that she might be lying down there, badly injured, in need of immediate help?" Thomas asked angrily.

"Yes, I admit it did when I saw how steep it was. But look, I didn't have a choice. Any moment I expected Gibson to be there and I figured

Julie was safer with a broken leg down there than back at Gibson's cabin! Besides, as soon as I had put enough distance between me and Madrone Flat, I called the fire chief to let him know where she was."

"I know you did," Thomas said icily. "But that was long after we had found her."

"I am very sorry, I really am," Andy said remorsefully.

Kim wanted to know what happened when Gibson finally caught up with him?

"Just a few minutes after I had come back and had called Julie's name, he came racing after me in his car. He jumped out and shouted four-letter words at me when he saw that she was gone. I was afraid he would shoot me any second–he was completely out of control. When he looked around, he also noticed the spot where Julie had plunged through the hedge. One look down the slope, and he saw that it was hopeless and too dangerous to search for Julie . He made a very nasty remark concerning the chance of Julie's survival and ordered me into his car. Then he tried to turn around on the narrow road. Swearing and screaming, carelessly hitting my truck, causing a bad dent in the left rear fender, he finally made it and careened off, toward Madrone Flat.

"He was absolutely out of his mind and determined to get away as fast as possible, because he figured that Julie would call the sheriff as soon as she reached the village. So he drove like a madman and ended up in the river. When I came out of the water, I also had only one thought–to get away. I was so scared about being considered an accomplice in the dope planting, and when I heard that the sheriff was coming, I panicked." Andy's voice had become quieter and quieter. Nobody spoke for a few seconds.

"You certainly fooled Ben. Why did you come back now?" Thomas couldn't help the indignation in his voice.

"I had been hiding out and when the panic wore off I realized that I had to face the music, otherwise my life would be destroyed forever. I decided to go back and talk to the Carters. They had been satisfied with my work and probably would be willing to help me. Of course, I was afraid how Julie would react. After all, she had seen and heard what kind of company I kept, but I saw no other choice.

When I drove up the road to the ranch, I got the idea to stop halfway and walk over to the hidden valley to find out if the plants were still there. You probably believe that I wanted to continue growing them. I swear, that was the last thing on my mind, it was idle curiosity that made me walk over there and I just happened to be there at the right time to help Julie.

"So far, I have never had any trouble with the law. But when that guy offered me the opportunity to make a lot of money by watering the plants all summer, I guess I closed my eyes and didn't want to see the criminal side of it. The though of presenting my parents with a check of perhaps up to fifty thousand dollars by the end of the summer was overwhelming, I just couldn't resist. As I said, I was very foolish and naive and the question is, how can I get out of this mess?"

"Quite a story, Andy. I think you need a good lawyer," Julie looked at Thomas, her eyes pleading for his help.

"Yeah, that probably would be a good idea. But I don't know anybody around here and besides I hate to spend my money on lawyers while my parents need it so desperately."

"I know a good lawyer who might help you for free if we beg him, he is sitting right next to you," Julie said, smiling at Thomas.

Andy looked at Thomas, whose anger was melting. "Really?"

"Yes. I'll try to get you out of this without needing an outside lawyer, Andy, and I hope you are worth our concern. Since I arrived last Tuesday, I have been involved in looking into the disappearance of the Carters and have also established a good relationship with the local deputy sheriff. We know quite a bit by now, especially how Gibson and that Olson guy were linked. You might have some more important information we could need. Do you remember when the Carters left?" Thomas asked.

"I don't know the exact day, but could probably get fairly close if I look at my calendar. Actually, I had not seen them long before they went on this trip. Let me see, I might pin down the date more or less."

He pulled out a small pocket calendar and leafed through it.

"OK, I was there at the end of March when we had done some vegetable planting. Bret wanted to start a new asparagus bed and had planned to get the plants on his next trip to Garberville. He asked me to cultivate the area where the bed was to go. Next time when I came back, he would have the plants. I went back the next week, yes, that was the sixth of April, and they were not home. Nobody was home on the eighth–I couldn't make it on the seventh. I had left a note each time I went there and on the tenth, I found a letter attached to my gate saying that they were sorry they had missed me. Bret had forgotten the asparagus plants, could I bring them along next time I was in Garberville. They had included one hundred dollars. After that, we always seemed to miss each other. They left notes or money, and eventually they had no more jobs for me. And then finally, they told me, also in a note, that they were going to Washington, could I do some watering until they would be back. After that, I received a picture post card from them and that was the last I ever heard."

"This is interesting what you told us. By the way, how often did you meet Gibson and talk with him, you know, just chatting? And could it be possible that you made remarks about the Carters, that you had missed them, or that they had forgotten the plants, and so on?"

Andy paled, all of a sudden it seemed to dawn on him what Thomas was suspecting.

"Oh my God, that's awful. I see what you mean. Yes, we did talk sometimes. Once in a while, he would come in the evening when I was watering the plants, checking up on me, I guess. And I might have made little remarks, talking about my jobs, including the Carters." Andy was devastated. "Don't you have any clue where the Carters could be or what could have happened?" Looking at all the faces around him, he saw the answer, there was very little hope left in their eyes.

They all sat silent for a while until Thomas broke the spell and addressed Andy. "Did Gibson ever mention that he was working together with the people in Oregon?"

"No," Andy replied. "Although, I had the feeling that he was getting orders from others and this action was not his own thing. He made vague remarks that he needed more money for fertilizer, and that 'they' were kind of tight."

"What about any names–Merv Olsen, Jessica or Milt Undell, who is the owner of Olsens' car dealership in Medford? Did you ever hear those names?"

Andy shook his head. "Sorry, but I never heard him mentioning these or any other names."

"We will have a breakthrough soon. Even if Olson is still unconscious, Jessica might talk. Stenton promised to call Charles as soon as he had any information. However I should call him later this afternoon anyway and ask if we can see him. Are you ready to go along, Andy?"

The answer came promptly, yes, the sooner the better, he wanted to get this burden off his shoulders.

"I'll stay around for a while, doing some work in the garden. Paying for my lunch, you know. So any time you are ready to leave, I'll come along, Thomas."

CHAPTER 20

After lunch, Andy went down to the basement and got out the garden tools. He was busy at work in the garden when Bonnie joined him.

Ralph and Thomas had returned the Olsons' car to Rosy's B and B in Madrone Flat and just came back in the Cadillac. Nick was waiting for them down at the river where he had taken the Carters' kayak.

Julie was lying down, the morning's distressing events had sapped her energy. After Kim had cleaned up the kitchen, she came out to the deck to see if Julie was all right.

"Before I get busy helping Andy and Bonnie in the garden, I just wanted to check up on you. Are you OK?"

"Sure, I feel fine, I am just a little tired. I'll come out to the garden in a while."

"Don't overdo it. It's not even a week since you had the accident, Julie." Kim left and walked down a few steps, but turned around and came up to the deck again. Hesitantly, she sat down at the end of the lounge chair. Julie could tell that she had something on her mind, yet, was reluctant to mention it.

"What is bugging you, Kim? Tell me, I know you can't keep it much longer to yourself. I hope it is nothing unpleasant?"

Kim grinned, "No, it's just the opposite, very exciting. I have the feeling that Thomas told you this morning that he loves you, didn't he?"

Julie blushed and looked at her friend in amazement. "How did you know? You weren't there? Or did you hide in the bushes?" she joked.

"Because you and Thomas looked so radiant when you came back from the hidden valley. You almost had an aura of happiness around you in spite of the frightening confrontation with Olson and his tragic accident. I wish you luck, Julie. Thomas is a wonderful person." She kissed Julie on the cheek and left.

Although Julie had done some weeding previously, the garden needed a lot more work. Now, with three people pulling weeds and cultivating, they could do a thorough job. Julie joined them a little later and picked raspberries, blueberries, and some vegetables. Around four o'clock, after Bonnie had dumped another five gallon bucket of weeds on the compost pile, she declared it was time to quit.

"After all, it's Sunday! As much as I love gardening, we should relax now. Let's go down to the river for a swim. Are you all coming along?"

Kim and Andy followed Bonnie's suggestion and walked with her down the hill. Julie carried the vegetables and berries to the kitchen and then lay down again on the deck.

Buttercup had followed her and was stretched out across her ankles now. Julie was tired and the pleasant heat and the humming of insects lulled her into sleep. She was just about to doze off, when she heard footsteps coming up the road from the river. Someone walked quietly up the stairs to the deck, it was Thomas.

Slowly, he came closer. "I hope I didn't wake you up? You look tired."

Julie assured him that she had not been sleeping yet. Thomas kneeled down on the floor next to Julie's lounge. He gently stroked her hair and then leaned over and kissed her.

Julie put her arm around him and smiled, "I hoped you would come," she whispered.

Buttercup had been sleeping, lying on his side, in complete relaxation, all four legs stretched out as only cats can manage. He woke up when he heard Thomas coming and slowly raised his head, carefully watching him as he bent down to Julie. Unhurried, Buttercup rose, and paw by paw, inched closer to where the action was. When he reached Julie's shoulder and sensed that Julie was in a good mood, in fact, in a very good mood, he curled up right there, purring contentedly with a smug expression on his furry face.

Startled by the sound, Thomas straightened up, saw the cat and laughed, " I thought it was you, Julie, purring away."

Julie petted the cat and smiled mischievously, "I do feel like purring when you kiss me, but I am afraid it was Buttercup this time. Poor Buttercup, he really is missing his people. He behaves like a dog, follows me everywhere, wrapping himself around my ankles. When I went into the garden, he came along and then again he followed me here. What will I do with him if Emily and Bret never come back? Would he survive in a small apartment in Berkeley?"

"You could seriously consider getting that teaching job at the local school and stay at the ranch, Julie. And I would come up every weekend by train to visit you. It's not that far from Santa Rosa and a pleasant trip. I could take my laptop along and get a lot of work done on the train."

Julie kept petting Buttercup, a dreamy expression on her face. "That would be lovely, Thomas. The idea of staying here has grown with me since I first thought about it. After New York, just a year of this would be marvelous."

Thomas sat down in a chair next to Julie. "It's a promise, Julie! You can count on my company every weekend, I love the house and its owner. But, getting back to Andy, I am glad that he did come to the ranch and waited for us, and that you were right about him. I hope I can get him out of this mess that he made for himself, he seems to be a decent guy after all. Sorry I was so angry with him…"

"I am glad that he came back–and of course, just when he was needed. Nevertheless, I shouldn't have gone with you this morning. By being so helpless, I endangered you and the whole project. Under normal conditions, I would have quickly scrambled up the hill when I noticed that Olson was going to climb up the path. And I am sure I would have outrun him."

"If you had not given Andy the chance to defend you against Olson, Julie, we might never have believed him. Too bad, that Olson was seriously hurt in the process, yet he has himself to blame, after all.

We probably should be leaving for the Kendars as soon as they all come back from the river."

After a while, Julie decided it was time to get back into the house and to see about dinner. She poured two glasses of homemade apple juice and they sat down at the kitchen table, Thomas shelled the peas and Julie hulled the strawberries.

"You two look like an advertising for a fruit and vegetable seed catalogue!" Kim exclaimed when she came in, almost dripping wet. She had gone swimming in her shorts. "We had fun while you were working, or did you have some fun too?" she joked. "The water was great, but I guess I have to change, I feel kind of cold in my wet stuff."

She went upstairs to put on dry clothes. Eventually, everybody was back. When Andy came into the kitchen, Thomas mentioned to him that they should go and call the sheriff from the Kendars now.

He was finishing his juice, and getting up, when Julie said, "You don't have to leave, Thomas. The sheriff is already coming." She pointed up the hill where the sheriff's car was coming down the road. Thomas went outside to greet him. They came back into the kitchen, and everybody was anxious to hear how Olson was doing.

"You lucked out again, Ms. Sutten, Olson did not. He is in serious condition, they just made it to the hospital in time. I will tell you all about it, but would like to talk to Andy first. Is he here with you?" Stenton asked Thomas, who confirmed it with a nod.

"Good, could I talk to him privately, in another room, I mean?"

Julie suggested the study. When Thomas introduced Andy to the sheriff and wanted to go along, Stenton said he preferred to be alone with him.

Thomas smiled at Julie, "I will act as his lawyer, Calvin, then, can I come along?"

Stenton was surprised, but agreed and the three went into the study.

Kim, Julie and Bonnie got busy with getting dinner ready. While cleaning, washing and chopping vegetables, they speculated how Andy would come out of this. After at least three quarter of an hour, Stenton, Thomas and Andy came back. One could tell from Andy's and Thomas' faces that things must have gone all right. By now, dinner was ready. They invited Sheriff Stenton to stay and eat with them.

He was reluctant, "Okay, but I will have only a small portion. It's my wife's birthday and I promised to be home by eight. I'll make it if I keep this short. I'll tell you quickly over dinner what happened to Olson, if you don't mind.

After everybody was seated and served, Stenton gave his report.

"Olson has internal injuries and a severe concussion. The doctor hopes that he will pull through. Although, when he wakes up and realizes that he lost all the dope, he'll probably wish he were dead. All his dreams vanished. It can be days before he regains consciousness or is clear enough to talk."

"What about his girlfriend?" Bonnie asked.

"Well, at first she wouldn't talk at all. She was so distraught about what happened that she cried or sobbed most of the time and wouldn't even answer. I finally made it clear to her that I had enough reason to arrest her. If she were willing to help us find out what had happened to the Carters, we could strike a bargain. Eventually, she was cooperative and I know a lot more now, but it still does not help us much further. She admitted that Olson was not at home last Saturday around the time the call was made from the pay phone at the hospital to the Highway Patrol. And she also remembers that earlier that day Gibson had called Olson at home. She does not know the details–or pretends she doesn't–although she believes it had to do with the Carters.

"Jessica knows all about Gibson's dope plantation down here. When Gibson left their place in late February, he first went to Santa Rosa and picked up the marijuana seedlings. They got several calls from him that everything went well until early April when he told Olson that he had run into trouble with the Carters. Olson was not home when Gibson called and she told him to try the office in town. She claims that Olson never gave her details. He just mentioned to her that Gibson had run into some problems and that he–Olson–had reported the incident to the to 'big boss', and that was it, it was not his responsibility any longer."

Bonnie and Julie looked desperate when they heard this, it could mean the worst and would they ever find out?

"When Olson called the so-called boss, didn't she get any indication of what could be in store for the Carters?" Ralph asked Stenton.

"She said that Olson never talked to the boss in their house. He would call a number and leave a message. Then the boss would call him back, and Olson would leave, and call the boss from a pay phone. She never overheard a conversation," Stenton answered.

"This sounds as if we are dealing not just with a few people but a well-organized gang. They have really thought of all the angles. I guess Gibson was in the lowest ranks, Olson a little higher, and who knows how many steps his boss is still away from the real boss," Thomas said in frustration.

"I know," Stenton agreed. "We probably have only scratched the surface. When I had looked through Olson's wallet earlier, I couldn't find any phone numbers or addresses. After I had finally been able to get some information from Jessica, I persuaded her to let me look through Olson's belongings at Rosy's B and B in Madrone Flat. She agreed to do that–I could have gotten a search order had she refused–and so I drove her back. Olson's address book was in his suitcase and I will check out some of the numbers later from my office. I called one number in Seattle, with only a big 'B' in front. It turned out to be one of those message centers. This could be the number Jessica mentioned. So far, I couldn't reach a supervisor at this place. Tomorrow I will try again, although I doubt that this will get us anywhere. Of course, the owner of the used car lot which Olson manages, also lives in Seattle, there could be a connection ...." Stenton finished.

"What about the possibility of letting Jessica call this number and report to the 'big boss' what has happened to Gibson and Olson? She could give him a number where she could be reached and you could put a tap on it, thereby finding out the number he calls from?" Ralph suggested.

"I have considered this, yet I am afraid this guy will most likely also call from a pay phone which would not help us much. Besides, Julie heard Olson saying–when he was working on the pump–that he had not called the 'big boss' yet, right?" Stenton said and Julie nodded in agreement. "If the boss indeed is not informed yet, we might save this piece of information–it could come in handy. I am sure Jessica will not call him on her own.

"I will talk to the Seattle PD about it tomorrow. I'll also call your friend Weaverly in Medford, Thomas, and get more background information about Undell, the owner of the car lot."

"Did you find out whether Olson has a criminal record, Calvin?" Thomas asked.

"It all came out negative. The guy is either new in this line of work or very careful and I think the latter is the case. Jessica told me that they lived in New Orleans until last year and that all of a sudden Olson got this job in Medford and they had to leave in a rush to get there. He probably got into trouble down there and the boss transferred him to

Medford. Olson had been the manager of a night club. Perhaps there were drugs involved. Have to check with the New Orleans PD to find out if there was a problem with any of these places around that time.

"Jessica is only twenty-one. She grew up in a very strict Christian Fundamentalist family, her father is a preacher. Jessica never liked her life and ran away from home right after high school. Trying to get a modeling job in St. Louis, she met Olson. He got her a job as a hostess in a nightclub where he worked as an assistant barkeeper. They fell for each other and when Olson got a new position in New Orleans, she went with him. I guess this is where she started to wear those fancy outfits you have seen her in, Thomas. But this doesn't get us closer to the truth about the Carters. If Olson dies, we might never find out. You remember, I told you to be careful about your surveillance up in the canyon and not to lose it?" Stenton looked reproachful at Thomas and Julie.

Julie looked unhappy when she responded. "What happened was not Thomas' fault at all. I admit, I shouldn't have gone along, that was foolish of me. Without my injuries, I would have been able to get up the hill fast and Olson might not have seen me. Somehow, I felt really well this morning and wanted to do my part finding Emily and Bret. And we were very careful, but anyone can get the urge to sneeze. Of course, I regret that this man was hurt so badly, but it was caused by his own actions. Andy and I heard him clearly when he threatened me, saying that I would face the same fate as my friends. And when he tried to reach into his pocket, we both thought he had a gun, and that's when Andy attacked him."

Stenton sighed, "I guess it's the cop in me who dislikes the involvement of lay people who are trying to solve a crime. Although I do admit that all of you have been very helpful.

"Having read the Carters' books to my boy, I almost feel as if I know them personally and their fate concerns me deeply. It is depressing. In spite of what we know now, we are still stumped."

Thomas looked at his notes, "I suggest that we should focus on Seattle, specifically Undell. This is the only name we know for sure at this point, right?"

"Yes, your friend Dean gave me the name and the address. But where does that get us?" Stenton replied.

"You remember, when you called the owner of the cabin back here, where Gibson lived? He told you that someone from Seattle had leased the property for the summer. You had called the number he had given to you and it was disconnected."

Stenton rubbed his nose. "Yes, I should look into that more closely, just haven't had the time. I meant to call the Seattle PD and find out who was the person behind that phone number–would it be the same name the owner of the cabin property had given me? I'll look into it again tomorrow. You're right, Seattle could hold the key. I also will try to find out more about the owner of the Medford property."

"What about flying up there and talking to him? You might catch him by surprise." Ralph suggested, "if your department is short of funds, I'd be happy to pay for the trip, if that's possible."

Right away, Bonnie joined Ralph in offering financial help.

"Well, thank you for your offer. I have to talk to my boss and see if we can accept your assistance in this matter. However, I have to get a few more facts. It will be my first task tomorrow morning when I get to the office. Usually, I start around seven o'clock, don't know if the other departments are in so early too. Try to call me back by midmorning. If I have anything earlier, I'll leave word with Charles Kendar."

He looked at his watch, "I'd better leave, it's getting late. I have to stop in Madrone Flat and pick up Jessica to take her back to Garberville. Can you believe this, she doesn't know how to drive?"

Andy also had to leave. As they watched the two cars climbing up the road, Bonnie sighed. "It's a tough job being a policeman and often not appreciated by the public. That's the first time in my life I have gotten involved with the police in such a close, personal manner. I like Calvin Stenton, he really tries hard to find out what happened. He also accepts our help and lets us work with him, even if he was a little disgruntled today. Yet he relented, and that is important. One often hears that the police are secretive and don't allow any participation." Thomas nodded, "I agree, Bonnie. I like Calvin, too, he is intelligent, tolerant and dedicated to his job, the kind of person we need in law enforcement."

CHAPTER 21

Monday morning, right after nine o'clock, Ralph, Julie and Thomas drove to the Kendar ranch. Charles was alone, his wife and grandfather had left early for a doctor's appointment in Willits. The old man had insisted taking the train. This would be his first trip since the passenger service had been reintroduced. His rehabilitation was going well, he managed to walk a few steps without assistance, and he had been looking forward to the train ride.

Deputy sheriff Stenton had not called yet. Charles was anxious to hear about Olson and very disappointed that no new leads had come up. They talked for a while halfheartedly about the possible steps that could be taken now, hoping that the sheriff's call might bring some better news. It was just about ten o'clock when Stenton called. Thomas talked to him for at least ten minutes. The others listened intently for signs of progress, but by the time he put down the receiver, they could tell that things were as hopeless as before.

Thomas' voice revealed the strain of disappointment when he spoke. "Calvin is trying to set up a meeting with Undell, who lives in Seattle. This is about the only chance we have left, short of Olson telling us the whole story. His condition has improved, but it still could be days before he talks, and according to Jessica, he really does not know what happened to Emily and Bret.

"Calvin checked out the various phone numbers this morning, the three we know of that are connected to the case. Number one supposedly was a Mr. Lancer's number. He is the person who leased Gibson's cabin from Mr. Mellet, the owner, who lives in Los Angeles. We know already that this number is disconnected. About an hour ago, Calvin talked with someone from the Seattle PD, and they were right on the ball, within minutes they had the address under which this disconnected number had been listed. Being a rental property, they contacted the owner and found out that a Mr. Lancer had lived at this address for four weeks only and moved without leaving an address. So much for that.

"Telephone number two is the one Calvin found in Olson's address book under 'B'–which could mean 'big boss–and he got a message center when he called. This morning, he reached the supervisor for the center and got a Post Office Box address and a name. His Seattle connection got one step further, finding a real address. But, they have not had a chance to check this address out.

"Telephone number three is intriguing and turned out to be a masterpiece of deception. Mr. Lancer, the person who leased Gibson's cabin, had sent a letter of reference from a Seattle bank to Mr. Mellet before the lease contract for the property was confirmed. Mr. Mellet faxed this letter to Calvin today. When Calvin called the number on the letterhead, hoping he finally had a real lead, the number was also disconnected. From Information, he got the bank's current phone number and found out to his dismay that they never had a Mr. Lancer as a customer. Their real telephone number on their letterhead had been replaced by this fake number. He later learned from his contact in Seattle that the number had also been active for four weeks only during the time when the lease for the property had been negotiated. Seattle found the physical address to this phone number and it happens to be the same one as number one, which of course makes sense.

"I am afraid, we are dealing with some very clever people here, who are experts in covering their tracks.

"Getting back to a possible appointment with Mr. Undell, this is a touchy subject. This man is extremely wealthy and well connected. He sits on the boards of several corporations and institutions. At the moment, he is in town and available. The question is whether Stenton will get the go-ahead to schedule an interview with him. Both Seattle and Eureka have to support this move."

Ralph had been pacing back and forth and was sitting down now in one of the deep armchairs. Leaning back, he looked defeated and tired when he said, "I'm skeptical that anything will come out of that meeting, but who knows. These people are real pros, there must be a whole bunch of them working together. Will anybody be able to break this ring?"

Thomas continued, "Calvin also talked to the New Orleans PD. There had been major trouble with the nightclub Olson was managing. A large batch of cocaine had been seized by the Coast Guard. The skipper of the small vessel panicked and told the police where he was supposed to deliver three individual packages. One of the places was Olson's club and when they came to question him, he had disappeared. The skipper later retracted his statement and named a swanky Cajun restaurant as the main place for drop-off. That's why they didn't pursue Olson. Interestingly, the new manager of the nightclub came from Seattle. They all seem to be connected, just as Ralph said. Anyway, Calvin wants to fly to Seattle as soon as he gets the OK from his boss and the Seattle PD. He suggested that I come along for the appointment with Undell. But first, he wants me to talk to his boss in Eureka. So, I will take the next train to Eureka and there is a chance that we might even fly up tonight."

"I would like to come along, Thomas. Not necessarily for the talk with this Undell, I realize that this might be too much to ask, but for the flight. Who knows what might develop up there," Ralph said and his tone indicated that he had made up his mind to go.

"I would very much appreciate it if you would come along, Ralph," Thomas answered him. "In fact, I was just going to ask you. So let's go back to the ranch and get ready for the train."

Charles went with them to the car and wished them the best as they drove off.

When Bonnie heard of their plans, she also decided to go to Eureka with Ralph and Thomas, and, if possible, to Seattle. They quickly ate lunch, packed, and Julie, Kim and Nick walked with them down to the train and saw them off. They waved until the train had disappeared in the tunnel. Then, instead of going back to the house, they strolled down to the river. Each of them was absorbed in their own thoughts. Reaching the water, Nick kicked off his shoes, pulled the T-shirt over his head and dived in. Kim sat down on a big boulder, with her legs suspended in the water, and Julie lay down in the sand. The ground was pleasantly warm from the sun and she felt comfortable. She would have loved to go along with Thomas, but the experience on Sunday had taught her to stay out of critical situations until she was completely well again. Besides, the little money she had left had to last until she started her job in September. Watching Nick swimming playfully back and forth, happily at home in the wet environment, Julie prayed that his young life would not be marred by the final, terrible news they all feared.

CHAPTER 22

Deputy sheriff Stenton had organized things well. When the train arrived in Eureka, a deputy was waiting to drive them to the sheriff's station. Within minutes, Sheriff Halls came into the waiting room and invited them to his office. He was surprised to see all three of them, but understood why Bonnie and Ralph had come along. He had no problem with Thomas, being a lawyer and PI, to accompanying Stenton to the interview with Undell as long as the officials in Seattle didn't mind.

While they were talking, the sheriff got a call from Seattle. Undell had agreed to see Stenton and Thomas at his house tomorrow morning at eleven o'clock. Halls glanced at his watch.

"Calvin should be here any minute. Let me call the airport and tell them that they will have two more passengers. I am pretty sure they have seats available."

He made the call, and there was space left on the plane. "Everything is set. Now all of you have reservations. The plane will leave in an hour. I hope to God that your trip will bring results. What a tragedy, I feel for you. In the meantime, we will keep an eye on Olson in case he should be able to talk. And of course, we will be alert for anything else that should come up," he said, addressing Bonnie and Ralph.

They had been back in the waiting room for about five minutes when Stenton came in. He didn't look happy when he saw Ralph and

Bonnie. They reassured him that they didn't expect to participate in the meeting with Undell. They just wanted to go along in case something should develop up there.

Stenton's mood improved, hearing this. "I was envying Thomas when I drove up here. I pictured him sitting relaxed in the train, enjoying the scenery and not having to watch the traffic every second–and in addition, he had pleasant company," he smiled at Bonnie. "Why didn't they build the railroad through the more populated areas?"

"I believe they had considered the other route–along the south fork of the Eel River–as well, originally. Supposedly, this set of plans got lost during the 1906 earthquake and so they built it through the other valley," Bonnie explained.

Stenton looked at her–was she joking? "I've never heard that story. Actually, Highway 101 wouldn't be that bad if we had fewer trucks on the road, especially in some of those narrow sections. They should do much more freight shipping on the railroad, that certainly would help. There was another bad accident coming up, involving a big rig. Fortunately, they had it almost cleared away when I came by and there was very little delay."

With these words, he disappeared into Hall's office for final directions. As soon as he came back out, they left for the airport, and were up in the air thirty minutes later.

The flight to Seattle went smoothly. The weather was perfect and they had an unobstructed view of the snow covered mountains of the Cascade range all the way up to Mt. Rainier.

On Tuesday morning, they met early with Lt. Earnest Somes of the Seattle PD at his office to discuss the case in detail. Bonnie and Ralph came along but made it clear right away that they didn't expect at all to be present at the meeting with Undell. They would stay at the hotel until Stenton and Thomas came back.

Thomas liked Somes right away. He was in his fifties, an intelligent, unpretentious man of medium height, a little on the heavy side, with a pleasant face under a shock of almost white hair. He told them that he had discussed the matter thoroughly with his boss. Several of his colleagues in law enforcement, including his immediate boss, were sure that Undell was deeply involved in all kinds of illegal deals. However, he was a powerful and very wealthy man who had influential connections.

So far, the police had not been able to prove anything. Undell had survived a number of law suits and investigations. With the help of several high-paid lawyers he had slipped through the nets.

"He is a slick customer, and his lawyers are worse," Somes prepared the others for what they were about to experience.

"Have you ever had any dealings with him?" Thomas asked.

"No, that's why they chose me to go with you. I have never met him personally. However, I have done extensive background work for some cases he was involved in. Believe me, I know the guy pretty well just from the paperwork. I have observed him or his lawyers in court and experienced how he operates. Honestly, I have very little hope that this meeting will bring any results, there is just not enough factual evidence to implicate him.

"Anyway, here is the strategy my boss suggests. Don't get him angry by implying that he is in any way connected. Rather pretend to come to him for help. We have this major problem that two people disappeared. The only suspects in this case we know of, Gibson or Olson, are either dead or unconscious. But he, Undell, is Olson's boss and might have information that could help to shed some light on the case. I expect him to categorically deny that he knows anything about it. The best thing we can hope for is that unintentionally, he might make a remark that would tell us that he does know what's going on. Most likely he hasn't heard about Olson's calamity or Gibson's death yet. If he is a participant or perhaps even the 'big boss', it might rattle him and perhaps cause him to make an unwise comment."

"Do you expect his lawyer to be present?" Stenton asked.

"No, because if he is involved, he knows the real reason for our visit. Having his lawyer there, he would somehow admit that he needs to defend himself. And if we are wrong and he is not involved at all, he doesn't need a lawyer anyway. I predict that he will play our visit down, give us a lot of small talk and make himself look like an outstanding, honest citizen. In case he should make a careless remark, indicating that he is a partner in this dope deal, it might be wise to treat it lightly, perhaps pretend that we haven't noticed. Otherwise, he will act much more cautiously in future dealings with us."

As they were driving north to get to Undell's house, Somes was sitting with Stenton and Thomas in the back of the police car. The driver and another officer were sitting in front. A few minutes before eleven, they reached the gated subdivision where Undell lived and were cleared to enter by an armed guard. From a well maintained road–winding through a lovely wooded area for about a mile–they noticed several houses tucked away behind trees, and caught occasional glimpses of Puget Sound far below. Eventually, they came to another gate, the entrance to Undell's property.

Again, a guard waved them in, and at the end of a long driveway, they arrived at the house. It was surrounded by a vast expanse of lawns, colorful flower beds, several small lily ponds and beautiful old trees towering over this magnificent estate. To use the term house for the building before them was an understatement, mansion was the only way to describe it. It was old, probably built around 1900, by one of the lumber barons of the Northwest with the intention of recreating an English country house. The driveway ended in a circle in front of the entrance. Several wide steps led up to a huge terrace, made of flag stones, broken up here and there by small flower beds. The front door, or rather doors, were tall and wide and would have been big enough for a church. As the car came to a stop, the door opened and a man, conservatively dressed, came down the steps. He introduced himself as Undell's secretary and invited them in.

The interior was as impressive as the outside and Thomas tried not to stare, but he was awed by what he saw. He recognized two large paintings as a Gainsborough and a Constable, and they looked real. Undell had spent millions to make his home as authentic as possible.

Occasionally, Thomas had gone along, when his father visited clients to render his professional opinion on paintings or other art objects. He had seen many grand houses, and this place would rank among the finest. Thomas made a mental note to mention it to his father next time he talked to him. His father had literature on famous houses in the country and Thomas was sure that this house was included. It would be interesting to find out who had built it and who had owned it until Undell made it his castle.

The secretary led them into a room that he called the study. Shelves filled with books from floor to ceiling covered all the walls of the huge room. It was big enough to serve as a public library for a small town. There were several groups of tables surrounded by leather-upholstered armchairs, and an enormous desk in one corner. Through the windows of the tall French doors–one was partially open–one could see a large terrace leading to the garden. The secretary pointed to the group of chairs closest to the French windows and after the three sat down he told them that Mr. Undell would be with them in a few minutes.

"Quite a spread, but I guess my wife would revolt, too many windows to wash," Stenton joked, as they were waiting for the master of the house to arrive. Thomas stood up and took a few steps through the open door, admiring the view of the garden. The sun was streaming through an opening in the tree canopy onto the terrace and was reaching into the library, softening the austere atmosphere of the room. The garden beyond the terrace was as beautiful as the one in front of the house, and lovely fragrances from hundreds of blossoms wafted into the room.

After five minutes, Mr. Undell entered the study, together with his dog, a sleek Doberman. He was a tall man, in his mid-fifties, broad shouldered and overweight. Everything about him oozed money. From his Italian tasseled loafers, expensive-looking gray wool flannel slacks, an intricately patterned, dark-green Cashmere sweater showing a light green silk shirt, several large diamond rings on his pudgy fingers, to the Rolex watch–this man had spent a small fortune on his person. The only thing lacking was an expensive haircut–for good reasons, because he was almost completely bald.

He had a thin smile on his lips when he introduced himself. But the smile was completely missing in his small, dark eyes which were alert, intelligent and very cold. Thomas shivered. His immediate reaction was an intense dislike–this was a ruthless man.

"Good morning and welcome, gentlemen. What a beautiful day to come out and visit me here in my neck of the woods." As he petted the dog's head, he added, "Don't worry about her, she is a very friendly puppy… As long as my visitors are friendly too, aren't you, Missy?"

The dog sat down, watching her master and then turning her attention to the visitors. Her brown eyes were as suspicious and cold as her owner's.

Undell pointed to a bottle of French Cognac and some glasses on a side board.

"Could I offer you some of this superb Cognac? I get it shipped directly from France and can recommend at least a taste."

He didn't have any customers, all three declined. With a little shrug, he poured himself a small amount into a huge crystal snifter, picked up the glass and took a small sip.

"Ah, this is heaven, you don't know what you are missing. Well, shall we begin? How can I help you today?"

Lt. Somes introduced his two companions and himself and then explained to Undell why they were here, along the lines he had mentioned earlier to Stenton and Thomas. He was joined by Stenton, making a convincing plea for help. Thomas explained his presence as the lawyer and private investigator for the family of the missing Carters. Undell seemed to be completely at ease, until Stenton and Thomas reported on the latest events, closing with Olson's severe accident.

Thomas noticed that Undell raised his eyebrows and it was obvious that this was new and very unpleasant information for him. His eyes seemed to look even colder and more menacing than before.

He managed to control himself quickly. "I am very sorry to hear about the accident. Mr. Olson was a good manager and I sincerely hope that he will recover. On the other hand, I regret what he has done, that was very foolish of him, I certainly paid him well for his work. He had no need for an extra–and illegal–income. Now, I realize what he meant when he said a few months ago that he might give up the job because he expected to inherit a bundle." Undell snickered unpleasantly. "He has inherited all right, a lot of pain and trouble and most likely a prison sentence."

"Unfortunately, I cannot help you any further in your search for these people. And frankly, I cannot quite understand why you suspect that Olson's dope plantation was in any way connected with the disappearance of your clients' relatives, Mr. Millon?" Undell said, addressing Thomas. "That they have not yet found the car or the bodies in the Columbia River doesn't mean that the accident did not happen. This is a mighty river, very powerful and swift, and with all the rain we had recently, it probably is higher than normal."

Thomas' answer caught Undell off guard, "We have a very good reason to assume that these two things were connected. Just before he had the accident, Olson made a remark to Miss Sutten, indicating Gibson's involvement in the Carters' disappearance. And the Carters' dog was found near the plants, dead, shot twice. Everybody agrees, that if the Carters had gone on a trip, they would certainly have taken the dog along."

"I didn't..." Undell started out, but stopped short, showing signs that he was ill at ease. The dog, which had been lying at Undell's feet, sat up and started to growl, sensing her master's discomfort. She lay down again, when Undell stroked her. He continued, "I didn't... wouldn't have thought that there was any connection between this man who drowned, Olson and the missing couple. But what you just said makes me wonder... What a shame. I had only strictly business dealings with Olson and most of that was done through my accountant. However, I must admit that I liked the man and I am very disappointed."

By now Undell had recovered, and he didn't like Stenton's question.

"I thought you had known him already when he was still in New Orleans? His girlfriend told us that Olson left New Orleans because you had a new job for him?"

Undell fidgeted for a few moments. Now, he probably wished his lawyers were there. Finally, he said, "To say that I knew him would probably be an exaggeration. I had heard about him–he was recommended to me, so I offered him the Medford job because I had just fired the manager there."

"We heard that Olson left New Orleans in a hurry because the police were just about to question him in connection with a cocaine delivery. Had you been aware of that, Mr. Undell?" Somes asked.

Undell didn't like this question at all. He took his time to answer and finally said, "I heard that there was some trouble when Olson left New Orleans and when I found out about it, I regretted having hired him. Fortunately, it turned out that he was not involved in any way and I was also very satisfied with his performance, working for me."

He took another sip from his glass, apparently happy that he had managed that hurdle.

"Could you think of someone else in Medford who could have been involved in this operation, with Olson? Did he have any close friends among the staff we should talk to perhaps?" Thomas asked, wondering if Undell might be ready to throw one of the other employees to the wolves, just to show his willingness to comply.

"I have no idea. I only dealt with Olson. He hired the salesmen and the office help. In spite of what he did now, he was the best manager I have had for years. I really had trouble with some of the others. They stole cars from me right and left." he took another sip of his Cognac and was putting the glass back, when he asked, "What happened to the Jeep the guy drove into the river?"

That was the opportunity they had hoped for! The careless remark by Undell that might prove that he had known what was going on. He realized his mistake the second he did it and tried feverishly to smooth it over with small talk. He complained how little one could depend nowadays on one's employees even if they were paid well, and on and on. Somes didn't let him off the hook so easily, yet employed the strategy he had advised earlier.

"Do you remember perhaps who told you that it was a Jeep? Did someone from Medford tell you? This could be important."

Now Undell was in a bind. After describing his relationship with Olson as strictly businesslike, he couldn't admit that he knew from Olson about Gibson driving the Jeep. He didn't have much choice but to lie as convincingly as he could.

"It was Mr. Millon here who mentioned the Jeep, don't you remember?" he looked at Thomas with a big smile around his lips and cold anger in his eyes. It was a cheap shot to pick out Thomas for having mentioned it, he was not law enforcement and therefore easier to dismiss should this matter be brought up again later.

Thomas's first reaction was to deny that he had mentioned the red Jeep, but he caught himself just in time and kept quiet.

Undell continued quickly before the others could say a word, "I am sure you mentioned a Jeep, Mr. Millon, unless I misunderstood you, I sometimes have problems with the different accents." He beamed when he said this, and looked at Thomas with a disparaging smile.

Thomas was furious. From the very beginning, Undell had behaved as if he was meeting only with Somes. He had ignored both Stenton and Thomas as much as possible, had made little eye contact with them and had addressed only Lt. Somes when he talked.

Undell was still rambling on, telling his audience how much he abhorred drug use and what he had done to prevent it. Thomas didn't listen, he tried his best to get rid of his anger, taking deep breaths, and calming himself down.

He had shrugged as a response to Undell's explanation about the Jeep, trying not to show his feeling, and sensed that Calvin and Somes were just as upset. But, after all, this was part of the strategy they had planned for this meeting, trying to get as much information as possible without making him aware unnecessarily that he had slipped up.

As a last word, Somes reminded Undell to contact him, in case he should hear of anything pertaining to the case.

Undell walked with them out to the terrace. He stayed on the upper step when he said good-bye to them, trying to look as benevolent as a pastor who was sending his flock home after church on Sunday. He waved as the car started to move.

For a while, nobody spoke. Somes finally broke the spell. "I am sorry that you had to put up with that, Thomas. I was just as angry about him as you are, Thomas. But, as we had said before, it was wiser not to antagonize him. The less we confront him the easier it will be to catch him."

"I just hope that eventually you will get him, Earnest, he deserves it. At least we know now that he is involved. Hopefully, he believes that we didn't catch on. The question is, how can we prove that he is part of the operation, perhaps even the brains behind it, and do we have any time left to save the Carters?"

"Checking out again the addresses behind those telephone numbers is all that we can do at the moment, and I hope it will get us a little further. I'll look into it right away when I get back to the office," Somes promised.

Thomas offered his help, "Our plane does not leave until six this evening. We have quite a few hours to spend here. If it is OK with you, Earnest, I would be happy to help. I could investigate the one address you have not looked into yet, that will save you some time. I guess Calvin has given you some idea concerning my background, I do have experience in this field."

"Thomas also worked for a while for C & O here in Seattle, Earnest, I might not have mentioned that?" Stenton broke in.

Thomas sensed that at first, Somes was reluctant to give him the go-ahead, but when Stenton mentioned C & O, his attitude changed.

"OK, Thomas, why don't you see what you can find out. But listen, this is not an official arrangement, you are doing this on your own. I guess you understand? And don't probe too far, leave this up to us."

"Thank, you, Earnest, I'll do my best. One question. Yesterday, when you checked out Lancer's address, which was also the address behind the fake bank telephone number, you only talked to owner of the house, right? You didn't check with any of the neighbors?"

"No, we only contacted the owner. Why?"

"I thought it might be interesting if any of the neighbors remember some details about Lancer. Maybe I should look them up also."

Somes tore off a piece from his note pad and handed it to Thomas, "Here are the two locations, you can have this slip, I have the information at the office."

"Thanks, I will call you when I am through with it this afternoon. I hope that I come up with some leads from where you can go on."

Stenton decided to accompany Somes to his office. He would meet Thomas, Bonnie and Ralph later at the airport.

Thomas dreaded telling Bonnie and Ralph the bad news. To his amazement, both had prepared themselves well for a negative result. They had talked about the case all morning and knew that it would be a miracle if Undell would admit to any involvement. His lapse about the Jeep confirmed what they all had suspected and at least for this knowledge alone, the trip had not been in vain. Both were eager to come along, checking out the addresses.

"We don't want to interfere, we'll wait outside while you do your job. We just want to be there should you need us," Bonnie assured Thomas.

They located the two places on a Seattle street map. One address was right in downtown and the other one near the Space Needle. As they took the elevator down to the lobby, Bonnie suggested that it would be a good idea to have a photo of Undell.

"I probably can get one quickly," she said, as they stepped from the elevator. She walked over to the reception desk of the hotel, leafed through the telephone book, and came back. "I'll be back in a few minutes."

Ten minutes later, she presented them with two newspaper photos of Undell. One was taken at a reception at City Hall and the other one during an interview in his own house.

Ralph stared at his sister-in-law as if he was seeing her for the first time. "You are a wizard, Bonnie. How did you manage this?"

"Working for several nonprofit organizations has taught me the ropes. It is usually easy to get photos from newspapers, they have always a good archive, and one of the local newspapers was just across the street."

The first address, where Lancer supposedly had lived, was a small house in a slightly run-down neighborhood. The cab driver was willing to wait. Bonnie and Ralph stayed in the car, it had started to rain. They watched Thomas heading for the house on the right side of Lancer's address. Nobody responded when he rang the bell or knocked against the front door. He walked over to the house on the left, which looked better cared for than most of the others around. This time, he lucked out, an older woman opened the door. Thomas identified himself.

"I'm sorry to bother you, but perhaps you could help me with some information. A few months ago, a Mr. Lancer had rented the house next door. Did you by any chance see this person occasionally and could you give me some description?"

"You said a Mr. Lancer? When exactly did you say he supposedly lived here?" the woman inquired.

"I couldn't precisely tell you the dates when he moved in or out, but apparently he lived here in January or February and only for about four weeks." Thomas replied.

"Would you mind telling me what's this about, young man?"

Although Thomas liked the woman, he didn't want to risk anything by telling the truth. He invented a plausible explanation about an insurance inquiry. Though he had the feeling that the woman saw right through his tale, she nevertheless seemed to trust him.

She smiled a little and answered, "Perhaps a Mr. Lancer rented the house, but I never saw him." When she saw the disappointment on Thomas' face, she quickly added, "But a woman lived there around that time. She moved in at the beginning of February and moved out again on March 4th. I happen to remember the date so well because it was a day before my daughter got married. The renters before this woman–a young couple–had lived there for two years. The house was empty until two weeks ago when the present renters moved in. I saw very little of the woman and I don't know her name either, but I can tell you what she looked like. She was about 5' 5" tall, short, blond hair, expensive hair cut, medium size figure, conservatively dressed, mostly in skirts, nylons and heels, and she had a slight limp. I never saw visitors and believe that she was gone a lot, too. Mail–mostly junk mail–would pile up for a few days and then, one day it would be gone. I often saw lights at night and heard the radio, but somehow, had the feeling that they were timer-controlled."

Thomas was impressed, this lady was observant. He asked, "And you never saw a man?"

She shook her head.

"Thank you very much for your excellent description, I might need it after all. Before I knocked at your door, I tried the house on the other side, but nobody answered. Any chance that those people had closer contact with the woman?"

"No, not at all. These people bought the house in April, they never met her and it had been for sale–empty–since last fall. Knowing the neighborhood well, I am pretty sure you would waste your time trying to talk to anybody else. I am home most of the time, I do some freelance art work and my workplace window faces the street. I can't help seeing what's going on," she smiled.

"Thanks, I really appreciate your help. I guess I have to contact the owner, perhaps he has some knowledge about this Mr. Lancer or even a forwarding address. I suppose you wouldn't have that by any chance?"

"No, certainly not. And the owner is not a 'he'. She is an old lady, almost ten years older than I. We have been good friends from the time when she lived here. But, she left the dealings with her tenants to a real estate office, all she would know is the name. So she wouldn't be of much help, besides, she left last night for Hawaii." Sensing Thomas' disappointment, she added, "Why don't you contact the real estate broker who handled the rental? Come in for a minute, I'll look it up in the phone book. I don't remember the name but if I see it in print it will come back to me."

She led Thomas into a pleasant, bright living room. The furniture was old but well-kept, the upholstery done in pastel colors, very clean in spite of two cats and a small dog lying on opposite ends of a large sofa, eyeing Thomas suspiciously. As she had said, a huge work table was arranged in the bay window toward the street and many examples of her art work–mostly plants–were displayed on the walls. Going through the entries for real estate brokers in the yellow pages, she quickly found the company.

"Here it is, Sunset Realtors. And here is the address and the phone number."

Thomas accepted the slip of paper, thanked her again for her help and left. When he came back to the cab, he asked the driver to take them to the real estate office. On the way, Thomas gave a short report to Bonnie and Ralph. Arriving at their destination, they dismissed the cab driver and went together into the office. The Realtor who had handled the rental–a man in his sixties–happened to be in. He was familiar right away with the house and after consulting his files, gave them detailed information. He had never heard the name 'Lancer' in connection with this woman renter. His description of her was very much the same as the neighbor had described her to Thomas. She had responded to an ad in the paper, wanted the house for six months, but had to move after four weeks, leaving the house in very good condition. Her name had been Muriel Laner. When the deputy had talked to the owner, she had probably mixed up the name with Lancer. The Realtor had no forwarding address.

"Well, we didn't learn much, but at least we now have two people who could identify this mysterious Mr. Lancer/Ms. Laner if we ever find her. Let's take the Monorail to downtown, the station is only two blocks away. We can walk, it stopped raining," Thomas said when they had left the office.

They enjoyed the ride on the Monorail back to downtown. The second address, as Thomas had predicted, was only one block away from the terminal. It was a high priced, many-storied apartment building with a very elegant lobby. Bonnie and Ralph relaxed on one of four modernistic, pale leather sofas that were placed around a black marble fireplace. Thomas told the liveried doorman–who was controlling the access to the elevators– that he would like to see the building supervisor.

He had to wait almost twenty minutes until the supervisor was available. When he finally led Thomas into his office, it took him only a few seconds to find the tenant in question on his computer. He had been an artist from London, and had rented a one-room apartment for only six weeks. When he described the person as a tall, overweight man, Thomas showed him Undell's photos. Fortunately, the supervisor didn't seem to know Undell. He was pretty sure that he was not the person who had rented the apartment, although his build had been similar. His tenant had sported a long beard, fairly long blond hair, tied into a pony tail, and wore glasses. He had only a few visitors during the time he lived there, and had left the apartment in absolutely perfect condition.

Over a cup of coffee, Thomas gave his report to Bonnie and Ralph.

They all three agreed, that this English artist could have been Undell in disguise, at least as far as his dimensions were concerned. But where could this information lead them now?

Lt. Somes was not very encouraging either when Thomas called him, relating what he had found out. Somes promised they would take a close look at Undell's staff. Perhaps there was a woman employee who matched the description of the tenant. If that should be the case, the woman who lived next door to the 'Lancer' house and the real estate broker would make good witnesses. In any case, they would get started right away.

They debated whether Thomas and Ralph should stay in Seattle to check out some more leads, but decided that it was better to let Somes get into the act first.

The cafe happened to be opposite from a light-rail station. Ten minutes later they boarded the train to the airport, where they arrived in time to have a quick meal before takeoff. They met Stenton at the gate and soon were back on their way to California.

CHAPTER 23

The call came a few minutes before midnight. His wife shook him awake.

"Wake up, wake up, I am sure it's the boss."

He sat up with a start. Still half asleep, he picked up the phone, "Hello?"

"It's me. How is everything?"

"OK."

"Good, listen carefully. I put a package for you in the mail today. You might get it tomorrow or the next day. It contains, among other things, a letter with instructions I want you to follow exactly. As before, the key to the room and for the car will be enclosed. Again, follow my instructions EXACTLY as I wrote them down. You understand? Follow my instructions EXACTLY.

You had mentioned that you and your wife wanted a vacation. You can leave after you have followed my orders, OK? I will not need your services for at least four weeks. I'll probably call you again around the middle of July, and will have further instructions at that time. There is some cash enclosed for necessary expenses. As soon as I know that you have done as I have told you, your payment will be in your checking account. Any questions?"

"No, I'll wait for your letter. If I have any questions after I get the letter, can I call you?"

"Any time, the old number. But, I am sure that you will have no problem. It's very simple what I am asking you to do. If the letter has not arrived by the day after tomorrow, call me back. That's all."

The line went dead. He looked at the receiver in his hand and slowly put it back. His wife had been watching him, worry in her eyes. "What does he want now?"

"I don't know yet, Conchita. We will get a letter with instructions. It should be here tomorrow, or in two days. No, it's already tomorrow," he looked confused, turned out the light and slipped back into bed. Why worry about it now before the letter arrived? But Conchita was distressed. He had avoided looking into his wife's eyes, because he didn't want to see her fear. Now, at least it was dark and he couldn't see her face any longer. If she started to talk he could pretend to be asleep.

If only they could get away from it all for good and not come back after four weeks. Start somewhere else all over or do what she would like to do more than anything, live in her native country, in Mexico.

By Mexican standards, her family was well off. She had always told him that they would welcome him and have a job for him. Yet, he felt too proud to go begging, at least that's the way he saw it. So, he had done a most foolish thing, he had gambled, hoping to come out with lots of money and then go to Mexico, and impress her family. That's how he had ended up in this dreadful situation, doing all kinds of odd jobs for a man whom he feared. Sure, he couldn't really complain. They lived in a decent house, had a nice car, enough money to take care of their needs and didn't have to work hard. So why did he worry?

He had never met the boss personally. When his gambling debts had grown so high that he didn't know how to get out of his problems any longer, he had desperately grasped at straws. Then it was too late. After he had performed several tasks for the boss–even though they seemed to be harmless on the surface–he knew in his heart that these jobs made him an accomplice in illegal deals. By then, he was hopelessly trapped.

One of the jobs he had to do was to care for occasional 'guests'–serve three meals a day. In reality, these 'guests' were nothing but prisoners, housed in a small room built and well insulated in an old barn at the end of the ten-acre large property he took care of. This had happened several times so far. In the previous two cases, he eventually received the order to drug these people, and then drive them at night to an isolated, specified spot. A car for this action had been left at a designated place in the neighborhood. The car keys and the key to the room were enclosed with the boss' instructions. He would get the car at night, drive it into the barn and move the 'guests' into the back seat and take off, with Conchita following him in their own car.

Afterwards, he and Conchita had cleaned the place, making it ready for the next people. Eventually, new 'guests' would be brought in at night by using the back road leading into the property. At that time, a new lock would be installed, making it impossible to open the door with the old key.

Often, he and Conchita had speculated what might happen to these people–both feared the worst and he was glad he didn't have to bear it alone. They had tried to treat the 'guests' as well as possible, serve them decent food and take care of their needs. But, no matter how he looked at it, there was no question that he was a willing partner in a kidnapping operation.

Now he probably had to do it again. This time, he felt much worse about it, because he liked the couple who was living back there, they seemed to be good people. He had never talked to them, his job was to watch them occasionally and report what he saw or heard. What about letting them go, and he and Conchita fleeing to Mexico? Although he knew he would never dare to do this in reality, he had toyed with this idea, forgetting completely that he couldn't set them free anyway because he had no key to the very complicated lock in the door to the small room.

There was no way out, the boss had already too much control over their life, he probably had all their movements watched. He and Conchita wouldn't even make it to the Mexican border. What else could he do? Go to the police? He almost laughed about his own joke. No, they were stuck, there was no hope. At last, he fell into a fitful sleep.

CHAPTER 24

She woke up, but kept her eyes closed. Treasuring those minutes of drowsy, cozy, semi-consciousness between sleep and awakening, she pretended that she was lying in her own bed at home, in her airy and cheerful bedroom, looking into the trees and the Eel River valley below. As soon as she would open her eyes, reality would prevail–this dreary little room, where they had been imprisoned for the last two months, and the nightmarish encounter in the canyon, which had resulted in Bret being knocked unconscious, and old Toby shot dead. She dreaded the memory of lying on the dirty floor of the filthy cabin, gagged and bound, exposed for hours to cigarette smoke. Eventually, they woke up in this room, without having the slightest idea how they got here, where they were and what would happen to them. Except for the man who had attacked them on that beautiful spring day in early April, they had not seen a human being since. They had found a small note, addressed 'To the Carters, lying on a table. It explained in a few sentences that they would be held here until 'the crop' was harvested. They would receive three meals per day, and 'laundry services' were available! In case of an 'unforeseen' medical emergency, they should leave a note on the food tray. Someone was out there feeding them. The meals were delivered each day through a tiny door in the wall. There were no windows in the room, only two doors. One leading into a small bathroom, the other one to the outside, a metal door without a handle or lock on the inside, but tightly locked from the other side.

Whoever kept them imprisoned seemed to know about their profession. An old, but functioning typewriter, as well as plenty of paper, pens and pencils were placed on the sturdy table in the corner of the room. After the initial shock had worn off, they had tried to do some work, but gave up, their creative flow was gone. They felt like streams that had dried up during a drought year. What kept them mentally alert and enabled them to tolerate their captivity, was a large book case, tightly filled with enough books to keep them going until the end of the growing season, which, they hoped, would be the time of their release.

The books were the biggest mishmash of titles they had ever seen. There were perhaps fifty classic mysteries, many modern ones, at least twenty romance novels and more wild west stories. In addition, there was a large selection of classic novels, as well as many newer ones. There were books on how to raise rabbits and chickens, crossword puzzle books, income tax guide books, dating back to 1963, and at least five cook books. Also, books in foreign languages, some Spanish novels, a book by Friedrich Nietzsche in German, some Russian books and Ovid in Latin. Fortunately, there were also a number of books on political, philosophical and environmental issues which kept them busy mentally. And of course, there was the Bible. Bret's dry humor "every decent motel provides a Bible for its guests" caused Emily to laugh for the first time since they woke up in their prison. They didn't have much knowledge of this book, because they had never participated in organized religion. Now, they had the time and the opportunity to become acquainted with the book's overwhelming wealth of historic information.

The food was adequate and actually quite good. At the beginning, they hardly touched it, but after a week, they started to look forward to the meals. It was good Mexican home-cooked food. As time went on, the trays became more personalized, with some special touches–a few blossoms, prettier plates and some elaborate desserts once in a while. Whoever the cook was–both Emily and Bret were convinced it was a woman–was enjoying her job and they left small notes in the empty dishes, thanking her.

Although there was this continuous nagging fear whether they would really be released at all some day, they had decided to make the best of the situation. After about a week, they settled into some sort of a fragile routine–taking care of their appearance, keeping the place clean, eating, reading, exercising and meditating on a regular schedule.

Each day, they discussed the books they were reading to keep their minds focused. One book that positively influenced their life here was a book on Buddhism. They had become interested in Buddhism several years ago, had read a number of books and also attended some gatherings. This book now renewed their belief. When outrage, fear and despair had been the dominant feelings at the beginning of their ordeal, they eventually lost their anger and were now ready to forgive.

One chapter of the Bible, Matthew's Sermon on the Mount, attracted their undivided attention. It mirrored their own philosophy on life and was in many ways similar to Buddhist teachings. These writings supported them in trying to turn their ill fortune into a constructive experience, and not to look at it as a wasted part of their life. It certainly was different than life at home, a very passive life. Just as the temperature in this little room seemed to be constant, their life was flowing along on a level path–missing the rivers and streams of creativity, the hills of excitement and the valleys of frustration. A few days, after they had found themselves in this prison, and when the original fear and panic had subsided, they had made love one night. Only, their hearts were not in it, instead of nourishing their souls, it had turned into a frantic exercise. They had abstained since, patiently waiting for the time when life would be their own again. But, they usually slept in each other's arms, or at least holding hands, finding consolation in their embrace.

Emily realized that her mind had wandered. Instead of pretending to be at home and imagining the view from her bed into the valley, or hearing the birds sing, she had again dwelt on their present state. She felt sad that they had missed the beauty of the two spring months, being awakened by the chatter of the swallows, building their nest under the eve of the roof; or the melodious calls of the red-winged blackbirds, and the lovely, early morning songs of the thrushes. In this tightly-sealed room, they didn't hear any outside sounds, let alone a bird. But all of a sudden she became alert,–she did hear a bird! Or was she just hearing noises in her mind? No, there it was again, a trill, a twitter? Emily opened her eyes, and didn't believe what she saw. They were no longer in the room that had been their home for the last two months, they were in a car!

Feeling kind of woozy, she slowly sat up and looked around. Bret was lying next to her, sleeping soundly. It was getting light, and what she saw through the windows explained why she indeed had heard a bird. They were in the middle of a forested area! It looked like a campground with picnic tables and benches along the bank of a rushing creek. She saw some other cars and tents through the trees further up the road. There were no people around or up yet, it was still too early.

By now, she realized that they were in their own van. And then she noticed that she wasn't wearing a nightshirt, she wore the jeans and sweat shirt she had worn yesterday. They must have put some sleeping pills in their food last night and then carried them off to the car. No wonder it had taken her so long to wake up and not realizing that she was not lying in a bed! She still felt very tired, not quite normal. She had no luck waking up Bret, he just grunted and slept on. Very quietly, yet as fast as she could, she got out and opened the left front door. Perhaps she could release the brakes and get the car rolling, at least out of sight, away from the other cars? To her amazement, the car keys were lying on the seat, next to her sneakers. She didn't bother putting on her shoes or fastening the seat belt. She had only one thought–getting away from there as fast as possible. The engine started on the first try. Quickly, she drove out of the parking space onto the road which led her within minutes to a regular highway. Every few seconds, she glanced in the rearview mirror, expecting one of the other cars to race after her. Nothing happened. The question was now, which way to turn? She had no idea where she was. Judging from the vegetation, this place could be in the foothills of the Sierra, perhaps 4,000 to 5,000 feet high? There were black oaks, still in their first spring green, Douglas-firs and ponderosa pines. There should be a sign somewhere, showing the name of the campground. But she wanted to get out of here quickly. To the right, the sky seemed to be lighter, which would be East. If she really was in the foothills, she should turn left, toward the West, the Central Valley. She quickly followed her instinct, turning left onto the highway. There was no traffic at all and soon she was going at a good speed, hoping to find out within the next few miles where in the world she was. The first highway marker she passed indicated that she was on Highway 32. Where was 32? It didn't ring a bell. Should she take the time and look at the map? Better not, she wouldn't feel safe until she reached a more populated area. So far, the road behind her stayed empty of cars, but a small pickup truck was coming from the opposite direction. As it passed, Emily wondered how the driver would react if he knew that he was the first person she saw since April. She turned on the radio, expecting to get some clues on their whereabouts and also opened the window, hoping that the fresh, cool air would clear her mind faster. After about five minutes, one of the radio-advertisements mentioned a Sacramento store, which confirmed the foothill theory all right. Apparently Highway 32 was one of the routes leading into the Sierra, and since the road seemed to descend, sooner or later she would reach the valley. With each mile, Emily felt a little safer, but still kept a close watch on the rearview mirror. Suddenly, a vehicle did appear on the road behind her, but to her relief it was a huge Safeway truck, going at a good speed and passing her a few minutes later.

Bret was still sleeping. As soon as she reached a village, she would stop and try again to wake him up. Perhaps she could get some coffee, she was not really completely awake yet and would have liked to lie down and sleep. The area became more open. There were a few houses here and there, a gas station that was not open yet, and a very seedy-looking motel, displaying a 'Vacancy' sign. At the sight of it, the desire to fall into a bed and sleep–any bed–made her slow down for a few seconds. But no, this place was too isolated, too close to the campground–she had to keep going.

Eventually, the traffic increased and soon, she reached the outskirts of Chico. As Emily scanned the roadside businesses for a coffee-shop–she needed a strong cup of coffee to overcome the fatigue–she heard commotion behind her, Bret finally was awake.

"What's going on, Emily? Where are we? How did we get into the car? Are we free?" Bret was sitting up, staring at her as if he were seeing a ghost.

Emily slowed down and told Bret that she would stop in a minute, she was just looking for the right spot. At the next corner, she noticed an open coffee-shop and turned off the road. As a precaution, she drove behind the building where the car was not visible from the road and parked it in the very back, in a narrow alley, separated from the parking lot by a dense hedge. Without bothering to put her shoes on, Emily hurried to the back door. Bret had gotten up and was staggering toward her, rather shaky on his feet. They fell into each other's arms in a tight embrace, kissing and laughing, until they were interrupted by a pickup truck passing by. The driver grinned when he saw them and honked his horn.

Emily told Bret what had happened since she woke up this morning. Then, concerned, she looked at Bret, "Are you all right? I tried to wake you up but you slept on. I am sure they drugged us last night and then carried us into our car and drove us into the mountains. The car keys were on the front seat, so I tried to get away as fast as possible and here we are."

Bret took a deep breath, "This is unbelievable, Emily. I wonder if this was by design or accident that we got away?"

"I still cannot believe it either. Whichever way I pictured our release, it certainly did not include waking up on a campground in the Sierra early in the morning. But I think it was by design, this was no accident. It's our own car, with the keys–and a full tank. Oh, by the way, my shoes are in the front, I wonder if yours are around too?" Emily sat down and put her sneakers on, while Bret searched for his.

"Here, I found them in the back, together with this, I wonder what's in it." He was opening a small white box. "Wow, look at this, Emily!"

The box was filled with oranges, apples and a clear plastic container with cookies. Bret picked up a note card and read its message to Emily.

"Dear people, I am happy you are allowed to go home now. I was worried. We go to Mexico and live there, we not come back, the boss is a bad man.
My best wishes, your Conchita.

That must have come from our cook. These cookies look like some she made, you remember? I am sorry we will never be able to say thank you. I guess it would be impossible to find 'one' Conchita in Mexico. But do you realize, Emily, that her phrase–'you are allowed to go home'–means that we are free, officially? "

"Yes, I do–but I still cannot believe it. Why would they let us go? They must know that we will inform the police as soon as we get home–or even right here, right now? This doesn't make sense."

"I guess the plants got raided and the guy was caught. And now the man behind this scheme–perhaps the boss Conchita mentioned in her note–feels there is no reason to keep us in prison any longer. This man who attacked us didn't act alone, he was probably nothing but a hired hand, in a way. If he had been in charge, he most likely would have killed us." Bret had finished putting his shoes on. He stood up, moved out of the shade of the trees to the back of the van which was fully exposed to the sun. Although it was still early, it was already getting warm. Leaning against the car, he soaked in the sunshine. When Emily joined him, he put his arm around her and told her with a brilliant smile on his pale face how much he loved her.

"I was hoping to get a cup of coffee to really wake me up, but I just realized that we don't have any money, Bret."

"Perhaps there are a few dollars in the glove compartment? Let's take a look." Bret suggested.

To their amazement, they found their wallets in there, apparently complete with Visa cards and other identifications, and there was even some money.

"I wonder how they got our credit cards and all the rest?" Emily asked.

"I suppose the man who attacked us in the canyon went to the ranch, got our wallets and also stole the car, otherwise the car would not be here, right? I'm afraid we might be in for a surprise when we get our next Visa statement. Well, I don't care about things like that at the moment–we are free, that's all that matters. I am not in favor of going to the police now, Emily. Let's do that when we get home. I'm sure the local police are already investigating our disappearance."

While they had their coffee and a simple breakfast at the coffee-shop, they studied the road map.

"We are now in Chico. How should we go home? South on Highway 20 to Ukiah and then north on Highway 101 or take 36 and come out in Scotia and then go south on 101? Either way it is a long trek, but 36 is the prettier route. What do you think?"

Emily's reply came fast, "Let's take the prettier route, Bret. After having seen nothing but that ugly room for two months, I am thirsty for beauty. It's still very early, we might get home around noon. I can't wait to see Julie. Now, that we are free, I can worry about her. These last few weeks, since she came home, must have been terrible for her, not knowing what happened to us. I hope she is all right, she could have easily gotten involved in this too. Also, I pray that she has not contacted our family yet, but I am afraid she has, we have been gone too long. We must call Charles or Rosy soon to let them know that we are on our way, but it is still a little too early."

"Isn't it strange that we have no idea where we were held? What is the last you remember? I know we had dinner and it was especially good with two glasses of wine. And I must have passed out after that, it was around seven o'clock."

Emily hesitated before she answered, "Yes, I would say that is about right. In other words, they had about eight to nine hours to take us where we woke up. That covers a huge area, even into Oregon or Nevada. Unless we remember anything else that would give us a clue, we will never find out where we were. Well, let's get home."

CHAPTER 25

Charles was still asleep Thursday morning, when the telephone rang. Nomi and his grandfather had stayed in Willits until Wednesday and had come back on the afternoon train. The old man had enjoyed the train ride and swore he would never make that trip by car again, going up and down on these winding, narrow roads. Charles hadn't found the time yesterday to drive over to the Sutten ranch until after dinner to find out what Thomas, Ralph and Bonnie had accomplished in Seattle. They had talked for a long time, it had been almost midnight when he came home. He was still sleeping when Nomi got up this morning. She was out for a walk with the dogs now and when the phone rang for the fourth time, Charles finally woke up.

He tried to sound awake when he answered the phone, "Kendar ranch, good morning." The receiver almost fell out of his hands, when he heard the voice coming over the wire.

"Charles? It's Emily!, I hope we aren't calling too early? We are coming home, we are free, we were kidnapped. I am sure the police have already searched for us all over the area? And you were terribly worried?"

Charles was speechless. He was sure this was not a hoax, this was the real thing. It was Emily, no question. His voice was shaky, "Emily, I cannot believe it! This is the best phone call I ever got in my life! Are you all right? And Bret?"

Emily didn't know where to begin. She burst into a torrent of words and sentences, starting at the end of events, jumping to the beginning and mixing it all up, but the main thing he heard was that they were both healthy. They were calling from Red Bluff and coming home on Highway 36, hoping to be in Madrone Flat by noon. Could he drive over and let Julie know that both of them were all right and would be home soon?

"You have no idea what it means to me to deliver this message," Charles assured Emily. " Julie and your sister Bonnie with her son Nick, as well as Bret's brother Ralph, Julie's girlfriend, Kim, and Julie's boyfriend, Thomas, they are all at the ranch. They will be ecstatic when they hear that you called, that both of you are OK and are coming home. I will drive over right away."

"I was afraid that Julie had contacted our family," Emily replied. "What else could she do? They all must have been desperate. But what did you say? Julie has a boyfriend? This is completely new to me. When did this happen? And where did she meet him? Did he come with her from New York?"

"Too many questions, Emily! We will answer them all when you get here. But I will tell you about Thomas, Julie's friend–who is a young lawyer who helped searching for you. She met him in Willits where she had stopped at Frank Rodgers' house. He came up to the ranch to support Julie and that's how they got to know each other. They all have been working around the clock to bring you back. But as I said, they will tell you all the details when you get here. Listen, don't rush, take it easy, we don't want you to have an accident now, it doesn't matter if you come an hour earlier or later, the main thing is that you do come home!"

Emily promised and hung up. For a minute, Charles was not sure if this call had been real. He got dressed in a hurry. His grandfather was still asleep, so he left a note for Nomi and took off for Julie's ranch. Never had he driven this stretch as fast as today. Here he was giving advice to Emily to drive slowly and he himself was behaving like a race-car driver. All the events of the last week came back into his mind. He had no hope left when he drove home last night–and now he knew they were alive and well–it was a miracle!

They were eating breakfast in the kitchen and looked at him with surprise when he came rushing in.

"Emily and Bret are coming home, she just called, they were kidnapped. They are both all right and hope to be here by noon," Charles sat down, as if exhausted by bringing the message.

Julie was speechless and started to cry, Bonnie hugged her and cried too, and everybody started to talk at once, asking questions over questions. Charles finally managed to tell them as much as he remembered from Emily's emotional call. He still saw some doubts on Julie's and Bonnie's faces, but eventually they all understood that this was not another fake phone call–they were really coming home.

Charles excused himself soon, Nomi was probably waiting already, and he was eager to tell her the good news. He promised to call Ralph's wife, Rosy, the fire chief and of course, also sheriff Stenton. And he and Nomi would come back later in the day if they all felt ready for company.

"We will fetch you, Charles, we will come over to get you!" Julie told him when he got up, walking with him to the front door and giving him another hug for bringing the good news.

Back in the kitchen, they were still discussing the bits and pieces of information, and speculating whether the meeting with Undell had precipitated Emily and Bret's release.

"When we talked to him on Tuesday, we were pretty sure that he didn't know that Gibson was dead or that Olson had a severe accident," Thomas said. "And this was, of course, the end of this pot plantation. So he probably figured why keep the Carters imprisoned, now that it did not matter any longer? I guess this leaves no doubt that Undell was the 'boss', the mastermind. Was he also responsible for that terrible idea to fake the accident at the river? I'm afraid he had his hands in that too. He was quite serious when he suggested that the Carters' bodies and their car might never be found. It is a miracle that they are still alive. The man is not as evil as I perceived him to be," Thomas said.

"But, it also means that this man is extremely sure of himself. Obviously, he must expect that we will draw the conclusion now that he was behind it all. And still, he sets them free. I suppose he has all his people under tight control and is not afraid that anyone will talk and endanger him," Ralph added. Thomas nodded in agreement.

"You know, it is quite possible that most of the people who work for him, have never met him, and that he conducts all his illegal business by phone, pay-phones preferably. Jessica had actually mentioned this to Stenton," Kim concluded.

Lunch was ready and waiting on trays in the kitchen from noon on, and every few minutes someone looked up to the hill, expecting the Carters' van to appear at the ridge.

About ten minutes to one, Bonnie excitedly pointed up to the road, cheering, "They are coming, they are coming!"

Everybody rushed to the front door, where they stood now, watching impatiently as the light green van came slowly down the hill until it stopped before them. They all crowded around the doors of the car, hardly giving Emily and Bret a chance to get out. When the Carters finally emerged, they were greeted with endless hugs, kisses, tears and laughter. After the first wave of greetings had calmed down, Julie introduced Thomas, explaining to Emily and Bret how important his help had been in getting them out of their prison.

Bonnie mentioned that lunch was waiting, would they all please come out to the deck where the table was set, they could continue talking there, sitting down comfortably. But then, glancing at her sister's and Bret's clothes, she had second thoughts.

"Are you very hungry, Emily, or would you rather change first?"

Emily smiled at Bret, who nodded. "We are hungry but I think we can wait ten more minutes, it will taste much better after we have shed these rags that we have worn now for two months. I promise we will be quick."

They all went into the house and Bret and Emily disappeared to their upstairs apartment. Ten minutes later, they came down again, they had showered and changed. Emily looked much more attractive now in a pretty summer skirt and a white blouse that made her look less pale than the navy-blue T-shirt she had worn before. She had shampooed her dark-blond hair and wore it in a loose, hastily tied French knot. Buttercup lay relaxed in her arms, his eyes closed, purring contentedly. He had been sitting in front of their door when they came upstairs. Emily put him on her lap when she sat down at the table and he seemed to be determined to stay there for a while.

Bret was as tall and slender as Emily. His dark hair, slightly thinning at the top, showed some gray that Bonnie had not noticed when she had seen him six months ago. She also thought that his nice trim beard looked a bit grayer. He was a quiet, pleasant man, with a friendly, open face.

Eventually, they all sat down for lunch. Between bites, Emily and Bret told their story. In turn, their audience filled in some of the gaps from their experiences, events at home or during the two trips to Medford and Seattle.

"I am the only one here who met Undell in person," Thomas said. "After our visit to his house, I almost had given up any hope that we would find you alive still. He struck me as a ruthless person, also as being very conservative and arrogant. To let you go now certainly points strongly to him as the mastermind behind the whole operation. But it also appears reckless from his point of view–like playing with fire. As Ralph said earlier–this man is so sure of himself, he doesn't care what we think. He must be convinced that he has left no trail that could confirm his participation. Unfortunately, we still have only little factual evidence that he is the boss. And, setting you free now, two days after he found out about Olson's accident–which also meant the end of the dope plantation–is, of course, no proof either, it's not even circumstantial evidence."

They continued talking about the various aspects of the case. Emily and Bret were surprised to hear that Gibson had died in the car accident and they also knew nothing about Olson.

"You must realize that after we were attacked by Gibson in the canyon, we never saw anybody during these months. And we didn't have the slightest idea where we were. We had no radio or television that could have given us a clue. By the way, I am very surprised that Andy was in cahoots with this Gibson, we really liked him and trusted him. That makes me feel rather sad and disappointed," Bret concluded.

While she petted Buttercup, Emily replied, "I feel sorry for Andy. He had been very depressed about his parents losing all their money to pay for his father's medical care. He wanted to earn as much as possible this summer to come back home with a considerable amount. He was working several jobs in Garberville besides working for us. Starting the end of April, his uncle had promised him a well-paying job in his saw mill. It's a pity that he fell into this dope trap, I am afraid he might not have seen the fruits of his labor anyway. Don't feel too bad about him, Bret. I guess he didn't realize what he was getting into and after all, he came just at the right time to help Julie."

Bret looked at Emily and smiled. "You are right, love! I am glad you are so understanding, it makes life more peaceful." He put his arm around her and kissed her, and then, as a second thought, scratched Buttercup under his chin, stroked his back and ended up with the cat on his lap.

"You mentioned that there were a lot of books. Did you check them out for names, or perhaps stamps from libraries?" Thomas asked.

"That's a good question. In fact, we carefully leafed through each book, hoping to find some names or addresses. Yes, some of the books had library stamps, from all over the place, usually big cities, like Los Angeles–I believe there were at least four books from there–San Francisco, Seattle, Vancouver and San Bernardino. These are just a few I remember, and they didn't help us at all pointing to a specific area," Emily responded.

"What about sounds from traffic–airplanes or cars, anything like that?" Kim wanted to know.

"We very seldom heard the sounds of cars. Wherever we were, it must have been an isolated area. And there was hardly any noise from airplanes. This was all negative."

"Where did Gibson attack you? Right in the hidden valley or were you in the vicinity?" Julie asked.

"We had been down there several times. It is a very special place, so beautiful that it is almost unreal. It had been warm the day before and we decided to go there for our morning walk, the first time since last fall. It was rather early. We had come down from the northern slope, had stopped at the waterfall for a while and were just walking through the valley–planning to climb up the cliff to go back to the ranch–when we saw to our dismay all the tiny marijuana plants. Bret said right away that we could be in trouble if the owners of the plants showed up. So we were just hurrying across the meadow, ready to cross the creek, to get to the path leading up to the ledge, when the car drove into the valley and the guy jumped out with a gun. It was the most frightening thing I have ever experienced. He knocked Bret unconscious and shot Toby."

Emily started to cry when she mentioned the dog. They all sat there, realizing how lucky they were to have Emily and Bret back in their midst.

"At gun point, I was told to get into the car, and he tied me to the seat. Then he went back and dragged Bret to the car and shoved him in. It was awful," Emily started to cry again. "He kept us in his dirty cabin all day. Bret woke up about an hour later, but Gibson had bound and gagged him in the meantime, so he couldn't talk. The last thing I remember of the cabin was that it started to get dark. When we woke up, we were in the small room where they kept us until yesterday."

"Do you still have plans to hire the investigation agency to find out more about Undell?" Thomas asked Ralph and Bonnie, explaining to the Carters that they had decided to do that when they came back from Seattle two days ago without any results. In spite of having Emily and Bret back safely, both Ralph and Bonnie felt that Undell should be further investigated. This man–if indeed he was behind the kidnapping–was an extreme danger to society. Ralph and Bonnie suggested that Thomas should talk to his former colleagues in Seattle about setting up a contract.

"While we were imprisoned, we often talked about this. Would we ever find out who did this to us?" Bret said. "We came to the conclusion that we would not seek revenge. We expected to be in that room until perhaps September, for about six months, until they had harvested the stuff. There was no way to break out. So instead of ranting and raving all the time and making our life miserable with hate and anger, we knew we had to accept the situation and make the best of it. Emily and I had studied some concepts of Buddhism for several years and that helped us a lot to live through this ordeal and come out as whole persons. No, we are not vindictive. Why waste perhaps years, trying to find the person who was responsible for this, hire a lawyer, go to all the court dates? Fortunately, because of your involvement, we got out after two months and we are very thankful to you. We feel pretty good health-wise now–who knows, what three or four more months without sun would have done to us. So, we were lucky. Why should we add new misery to our lives going after the person who was responsible for it? And besides, all I hear from you concerning Undell is that there just isn't enough proof that he is indeed behind it.

"Nevertheless, I must say that I am very angry that this man–whoever he is–cruelly deceived all of you with the fake accident. When I heard this I felt different. Still, we probably would not pursue an investigation on our own, rather leave it to the police. But since you want to go ahead with this, we will join you and certainly help with the expenses." He looked questioningly at Emily.

"I also felt the best way to get over this terrible experience was not to dwell on it any longer and actually forgive the person–whoever it may be. But now, I realize that we are not alone in this–you all suffered–and would have gone on suffering until we finally may have been released.

If eventually he gets caught, he will not be able to inflict this kind of hurt on other innocent people any longer. So, yes, go ahead with your plans, and I agree with Bret that we share the cost with you."

"I certainly can understand your reluctance to investigate further." Thomas said. "But this can be done without involving you–or at least keep the involvement as minimal as possible. I can vouch for the people at the Seattle branch of C and O–which stands for California and Oregon Investigators–the case will be in good hands, and they are working closely with the police.

"Getting back to your release–I was just wondering if any of the other campers on that campground might have heard or seen the person who took you there, or perhaps have seen the car when it drove away? If you can describe the campground, the sheriff could get in touch with the rangers in the area."

"I doubt anything will come out of this, but, yes, I can give you a pretty good description," Emily replied. "It was a Forest Service campground on the south side of route 32. Bret actually found it on the map, he can show it to you. The other cars, three or four, were at least one hundred feet away."

Thomas thanked her for the information and promised to mention it to Calvin Stenton.

Bret brought up a different issue. "We often have wondered how Gibson ever got the idea to grow marijuana in the hidden valley? He was not a local man from what you have told us now. Where did he get the information? I agree with you, Julie, that Andy was only superficially involved. So how did Gibson ever find the valley? I am afraid we will never know unless Olson gets better and tells us some details."

"By the way, Bret. Do you happen to know how many miles your car has been driven since April? This could give us some rough idea how far away your hiding place was." Ralph asked his brother.

"We thought of that when we started out on Highway 32 this morning. Yes, I knew pretty much the mileage before this all happened. Deducting today's mileage, the van was driven about seven hundred and fifty miles. But again, this does not lead anywhere. The area in question is so large, it will be impossible to find the spot where we were held," Bret replied.

"I cannot understand why Undell–if he really is the big boss–even bothered with this fairly small operation? Small in comparison from what he seems to own? You mentioned where and how he lives, Thomas, he must be incredibly wealthy. Does he need the proceeds of a pot harvest in northern California?" Emily was wondering.

"It was not that small an operation, Emily. He probably would have gotten several millions out of it. But I am sure, he has several others like this going–so you lose some and gain some." Thomas replied.

Bonnie observed her sister with growing concern, "You both look very tired. We really should not bother you any longer with questions, you need to get some rest."

"Only one more thing," Julie said. "Charles Kendar would like to see you too. Would it be all right to invite him for dinner with his wife?"

Both Emily and Bret were eager to see Charles and his wife again. So it was decided to have dinner at seven o'clock and invite the Kendars.

And then, Emily was finally able to lie down in her own bed and look out into the trees. This time she didn't have to keep her eyes shut and pretend, only she was too tired to enjoy the scenery for very long. After a few minutes, she was fast asleep.

Thomas and Julie drove over to the Kendar ranch to invite Charles and Nomi. Their housekeeper agreed to come in the evening and take care of old Mr. Kendar. Although Charles' grandfather was alert mentally, he tired very easily. Sometimes, he fell asleep even when they had dinner together. Charles had told him that Emily and Bret had come back and his grandfather remembered who they were, and that they had disappeared. He was glad to hear the good news, but had no desire to come along to the dinner. "Too many people", he said, dismissing the matter.

Thomas made several phone calls to let everybody know about the Carters. He called Stenton again, Charles had only left a message because he had been in a meeting. Now, Thomas reached him in his office. Stenton could hardly believe the story, it was the last thing he had expected. He told Thomas that he would come over to the ranch the next day to talk to the Carters. He was relieved and happy that they had been released. Thomas gave him the name of the campground where the Carters had been left, and Stenton assured him that he would call the Forest Service right away.

Olson had shown the first signs of consciousness, responded to questions with a nod or shaking his head. He had talked a few words and seemed to be fairly clear, mentally. Thomas also called his friend Dean and Maxine Cooper in Medford, Lt. Somes in Seattle, and left a message for Andy in Eureka.

On the way back, Thomas stopped at the entrance to the hidden valley. "How about taking a short walk up to the valley, Julie?"

She liked the idea. They held hands as they were walking up the trail along the creek. When they reached the valley, they stopped at the same spot where they had been standing on Sunday, watching the two men carrying Olson down to the car, and Jessica trailing behind them.

"A lot has changed since Sunday, hasn't it?" Julie said when Thomas put his arms around her and kissed her again. "I was happy when you kissed me on Sunday, but today I can enjoy it thoroughly."

They strolled to the end of the valley, to the foot of the waterfall, and sat there quietly, listening to the sound of the water, the humming of insects and the occasional twitter of birds. Thomas put his arm around Julie and kissed her again–it was one of those rare, exquisite moments in life they would always remember.

"Today I can really appreciate this paradise," Julie said. "Not only do I know that Emily and Bret are safely home again, I am also here without fear–and I am here with you, Thomas. I am sorry that you have to leave so soon. Can you stop for a visit on your way back? Or will you drive with Ken?"

"Ken is also taking the train to and from Eureka, so I will come back by train, and visit with you for one more day, but then I have to get down to Santa Rosa and get ready for my job. I would love to come up every weekend, but now that Emily and Bret are back, you won't be alone any longer. I will come as often as I can, Julie–but perhaps, you could also come to Santa Rosa some weekends? We could go to a play or a concert?" Thomas suggested.

The summer stretched out before them like an endless succession of beautiful and happy days. Julie sighed, life was all of a sudden a sheer delight!

After a while, she broke the contented lull in their conversation, "You know, Thomas, I still owe you an explanation why I acted so strangely when we first met in Willits. You remember, when I was waiting for my luggage from the train?"

"Sure, I do remember. I must admit that I actually have been wondering about this guy who supposedly resembles me and who evoked such a strong, emotional reaction in you. He either was your enemy, or you loved him dearly?" Thomas joked.

"It's just a simple story. Benji was at Columbia for a year–at the department of archaeology–on sabbatical leave from the University of New Delhi. He had arrived while I was working on a dig in New Mexico, and I therefore missed his sad story. His little daughter had become seriously ill with polio two weeks before the family's departure to the States and his wife had to stay home with the child. He was introduced to me when I came back, but nobody mentioned his family. We worked closely together on the same project. I liked and admired him a lot, both as a scientist and a person. When he came alone to some parties, I assumed he was single, and started to fall in love with him. Fortunately, I kept my feelings under wraps,... why are you laughing, Thomas?"

Thomas grinned, "Your face is like an open book, Julie. That's one of the many things I love about you, you look so innocent and honest. I doubt very much that Benji didn't notice your affection. I can't imagine you with a blank face."

"You can't judge from that meeting in Willits, Thomas, you caught me by surprise. I have long overcome my feelings for Benji, but for a second, you looked like him. You have the same coloring, same height and figure, dark curly hair, and you wore sunglasses–Benji wears glasses regularly, you see? It was kind of a shock, until you took off your sunglasses and became a stranger.

"So eventually, you found out that he was married?"

"Well, perhaps a month later, just by accident. We had been so involved in our project that we hardly ever talked about personal matters. I was glad I had hidden my feelings so well. Please, don't laugh again, Thomas, because I am sure that he had not noticed my affection."

Thomas took her into his arms. "I am happy that you didn't hide your feelings for me, Julie, and also, I swear, I am not married! So he went back to India?"

"Yes, his year ended in September. Actually, the longer I knew him, the more I realized that we differed greatly on some basic issues. And this cooled my affection down to friendship level fast," Julie smiled.

"Political or religious differences?" Thomas asked.

"No, it was more philosophical–well, perhaps you could call it political. His wife is a physician and after their daughter was born, she went back to work at the hospital twice a week–against Benji's and his mother's explicit wishes. He felt a mother should be with her child, and should not work outside the home as long as the child was young."

"I would agree with him, Julie. This is one of the worst problems we face in our society today. Too many mothers are working and too many children grow up without enough support. Unfortunately, many women have to work, but there are also many who would have the means to stay home, but don't," Thomas responded.

"I do agree with you, Thomas. My mother stayed home when we were little. My parents were archaeologists and worked together, but Mom quit until we both were in school. Then she went back, working half days."

"So, where is your difference of opinion, Julie? I don't get the idea?" Thomas asked.

"It's the way he approached the issue. It was not to be his wife's choice, he felt he was the one who should make this decision. Pater familias, you know? They lived in his mother's house–the father is dead–and she controlled the household staff, his wife had very little influence. So it is understandable that she liked to work twice a week; days when she became her own person. Besides, she didn't need outside child care, the child was well cared for by the family in her home and didn't lack support. Benji couldn't understand why I sided with his wife. After all, the husband was the head of the family. You see what I mean, Thomas?"

"Yes, now I do and I agree with you, Julie. Do you think you had some influence on him?"

"I am not sure, he didn't admit it, but perhaps I slightly changed his attitude. We also had very different opinions on family planning. His ideal was a family with at least four children, and his wife didn't go along with this either. Benji's argument was, that both he and his wife belong to the well-educated, intelligent portion of the population. If they would have only one or two children, the poorer, and less intelligent would soon outnumber them and overall, future generations' intelligence would decline steadily."

"Wow, how presumptuous! Very few geniuses have children that are as intelligent as their parents, but I know other guys who have the same opinion. And how often are we surprised by kids that come from very poor backgrounds and are brilliant? Our genes have been so mixed up over thousands of years, any combination can happen. What counts, however, is that there are too many of us. We all have to keep this in mind, not only the poor."

"I believe I made a difference there. Later we often talked about over-population and I think in the end he saw my point," Julie concluded.

She stood up and stretched. "I am afraid we have to get back. I could be with you here forever."Reluctantly Thomas got up too. "We will come back, Julie. This place has by now a very special meaning for us."

Kim and Ralph had walked to Madrone Flat–Kim wanted to call her husband and Ralph his wife. Bonnie and Nick were in the garden, picking things for dinner. Julie mentioned that both Kendars would come over this evening and she helped harvest some more vegetables. They went back to the kitchen to get dinner started. All the vegetables and berries needed washing and cleaning. Thomas wanted to help too, but Bonnie persuaded him to relax, pretty soon he would have a full work load every day.

"There is one thing I would love to do, Julie, yet so far, have not felt in the mood for it, as long as Emily and Bret were still missing. Would you mind if I played the piano for a while? Or do you think it would disturb your sister, Bonnie?" Thomas asked.

Bonnie looked up from shelling peas, "As long as you don't play Rock and Roll, she hates that with a passion."

Thomas smiled, "I had planned on something a little quieter, like Mozart or Bach? Along those lines? I could close the doors to the deck, they probably have their windows open upstairs?"

"No, don't do that, this is the kind of music Emily and Bret love, leave the door open, please."

"And also leave the door open to the living room, Thomas, we want to enjoy your music too," Julie added.

A few minutes later Mozart's concerto in A Major, played astonishingly well, drifted in from the living room. Bonnie listened, interrupted her work, and leaned back, "He plays very well, your Thomas, he is a man of many talents. I like him, Julie, I like him a lot. You are a lucky woman."

Dinner was special this evening. Bonnie had prepared a scrumptious chicken dish with dumplings, which was Emily's favorite. In addition, there was a big salad, steamed asparagus, and strawberry pie with real whipped cream for dessert.

After they were through with dessert, Charles, rather ill at ease, told them that he had to make a sad confession.

"We all have been wondering how Gibson had found out about this valley that was so convenient for his purpose? I talked with Nomi about it a few days ago and she discovered the link, which–I am ashamed to admit–rests with my family."

Very much surprised, everybody stared at Charles, who looked uncomfortable. Nomi put her hand on his arm.

"Let me finish dear, they will all understand. You have nothing to do with it, it was not your fault at all. "

She turned and faced the others, "Charles' half-brother Jason is responsible for what happened. It occurred to us that Jason had been in jail. What if he knew the hidden valley, saw its potential for a well-hidden pot garden and told another inmate about it and somehow Gibson found out? Anyway, Charles called Deputy Stenton and talked with him about his suspicion. Stenton quickly found out that Gibson and Jason had been at the same prison at one time. So, Charles went to Santa Rosa, prepared to have an angry confrontation with Jason. Fortunately, it went much smoother than he had expected. Jason has changed a lot since he has been released. He had no idea what had happened here. When Charles questioned him, he readily admitted that he had been so foolish to mention in prison how perfectly suited this hidden valley was for growing marijuana on a large scale. Apparently, he himself had grown some plants for a few years, after all, he had studied agriculture. He very well remembered how fast Gibson had responded, questioning him in detail. And Jason had received a number of favors for this information from Gibson for about two weeks–cigarettes, some joints, a small amount of cocaine. Then Gibson had been released on probation. Jason had lived in fear that his stupid mistake could cause some problems for Charles. Several times he had been on the verge of warning Charles, only had never found the courage. Now of course, he was very sorry that he had kept quiet and that he was ultimately responsible for the disappearance of Emily and Bret."

Nomi put her arm around Charles and gave him a kiss on his cheek. "We are very, very sorry about this. Charles, of course, had not the slightest idea about this connection. We have not mentioned it to old Mr. Kendar, it could cause another stroke."

They all were moved by Nomi and Charles' story and happy at the same time for them, that it all had ended well, with Emily and Bret safely back home again.

"By the way, Charles, Julie told me about another item this afternoon that I want to clear up," Emily said. "We didn't give your telephone number to Fred Mendell, so that he or Julie could leave messages for us with you. We would never have done that to you. Whoever faked those postcards used your phone number–I guess to make them look more authentic," Emily said.

Charles nodded, "I had already come to the same conclusion, Emily. But at the time when I got those phone calls, we had no idea that you had been kidnapped, or of all the other evil things that had been going on."

Before the party broke up, Emily thanked Thomas for playing the piano. "Your music was lovely, you play very well. How about a nice, quiet piece to end the evening?"

Thomas went into the living room and sat down on the piano bench, considering for a minute what to play. Julie had come along and opened the bay window to the deck. She sat down on the wide, cushioned window sill, waiting for Thomas to begin. He chose the second movement of Mozart's Piano Concerto No. 20, a delightful answer to Emily's request, and the right music to end this eventful day.

At breakfast next morning, Emily persuaded Thomas to stay at least for another day. She had observed the growing intimacy between him and Julie, and liking Thomas a lot, she wanted to support the relationship.

"You have worked so hard since you came here to help us all and have not had much fun. Why not stay until tomorrow? Your hike will not start until Sunday? We'll make it a day of relaxation; spend some time down at the river, swimming, kayaking or doing nothing."

Thomas gave in, after all he cherished every minute he could spend with Julie. Ralph would also stay two or three more days at the ranch. Bret had noticed a maintenance problem with the solar power system and Ralph was going to help him getting it repaired. Bonnie had decided to leave with Ralph. They were all going to take the train south on Monday or Tuesday. Bonnie had promised Nick to stop in Willits and ride the Skunk train. Julie had told him enthusiastically about the scenic trip. Bonnie's family would be back later in the summer for a visit to the ranch when her husband and daughter had come back home.

The river was as beautiful as ever. The water had warmed up during the last few days, and they all went in for a swim. Later, Emily lay in the sand, resting under a willow tree, enjoying the warmth of the sunlight, filtering through the branches and leaves of the tree. She was completely at ease, listening to the sounds of the river and the laughter and shrieks of the others, who were playing around with the kayaks. Bonnie sat quietly at Emily's side, as if protecting her sister from any unexpected intrusions. Julie and Thomas had walked upstream along the river, and were sitting now near the water, talking to each other.

Sheriff Stenton had just arrived when they came back to the house for lunch. He congratulated the Carters for having survived this terrible ordeal so well, and told them how happy he was to meet them. They spent almost an hour in the study. Stenton took down their testimony on tape. He respected the Carters' decision not to get too much involved in the case, but appreciated the decision to employ the detective agency. However, he made them aware that their testimony would be needed at some time in the future, here in the county against Olson and perhaps even in Seattle, if eventually substantial evidence against Undell could be brought forward. Bret and Emily had no problem with that.

During lunch, Stenton told them about his first talk with Olson this morning who had admitted that he had known Gibson and that he had supplied him with the Jeep in Medford–supposedly without Undell's knowledge–and had stayed in touch with him after he had left for Madrone Flat. He denied that he had made the phone call to Charles, pretending to be Bret, or that he had made the call from the hospital pay phone, reporting the fake accident.

Stenton looked at his notes and continued, "When I mentioned to him that he had threatened Julie last Sunday morning, warning her that she would share her friends' fate, he offered a flimsy explanation. He pretended that he had not known about the Carter's abduction. He had assumed that Gibson had given them a strong warning, perhaps beaten them up. He claims that's what he meant when he warned you, Julie, and that he only wanted to scare you.

"In the meantime, your friend Dean in Medford, Thomas, checked the telephone records of both the Olson residence and the office. There was a call to the Seattle number marked 'B' in Olson's note book, just a few minutes after the April 5 call from Madrone Flat to Olson's office, which you had found. I will keep this evidence for the trial. I am sure that Olson will eventually tell the whole story. He did admit that the Seattle phone number, the one marked with a 'B', had been the big boss' number and that he had to call him whenever decisions had to be made. But, he had never met him in person and doesn't know his name. He tried to convince me that there was definitely no connection between the big boss and Mr. Undell, whom he knows, of course. Unless we nail Undell, we will never be able to prove this one way or the other. Gibson is dead, so we have only Olson's word for it."

After half an hour of interrogation, the nurse had come in and told Stenton he had to stop now, the patient needed a rest. He was hoping to continue perhaps later, although he was not very optimistic about getting much more out of Olson.

"I did call the ranger who is in charge of the campground on route 32. He drove there right away to investigate and called me back this morning. Only one car was still there. The woman had gone to the rest room just at the time when the Carters' van drove in, it was around 4:30. She saw a person get out of the van and walk back toward the entrance of the campground. She believes she heard a car in the distance leaving right after that, but is not sure. It was still dark and all she saw was a vague figure. The ranger gave me the addresses of two other campers who had been there during the night, one from San Francisco and the other one from Oregon. So far, I have not been able to reach them.

Stenton leaned back in his chair and was quiet for a while, and then added, "You know, this was the typical case where the criminal dug his own grave. If Gibson had been more trustful when Andy told him that you, Julie, would not take any action concerning the plants, nothing would have happened. You would have gone with Andy to Madrone Flat, and walked back with Thomas to your station to meet Kim. You would have remained suspicious of Charles and avoided him wherever you could. Possibly, you wouldn't have found out the truth until the Carters eventually had returned to the ranch, after spending all those months in their prison. It would have been a terrible summer for you all."

Thomas took exception to Stenton's scenario, "Not quite true, Calvin," Thomas interrupted, "I had already learned that morning, when I called a friend of mine in Santa Rosa, that it was not Charles Kendar who had been in prison. And I certainly had realized that the car in the canyon had a gasoline engine, while Charles' Land Rover was a Diesel. In other words, we were most likely dealing with two different people. Still, you might be right. Who knows how things would have gone? I might not have given it that much thought, considering that Julie was not alone any longer after Kim arrived and I would have left for Eureka a few days later. In any case, we all can be happy that it ended as it did, sparing Emily and Bret perhaps another four to five months in captivity and anguish."

"Somes called me this morning after he had heard the good news," Stenton continued. "He was very happy that Emily and Bret are back in good health. They have checked out all of Undell's employees–back to three years ago–and there was no one that fitted the description of the woman who rented the house near the Space Needle. He was pretty discouraged, but assured me that he would keep his eyes open. Sooner or later, Undell would make a mistake."

They all were quiet for a while, wondering if Emily and Bret's kidnappers would ever be brought to justice. The silence was interrupted by a loud and cheerful "Welcome back". Rosy came around the corner of the house, hiding behind a huge bouquet of summer flowers which she dropped on a chair to give Emily and Bret a big hug.

"I can't believe it–what a blessing that you are back, I am so happy for you and all of us," she wiped her eyes and picked up the flowers again to thrust them into Emily's arms. "I also brought you something for dinner, two pans of lasagna and a chocolate pie. I left it in the kitchen."

"What a beautiful bouquet, Rosy. I love the combinations, roses, delphiniums, daisies and those pretty lilies. Thank you so much, I'll get a vase right away."

When Emily came back with a tall, blue vase, she also brought a pitcher with more apple juice and poured some for Rosy, before she arranged the flowers.

"You cannot imagine how happy we are to be back with you!" Emily said. She was still standing, addressing them all. "In spite of having gone through this nightmare–today, I feel almost normal again. Relaxing this morning down at the beautiful river, brought my life back into balance."

"I have a suggestion how to make your life even more normal again, Emily," Rosy said. "Why don't you all come over to the school tonight? We have a big community square dance at the multi-purpose room. Didn't you and Bret used to square dance anyway?"

Emily's face lit up, "That's a wonderful idea, except we are a little rusty and have forgotten many of the figures, and I hate to mess up a square."

"It will be at a very low level, I was told. All of you can participate. The caller is supposed to be very good and a lot of fun," Rosy replied.

Looking around, Bonnie said, "We are actually a full square right here, Emily. You and Bret, Kim and Ralph, Julie and Thomas and Nick and. . . ."

"Mom, do you really want to make my life miserable? I will stick out like a sore thumb in that crowd of middle-aged people, don't do that to me!" Her son looked at her as if she had ordered him to wear a three-piece suit to school.

"This will be a very mixed crowd, Nick," Rosy tried to persuade him. "There will be a lot of young people. The girl who works for me is also going and she is only eighteen. And besides, I wouldn't call Julie, Kim and Thomas middle-aged. There will also be line-dancing, wouldn't you like that?"

After Nick, Ralph and Thomas had overcome their reluctance, they all decided to go. It turned out to be a great evening. Nick very soon abandoned his mother's square to join the younger crowd and didn't feel out of place at all.

When they came back to the ranch after ten o'clock, they all agreed that the dance had been the culmination of Emily's and Bret's homecoming.

EPILOGUE

The second Saturday in August was a beautiful summer day–pleasantly warm with a light breeze, the sky of the deepest blue and the air crystal clear. Exuberantly, Julie skipped down the road to the railroad tracks. She was early, the train from the south was due in about thirty minutes. Emily and Bret would follow with the car in time for the arrival of all the guests.

She needed a few quiet minutes by herself–as soon as the train arrived, a whirlwind of impressions would bear down on her. And Thomas was coming, this alone was reason enough to be excited! After he had left in June, he had stopped for a day at the ranch on his way back to Santa Rosa, returning from the hiking tour. But frequent weekend visits, as they had planned so enthusiastically, had not become a reality. His new job was very demanding, and Julie had not been able to get to Santa Rosa either, there had been a string of visitors to the ranch all through July. They had stayed in touch with several phone calls and letters, but Thomas didn't know yet that she had made the decision to teach school in Madrone Flat, starting in September.

When she had called the archaeological department at UC Berkeley to tell them that she wouldn't take the job this year, she found out that the grant had not come through anyway. They had assured her that it would work out next year. She left it at that, the teaching job was perfect for now.

She thought of the many times she had already come down here this summer, expecting company–exhilarating and exciting– and seeing them off again, always a little sad. First Thomas had left, then Bonnie, Ralph and Nick, and a few days later Kim. Then new visitors came–Clara Winters, the young woman she had met on the Amtrak train–Helen and Josh, Doris and Fred with Julie's grandmother and Alma Read.

And then Maria and Ken came, and their visit had sparked the event that was happening this Saturday. Thomas had told them about the disappearance of the Carters, in connection with the marijuana crop. Maria remembered Julie's interest in the hidden valley, and hearing about this multi-million dollar dope plantation in a place that possibly had been a spiritual retreat for her people, made her angry.

They had hiked into the valley and were deeply disturbed seeing the ugly scars in the meadow, caused by the uprooting and confiscation of the plants, which had happened a week after Emily and Bret had come back. Maria suggested recreating the original meadow, and they talked with Charles and Nomi about it. Both supported the idea. The revival process got under way within a few days after Maria's and Ken's visit. Everybody helped, including Andy who came by train from Eureka, and even Jason Kendar, who turned out to be a very effective worker. He truly regretted his irresponsible behavior in prison that had led to the Carter's kidnapping.

Ken and Maria came back again to help, and Maria and Julie had a chance to look for signs of Native American artifacts in the valley. They found a number of arrowheads made from obsidian or chert, randomly scattered around the valley floor where the plants had been uprooted. The most exiting find was a small cache of beads, shells and pieces of obsidian under a rock near the waterfall. They added the arrowheads to the beads and shells and put the rock back in place.

After two weeks of heavy work, the battlefield-like valley floor had been smoothed out and grass had been sown. Maria suggested having a consecration ceremony as soon as the valley was restored to its original beauty and the date had been set for the second Saturday of August.

Julie heard Emily and Bret ‘s car coming down from the house, and a glance at her watch showed that the train would be here in a few minutes!

The first person to get off the train was Thomas and Julie rushed into his arms. By the time the train continued to Madrone Flat, Julie and the Carters had welcomed all their guests: Maria and her parents, Ken, his parents and sister, Ralph and his wife Roberta, Kim and her husband Martin, and, of course, Thomas.

Bonnie and her husband Jeff had already arrived two days ago, together with Nick and his sister Esther. Bonnie and and her daughter had lunch ready at the house.

In the afternoon, they all squeezed into the Carters' van and the Kendar's Cadillac, which Julie had borrowed again for this special occasion, and drove across the hill to the Fir Creek bridge. Charles, Nomi and Jason were already waiting, and a few minutes later, Rosy drove up with her husband George and Andy, followed by Ben Wilson, his wife and daughter, and Calvin Stenton, also with his wife and son.

The entrance to the valley was closed to cars now. The potted trees had all been planted randomly across what had been the road and only a narrow, unobtrusive trail along the creek remained.

The group strolled leisurely up the path into the valley. Maria was waiting for them at the pond by the waterfall. When everybody had arrived, she raised her arms, and looked at each person present.

"Thank you all for coming today and celebrating a new beginning! And thanks to all of you who worked so hard to restore the valley's beauty.

"I also want to thank my grandmother who counseled me how to conduct this ceremony–in her thoughts, she is with us today. My grandmother is old, but even she was not born when our people lived in these hills, free, before all the tragic events happened. Yet, she remembers stories about similar ceremonies in special, sacred places to overcome evil influences or actions. She told me of valleys like this and in my heart I believe that our people regarded this valley as the home of their Spirits. Look around you, how could it be otherwise?

"During the last few weeks, when we tried to heal the wounded earth, we found some small treasures that our people left long ago, and we put them back where they had been hidden. All of us who come here feel it–this is sacred ground! I thank the Spirits who have guided me here and I thank you who have promised to protect this place in the future. Except for my parents, none of you are of my people. I even fell in love with a man who is not of my people. But that's all right–we are all humans.

"Some of you have dark skin," Maria smiled at Thomas and Calvin Stenton. "And some of your ancestors came from Asia." She looked at Nomi, Kim and Carol Stenton, an attractive Chinese woman, and her little boy.

"My parents, Rosy and I are from the Americas, and the rest of you are just plain white folks." Everybody laughed, and Maria continued, "But you are also not all the same. Your ancestors came from different countries and cultures and spoke different languages. And now we are all here together. No matter the color of our skin, our hair or how we look or speak, the most important thing is to respect and love each other–and if we do, we also respect our spirits, whatever they are named or wherever they are dwelling. I love you all, we are all one."

She picked up a basket that was resting at her feet and took a handful of rose petals out.

"My grandmother told me to scatter the petals of wild roses whenever you want to free a place of Evil Spirits. She doesn't remember where this ritual came from, and I have not found any reference for it studying our people's history. But I like the idea, as I like the wild roses in our hills, and if we use a custom today that perhaps was not part of our people's ceremonies, I hope the Spirits will accept it kindly.

"Unfortunately, there are no wild roses flowering this late in the summer. So, I picked some roses in our garden this morning, together with leaves from manzanita and ceanothus, may they keep away the evil from this lovely place forever!"

She scattered the petals over the pond until her basket was empty. They drifted around for a while and then slowly started their journey down the stream.

Esther and Nick began playing a tune on their flutes–the enchanting melody accompanied the sound of the water cascading down the rock wall. When the last tone died away, there was complete silence and nobody moved, as if a spell had been cast over them. Nick and Esther explained that Maria had taught them the melody which she had heard from her grandmother many times as a child.

They picked up the recorders again and repeated the last part of the tune. As the sound faded out, they made room for Julie, who came forward.

"Thank you, that was lovely, and what I am about to say goes with your music," Julie said. "When the grass we planted started to grow and came lush and thick, I was sitting up there on the ledge one day," she pointed to the top of the cliff. "I was quietly enjoying the beauty of the valley, when I got the idea putting my feelings into words, to write a poem about the valley." Julie blushed, "I don't pretend to be a poet, although I wrote a few little poems in high school," she smiled and continued. "But somehow, sitting up there and gratefully appreciating this jewel, the lines just poured out of me, all I had to do was write them down, and here they are:

SACRED GROUND

The Valley was the same–for many, many years.

The storms of winter swelled the winding, little stream,
And spring rains dyed the meadow bright with colors,
The fogs of summer kept the valley moist and green,
In fall, the rusty leaves of autumn closed the cycle.

The valley was the Spirits' home,
And people came to worship, came to serve,
They came to learn the art of healing,
To listen and to ask for guidance.,

The Spirits lived in trees, in flowers, in the creek.
They were the gentle breezes gliding through the valley,
They lived in all the creatures, wild or meek,
And in the earth, in soils–so rich and fertile.

Change came, when strangers found the valley.
Tight were their souls, and closed their eyes and ears.
They didn't come to learn, to listen or to heal,
They came to own, to rape, to steal.

The strangers pulled the people from their roots,
And ousted them to cold and alien lands.
From far away, the Spirits sensed their woes,
And heard their moaning, felt their suffering.

The valley was the same no more.

When many moons had passed,
New strangers came into the valley.
Strangers, who did respect the Spirits' homes,
Strangers, who understood the Spirits' voices.

And so the valley was, for many years.

Change came again–a bad One plowed the lands,
Greed was his motive, healing not his wish.

He raised a crop of thousand magic plants,
To bring him riches, power and success.

The Spirits watched him warily, not liking what they saw,
He had defiled their home and earned their punishment.
By shooting old dog Toby, he broke the valley's law,
The Bad One was condemned to face an early end.

And now the Spirits' home is pure again.
Be still, and listen to the falling water's sound.
Treasure the trees, the flowers and the creatures.
Honor the laws of nature–this all is sacred ground.

When Julie had ended, Maria embraced her, "That was beautiful, thank you. You found the right words to describe what happened, so many years ago, and again this spring."

And then Emily joined them, putting her arms around Esther and Nick to her right and Julie and Maria to her left.

"Thank you, all of you, you have made this a day to remember. Bret and I are deeply moved. We thank you for coming and celebrating with us. This valley has been a special place for us since we discovered it a few years ago. Yet, for two months, we avoided thinking of it, because it held terrible memories. Not only were we brutally attacked here, but–as Julie mentioned in her poem–our old, faithful Toby died here. Now, with all your help, the valley is alive again.

"We are sure, had it not been for your persistence, we would still be imprisoned. Instead, we can enjoy this beautiful summer day together with you. Thank you all again!"

SOURCE NOTES

1. *Environmental History and Cultural Ecology of the North Fork of the Eel River Basin*, Thomas S. Keter, Heritage Resource Program, U.S. Forest Service
2. *Genocide and Vendetta*, Lynwood Carranco and Estle Beard, University of Oklahoma Press
3. *The Headlight*, Northwestern Pacific Railroad Historical Society Newsletters, Santa Rosa, CA
4. *History of Mendocino County Timber Production* - California, Statistical Abstract, State Dept. of Finance, 1996
5. *Laytonville Loose Ends*, Kate Mayo, Willits News
6. *Logging the Redwoods*, Lynwood Carranco & John T. Labbe, The Caxton Printers. LTD.
7. *Maximizing Forest Productivity*, H.J. Burkhardt ,Fort Bragg, CA
8. Mendocino County Railway Society Newsletters,Fort Bragg, CA
9. Modern Transit Society Newsletters, *Moving People*, Sacramento, CA
10. *The Northwestern Pacific Railroad*, 2 Volumes, Fred A. Stindt, Kelseyville, CA
11. *Redwoods, Iron Horses, And the Pacific*, Spencer Crump, Trans-Anglo Books
12. *Redwood Railways*, Gilbert H. Kneiss, Howell-North Press
13. *The River Stops Here*, Ted Simon, Random House, New York
14. Roots of Motive Power Inc. Newsletters, Willits, CA
15. *Watershed Analysis Report for the Upper Main Eel River Watershed*, U.S. Forest Service Dept. of Agriculture
16. World Watch Papers, Numbers 84, 98 and 118